'Peter Preston didn't get to where he is today without knowing what makes a good story and *51st State* is a fine yarn'
Erica Wagner, *The Times*

'Preston writes pacily . . . What *51st State* succeeds in conveying, albeit in a heightened form, is the tide of politics . . . He appreciates the way sexual passion or private pique can nudge history along, and he uses these Macmillanesque "events" to lend drama to his narrative'
Michael Gove, *The Times Literary Supplement*

'Preston does a brilliant and surprising job of rendering plausible this seemingly preposterous premise . . . an admirably climactic sting in the tail' William Sutcliffe, *Independent on Sunday*

'Unusual and entertaining . . . brilliantly captures the prevailing, patronising attitude of the US government towards its British counterpart'
Andrew Stephen, *Observer*

'It is probably one of the lightest and most scurrilous reads any devotee of the *Guardian* will have, and, taken in the right spirit, one of the most entertaining' Conrad Black, *Literary Review*

Peter Preston edited the *Guardian* in London for twenty years. He is a member of the Scott Trust, which owns the *Guardian* and the *Observer*, and now writes columns for both papers.

He had a front seat in the political stalls through five premierships and has reported first-hand on many American elections. He has also had less welcome front seats in many courtrooms from *Spycatcher* onwards. He is the 'hound from hell' who began the investigations into Neil Hamilton, Tim Smith and Jonathan Aitken.

Preston was born in Leicestershire and went to St John's College, Oxford, slightly before Tony Blair. He has worked, mostly for the *Guardian*, as a political reporter, gossip columnist and war correspondent. He is married with four children and lives in south London. This is his first novel.

PETER PRESTON

51st State

PENGUIN BOOKS

PENGUIN BOOKS

Published by the Penguin Group
Penguin Books Ltd, 27 Wrights Lane, London w8 5tz, England
Penguin Putnam Inc., 375 Hudson Street, New York, New York 10014, USA
Penguin Books Australia Ltd, Ringwood, Victoria, Australia
Penguin Books Canada Ltd, 10 Alcorn Avenue, Toronto, Ontario, Canada M4V 3B2
Penguin Books (NZ) Ltd, Private Bag 102902, NSMC, Auckland, New Zealand

Penguin Books Ltd, Registered Offices: Harmondsworth, Middlesex, England

First published by Viking 1998
Published in Penguin Books 1999
1 3 5 7 9 10 8 6 4 2

Set Monotype Sabon
Typeset by Rowland Phototypesetting Ltd,
Bury St Edmunds, Suffolk
Printed in England by Clays Ltd, St Ives plc

For Jean

The Movers

Rupert James Grosvenor Warner: Leader of the House of Commons – and then much else
Jennifer Margaret Warner: his wife, and much else
Curtis Michaelson: Prime Minister, in the beginning
Polly Jane Gurley: Conservative MP for Leeds South-West, in the beginning
Tim Broadbent MP: a Euro-sceptic balloon
Brian Carstairs MP: his fellow-travelling companion
Neil Forrest: the new Leader of the Labour Party
Arthur Palmer: the dead, old leader of the Labour Party
Lord Ray Sandlewood of Powburn: a decrepit fixer
Robin Groom MP: a buoyant, fresh fixer
His Majesty The King: whom nobody can fix

The Shakers

Guillermo Milhous 'Wild Bill' Angeli: the forty-seventh President
Senator Mark Henry Tate: the Maine chance
Marti Tate: his First Lady
Governor Pedro Bordon: the Illinois Mex. A winner?
Senator Nate Plummer: the Alabama Good Old Boy. A winner?
Vice-President Wilbur Richard Galt the Second: a loser
David J. Simmons Jnr: the American counsellor with the big idea

Significant Others

Hermann Gross: the Chancellor of Germany
Alain Peyerfitte: the President of France
Egipane Engibono: a handy Ethiopian man
Gloria Bradshaw: the President's Lady's lady
Joe Harris and Bobby Kraft: the campaign words men
Nicos Papadopoulos: the campaign ideas man
Jeffrey Irving Crew: the pocket Rupert
Julianna Ekpu: the reporter who lays it as it plays
Mujib Khan: the money man
Governors Treneman (Ireland); Mills (Wales); Angus (Scotland); and Jeffreys, the Belfast bawler
Jimmy Bannon and Dwight Schultz: Security Inc
Shorty Maddox: Snap! Gotcha!

PHASE ONE

The more developed country shows the
less developed the image of their futures.

MARX, *Das Kapital*

Yankee Doodle went to town
A-riding on a pony,
Stuck a feather in his hat
And called it macaroni.

RICHARD SHUCKBURGH

Chapter One

The house, a grey pebbledash box from the 1930s, was called Cliff Farm. But there was no farm, only a caravan site huddled in a gully a couple of hundred metres away. And there were no cliffs either. The box, marooned on a concrete island of packing cases and dismembered, rusted trucks, stood high atop the slope of the Dorset coast, rolling down towards the thin strand of Chesil Beach.

He looked down at the wreck of his father, gasping for breath, in the bed. The flimsy yellow curtains were drawn tight, but shafts of winter sun gave the room pallor and the face a waxen sheen. For two hours, neither said a word. The son, leaning forward on a wooden chair, shifting uneasily from time to time, merely held the outstretched left hand. They were drained of small-talk, unable to discuss the death they both knew could not be far away.

'Rupert,' said the old man at last.

He might have talked of the warm days when Elizabeth was alive. He might have remembered the young family he had been left alone to bring up. It was the time for remembrance, the approaching time when mind and body become somehow detached from each other and seem to float in a world where the pain is dulled. But, in fact, he was talking bloody politics again; worse than that, bloody referendums.

'This new vote, Rupert,' he said. 'Tell me about it again.'

'It's just the same stuff, Dad. Tidyings up. Nothing amazing. I told you about the treaty of Delft. There was monetary union,

3

but there wasn't all the political union we wanted to go with it. This gives us all a tighter combined Foreign Office in Brussels and a full list of shared embassies. That way there's a European foreign minister who operates, when it's sensible, with his own machine alongside the defence minister. It will save a packet. And they're combining what's left of our select committees with the ones in Strasbourg so that the monitoring works better. Totally co-ordinated, that sort of thing.'

He paused, bored already with the sound of his own voice. 'Oh, and there's a new approach to majority voting because of that Slovak veto shambles last year. An extension of what we used to call variable geometry. Now it's constructive abstention for second-tier membership. If the Balkans don't like it, the Balkans can sit on the sidelines and lump it. We can just leave the tiddlers behind for a while if we want. I told you. Nothing big.'

The clutch on his hand grew tighter and the chill lips began suddenly to move in agitation. The voice seemed to come from far away. It wandered and drifted through childhood and marriage, through long months of duty and absence and pining. It dwelt in a simpler world of simpler values. It spoke of hearth and home and the endless fight to make ends meet, to give two tiny children a start in life. The personal and the politics were not separate. They were part of the same old restless mind and the same broken, failing body.

'No, Rupert, no. I remember the Falklands, I remember Goose Green. A night darker than sin, and bodies falling all around me. Do you think we did that so that our foreign secretary could piss like some Belgian dwarf in the square? Did we sail to the ends of the earth to share an embassy in Buenos Aires with the Eyeties and the Huns? Wasn't that the big and the little together, standing firm? Did my men die then to make us part of the bloody Balkan problem?'

The son groaned softly. He had heard it all so many times before. But he was expected to argue back. It was his role. 'Dad,

4

that was another time and another place. We've done all this to stop wars. And we have. We used to be fighting always, and now we don't. I know we've given things up and I know you don't like it. But you mustn't let the crazies in the press foul you up. When I go into Dorchester shopping, there aren't crowds in the marketplace shouting, "Bring back the pound," or any of the tabloid crap you were fed. People understand about the Central Bank now. They don't worry about inflation gobbling up their pension like it gobbled your family's. They don't bang on about the sacred right of the chancellor to foul things up every election. Nobody under thirty can remember anything but a euro.'

'But are they happy, Rupert? Are they happy?'

He shifted uneasily on his chair. What was the real answer to that? Some were, and some weren't. If you were young and trained and mobile, you were happy – and probably off to Montpellier or Munich before breakfast. But Dorset hadn't survived the disintegration of the agriculture policy without its farms, and farmers, being literally set aside. And the people who were left were ageing, finding too little work and too small a pension at the end of it. They survived on the backs of the moneyed geriatrics who at the end of their days came to pretend to be country folk, taking the City pension cheques and tarting up their cottages. The currency was fine where the cities – London or Lyon – bustled; fine somewhere, not fine everywhere.

There was no need to reply. The grip on his hand tightened again. 'I want you to promise me one thing, Rupert, one last thing. I came from a country which had its roots and its history. I was proud to be an Englishman, to serve the old Queen, to salute the flag. My men, my friends, were the same. We did it for England, and now there's nothing of England left but pots in the curiosity shop.

'When we came home to Portsmouth, you know, there were thousands cheering on the harbour. And your mother, with you kids at her side, all waving. I'd been away for months. I didn't know that she was ill. She never said anything. It was the biggest sacrifice of all. It had to be for something. Promise me to remember that. Promise.'

Words were cheap. Rupert squeezed his father's hand back and solemnly found eye contact. 'Of course I promise. We must never forget. I'm not just saying this. There's always a balance, always something worth holding on to.'

The glibness unsettled him and he got to his feet. 'I must be going. There's a meeting and a lot to do.'

The wax lips smiled politely.

'I'll be down again at the weekend. Please tell Hatty if there's anything you need. Maybe a referendum form?'

A joke too far. The lips curled.

Rupert kissed the dank forehead and hurried downstairs, calling a perfunctory goodbye to his sister in the kitchen.

In the mud and chaos of the yard, by the rusted Ford pick-up, he pulled out his mobile and summoned Fairfax, who'd been waiting quietly in the car park of the Hardy Arms down the road. Rupert had not wanted to signal his visit.

The silver Daimler reversed into the yard. The minister left for London.

The new secretary Rupert Warner had picked for her singular, gossip-quenching lack of any redeeming attraction was poised at the office door, pacing for his return. 'Your sister called an hour ago,' she said. 'She hadn't got your mobile number and wanted to know how booked you were. Well, don't forget you've got the PM at eight. But she seemed a bit odd, a bit anxious.'

'Thank you, Miss Bowen,' Rupert said. What the hell was her first name? Muriel? No, Violet. He kept thinking of her as Eva, as in Braun.

Her short, thin arms settled briefly on bulbous hips, urging him to instant action. Marching orders.

Rupert sighed. Had he walked out and left something? Harriet answered on the second ring.

Her voice was the usual cold whine. 'You went two hours too soon,' she said, almost triumphantly. 'He's dead. He cried out for you, but by the time I got there the heart had gone. The doctor says that often happens with cancer. One thing then another. It was a pity he had to go alone.'

She didn't want him to return. What was the point? Their father had been dying for weeks. The arrangements had been made long since: one call to the undertakers in Dorchester and the body would be gone in the morning. Rupert muttered a few soft phrases of comfort and regret, and put down the phone.

RIP, as expected, but his head still swam and his eyes still smarted. His father and he had never been easy with each other. Captain James Hector Lionel Warner, 2 Para, away in the Gulf; away in Germany; away in Ireland and the Falklands – with Lizzy trailing the two children fitfully in his wake. But when she'd found the lump in her left breast, and that it was too late, that the lymph nodes were gone, he had abandoned everything in life he loved, including the promotion of the medalled hero, to be with them. Not much of a businessman. The hotel had gone belly-up. The farm, the proper farm near Tiverton, had followed in a snowstorm of botched paperwork and bitter winters where the feed ran out. Captain Warner MC, Keeper of the Caravans, eker of a frugal living. But too bloody proud to take any of the help Rupert had offered. 'No,' he'd say. 'Life dealt me my cards and I must play them that way. I gave you what I could, a proper education and a start. Those are your cards. I don't want anything from them.'

Rupert got up, walked slowly through the maze of corridors from the Leader of the House's rooms towards New Palace Yard; then, coat collar turned up against the wind, across Whitehall and past the shivering policemen into 10 Downing Street.

The Prime Minister and Rupert Warner were not, in any true sense, friends. Michaelson had no friends. But they had been together for twenty years, since one party conference night in

Blackpool. It had been tipping down. Michaelson scuttled out of the Queen's Hotel shouting for a taxi and, as it splashed to a halt, a big man in a trench coat and a pork-pie hat appeared from the spray and opened the door. 'I say,' said Michaelson, squeaking. 'I think that was mine.'

'Sorry, old son. Why don't we hop inside and see what we can sort out?'

Easily done. They were both, it emerged, going down to a south coast agents' cocktail thrash at the Pleasure Beach. Necessary cheap plonk and pleasantries, pressed flesh and sausage rolls. Warner was starting out on the candidates' obstacle course, fighting a chunk of nether Dorset with a Lib-Dem majority of 9,000; Michaelson was senior partner, hero of the New Forest West by-election. But Rupert Warner skipped the deference. He wore thick wool suits and check waistcoats and brogues, and he talked of the land as though he owned it. 'Come over for the weekend,' he'd say. 'We've got the point-to-point in Foggy Bottom.'

He was not really a country gentleman. The family came from Birstall, urban sprawl three miles north of Leicester. His grandfather had made socks and sweaters till the Poles and the Chinese took him apart. The Captain, though, believed in proper schooling for a proper life. Elizabeth's parents – poor dead Lizzy's grieving mother and father – had retired to Dorset. Sherborne, with its quads and parks and cut-glass accents, was the proper choice, paid for from the last toe of the last sock. Rupert, with his easy smiles and natural courtesy, somehow became a toff, a character, a charmer. That charm got him to Oxford and a third in geography – though not quite the Boat Race slot he'd coveted. A bit short of puff in the last half-mile, he would grin ruefully, and promise to train harder next time.

Rupert had drifted into politics. His year off after university was spent, to his father's manifest amazement, on a cattle ranch in Queensland. The ranch owner wanted to be a state senator. Rupert had found himself part-time cowboy and election agent, canvassing by radio. They won, and were drunk for two days.

When he got home, the farm was going down the pan. No choice. First he joined the Country Landowners' Association, and then the Conservatives. People seemed to like him. They liked his chuffling jokes and his inexhaustible good humour, the way he could hug them in an instant. And they liked Jennifer, a foot shorter, seven stones lighter, and the smiling baby she carried to meetings. Politics became what he did. Westminster just happened. The blissful Boundary Commissioners' report that carved through Weymouth and ditched the Liberals just happened. The Michaelson opportunity – the death of Palmer, the bust-up, Labour's implosion, the need for a Tory leader who had kept his European powder dry – seemed merely to happen too.

They made the perfect campaign team: little and large, thin and playfully thick, Roundhead and laughing Cavalier. Rupert glad-handed the lobby, building up Michaelson as the brain of a coming Britain, the master calculator of classlessness, smoothing his path with the party nobs, warming up audiences with unexpected tales of the humanity that lurked behind the candidate's thin smile. He never stole the limelight. But he bathed bloodlessness in a rosy warmth.

Michaelson had not thought, for a second, of giving him one of those head-banging ministries of detail like Social Security or Environment. Rupert was good at people, not flow-charts and figures. Mine's a large Bell's with a spot of soda, old boy, and even then he often lost count through the evening. He was chief whip for two smooth years and then Leader of the House; Luncher Supreme, Head Chef of chumminess to a ravenous press.

The Prime Minister didn't look up for a while after Rupert had come into the room. He turned a page, finished a paragraph. 'Oh, Rupert,' he said, as in 'Oh, coffee.'

'You said you wanted me, Curtis.' It was and would always

be a ridiculous name. Michaelson's father, late into middle age when the only son arrived, had been a golfer and – drunk with celebration – had stuck a pin into that year's Ryder Cup list. The Prime Minister hated him and hated the result. But the image makers had worked hard on it. Clipped, technocratic Curtis: prematurely silvered hair cut almost crew length, matching silver spectacles, grey suit, grey face. Corporation man. Mr Efficiency for the new Efficiency Britain, the country that would take Singapore to the cleaners.

'It's the bloody referendum,' he said. 'It will have to be March the seventh. The Bratislava summit is bound to be a shambles. We'll need Christmas to make them all forget. Then there's my South African visit and the Central Bank governors' meeting. January is a nightmare – and, anyway, it's always best to let the Fritzes have their vote first. That will pull the whingeing mini-Fritzes into line, remind them who butters their pumpernickel. We can time it near the end, a kind of dot-and-comma exercise. They've all signed up again. You do the same.'

Rupert had his diary out and was hunting through it. 'I think February would be better,' he said. 'The less time the buffers have to get organized, the easier it will be. It's not the result that worries me, it's the cash we have to keep spending. What about the fourteenth?'

'Wonderful,' said Michaelson, breaking his pencil and lobbing it into the basket. 'Genius. Twenty years since the Queen died. Westminster Abbey running hot and cold with the tear-stained populace. Our bald little apology for a king doing his Runnymede add-on. And you want to hold a referendum over lunch. For God's sake, Rupert, put a sock in it.'

'I'm sorry,' said Rupert. 'I'm not in top form. They told me my father died just before I came over.'

The Prime Minister was not really listening. He was rummaging around in the waste for the pencil.

'I'd only just got back from seeing him, and it was pretty awful. He got very agitated about Europe. Said that we'd gone too far, that we were betrayers. Said we'd let my mother down. I know it's silly, but it was the last time. There's no second chance to sort it out.'

Michaelson found the pencil and jotted something on his pad. 'It's a loss, Rupert. I can see why you're upset. But for heaven's sake don't get Europe all bogged with natural grief. Your father was what? Seventy-three? Not a bad innings. He'd been ill for ages. He was waiting to die, in pain. People in that sort of state say all sorts of things, silly things, emotional things. How can you possibly understand anything at an end like that? You and Jenny have all my condolences. I'll write you a letter and make sure we're properly represented at the funeral. But you must keep stupid issues and ramblings out of this. One word out of turn to the lobby and they'll be turning a sick old man into some sort of British hero figure.'

Rupert said nothing, but he could feel the area of neck above his collar pulsing redly.

'Now,' said Michaelson, 'I can see you're not really up to thinking clearly. Why don't we cut this short and try again tomorrow? Say one forty-five, just before Questions.'

The pencil point snapped, and he threw it back in the bin.

'You might have told me.'

It was the first thing Jenny said when he came through the door.

'The *Dorchester Echo* rang, wanting some quotes. I didn't know what they were talking about. I didn't know he was dead. They obviously thought I was a fool – and I felt like one.'

Rupert, as ever, shuffled back half a pace. 'Oh, God,' he said. 'I'm sorry. They only told me when I got back to London. Then I had Michaelson and a pile of business questions to sort. I didn't have a moment. I'm sorry.'

She turned away from him and went into the kitchen. No longer slim; no longer young; no longer the girl he'd married or the mother of his babies. But strong. Jenny Cochran had been seventeen when they met – a temporary secretary in the fertilizer agency, earning some money and thinking about university. Her father's little business in agricultural machinery had just collapsed in a pile of debt. She was on her own. She instantly found Rupert.

Jenny supposed that the big, bumbly man on the way up had seemed some sort of substitute father to her. For a while, when Richard and Piers had been tiny, they'd been happy enough. She'd become immersed in his life and his politics, and found how she could be useful to him. She charmed the constituency chairmen, opened garden fêtes, always knew how to get one of her golden babies on the front of the local rag. But she had abandoned her own life too early. When the boys went away to school, she'd gone to university in Exeter, commuting back and forth at weekends, and done social sciences. She was ferociously clever. By thirty-two she was head of the county's social services committee. A handful of years later, when Rupert made cabinet, she turned quango queen: Arts Council, mental health tribunal, community care advisory commission, the Broadcasting Morality Board. She was on television far more than him, a statutory panel-show woman. Her *Who's Who* entry ran two centimetres longer than his.

There was always a murmur of speculation about her. One craggy professor at Exeter. The boyish director of the Royal Shakespeare Company, who'd done so amazingly well in the grants stakes a few years ago. The Oxford head of psychiatry with the ginger shock who occasionally advised her tribunal for a carefully negotiated fee. You could see the possibilities. Jenny's plump shoulders and jutting bosom were toned by hours of swimming and gym sweat. Her full little face was unlined. The blonde-streaked hair was cut short and tousled. Her business suits always hovered on the brink of the incongruous, wrestling anxiously with the swell of her breasts. When she tossed her glasses aside, you suddenly noticed the thin mouth flexing.

But somehow no tabloid, fretting over more privacy laws,

had ever laid a finger on her. Nor did Rupert say a word. They maintained more than pretences. Sometimes, on a Sunday morning, she would stretch towards him and make herself briefly available. She did not miss constituency events or cabinet dinners. They were a team, a limited company. He was her passport to the life she had carved out. He had settled for a steady, emotionless state.

Jenny made camomile tea and brought him a cup through into the study. 'Do they know about the funeral yet?' she asked tonelessly.

'Not certainly, but Saturday I hope. Hatty had the undertakers on stand-by. They've been told that the weekend's easiest for me.'

He talked to her awkwardly about the last hours, and what Michaelson had said. 'I know he's a cold bugger, but that was tops. He's changed, you know. He never was any good with people, but there was always a small red light somewhere that told him to switch on the charm. Tonight the bloody fuse went phut.'

'I'll need a hat,' said Jenny. She had left him already, running through tomorrow's diary in her head, wondering where to find thirty minutes for Bond Street.

They went to bed. She gave him a brisk, chill embrace before he churned into sleep.

The parish church at Abbotsbury stood on a small plateau of another hill overlooking the village. Look west, and you could see the slate Dorset roofs and smoking chimneys banked like a stage set. Look south, and a scoop of valley led straight to the sea. In summer, Rupert thought, it was one of the most beautiful places in England. In winter, with the rain gusting in from the Channel, there was no time to pause and look as they scuttled from their cars and raced up the steps.

His father had few friends left. A depleted watch of old soldiers, a scatter of villagers and farmers. Harriet wore her lovat Burberry and a dark green headscarf pulled tight under the chin. The rest were there because of Rupert. The mayor of Dorchester had his chain. The local Conservative Association had its three-line whip. Four photographers cowered beneath umbrellas at the gate.

Rupert sat next to Jenny and bent his head. Somehow he could not pray, but he had to close his eyes. There was a sudden whisper of excitement. Michaelson appeared on the pew beside them. 'I had a meeting in Poole,' he said. 'I thought I'd come and pay my respects. I hope you don't mind. It just seemed appropriate.' Rupert nodded. The small red light was working again.

'Dearly beloved, we are gathered here this morning, in the sight of God, to celebrate the life of Captain James Hector Lionel Warner, a member of this church and citizen of this parish . . .'

'Rock of ages, cleft for me.' Jenny put down the battered blue hymnal and it slipped to the floor beside her. Michaelson was bending in an instant, handing it to her. She looked at him. He smiled.

Rupert did not need to be told. He had seen that look and that smile before. His neck began to pulse again.

Chapter Two

The referendum was no big deal, any tension staled by repetition. Blair's old government, nearly three decades before, had strewn them around like confetti. One to change the electoral system, one to change it back; one to regionalize, one to centralize; one to marry the Liberals, one to divorce them; and so interminably on. This was the ninth specific European question since, long ago, Britain had finally, finally opted to become a part of the mark two, post-Maastricht version with all the monetary kit attached. For years the press had drummed up the drama, and ambitious politicians – flailing back and forth – had laid bets for their own futures. Stay out, it won't work. Told you so. No, wait! Get in, it's working.

But now the argument was over. All of the Union held referendums all of the time: it was one price paid for Swiss membership. Because the burghers of Berne didn't have proper prime ministers and presidents and charismatic leaders on the make, they insisted on hanging on to the votes they had, and the thing got contagious. Sometimes there were minor hiccups, especially from the minnows of the Mediterranean and the Baltic. Malta and Latvia were continuing pains. The waves of voting, however, the constant affirmations, contrived to keep stroppy flag-wavers in order. The question put, from habit and experience, always upped the ante and loaded on the threat. Do you endorse the treaty of Superblank as solemnly negotiated by your government with the thirty-two other nations of the Union or do you renounce that agreement? In Britain alone a distant amendment to the

Referendum Act, as supervised by the Standing Commission on Democratic Accountability, made it explicit that renunciation of anything implied renunciation of everything. Submit or we quit. The Law Lords had trawled over the text fifteen years ago. A vote against, their exalted wigships solemnly ruled, was a vote to get out. The Labour government hadn't liked that and stomped off to the Court of Justice in Luxembourg, but the Swiss judge had his own *rösti* to fry and the French judge saw no reason to help the Brits off another bloody hook. Everyone, in the end, lacking the relevant Westminster majority for further change, feigned principled agreement: subsidiarity meant asking the question the way local parliaments wanted. And, anyway, it helped keep the back benches in order.

Michaelson sighed as he flipped through the private polls from Central Office. If the referendum were held today (which was, anyway, last Friday, two useless months before reality) then 61 per cent would have said yes, 28 per cent would have said no – and the rest would have been stewing around in familiar inertia. That was more or less par for the course. There would be the usual thrashings until the final week. The tabloids, with their Australian and Canadian and American owners, would enjoy waving the flag for a while. But they, too, knew which bowl held the double cream. They were corporations with interests to protect. They'd begin to balance it out at last knockings.

Dear Lord, it was such a pointless ritual. Any card you like, sir, so long as it's the ten of clubs.

He didn't know why Warner had asked to see him. There was nothing much afoot. The usual sceptical crew were making the usual noises, but there couldn't be more than twenty-five of them topweight – and they were mostly ageing idiots, parroting the futilities they'd learned in their twenties. Ten more years, Michaelson reckoned, and nobody who mattered would remember what it used to be like. They said we'd become a cypher; that Downing Street would be a shell. They hadn't the gumption to realize how a prime minister who played Westminster against Brussels and Brussels against Westminster had two power bases rather than one. Next year, the one thing that never changed, he'd have his six months as President of Europe. That would be the picture to frame in the library.

Rupert knocked. It seemed a daft thing to do, he thought. This man, this metronome, this dry, fornicating bastard, was supposed to be a friend.

'Have you got fifteen minutes?'

'Ten,' said Michaelson, glancing at his watch. 'The Spanish foreign minister is due at eleven. Problems come and problems go, but Gibraltar goes on for ever. The Royal Navy should have towed the bloody Rock into mid-channel and sunk it.'

'Right,' said Rupert. 'I don't want to say this over a desk. Can we go and sit by the fire?'

He poured himself a glass of Malvern water.

'I'd appreciate it if you'd hear me out. I've decided to resign, and I want you to understand why.'

Michaelson said nothing.

'In a way, it was my father. You were right, of course. He was a sentimental old fool. The Britain he remembered was never up to much. But he felt a passion for it and he knew where the roots were. He came from somewhere. And when you laughed at him, I asked myself: Where do I come from?

'There doesn't seem to be a focus any longer. You know, when you're part of something big, how difficult it is to see where the decisions get made. You always assume it's the committee you're not on that matters. That's me now, and I think it's us. Oh, there's still a House of Commons and I'm Leader of it. We tog out in fancy dress every so often. The King polishes up his silverware and comes down to do the opening bit like his father and his grandmother before him. We meet. We debate. We vote. But, really, we're going through the motions.

'And yet, when I go to Brussels, it's just more of the same. They say they're servants of the greater Union. That it's

Strasbourg that counts, with all those shiny new powers we've given them, sitting round counting their expenses. But when you pinch an MEP, he'll go on about how much better Westminster still is – or wish he was a frigging Central Banker, taking the real decisions way away from contaminated politicos. Who wants to be a servant of the people when you can be a heap big Kraut writing cheques?'

Michaelson grimaced. Warner had never been much of a political thinker. You wound him up, pointed him in the right direction and let him ladle out the spluttery charm. But this was pathetic. 'Please,' he said, 'spare me the useless jingoism. At least try to talk policy. You sound like a cheap newspaper editor.'

Rupert barely paused. 'That is precisely what you don't understand. Of course, these things can come out cheap. I hate that. But at least there's a real feeling there. Say something like that in the pub and you'll get ordinary people agreeing. They understand. They don't understand a constructed continent. They don't know where to turn any longer.

'Oh, of course you can sit on top of it all – sneering, weaving, playing the odds. Devolving this down and that up. Filling the cracks. Phoning your chums in the chancelleries. And so we go slowly down the road, step by step, until we live in a country that doesn't function any longer. Perhaps my father was a fool. But he was at least a warm fool, not a cold, desiccated one.'

'Have you talked to Jenny about all this?' Michaelson asked, no red light flashing, the tone of voice swilling with solicitude.

Jenny. The match that lit the fire. Did he realize what he was saying?

Rupert got to his feet and walked five steps to the door. 'Look,' he said, 'there's no point in trying to bodge our way through this. We ought to understand each other after all these years. I've been useful to you because you need somebody who looks like a human being to open the batting with. I can't begin to compete on the brainbox front. You're a bloody genius at manipulating things, but you're no damn good at people. I'm calling it a day. You probably weren't going to give me another job anyway, just a fat armchair in what's left of the Lords. Now, at least, I can begin to live again.'

The Prime Minister shrugged. God save us from middle-aged ministerial menopause. There was a lot of it about; and it made proper planning difficult.

It seemed the smallest of earthquakes, with nobody much hurt. Rupert put in his formal resignation note at nine on Saturday evening, too late for the Sundays to make a number of. He talked, briefly, of personal circumstances and the need to step out of the government spotlight for a while. Michaelson cut loose with the adjectives, hailing a vital contribution that would be greatly missed and wise counsel that surely could not be replaced. The lobby was told, far off the record, about the strain of office after a death in the family that had hit hard. Poor old Warner. Soppy cove. Let him go away quietly and try to get over it.

No interviews. A one-day wonder. By Monday morning the story was all about the promotion of the chief whip they called Himmler. Was he too brutal to lead the House? Was his oily deputy up to taking over? High tedium without a TV picture worth the glance. Except in the eating houses of central London, by Wednesday Rupert was a forgotten man.

Jenny treated him as though he'd had a mental breakdown. She didn't shout. She lowered her voice and spoke very softly. 'You nit. You poor, stupid, deluded sod. It's not just your life, it's mine – and I'm not going to let you take it away from me.'

The Broadcasting Morality Board had a two-week tour of California scheduled. At short notice, she said, she'd decided to lead the delegation.

There was a press conference at Heathrow when they left. 'We hear about some new screening chips that can be automatically activated – fifteen seconds ahead of transmission – by the pending prospect of bad language in live speech,' she said. 'They call them flexible prior constrainers. They analyse, they predict and then they bleep. Ninety-seven per cent of swear words and unsuitable images gone in a trice. If we value our children's innocence, it's just our duty to investigate.' Duty called. Rupert was left alone.

He sat in the front room at Draycott Place while the dark of winter extinguished the last grey light of afternoon, the crunch of car doors echoing outside as the mothers of Chelsea picked up their kids from the school five doors down. There were squeals and howls and coos. Life was going on as usual. Young life, renewal. His phone did not ring. It was as though he had suddenly ceased to exist.

Do I simply pull the blanket over my head? Do I give them what they want? Or do I, at least, say my piece?

The Second Reading of the Referendum Enabling Bill wasn't a crowd-puller. A wet Thursday heading into a long weekend. The House maybe a quarter full.

Michaelson, as had become custom, opened the debate. Forrest, still finding his feet, did Labour's stock turn, moaning and questioning – but not really opposing. He wasn't Palmer, the great lost leader. He hated the comparisons.

Rupert sat quietly on the third row back. He was the fifth to be called.

'Mr Deputy Speaker,' he said, fiddling with his glasses, thumbing through a dishevelled file of notes, 'this is my first speech from the benches of honour, the back benches from which I started out nineteen years ago and to which I now return with a full heart.' The press gallery yawned. A few more men of honour headed for the tea room.

'I speak here today, however, on a matter more vital, more crucial to the future of this country than I have ever previously addressed. I speak to oppose this motion. I speak – after years of silence, after years where I had eyes but could not see – finally to call a halt to the quagmire of Europe, which has swallowed us all so silently but so inexorably.'

The tea room began to empty. The parliamentary sketch writers, spinning their cobwebs of words, began to call urgently for the hard-news types who could do the front-page stuff.

Warner would never be an orator. The metaphors were bargain basement. The warmth he could contrive one-on-one faded amid the artificially plummy tones he'd cultivated since Sherborne and he found he could play the toff. There he stood. Just fifty-one, but looking older: hair a shade too grey and a shade too wispy, blue waistcoat harassed by pink stomach, talking about England. No one had ever heard a word of dissent from him before. Big Rupe, Michaelson's dummy, suddenly answering back.

'There are those,' he said, 'who find any thought of a pause, any question of a moment for reflection, almost contemptible. We have had our arguments, they say. We've had our European votes and our upheavals. Now we must put all that behind us. These people do not look back with pride on the Britain that has gone and the days when we ruled ourselves and traded in our own currency. They have no time for such sentiment. Why, they wonder, do we complain so? Why don't a few new chemical factories, a few thousand new jobs, shut us up? Why – bloodlessly, technocratically, impatiently – is there no gratitude in their brave new world of frigid calculation?'

He was looking straight at Michaelson's back, its shoulders somehow hunched under fire. Those who could see the Prime Minister saw him grey with anger, lips clenched into the thinnest of slits.

When they reached for Hansard next day, it was not a speech of originality or eloquence. It was banal. But the confrontation and the surprise gave it a force beyond words.

'Mr Deputy Speaker. I oppose this motion with all my heart. And if I lose here, in the House I love, I shall fight the referendum with every sinew of my being. For, sir, the time has come. The time – whether ideal or not, whether the question to be decided is crucial or not – to begin rowing back to a better world which, if we are honest to ourselves, we remember. The time to say, "No more".'

He had not thought what to do when it was all over. The lobby hacks would be looking for him, the TV crews shouting for a few sentences of recyclable defiance in their arc-lights. He groaned and mopped his forehead, sweating and shivering together. He wanted a moment of peace in the cocoon of the Palace. He wanted a cup of tea.

Rupert loved the Members' Tea Room. Heavy panelled walls, thick green carpets, waitresses called Kylie and Sharon in white pinafores who knew his name but nothing of politics.

'The usual, Mr Warner, dear?' said Kylie. 'We've got mince pies as the special this afternoon. Christmas is coming. Very festive.'

He did not feel like Christmas. He ordered a pot of Darjeeling and a slice of Bakewell tart and sat in a corner picking at its thick pastry, slowly separating the heavy yellow sponge from the seam of strawberry jam; eyes down as the room glanced at him and muttered behind its hands. Alone again.

'Do you mind if I join you?'

Rupert looked up, startled, a nodule of sponge tipping from his fork into the tea-cup.

'No. No, of course not. Miss Burley, isn't it?'

'Gurley,' said Polly, frowning in case he made the joke that always set her teeth on edge.

The sponge was soddenly spreading across the cup. He reached for a teaspoon and began to fish it into the saucer. Gurley. Polly Gurley. That was it. Elected for Leeds Somewhere-or-other last time. Used to be a high flyer in the Cabinet Office. Permanent-secretary material. Maybe a dame three decades down the road. Nobody quite knew why she'd wanted to trade all that in for politics and mushing around in the backbench pits waiting for the whips to take notice.

She was not, he thought, dressing to get noticed. She was thin, in an angular maroon suit that seemed to make hard edges of her body. The brown hair was pinned back, trailing a few strands of disarray. The brown glasses were square and severe. But maybe there was something more there? Her skin was clear and unlined. Late twenties, early thirties? And her grey eyes were steady, fixing him as he looked up.

'Forgive this,' she said. 'We haven't really met, and it may seem a bit of a cheek. But I just wanted to say how much I admired what you did this afternoon. It took real courage.'

Rupert found himself blushing. 'That's very white of you,' he said. 'I didn't have you down as a sceptic.'

'Oh, I'm not,' said Polly. 'Everybody thinks I'm a Union junkie, always trooping round on delegations to Vilnius and Bratislava, spreading the word. I don't really think I agree with a single thing you said. But that's not the point. I got out of the Civil Service because I knew I couldn't make a difference. We were there to take orders and implement them. Do that well, and you'd get a gong and a fat run of non-executive directorships at the end. Do it badly, and you'd be digging into your indexed pension ahead of time. Did I want that for the rest of my life? Not when I thought about it. I wanted, some time or other, to be able to make a difference, to say what I thought. That's what you did this afternoon. I admire that. I don't agree with you, but I admire you.'

He blushed again. A few more strands of hair were drifting down over her forehead. She pushed back the chair and began to squeeze to her feet.

'Hang on,' said Rupert. 'Have a cup of tea. Tell me about yourself. I haven't had a decent conversation with anybody for forty-eight hours. P-bloody-ariah Numero Uno. Let's not talk about Europe or the accursed Curtis. Let's have a chat. Would you like a mince pie? Doris tells me they're awfully good.'

And so, for half an hour, they talked. He told her about Jenny and the American trip and the two sons he never saw. She told him about growing up in Didsbury and the fruit-merchant dad who'd died when she was ten and the scholarship to Manchester Grammar School and the magic carpet to Cambridge. 'It was as though God was paying me back for all the misery,' she said. 'I can remember Mother weeping when he died, and there she was, eighteen years later when I got elected, jumping for joy. "Now you can make that difference," she says. But I keep waiting for the chance and wondering if it will ever come. Will I be like you? Will I have the guts to make a difference?'

Over her shoulder he could see three journalists peering through the door and pointing. He hunched, for a second, behind the cake trolley, as though the pile of pies could offer sanctuary, then began to clamber up. 'Duty calls,' he said. 'I can't tell you how nice it was to meet you. Really, v. appreciated.'

The grey eyes turned downwards. Was she blushing too?

For a few hours the damage limitation worked as the spinners spun their yarns. Poor Warner, off his head with grief. He got the boot, you know. The PM was trying to gloss that, struggling to save an old friend who needed a rest. Poor Warner.

The BBC *Nine o'Clock News*, as usual, swallowed the lobby line whole. Rupert got thirty seconds, five items in. 'There was fresh embarrassment for Curtis Michaelson and his government today as . . . And now over to our political editor at Westminster. Roger, how are ministers taking this intervention?'

'Well, Sally, more in sorrow than in anger, I think. Sources point out that the former Leader of the House has had weeks of bad health since his father died, and . . .'

'Thank you, Roger. And now we go to Antibes where Princess Alice and her new husband are enjoying the second day of their honeymoon as guests of Bahrain's Sheikh Gamal . . .'

The morning papers told a different story. *Et tu*, Rupert? PM's Great Chum Stabs Him in the Back. Europe Boils Over for the Tories Again. The Old Ghost Returns to Spoil the Feast. Mystery of the Michaelson Minister who Turned. Referendum Shocker for Fuming Mikey.

Rupert was suddenly famous. Old women stopped him in the street and shook his hand. Two TV vans were permanently parked outside the house. Anti-European groups obligingly staged daily demos in his drive, waving flags for the cameras and burning effigies of some parody Frenchman in a beret. Jenny called from Los Angeles to say she'd seen him on *Cable News*. 'You're off your head,' she said.

For the first time in years he was enjoying himself. His own man. Wanted. Carstairs and Broadbent, and the rest of what he used to call the Septic Tank, were round within hours, pleading with him to lead the referendum campaign for them. 'Better the sinner who can get us a few headlines, Rupert,' said Broadbent.

He didn't like the fat toad, all mouth and family banking money, all opportunism – a flag-waver of convenience after Michaelson, three years before, had tipped him out of the bottom tier of the Treasury and into the backbench gutter. In office Broadbent had had no views on Europe that stretched much beyond a five-course dinner menu at the Tour d'Argent. Out of office, with chatter about some matching grants that hadn't added up, he was suddenly John Bull. His British League – all-party and (the other joke) all-loony – operated from a mews office just off Grosvenor Square. They were not short of cash. Maybe the mad millionaires had dried up, but The Will and the Way Crusade – 'Leave us the money to fight on and in the end we shall overcome' – had been a marketing triumph. One rest home in Torquay had turned in over £500,000 in the last six months.

'Better than that,' said Carstairs. 'I think you can give us the gravitas we need, the feeling that heavyweights at the heart of things have seen the light. I almost cried when you got up to speak, you know. I was terribly moved.'

Rupert had more time for Carstairs: thinner, sandier, a junior Home Office minister culled in the last reshuffle after a snivelling row about balanced diets in women's prisons. He drank too much, but he had a kind of honesty to him. You couldn't predict which way he'd swing. And swinging now to Broadbent? Odd. Flaky judgement again. But at least he was a human being.

They lunched him at the Savoy Grill. They organized a press conference in Cowley Street. They hired him the latest helicopter and painted it red, white and blue. He made fifteen speeches a day minimum, learning that shyness and awkwardness could convey a sincerity Michaelson couldn't touch.

There were two dozen or so in the primary-school assembly room on Dog Kennel Hill, where the first lumps of South London struggle out of the Thames valley. The heating had broken. The Union Jack behind the stage was hanging slack, a drawing-pin short of a load. The audience, old men in mufflers, old women in heavy, shapeless coats, sat hunched together four rows back. Rupert had a cold. He croaked his familiar lines to the first swathe of empty chairs and watched as the chill turned his words to clouds of condensation.

'And that, my friends, is the signal we can send. That we are Britons who have learned, as the clock strikes twelve, that we have a Britain worth defending. That if we can fight together, as the world has cause to know, then we can always win.'

A smattering of applause. They clapped their hands, then rubbed them, then stuck them back into pockets.

'Questions?' asked Rupert. He had had to introduce himself, too. Five minutes before the off the chairman had called in pleading flu.

A young man in glasses was standing at the back, smiling. He raised an arm, and suddenly a camera team came through the door, running forward to poke a lens in Rupert's face.

'Hutchings from Granada Truthwatch,' said the smirk. 'Can you tell us what will happen if you win? How the pound will emerge from the euro? At what parity? Over what practical timescale?'

Rupert rubbed his nose and beamed. 'My dear boy,' he said, 'you're treating us seriously. I can't tell you how that warms the cockles of this ancient heart.'

The smirk turned to a scowl and began to talk about differential interest rates.

'Oh, I say, come on,' said Rupert, 'fair dos. Once sound-bitten, twice shy.'

There was a high, thin cackle of laughter from the depths of the hall, a ribald clacking of false teeth.

It was a fool's paradise, of course: an old fool's paradise. The polls barely moved. The Rupert Factor, the papers concluded after a couple of weeks, was three points max. The no men were going nowhere. The cameras began to melt away, catching him only in mute head shots miming the day's catchphrase. No Europe: No Worry. Your No is Our Yes. Take a Shot and Stop the Rot.

But, somehow, he didn't mind. Jenny came back three days later and sat on a few platforms for him. There was no alternative, she complained bitterly, to playing the loyal wife. 'That's in public, though. When the door closes, I don't want the stink of you in my nostrils.' He moved into the spare bedroom gratefully with only his mobile phone for company, falling asleep with it in his hand – and once waking the next morning to find it wrapped in his arms like the moulting teddy bear that had soothed his childhood nights.

Ah, well, only two more days, love, and then I can return to well-deserved obscurity.

Three in the morning, and a full moon bathed Whitehall, giving the lumpen edifices of state a shimmering life.

Michaelson sat immobile on a window-seat in the largest reception room, looking out over Horseguards Parade. Downing

Street was silent, seemingly lost in sleep, though he knew that couldn't be so. A pair of policemen patrolled beneath the trees at the edge of St James's Park. There would be many more of them outside the front of number ten, chatting quietly among themselves, brooding on the upheavals of the hours before and waiting for the wagons of the TV breakfast shows to start rolling in.

He stood up and began pacing from room to room, then almost jogging up and down the stairs, past the portraits of his predecessors, until his heart pounded with exhaustion to drown the frustration. Why did the bloody painters always do them grinning? Why did they always keep their hair? Thank God he'd told Susan and the children to stay in Lymington. The last thing he needed now was their whining and weeping.

At first, in disaster, he had turned in on himself, self-contained as usual, manufacturing a sporting smile for the cameras.

'You must be shattered, Prime Minister?'

'No. Just disappointed that the voters, the umpires we always obey, have given me out so narrowly and on such a poor turn-out. The pavilion was half empty. I'd expected a better innings.'

'Does that mean you're going? That there's no chance of you fighting back, calling an election, trying again?'

'I am not a quitter, gentlemen. But there is no alternative. We've seen the British people turn their backs on me tonight, and on Europe. They apparently want some other leader and a policy I can't begin to visualize doing anything but grotesque harm. That is their prerogative. Make no mistake, this was a vote to quit, to withdraw into our shell. I may only have lost by a hundred thousand votes but, as Churchill might have said, one hundred thousand is enough. It will be for others to sort this out. I wish them well.'

He seemed, for a second, to be a human being, to bleed in public. Then the lips pursed again. 'More than that,' said Michaelson. 'I shall remember them in my prayers.'

O Lord, mince Rupert James Grosvenor Warner, the shit of

the millennium, into a slurry of retribution, and strew his rotting remains across the Serpentine so that the ducks may devour his putrescent soul. Amen.

Rupert had not dragged himself home from Cowley Street until five in the morning. There had been too many interviews. His throat was raw. And too many glasses raised in triumph. His head throbbed. Jenny had come back hours before. He opened the bedroom door and heard her light, decisive snore, signalling unapproachability.

He shuffled down to the kitchen and groped in the cupboard by the fridge. Bloody hell! No Scotch. Two warm bottles of Orvieto Secco from some distant tombola. He poured himself a mug of cooking sherry and sat at the big wooden table, head in hands. Victory? What the hell was victory? He remembered the smirking reporter in the freezing school hall, banging on about the real world and the real questions that would come. Questions without anyone to answer them now that Michaelson had fallen on his paper-knife. There wasn't a government standing. There wasn't a leader in sight. Forrest? He filled the mug with sherry again. Christ, what a shambles.

The thump of the morning papers on the mat woke him. He peered blearily into the first glimmer of dawn. His tongue filled his mouth. The mug lay smashed on the floor, a stain spreading across the boards of the floor. He felt the stubble on his chin and lurched towards the window. What the hell was the time? Eight, at least. That was when the papers always came. And there, heading down the street, were four men, walking together. Men in grey overcoats hiding grey suits.

Pendrick, the chairman of the 2022 Committee; Wall and Crumpsty, his deputies; and the chief whip they called Himmler, hovering a yard or so behind.

The bell rang. Rupert sluiced his face in the sink and wiped it with a tea-towel. 'Gentlemen,' he said, 'this is a premature pleasure. What can I do for you?'

He did not know what to expect. Maybe they were here to expel him, to cast him into some Conservative outer darkness. God, there was plenty of darkness to spare.

'Well,' said Pendrick, suddenly bending from the knees and pivoting towards him. 'Well, we've been having consultations throughout the parliamentary party. And, well, we think it our duty, our national duty, to offer you the leadership. That is, if you'll accept.'

Rupert realized he was still holding the damp tea-towel. He hung it over his arm, like a wine waiter. 'Surely you can't do that. It's party policy to be in Europe and to be the party of Europe. What was it Mr Michaelson said about being the right ventricle at the heart of everything? The manifesto was absolutely specific.'

'And on the Conservatives' role as a listening democratic party, too,' said Pendrick. 'When the nation speaks, we listen. That is our paramount obligation.

'So the nation has spoken. So we're listening. I've been talking to colleagues through the night. They feel, overwhelmingly, that it is our job to remain in office and stay at the helm through these turbulent times. What, after all, would a general election accomplish – except for a few lost seats and the spectre of socialist revival? You are the moral victor this morning. We think it our duty to follow you.'

'But can you do that?' Rupert asked, pinging his braces. 'Aren't there rules about contests and constituency voting and all that stuff? You surely can't just waltz in and tell me I'm the man?'

'Oh, but we can,' said Himmler, striding to the front. 'Remember the Michaelson amendment to the Hague charter we passed at Brighton last year? In times of national emergency, the Conservative Party may suspend due process at the discretion of the properly constituted authorities. You proposed the amendment yourself.'

'But I didn't know that it meant that,' said Rupert.

They left, after ten minutes, with a swing of the door and a noisy round of backslapping.

'What the sod was all the row?' Jenny asked, tottering down the stairs. Last night's mascara smeared her eyes. The pink dressing gown hung open. 'More bloody TV people sucking you dry?'

'No,' said Rupert, twirling the tea-towel in a joyous arc. 'And please treat me with a little courtesy, at least for five minutes. I'm not something the cat brought in. I think I may be your next prime minister.'

Chapter Three

The day was textbook perfect. The long winter of chaos had gone at last. There was a bright sun; the first tulips dotted the gardens, red and white where the lawns turned to open fields.

Rupert sat on the terrace at Chequers wearing the yellow straw hat he'd found on top of his father's back cupboard. He thought he looked like a bit character from one of those 1950s costume dramas the BBC had lately found so popular: striped blazers, village cricket, P. G. Wodehouse meets L. P. Hartley, with a spot of rumpy-pumpy behind the pavilion.

Carstairs and Broadbent would be arriving soon for afternoon tea. Welcome, Foreign Secretary, welcome, Chancellor. Good to be here, Prime Minister.

Christ, what a turn-up for the book. He hadn't had a blind idea of what would happen next. Michaelson had folded like an envelope suddenly emptied. Was a legal challenge, home or away, possible? No, nor even a political one. Just over 50 per cent of the voters had come out to play, just enough. Labour didn't have anything to say. They'd wanted a weedy, carping Yes. The No left them with no policy worth a damn, mumbling and regrouping. And his lot, His Majesty's Government, majority 127 and three years to run, had simply jumped ship, dived overboard and paddled for the beach. He'd expected that the long wilderness years of European rejection would have made them cautious, that Palmer and Michaelson's struttings as model continental statesmen – Victory through Union – would have put down some resilient roots. Ahab Warner, the bringer of chaos. But not a bit of it. Himmler had blown his hooter and the Party turned like a bloody oil tanker, leaving only a dozen drips calling for lifebelts and recounts. Michaelson had opted for thirteen City directorships in three weeks and was making money, not waves. No one had even blustered about standing against Warner.

Carstairs and Broadbent walked slowly across the lawn, with Sir Patrick Flint-Richards in tow. Our man in Brussels, cocktail-consumer supreme. Not a happy bunny.

They sat at the round white table under the oak tree, drank Earl Grey tea and picked at postage-stamp tomato sandwiches.

'I don't think we can wait until Vienna,' said the fat chancellor, a sliver of tomato dangling from his chin. 'The markets won't wear it. The CBI and the City are going berserk. Shares are seventeen per cent off in six weeks, and they reckon that's only for starters. It's a black hole. We must have certainty quickly. A timetable for getting out and terms people can understand. Otherwise it's going to be mayhem.'

Rupert looked at Flint-Richards. 'Well, Prime Minister, I can barely give an opinion. There's been a lot of milling about, of course. Thirty-one countries trying to decide what day of the week it is with an Austrian president who doesn't know the time of day unless Berlin sends him a postcard. Hundreds of lawyers making a fortune, claiming there's no provision for any of this. We'll be lucky if Vienna has anything at all to say. Summits are only as good as their prior communiqués – and nobody has begun to write that yet. The sherpas don't even know which mountain they're supposed to be climbing.'

Rupert sighed. He'd thought there would be contingency plans, but that cupboard was bare. Carstairs had played a few sand-table games, and jolly futile they'd proved. All of them had assumed that Brussels would get its act together fast and offer some package or other, with decent terms to carry on trading. Then there would be a long weekend of haggling as per usual.

'If I were to advise,' said Flint-Richards unctuously, 'if my experience is of any value, I think that a truly secret meeting with Gross, a meeting that absolutely nobody knows about, is the only way of unlocking anything.'

Hermann Gross was the stick slender new Bundeschancellor, a Social Democrat from Hesse whose election the previous year had seemed to surprise everybody – except Gross himself. The press had instantly called him the Thin Man of Europe and cartoonists had put him and Michaelson together: Little Weed and Big Weed, in some obscure reference to a prehistoric children's TV show, which was back on Cable.

Ten days after taking office Rupert had flown to Bonn and shaken the German hand for the camera. But he'd had nothing useful to say so early, waited for Gross to start, and the Chancellor had merely ambled through a few generalizations about proper channels and careful consideration before the helicopter revved up on his lawn.

Broadbent reached for the teapot. 'Perhaps Patrick is right. Perhaps we won't get anywhere if we keep on playing this after-you-Hermann stuff. Let me get together a real negotiating brief and a proper timetable and see if you can sock it to him, persuade him that drifting around will drag us all into the mire. I know what their game is. Leave us dangling while the economy goes into a tailspin and hope that somehow we change our minds. But that's the absolute kiss of death.'

Rupert sighed. At the far end of the terrace, Jenny walked back from the tennis courts. There was a light mist of sweat around her lips. As she looked over and waved, Rupert saw Carstairs suddenly turn his eyes away. He knew, of course, what that meant.

'How long are we going to keep up this grieving stuff?' asked the President, tetchily. 'Seems to me just looking sorrowful and responsible while the dollar goes nuclear ain't much of a policy. The euro's shot to hell and the exchanges have got the shits, and we're standing here outside the funeral parlour like the goddamn hearse has lost a wheel somewhere.'

The man from State and the man from the Treasury said nothing. The chief of staff opened his notebook, then closed it again. The press secretary looked out of the Oval Office window, suddenly hypnotized by a helicopter buzzing across the sky towards the Potomac.

'Sometimes,' said State, at last, 'there isn't anything to do but do nothing. The Brits have exercised their democratic right. We can't poormouth that, at least in public. Berlin and Paris are going apeshit. So would we be in their place, I guess. But they'll get over it in the end. No option. Meantime, some currencies go up and some go down. Ours is way up. Is that comfortable? No. Business is squealing. But business is always squealing about something.'

'And,' said Treasury, 'the real problems are all still European ones. This is their mess on their porch, with a whole lot of investment going walkabout. We've got to remember there isn't much of a security dimension here that anyone's losing sleep over. The Brits are four per cent of the WEU defence detail, not counting the Ukraine. Them pulling out doesn't worry the Pentagon none. Even our brass can't see what enemies they're supposed to be defending themselves against.

'No, sir. We're gaining, not losing. We sit tight and let the people in the deep end swim their way out of this pool.'

'Watchful concern but still hands-off, then?' said Press. 'This administration would intervene immediately if it thought vital American interests were at stake, but continues to trust mature democracies elsewhere to find their own way forward.'

The President rocked back in his chair. 'OK,' he said. 'I just keep asking the question. I just keep wondering whether we can't make something that buzzes out of all the pieces on the damn carpet. But till I find out what it is, you guys can keep the shutters up. If I ever have a better idea, though, I'll call you. Day or night.'

*

Nobody had much use for the Fruchtheim air base any longer. Fifty years before, it had been a central pivot for the RAF in northern Germany, all NATO eyes turned to the menace from the East, all fighters primed for the illusion of action. When there was no illusion left, the British had gradually retreated through a maze of defence cuts and the Germans had taken over, though never with any great purpose. What remained of the base was an air training school – a solid two storeys of red brick half a kilometre from a single runway. Planes, and their pilots, came and went without remark. There always seemed to be a bone-cutting wind blowing in from the Baltic. You didn't linger and look.

Rupert was out of the cabin and into the back of the waiting black Mercedes in twenty seconds. The commandant's white-walled house was set back in a clump of pine trees a minute beyond the school. There was coffee and biscuits waiting in his living room, an incongruous mix of pink and sky blue – 'Like some bloody Hamburg bordello,' said Flint-Richards sniffily.

They'd agreed no more than two on either side, and only one to do the talking. Rupert had brought Flint-Richards. After all, this whole charade had been his idea and he'd enjoy kicking Sir Patrick's sparse posterior if it came to sick and tears. Gross, apparently, was bringing Neumann, his *chef de cabinet*.

But where the hell was he? Rupert peered out of the window and saw only grey clouds bringing grey rain to a grey land.

The Chancellor came in silently behind him, through the kitchen doors, and clicked his heels gently, as though calling the British to attention. 'Welcome,' he said, and perched on a pine stool. 'Now, gentlemen, what is it that you are here to talk about?'

Three hours later, Rupert had a crucifixion of a migraine and a dull, echoing ache of a stomach with nothing but a couple of biscuits to appease it. Typically, the RAF had only soft drinks and a few small bags of wizened peanuts aboard. 'It's the cuts, sir,' said the corporal with the dentist's smile and the body odour. Flint-Richards sat on the other side of the gangway as the SuperDart X7 rolled and roared through the cloud cover, saying nothing.

What was there to say? They'd only had half an hour to put together a minute when the session was over.

> Meeting: very sticky and curt. PM outlined need for urgent decision to dispel uncertainty on all sides. Suggested three-week timetable running up to Vienna summit to agree terms for euro withdrawal, with Central Bank support for six-month transitional period thereafter and willingness to intervene when turbulence for two years from severance date. British to leave all EU councils after Vienna and begin phased exit from CAP and Fishing. Farmers not to suffer unless absolutely necessary. Team of experts to examine free-trade access on continuing basis and report on need for changes, if any, before Copenhagen summit in December. He emphasized will of people, clear mandate and need for an ordered settlement which served interests on both sides.
>
> Bundeschancellor surprisingly passionate. Had no wish to stand in way of outpulling, indeed welcomed it. 'You have been the pain in our backside for too long.' But utterly unwilling to help. If we wanted to go, we should just walk out. Tomorrow. Couldn't deal with legal situation because no provision for withdrawal. 'If that means companies wanting to sue you, they will just have to get on with it and see.' German government would certainly be bringing case for continuing British contributions to EU programmes previously agreed. 'Why should we subsidize your folly?' Would be prepared to treat British-based euro notes as indigenous currency for nine months while total reprinting took place, but laughed at transitional suggestion. 'When you go, let the markets decide.' No prospect of managed outcome. Old pound had appreciated by 43

per cent since merged in euro, his experts told him. 'But that is our German triumph. Let's see what happens when you have to manage for yourselves.' Laughed at thought of continuing access for GB goods as before. Vowed the old barriers would be back in place within a month. And to hell with GATT. German bottom line crystal clear when F-R raised point about cutting off nose to spite face and need to ensure level trading field because we buy more of their goods than they ours. Kept laughing. 'You don't comprehend. We've built this thing for over half a century at huge cost to ourselves. It's our German monument. If we let somebody go, tamely, without a fight, then more of the thirty-one will want out the next time the economy catches a cold in the head. Watch the Danes and the Swedes. Watch the Estonians and the Lithuanians. Why should we make it easy to blow up our own memorial? My voters, and their fathers, have given everything to this project. They will not forgive me if we just smile and say sorry and carry on getting whatever benefits you wish. Do what you must. Do it tomorrow. But expect nothing but resistance from us, even if it causes us a little hardship for a while. Expect nothing.' Phew!

He had had the gall to click his heels on the way out too.

'Well,' said Flint-Richards, as the corporal brought more peanuts, 'now we know. This is going to be nasty so we'd better start playing our own nasty cards pretty damned quick. We shall fight them on the beaches. We shall overcome. Not cricket. That sort of thing. It could be your natural theme, Prime Minister.'

Rupert's hand shook as he took a can of ginger beer. 'Ruddy useless lousy trip,' he said. 'Ruddy prancing sneering Kraut. Please shut up. I think I'm coming down with flu.'

Polly Gurley smoothed the tight check shirt over her knees as she sat down. Message: the Prime Minister would like to see you. But what for, suddenly at seven o'clock in the evening? Was it a small, sour emergency of a meeting, a read-the-Riot-Act to the troops? Or a schmooze for the back benches? At any rate, she couldn't just rush over in her knockabout business suit. She had fished her emergency silk blouse – the blue one with the merest hint of translucency – out of the bottom of the filing cabinet, and spent five minutes brushing her loose hair until it shone.

There were no drinks, though, no canapés, no chattering guests. Only Warner, sitting on the sofa by the fireplace in his office, rumpled, ruddy, distracted.

'This is all very sudden, I know,' he said. 'But I need you.'

Her hands clasped her knees tight.

He laughed. 'No, sorry, damned stupid. I mean I have a favour to ask. I want you to be my eyes and ears in the House, my PPS.'

It was her turn to laugh. 'But why me? I'm new. I don't know how things work. And I absolutely don't agree with what you've done or what you're doing. The country is in a totally predictable mess, and sinking. But it's not my mess.'

She saw that his hand was shaking. She turned her grey eyes to him.

'Look,' said Rupert. 'Of course, you're right. But blame doesn't matter any longer. It's brain that counts. For good or ill, we're where we are. I'm surrounded by the old Septics and people who'll say anything for a car and chauffeur – limp people who can't help me sort anything. And you said you wanted to make a difference. If you come and help, I believe you will make that difference.'

For once, Polly didn't stop to think. 'Of course,' she said. 'Of course.'

He poured two fingers of Scotch and beamed like some happy schoolboy. 'The toast is, *vive la différence*.'

Chapter Four

Jenny had sex the way she wished to have everything else in her life. Professionally, expertly, tidily, an hour of exertion before the next meeting or, in this case, cocktail party. Carstairs sometimes wondered why she bothered. Fifty minutes of aerobics and ten of masturbation would have had exactly the same result, with none of the risks attached. She didn't love him for a second. She seemed to love nobody. She merely had a schedule, with the afternoon opportunity for exercise that party conferences occasionally provided. Warner had to be on the platform for the British Way Forward debate, Broadbent's increasingly familiar tale of grit and struggle for the City. Carstairs was supposed to be working on his speech somewhere. The Metropole knew what Do Not Disturb meant.

They were in no sense partners. They met at intervals – sometimes weeks apart – and briskly sated themselves. One day soon, perhaps the next available day, there would be no call and it, whatever it was, would be over, stored in a filing cabinet of sweaty memory. He was beginning to look forward to that moment. Four years of lonely divorce – of infrequent nights with women who might kiss and tell – had made him hungry for something more, and a prime minister's wife who could never tell, who reeked of a different danger, had provided the utterly unexpected. But it had been going on – what? – nearly seventeen months, only a few weeks less than this government. It was an even bet, the way things were, as to which would finish first.

She came back from the shower, bath towel neatly tied, and began the segment of political chat that always preceded the leavings. Never an endearment. Always, he had come to see, Warner plc business. He was obliged to give her a second opinion on the state of the Party, to sketch the plots and the mumblings and the crises to come. They were his loyalty check. They were her fix when Rupert needed steering.

'Is it as bad as they say?' she asked.

'Worse, I think, because it's not the Party that's the problem, it's the country. We don't have to worry about alternatives and by-elections and all that stuff because Labour's down an even deeper hole. They haven't got a way out either. We're just stuck with a situation where we can't go back without looking total idiots and destroying ourselves, but there's no belief that we can make a go of it alone. People are terminally depressed and the good old political classes haven't got a word worth hearing.'

Nothing had gone as expected. The pundits had all caught pneumonia. The spin doctors had packed up. We were out of Europe OK, the majesty of the pledge fulfilled. But everything else was a foul-up. The pound in your pocket, initially pinned a couple of points below the rate when we'd junked it all those years ago, had slid 40 per cent. That ought to have been great for exports, but the European markets had closed against us – just as the Germans had said they must – and the rest of the world wasn't exactly rushing to pick up the slack. Who wanted to join in the British dotty ditty? The Japs and the Koreans were relocating in droves to Spain and Serbia, leaving thousands more without jobs every week. It was recession as usual, but this time without any end in sight. Of course, the bloody Europeans had had it rough, too, but they were getting the car plants and the chip factories and starting to hail normality. Frankfurt was booming because it had taken the City to the cleaners. Who wanted a financial centre that didn't know where it was? We were beginning to be buried.

'It's psychological,' Carstairs said. 'We've done something

that might have worked fine if we'd really meant it. But this was an accident that nobody could admit and nobody can come to terms with. There can't be another referendum so that we can change our minds. The Germans don't want us back anyway, so you couldn't vote for a club that has locked its doors and chucked away the key. We're supposed to hate them again, which is where Labour's up a creek. There's no alternative to making a go of what we've got, but no one seems to believe that that's possible. It's just endless moaning and groaning, and nothing we can say – nothing Rupert can say – seems to cheer anybody up.'

'He's safe, then?' said Jenny. 'Why were the Sundays going on about Broadbent? I couldn't think that that stupid fat oaf had been briefing himself. He's deeper in this shit than any of you. He was always egging Rupert on.'

Carstairs didn't know what the Sunday tales had added up to, or quite where they'd come from. Treasury sources. The Treasury was a swamp of panic. Maybe Tim Broadbent thought he could do the Way Forward act better than Warner. Maybe he was the only one left who wanted to be prime minister.

'It's not real,' he said. 'Switch on the telly.' And there was Broadbent, a half second from the end of his final peroration, jowls wobbling as the rhetoric mounted. We could, with determination, with the spirit that had sustained us through centuries of independence, find the means to become Great again. There was barely a ripple of applause. A few ladies in blue suits on the front row tottered uncertainly to their feet, clapping, then looked round and sat down again.

'See?'

'Christ,' said Jenny. 'Rupert will be up here in three minutes. You'd better get going.'

It was only seven in the morning, but already the temperature was nudging eighty. Sundays started slowly in the relentless bake of a Utah summer. Give it a couple of hours and the first church-goers, with their floral dresses and their short-sleeved shirts, would be bustling and snapping, piling the kids into the back of the station wagons and Space Cruisers, wiping their noses, brushing their hair. But, for now, nothing stirred. The college boy on night duty at Texaco, just left off Main Street, hadn't seen a customer in over an hour, and he was flat out of coffee. Twenty yards away, in the little shopping mall, he thought he saw a light burning amid the shadows beneath the yellowing stucco of the arcade.

Maybe the old guy from the deli was up and around; sweeping up the scatter of flour, the scraps of pasta, the herbs of yesterday, and tipping them into the trash can by the fountain. Maybe he was in the back, wiping out the chilled cabinet where the gorgonzola and the dolcelatte lay, or sitting bolt upright on the oak stool behind his counter, writing menus for the coming week at the tiny restaurant beyond the spice racks. He didn't seem to sleep much, the boy knew. He was always shuffling around, thin and bent forward, leaning on his broom while he gasped for breath. God knows why he kept going, alone, deaf, the skin white and papery with age. It wasn't as though he couldn't afford something a damned sight better.

The boy liked him, though. Sometimes, on Thursdays, when the pay cheque came through, he'd eat at one of the bare, plastic-topped tables before starting his shift. Something cheap: spaghetti with clam sauce, or the lasagne turned crisp and dry at the end of a long evening in the big black oven. If it was the old man fretting around out there, he'd have coffee bubbling on the stove, the real stuff ground from bitter Arabian beans, not thin slop drained of taste and caffeine. I could be there and back in thirty seconds.

He walked out from the front of the forecourt, glancing left and right. Still nothing, bar the faded hum of traffic from the Interstate two miles away. He ran into the mall, past the Chinese laundry and the dry-goods store and Mandy's Fashion Centre, with its chipped dummies wearing check shorts and cheap cotton halters from Indonesia. If it hadn't been for the old man, he reckoned, they'd have flattened the whole place long since. It was what passed for a historical monument in this sprawling, thrusting town: three-quarters of a century gone since the fountain tinkled and spurted without leaks and the stained, cracked pillars stood pristine. But Angel's Fine Food Kitchen was a landmark for all St George, a heritage site. Occasionally even tourists from Tokyo or Turin would stop their buses and fill the parking lot, taking pictures of it and the proud blue plaque by the door. 'The first of the Fine Food Kitchens. Founded by Guillermo Angeli Senior. Birthplace of Guillermo Angeli Junior.'

He was right. The light over the counter was on, the door half open. But he could hear no shufflings. There was no drifting smell of coffee.

'Hi,' the boy shouted. 'Anyone home?'

He walked noisily over to the polished counter, picked up a large jar of artichokes and set it down again clumsily so that the clunk somehow signalled his presence.

Nothing. The stool was lying on its side, poking beyond the edge of the counter. He leaned over, peered past the piled tubes of tomato paste and the flagons of olive oil. The old guy, contorted and shrivelled, hands joined around knees, was lying where he had fallen, a pool of blood dried on the wooden floor where his head had hit the side of the great tin of mortadella from Bologna. He was rigid.

The boy had never seen death before. He ran back to the phone in the gas station, sweating and gasping. The police and the ambulance took twenty minutes to arrive. Utah started slowly on Sunday.

'I guess we don't need no autopsy,' said the sheriff, as he boiled himself coffee on the black stove and scratched the bulge of his belly.

'Naw,' said Doc Briggs. 'For the Lord's sake, he was pushing ninety. It was only a question of whether his heart or the rest of him gave out first.'

'The question is,' said the sheriff, scattering sugar amid the dried blood, 'who gets to make the call? Do you get to phone the White House and tell the President that his poppa is cold pastrami?'

'Your call,' said Briggs. 'You're the one that needs to keep running for office.'

Rupert sat on the edge of his single bed in his Downing Street single bedroom. She was away again. Manchester. The second round of public hearings on the sixteenth revised Website Morality Code for Narrowcasters. He felt dog tired and utterly decrepit.

Nobody had told him it would be like this, nobody had guessed. When he'd done the constituency bit last Saturday, they had not, for a second, been angry or accusatory. Ordinary folk, nice folk, people he'd known for almost twenty years. 'Will it be all right, sir?' 'Do you see your way, sir?' In a tone of voice you used to an ailing uncle recovering from a broken hip.

And no, he didn't see his way. If the Britain he believed in, the Britain his father had talked of so passionately, had ever existed, it didn't exist now. Mental breakdown. The Bank of England – used to finding out what Berlin wanted and saying 'Ja' – was utterly useless on its own, squittering round trying to construct a scheme where they shadowed every cough and spit from the Bundesbank. There was no reason, the chancellor's fifteen wise economists had said, in one of their impenetrably technical reports the other day, why the consistent pursuit of proper policies should not, within a measurable time frame, lead to the return of growth the year after next in the range of 1.5 to 2 per cent. But three of them disagreed with the other eleven about what proper policy was; and Sinclair from Cambridge disagreed with the rest anyway. He thought that the best anyone could hope for was some levelling off in the fall of GDP in Year Three. Since he'd been the only one whose pessimism had a remote track record (that bloody article eighteen months ago in the *Sunday Times* he kept quoting, with a dimpling of omnipotence) there was naught for any particular comfort.

One or two of the wilder right-wingers were starting to chunter about emergency coalitions and the smack of firm this-or-that. Actions, not words. Military discipline and short, sharp shocks from people – cocky industrialists, retired generals – who supposedly walked clear of political blame. Some CBI bigwigs were even touting the return of Michaelson, as in Dracula rises again. Who, the *Mail* had asked that morning, will give us HOPE? Who will give us PURPOSE?

Not a rabble of newspaper editors, reading their focus-group findings in the back of chauffeur-driven limos and recycling the results as the Voice of the Future. But it was still a good question.

Rupert had always talked out loud to himself when he knew he was safely alone. He hummed a tune. 'Land of Hope and Glory'.

'Look, old son. You're the sort of chap who is what he is because you know instinctively what other fellows and their wives want, for their kids, for their homes. You listen, you don't tell. You make the best of a bad job. Are you the right man now? Of course not. But you are the man. Come on, old son. Keep going. Something will turn up.'

He sang a long-forgotten music-hall song as he cleaned his teeth. 'Rolling round the world, looking for the sunshine'.

The President of the United States sat on the low grey wall that ringed the town and looked east over the valley, holding his dark sunglasses high over a dripping forehead. 'Damned old fraud,' he said. 'Always claimed you could see the towers of San Gimignano from here. Always told me it was those towers on the horizon that made him take off for Manhattan. Fact is, you can't see nothing. There's a great lump of hill in the way.'

His brother – short, fat, puffing Franco – clambered up beside him, tie already at half mast, white shirt puddled with patches.

'What's it matter?' he said. 'Pop liked to tell stories. Wherever he stopped, there were Italian stories, New York stories, St Louis stories. Remember how he told us he made the first tiramisu in Arizona and we told him it was Custard's Last Stand? Why'd you suppose it would be different back here in Castellina? Don't they like stories in Chianti or something?'

'Yeah,' said the President, 'but I been pushing that San Gimignano tower crap at every TV dame who wanted a bit of colour in their screwed-up lives since interviews were invented. And now I find it was all hogwash. That could have made me look pretty darned shitty – just like I was when we opened the will and found he wanted his fucking ashes spewed over some fucking Italian hillside. I mean, what kind of last request is that from a paid-up citizen of the USA? His mind was fettucine and shrimp sauce at the end.'

The two black limos were parked under the olive trees at the edge of the churchyard. Small curious boys, jabbering in Italian, pointing and giggling, were gathering behind the secret service detail in their shiny blue suits. Soon there would be a crowd.

'Let's get it over with,' said the President, plunging off down the hillside through the strew of granite tombstones and the grimy marble vaults. 'We gave him the full treatment back home. This is supposed to be the private bit.'

'Here's the place,' said Franco. 'See, they put flowers out like they said they would. Twelve generations of Angelis going way back to when Utah was Indian territory and Las Vegas was just a creek in the desert.'

'Spare us the history lesson,' said the President. 'Just think of it as the time before they invented tinned meatballs.'

He opened the plastic urn with the white Greek beading and held his arm outstretched, pivoting on the right foot. A cloud of ashes spread across the yellowed grass and, caught by a puff of breeze, drifted down the hill. The brothers stood silent for a moment, still, arms clasped behind back, heads bowed, in case there was a photographer lurking somewhere in the olive groves.

'*Arrivederci*, Poppa,' said the President. 'You had a good one.'

'Yip,' said Franco. 'Remembered for ever when tortellini need stuffing.'

'I can't breathe,' Rupert had said. 'I simply have to get some air.'

She looked across the hall at him and smiled a pitying smile.

'Not Chequers again,' he said. 'Maybe I could go down to Lyme for the day and feel the wind on my back. Maybe you'd like to come, too?'

Jenny shrugged. Why not? She hadn't been to the tiny constituency flat they kept in Lyme Regis for months. It would be useful to heat it for a few hours and check for the damp from the sea, which tugged at the wallpaper, and the salt, which devoured the paintwork.

He called his agent and fixed a surgery. 'But only thirty minutes, please. Then perhaps an hour in the snug at the Royal Lion. Try to get a few problems I can solve pronto. I want an easy time not another bloody grilling.'

Afterwards they walked along the narrow road of the front, past the tea-shops and the pink cottages and the hulk of hotels battened down until next season. The hanging gardens had begun to slip into the sea again and they hiked, stumbling, across the pebbles of the beach, rain driving in from the slate grey of the Channel.

He had come, he knew, because he wanted to stand again on the end of the Cobb, looking down at the waves as they drove against the stones of the long pier and tossed the fishing boats in the harbour. His mother had brought him and Harriet here every Sunday during the months of the Falklands. They'd been a family then, sucking sweets and laughing and watching the long rods from the hunched figures along the sea wall sweep down in search of fish. It hadn't changed. The town was a peel of genteel poverty. The cafés sold prawn salads and cod and chips. The future arched around Lyme on the by-pass and moved on.

Rupert edged back towards the harbour, body leaning into the wind, feet fumbling on the soaking slabs. He found himself suddenly alone. Where was Jenny? There, at the end, on the round platform of stone where the waters were fiercest, drenched time and again in a sheet of spray. She was wearing her purple gaberdine cloak with the hood pulled to her eyes, and her hands were clasped around her.

'Ah,' he said, as she finally came towards him. 'The English lieutenant's woman.'

She tossed back the hood. 'Bloody hell. It's sodding freezing, and all you can do is make useless jokes.'

They walked home in silence, keeping their distance.

Chapter Five

Bill Angeli had only fourteen hours to spare, but he wanted a decent night's sleep and the chance of a little business. You got fed up with cat-napping in the shaking single bed of Airforce One. He was sixty-four. His back ached continually. He had just fitted a Venice summit and the last rites for his dad into seventy-two hours. He had no more elections to fight and only two more of these goddamn G10 junkets to smile and shake his way through. The forty-seventh President would not pile straight on and head for a bleary Washington morning. He would fly in a properly civilized fashion to London, enjoy a quiet supper with his hallowed chum Ambassador Bonham, and get his head down on a soft, still pillow for eight hours. Then there would even be time for a consolation brunch at Chequers with Rupert Warner before he headed home.

Northolt didn't put on much of a show. The Brits seemed to have decided to let the stop-over go light touch, a friend passing through. A middle-ranking Foreign Office greeter stood along-side Bonham on the runway and bent fleetingly from the waist as he shook hands. A handful of press photographers took routine shots for the record. There was a studied air of polite uninterest and muted embarrassment.

Angeli was not surprised. Indeed, it was more or less what had been arranged. Nobody asked the British to their parties any longer. The UN Security Council seat was a distant memory, ceded long since to Brussels (and filled from Berlin). There had been no invitation to Venice either. Even the occasional rotating appearance as one of the two European faces at the table was gone. Next year in Kuala Lumpur? Forget it.

The President and his men tried, as ever, to be tactful about all this, like rich nephews visiting an old uncle who'd fallen on hard times, not mentioning the holes in the carpets. The Brits had their uses. Orchestrated royal trips to Los Angeles could still raise indecent money for decently disguised Republican causes. Whenever you needed a signature to turn a bit of uni-lateral arm-twisting into a 'world-community initiative', Down-ing Street signed on the bottom line by fax, no questions asked. Never kick an ancient retainer in the teeth unless he spills Haägen Dazs on the carpet.

'How's the handicap?' he asked Tug Bonham, as they wheezed into the helicopter and headed for the silence of the Ambassador's lawn and the walled enclave in Regent's Park, where Bonham shot rabbits from the terrace when there was nothing better to do.

'Oh, OK. You mean my golf or my ex-wife? I can't seem to get out of the bunker. She can't seem to get out of the hairdresser's.'

The ex's dad, forty years back, had been big in washing-machines. Bonham had been the brightest, blondest salesman in the front-loading section. Selling was what he did. Selling himself to the family. Selling the pair of them as Arizona's golden couple. Selling golf-course sprinkler systems and then back-porch whirlpool baths. 'We water the West.' He had also sold dozens of party candidates over the years, before payback time. The Court of St James. Selling soft soap to a stultified gang of know-nothings who didn't realize they'd been tumbled out to dry. Tug was no great shakes at policy, but he still had a boyish smile and a way with eye contact that made you think you were the only person in his universe.

Angeli and Bonham went back a long way. The President had sold Monument Valley SuperTurbos himself for a few weeks when he was working his way through Berkeley. Guillermo Milhous Angeli. And, baby, look at him now.

*

'Why Milhous?' Tug had once asked him. Easy. Guillermo Senior, rolling his pasta in Angel's Fine Food Kitchen, had been twitchy about too many Mafia movies. He needed to show his patriotism. So what better name for a second boy than the second name of the new President of the United States?

Bill Angeli hadn't made it from high school to college first time round. Senior needed someone who would deliver pizzas for nothing. Fat brother Franco had drunk himself stupid on *grappa* one night, smashed the van and shredded his driving licence. Bill spent two years on the pepperoni circuit by night and waiting table by day. He was a whiz, muscled, tanned and deferentially charming – with a knack of remembering every customer's name without pause. 'Great to see you again, Mr Feinstein. What can I get you today? The veal Parmigiana is awfully good.' Each night, before he went to bed, he'd collect the credit-card stubs and memorize the names, with a patent mnemonic that put faces and dishes together in an easy bank of memory. 'Hello, Mr Feinstein. Will it be your favourite veal again?'

One day Feinstein had drawn him aside in the parking lot. He was, it turned out, an accountant for the Silver Sands Casino and Resort Hotel down the Interstate in Mesquite, where the Nevada line suddenly grew a gambling town out of rock and sand. 'I know they're always on the look-out for young talent in the restaurant areas. What say I recommend you to one or two people?'

Within six weeks, Angeli was an assistant manager at the Silver Palm Bistrot and Cabaret and working his way through the chorus girls, rather to Feinstein's disappointment. Within six months, he was running all its accounting himself. He was organized and he was great on computers. They made him deputy and then manager of Slots. When the venerable chairman of Argent Investments, Guido Andreotti, arrived from Bermuda, he clutched Bill to his scrawny bosom and kissed him on both cheeks. 'My boys tell me you're a damned fine operator. Not one of the family, but damned fine. I put you on the fast elevator to promotion. Stick with us and you'll get a move to Vegas. You gotta great future here if you keep your nose clean, huh?'

Three weeks later Angeli left quietly and enrolled at the state college in Barstow, California, as a relatively mature student studying mathematics. In twelve months he was at Berkeley, with a Harvard Business School year at twenty-six. Poppa Pietro's, the second biggest Italian frozen-food chain in America, hired him at once. He did the family books in the evening. By thirty, Bill Angeli had sold nineteen of the Angel Kitchens to Poppa P for $17 million. By thirty-five, he was Lieutenant Governor of Utah, called Wild Bill Angeli because it gave him the cowboy touch. By fifty-eight, he was the four-time senator and majority leader who nicked the nomination when the Governor of Texas had trouble with under-age Mexican boys. By fifty-nine, he was President.

They shot a few rabbits with the infra-red rifles Bonham kept in his golf-bag, ate slabs of steak, and drank Jack Daniel's for old time's sake through an evening of joshings and stories from long ago. 'And she asked, "Where the hell are my panties?" and I said, "You put them in the goddamn diplomatic bag. They're on their way to D C by special courier."'

'But, hey,' Angeli said at last, 'I've got a stopover with Warner tomorrow. Anybody here got a script for me to follow?'

He knew Tug would have one of his political boys out there somewhere, lurking in the hallways, waiting with briefing papers and bullet points. The ambassador poured the booze and delivered the punchlines. The professionals, as usual, looked after the business.

'Sure. Dave Simmons has been kicking his heels for a couple hours. My top political guy. Used to work for Commerce and traded over to State a few years back. He don't move so fast since he fucked his knee playing football, but he sure knows what makes this miserable apology for a country tick.'

Simmons was long and lean, a loper with a limp. No spring chicken. Maybe late forties, black hair cut short with a peppering of silver, a Cornell tie and a button-down shirt, a constant flexing of the jaw as though he were chewing gum. Career diplomats had had a lousy run under this presidency. If you hadn't a fat chequebook, you didn't sniff the top. London was probably the last pending tray for his career. Blot no copybook and something juicy in the number-two line might be offered next. Maybe Jakarta or Seoul. He might yet make assistant secretary or ambassador to one of the important minnows, like Portugal. But time was getting on and faith more fragile.

'Make it fast, son,' said Angeli. 'I've got a load of shut-eye to get through.'

Simmons had a slow, low Texan drawl, but the diagnosis was crisp – and even Carstairs wouldn't have disagreed with it. 'This is a country which has just run out of belief, Mr President. They know they've been going nowhere for sixty years. They got off one tramcar because it was moving too fast. They looked round for another and found the service didn't run any more. The mood is simply dreadful, a Grand Canyon of pessimism. And Warner seems to me totally inadequate. He reminds you of one of those shire Tories they used to make prime minister decades ago because he sounded like a lord and wore green wellington boots, and he'll carry on playing that role for as long as he can. But he hasn't got an idea where to turn next, and I don't like the murmurs from those who want to do him down. You can't say they're dangerous. This place is too geriatric and too nervous for danger. But they're nasty, and they could cause us trouble.'

It was much as Angeli had expected. Brunch at Chequers would be hospital visiting.

'There is just one other thing, Mr President,' said Simmons. 'One wild notion I've had which hasn't been around since Pat Buchanan in the late nineties.' He began to talk trade and central banks and economic cycles, gathering momentum as Angeli looked at his watch. But he had his audience. An hour passed. Angeli still listened, and poured himself a slug of sour mash.

Rupert had chosen Chequers because there was no need for fuss. The helicopter could arrive and depart miles from any photo-call. If TV didn't show the President coming and going, there would be no scope for voice-overs with a touch of pity, casting Rupert as the idiot who'd lost his party invitation. Angeli could have stayed a few extra hours in Venice, glad-handing the Koreans over a gas pipeline to Fusan and Chemulpo, but he'd left his secretary of state behind for the bows and smiles routine. Rupert had told Carstairs to lie low at the FO. This was to be just an informal scrambled egg on toast between two old allies; an exchange of views without communiqué, or obvious point.

They took their toast and coffee and carried it through on to the terrace. Angeli was in the purple slacks, loafers and bright yellow sports jacket he sometimes wore to the golf course. An outfit for Venice airport, chosen to make him look the Westerner in town, not some second-remove emigrant crawling back in a dark suit full of awe and reverence. Rupert, anxious to catch his mood, had thrown away his tie and jacket and played edgily with the red braces that stretched towards his tummy.

The President had intended to treat Warner with the warmed contempt he reserved for well-meaning incompetents, speaking slowly as though to the deaf. They'd met twice before, once in Washington for the ritual turns last year, once at Oxford in January when the business school the Arabs had paid for made Angeli an honorary fellow. Both times he'd thought the Prime Minister a blustering fool. Now, though, he seemed more subdued.

'I was terribly sad to hear about your father,' said Rupert. 'I know what it's like. Your family had problems, and so did mine. Somehow my dad defined what I was, and I only realized that when he was gone.' He spread Oxford marmalade on a thick slice of toast and followed Polly's orders. Try to connect with him as a human being, she'd said. He's been scattering ashes all over Tuscany. He'll be feeling like crap. Maybe you can get through to him if you do the full funeral bit. Rupert talked about the Falklands and Michaelson and roots.

'Hell,' said Bill Angeli. 'I'm on your wavelength, OK. But it's a different station playing. My pa was just a difficult old cuss. Never changed, never bent, never took help or had a new idea in his life. He's probably in some hot kitchen down below just now, baking the pasta like he'd baked it for seventy years. I know what you're saying, though. The loss makes you think. It made you think about going back. To be honest, it makes me think about heading on.'

It was not what Polly had hoped for, but at least it was a conversation. Rupert stood up and walked down on to the lawn. He turned suddenly. 'You'll be seeing Gross in Washington one-on-one next week,' he said. 'I'd be terribly grateful if you can try him on tariffs again. We know we'll win on most things at GATT, but that's three years away – and, honestly, the cat may be dead for lack of nourishment by then. My chaps think an appeal to his higher instincts, standing together in a perilous world, binding up wounds for the sake of Western unity, that sort of thing, might stand a chance if you got one of your senior fellows to shuttle around a bit and play the honest broker. We don't expect much, but some idea of a timetable for tariff reduction would give us a glimmer of light at the end of the old tunnel – and get the moaners off my back.'

It was pathetic, Angeli thought, it was pleading.

'I may have a better idea for you,' he said.

Dave Simmons, in fact, hadn't left the President until two a.m. – and Angeli had been busy on the phone for forty minutes beyond that. Sometimes, Wild Bill would say, sometimes you just hear something and you know it's a cinch. You got to rope that buffalo while it's grazing on your land.

The Simmons wheeze was a buffalo herd. Since re-election,

Angeli had been looking round balefully for the trumpets of history sounding over his two terms. Toot, toot? Mute, mute. GDP was up; investment was steady; there were more jobs around than Americans qualified to fill them; and the euro staggered on, weak to feeble. But where was the record that would flesh a page or two and make students, fifty years down the line, remember an affable president who did more than preside? He worried about that more than he should.

It was the fusilli in the deli, the home-made ravioli, the pumpkin tortellini – Angeli would wake in the middle of the night remembering. Classically humble beginnings, the first ten minutes of a dream Hollywood bio. But the last half-hour, frankly, was just darned mundane. So he'd made it. So what? Everyone lived moderately happily thereafter. The nation drifted on, pocketing not quite enough money for its taste, working not quite hard enough, devoting more time than it should to sex and the crippling fluff of campaign spending.

But in a few passionate seconds Simmons had vaulted beyond all that. Here was something that would fill the news magazines for weeks and make Congress sit up straight. A big idea and, like the best of them, a simple stroke of imagination. Wall Street would love it. The snotty boys at State could hardly complain: it had come from one of their own. There was an old-fashioned touch of Empire to it that ordinary folks would love. Angeli's quiet hero was Teddy Roosevelt. And this was a ready-Teddy notion. Three telephone calls in the middle of the night made him sure he had a sale.

Polly came back with the computer runs before supper. 'This isn't such a wild idea,' she said. 'This could be gold. Look, the British economy and the European economy haven't been in true synch for thirty years. We were always heading out of recession when they were ploughing into it. We were always going off the boil when they were bouncing back. Just follow the graphs. We needed a central bank to keep us clean – but we chose the wrong one. Frankfurt never got it right for us. But, see, the Federal Reserve is a straight fit.'

Rupert was holding the graph upside down. 'Right. I'm sure you're right.'

'Good evening to you all,' said Rupert. He hated TV fireside chats. Try as he may, his eyes still pottered, transfixed, along the passing lines of text so that, five minutes in, he felt himself drifting into a goggling trance. If you had an interviewer, preferably a woman interviewer, you could make a few jokes and try a touch of charm. Straight to camera was like looking down a black hole. But there was no help for it. Prime ministerial broadcasts of national importance – so important that the BBC had postponed one of its Brazilian soaps – couldn't be unveiled with girls waving their legs at the front of the screen.

'I speak to you tonight in this way because I have something to say that impacts on the future for everyone, which puts us once more at the crossroads of history.' Christ, they'd vamped this bit up since he'd OKd it. Crossroads of history. Twenty-four hours ago the spin wizards were still arguing whether to play the whole wheeze as a technical thing with miles of boring statistics. That had obviously been bananas. But had they gone too far the other way?

The teleprompter ground anxiously to a halt, and hovered.

'It is eighteen months since the people of this country, you, the sovereign voters, chose to reassert our national destiny by asking us, your servants, to withdraw from the European Union.' Nothing to do with me, Jack. I only took orders. 'I make no pretence. They have not been easy months. We did not expect, and had no reason to expect, the bitterness, verging on male-volence, of some of our former partners, who have sought to exclude us from markets traditionally vital to our fortunes.' Blow you, Adolf, we're not all right.

'I want to make one thing clear tonight. Great Britain has never wished, or chosen, to go it alone in a world of increasing interdependence. We believe in partnership. But we can only be partners with friends who respect us and who recognize the role that our wisdom and our past achievements equip us for.' King of the knacker's yard. 'Our erstwhile friends across the Channel could not come to terms with that. But there is one friend who has always been there when needed, asking nothing, giving generously. Ladies and gentlemen, the United States of America.' Cue stars and stripes. 'And its great President, Mr Bill Angeli.' Cue portrait.

Rupert took a slow sip of water. 'Many of you may know that, for nearly forty years now, the United States has stood at the heart of a great trading alliance of nations called the North American Free Trade Area. In the beginning, it was joined by Canada, our old dominion, and by Mexico, one of the most teeming and vibrant new countries on earth. But now the membership of NAFTA, as it is called, spreads far beyond that original grouping.

'To the sun-drenched islands of the Caribbean. To Panama and Guatemala at the bridgehead between two continents. To Venezuela, with its riches in oil, and Colombia, emerging triumphantly from the dark shadows of the drug baronies. To the once tumultuous stretch of shoreline and mountain peak called Chile.' What had they done? He'd asked for a little contexting, not a bloody travelogue.

'Ladies and gentleman, a few days ago my dear friend Bill Angeli came to talk with me at Chequers. I explained our problems. He listened. And then he made the most generous of propositions. "Come live with us in our NAFTA homestead," he said. "There would be no United States if there had not been a United Kingdom. We are bound in blood from our very birth. Together, trading freely, we can find new directions in a new world for all our sons and daughters, and for their children yet unborn."'

That was the hump, over. It was, and was intended to be, an utter surprise. The cabinet had only been told at five, and

59

kept locked in Downing Street till the broadcast was finished.

Rupert began to relax. We would not be joining some fresh federal superstate seeking to drain us of our freedom, he said. This would be a pooling of economic possibility between equal partners. There was, of course, much work to be done. Detailed proposals had to be prepared and presented to the Parliament of Great Britain and the Congress of the United States. It was for them, in democracy, to decide.

'But, my friends, if there is a will, there is always a way. And with that will on both sides, I see no reason why, by next Christmas, we should not already have signed the necessary protocols and be the most optimistic, the most thrusting new member of the organization that President Angeli has offered to rename the All-American and North Atlantic Prosperity Area. Mark that well. ANAPA, an acronym with Prosperity built in. It is our capital road to better times. Take it and, truly, we can commence a new year together with hope high on our horizon. Thank you. And goodnight.'

'It ain't my style,' said the President, when Press switched off the set. 'That Warner's a dumb fool most of the time. A crock of posturing dung doing his bleeding-fart stuff. But maybe, for his audience, he pressed a few buttons there.'

'We shouldn't say anything, Mr President, but if you want a brief statement, perhaps we could welcome a statesmanlike rehearsal of a powerful case?'

'Naw,' said Angeli. 'Let's just lay back and see how it crumbles.'

Wall Street was up fifty points before the titles of the delayed soap had finished rolling. Rupert's incarcerated cabinet, locked around the big table watching him on a portable TV, had followed Broadbent's lead. The bulbous chancellor had been desperate: now he was a jelly of quivering enthusiasm. Himmler saw no difficulties if the newspapers were kind. Those papers were owned by Americans and Canadians, anyway, so he was cautiously optimistic. A few Labour backbenchers griped to reporters about capitalist coups and colonialism in reverse. But that actually helped with Rupert's own troops. By ten o'clock there was no doubt what the story was. Wizard Warner Loves Uncle Sam. Super Star Warner Wins his Stripes. Michaelson issued three clipped sentences to the Press Association, though no paper paused to carry them.

Rupert had told nobody beyond his private office. Not even Carstairs, because he knew the Foreign Office would want to tell the Treasury and the Treasury would want to consult the Department of Trade and Industry – and that way lay the mire of anticlimax. And not Jenny either – because he guessed she might murmur it to Carstairs. This was his baby. If it bounced, he would bounce with it. If it shrivelled and died, he would go, too.

She had not gone to bed. She made him a whisky and soda. She did not offer a word of reproach. 'That was very clever,' she said, as she passed his flannelette pyjamas, 'a real stroke. I didn't believe you had it in you, you devious old dog. Come here and give me a kiss. It's a night to celebrate.'

Chapter Six

The deal slipped a little, as soon as the experts and the professional negotiators got involved. But it was still in place by the end of February, due for full implementation on 1 May. Rupert's poll approval ratings touched 70 per cent. There had been nothing like it since the first heady days of Blair so long before. 'Trust me, please trust me,' said Rupert. 'I honestly believe this is the best for all of us.'

The pundits invested him with heroic stature. Their bag of wind had turned gale force. And Labour delivered their own severed heads on a plate to this modern magician. They griped; they mithered; they squeaked on about ethics and the CIA. And, in March, on an opposition supply day, they voted against ANAPA. Say no to All-American Prosperity. Rupert hugged himself and called a general election.

'Referendums have their place,' he told the same old BBC teleprompter, 'when the nation itself is divided beyond normal party boundaries. But here my government stands for the way of hope and prosperity, while Mr Forrest and those he supposedly leads cavil and dither and seek explicitly to sabotage it. You, the voter, must have your say, so that we can embark on this great adventure with the mandate it demands.'

See you in the polling booth three weeks on, he thought – and bring my 212-seat majority with you.

Opportunity knocks! he thought. Actually, opportunity was

kicking a hole in the bally door. After victory, the reshuffle. In triumph, a sluicing of the stables.

Broadbent had wobbled with indignation when Rupert had told him he was going to Environment. 'See whether global warming can't help you knock off a few pounds, old boy.' An offer made to be refused. Carstairs was on the way out, too. What else was the Home Office? Once and continuing graveyard of ambition. Three jail riots and he'd be ripe for the chop. Jenny had already moved on anyway: the prospect of seedy nights in motels near maximum-security prisons would make sure she never went back.

And then he got down to business, pensioning off or sidelining the rest of the gang of Euro-haters who had rolled in with Warner Mark One. He was sitting at the kitchen table in Draycott Place, scribbling frantically on the backs of envelopes, when Polly arrived.

'We have a hole at the Treasury,' he said. 'Froggy Gordon's wife has got stomach cancer and he won't take it. Any ideas?'

'It's got to be Robin Groom. There isn't another choice. I know he's not your sort of bloke. Too young, too pushy, too full of the Harvard Business School lingo that leaves us all trailing. But he's absolutely what you need.'

'A thirty-eight-year-old whiz kid with funny metal glasses whose only claim to fame is running umpteen supermarkets before he was out of short pants?' said Rupert, doubtfully. 'Think of the press jokes. Warner Picks a Basket Case. Warner's Off His Trolley. Last Checkout for the Chancellor.'

'But he's not a joke,' Polly said, severely. 'It took real genius to put fishponds in the middle of all his car parks so that kids could come and catch supper while Mum stocked up. Back to nature, fresh trout, the joy of the country in the heart of the city. The Pisces Experience. That wasn't just a gimmick. It was genius marketing. The Americans think he's great. They're building lakes with plastic waterfalls in the A and Ps so you can see the salmon leaping. And what if he thinks he's great, too? Don't argue. Really, just do it.'

Rupert sniffed and shrugged. 'On one condition,' he said. 'If I'm going to have him showboating round, offering air miles if you get your tax returns in on time, then I'll need a trade secretary who has a finger on all the damned shenanigans and can keep me up to speed. If I must have Groom, my dear, I also need you.'

When the list came out, they dubbed them the dynamic duo, Batgirl and Robin. And when Rupert (with the King in tow, because some Midwestern focus groups demanded it) turned up on the White House lawn for the signing ceremony, he made the covers of *Time* and *Newsweek*. That red, beaming face, which the computer artists crowned with a pastiche John Bull. Britain's Man of Destiny. The Old Country's New Miracle Worker. Bill Angeli saw no particular point in hogging the spotlight. He wasn't running any more. There was a gaggle of candidates already forming to take over when the lame duck limped into history – Yugoslavs, Greeks, Red Frigging Indians, and that pompous jerk from Maine, Mark Tate. He didn't need to keep leaping out, clutching glory. He could play a longer game. The shinier the trophy, the securer his spot in history.

'I knew there was going to be a worm in this apple,' said Rupert, 'but I didn't think it would start wriggling so bloody quickly.'

Polly smiled brightly and smoothed her skirt. 'It's only a crisis because things have come together, Rupert. One damned thing after another again. If we just had separate spots of bother, nobody would be at all agitated.'

'But that, my dear, is politics,' said Rupert, as though she were some decrepit golden retriever, searching astigmatically for a stick he'd thrown in a field of wheat. 'I go to the House expecting to talk about sanitary towels. TampCo shut down in West Hartlepool and open up in Guatemala City because the ladies of labour are cheaper there. Five hundred of the north-east's finest vagina stuffers get laid off. Problem. We're concerned, we're examining all options. Then that wretch Forrest, with his twisted, slobbering socialist lips, asks about the sewage that Santana are pouring into the Severn. Is it true that river weeds have turned orange and fifteen swans are dead? Do I know that Santana is now sixty-eight per cent Mexican-owned? Will I raise this grave threat to public health with the Committee on Sanitary and Psychosanitary Measures? And, while I'm phoning Washington, could I ask where the Rules of Origin working group have got to on the plastic cola cartons from Warrington the Venezuelans won't buy? Put all that on the *Nine o'Clock News* in ninety seconds and you can hear the chimes at midnight. It doesn't add up to a row of beans, any more than those lousy Spanish fishing rows we used to have did. Dead bloody mackerel, dead bloody swans. I tell you, it's like Brussels all over again. The beast lives and chews gum at the same time.'

Polly put on her glasses. 'Oh, surely it's not that bad, Prime Minister. You know the rules as well as I do.'

This, of course, was a flat lie. She doubted whether he had even read the original NAFTA treaty, let alone the ANAPA codicils.

'I question whether there's anything we want to do about TampCo. It would be a bit rich to go on about low wages and unfair competition when we've got delegations actually in Seattle, making speeches about lower British unit costs and trying to get them to shift some component factories here. Congress would make a meal of that. But the cola stuff has been referred to the Commission and the Secretariat. The Committee on Standards-related Measures has the paperwork. It's just that we haven't been able to decide whether we want arbitration on the binding or non-binding route. Perhaps we might choose non-binding there and put Santana to Sanitary and Psychosanitary on a binding basis. At least then everyone will twig about the twin tracks.'

She delved in her briefcase. 'See, here, Article 2015, because they're both "factual issues" the Scientific Review Boards can handle. I don't see arbitration under 2009 is much help. That would be ninety days minimum and a blazing great row about the Code of Conduct before we started.'

'And our nuclear deterrent?' snarled Rupert.

'Not Annex 2004 again,' she almost spat back. 'It's ridiculous to be going on about nullification and impairment at this stage. Anyway, we'd have to patrol off to GATT and do the whole Article XXIII routine, which would last for simply ages. Way past the next election.'

She could tell how frustrated he was. There was the slump to his shoulders she remembered from the pits of last year, and the big vein in his neck throbbing. 'Would you like me to call the solicitor-general for a legal opinion?' she said, with mock meekness.

'God, no. Let it pass. Not the stinking lawyers. That way we'll be buried for certain.'

Were all prime ministers like this, she wondered. Little boys who sulked and raged when life handed them a few rules they had to obey? Perhaps that was why he'd promoted her out of nowhere, plucked her, petted her. He knew she was good on detail. Seven years' flying high in the Civil Service before changing career planes.

She caught a glimpse of herself in a mirror as she turned towards him. Hair drawn back tight over the scalp again, those heavy glasses, that sensible green shirt and sensible brown skirt.

'Look, it's Thursday. We've got twenty-four hours till we need to brief the Sunday lobby. I'll get a team together and have a paper with you by breakfast tomorrow morning.'

I'm a nanny, she thought. A thirty-three-year-old nanny, with nice skin and a neat figure I bury in woolly cardigans. But this nanny has no children, no husband, no home beyond the little flat I sleep in. That's why he chose me. To look after him, humour him, nurse him through the things he doesn't understand, squeeze his hand in a jam. The Prime Minister's nanny, by special appointment.

Just behind Jenny's bedroom in Draycott Place, in the box room, which had once been the kids' toy store, she had installed a minute gymnasium. When there were no committee meetings or assignations or shopping afternoons in her diary, she would go in there and lock the door. Then she would run and lift and bike herself to the brink of exhaustion. But today that exhaustion failed to come. Jenny had spent an hour on the treadmill, turning its pace ever faster. Now, head down, teeth clenched, she was cycling ten miles. Sweat poured from her forehead, spattering the floor. Her leotard was dark and stained. Yet there was no voice inside crying for her to give up.

God rot the lot of them. She didn't like her new role. Who wanted to be a prime minister's wife, especially this prime minister's wife? Simpering and collecting bouquets from snotty toddlers, smiling with vacant loyalty at the Great Man as he floundered through his latest text. She was cleverer than him, she owned him. But now there was a takeover bid under way. He was pavilioned in civil servants, kept late constantly by that spindly girl with her awful glasses and her apology for a hair-do, coming home late to tell her – her, for Christ's sake! – how brilliant he'd been.

Suddenly, on the tenth mile, she began to ache. The calves shrieked protest, the thighs seized into a convulsion of pain. Her fury of adrenaline subsided.

I'll wait my time, she thought, in the needling ferocity of the shower. I'll go along. But this is my show in the end. And one day he'll have to realize that again.

Polly Gurley was right about nobody twigging. Suddenly we were back in Paranoia Gulch. The heavy papers began to excavate the ANAPA fine-print mountain and quiver with suspicion. Who was our minister on the Free Trade Commission? Robin Groom.

And he didn't seem very English. With his crew-cut and his Harvard jargon, he seemed like a White House man at number 11 Downing Street. And who headed the ANAPA secretariat office in Curzon Street? Why, David J. Simmons Junior, a Texas ball player straight out of the Grosvenor Square embassy and switched back to Commerce in unexplained circumstances. Television cameras descended. Simmons wasn't just a surrogate: he was an American with a drawl you could spread on a piece of pie. Worse, the chairman of Sanitary and Psychosanitary was a Californian. We, to be sure, had the deputy chair on Rules of Origin – but this Professor Smithers person had worked most of his life in Chicago and only been elected on the Mexican casting vote. At heart, they're all the President's men, said the *Sunday Times*. Neil Forrest began to play the concerned statesman with a vengeance.

Great men need great weekends. Rupert retreated to Chequers. Bill Angeli and Dana headed for Hurricane, Utah, and the place the press called the Blue Angel Ranch after the President's grey lady had endured a particularly vicious blue rinse. The Angelis liked that. They scrubbed Valley Forge Ranch off the signboard and adopted the sneer as though it was their own. Wild Bill called his favourite mare Marlene and threw a Lola/Lola barbecue for everyone in Hurricane County rich enough to be worth inviting. 'Call it the BAR for short,' he said. 'Always open to friends and those in need.'

Charlie Fairweather, who owned most of the valley and all of its water, sniggered into his Stetson. Who'd put up the money for the needy friend he called Guillermo twenty years back when the most importunate Italian in the West wanted a country home? Clap hands, good old Charlie. It might not be a ranch in any strict sense, just five acres set back from the road a couple of miles from the clapboard straggle of Hurricane City. But it was still prime land. Charlie could have sold it to the Wal-Mart corporation as a warehouse overflow. But he'd placed a private little bet on Angeli and, boy, had that come up trumps.

There were no barbecues this Saturday. Angeli had his chief of staff and a carload of aides along. It was 98 degrees and tinder dry. A routine July day in southern Utah, with a hot breeze pottering in from Kanab. They laid out the paperwork on the back porch table.

Christ, what an endless list of problems. Teenage pregnancies were up 15 per cent year on year. 'Put me down for a Hollywood gold plate supper in the fall,' Angeli said. 'It's time to tell those goddamn merchants one more time to can the filth that's degrading our young people.' The Vegas casino outfit, which had bought into Havana big twenty years ago when the last red menace gave up the ghost, had just had its front-of-house area blown up and was bleating for protection from the Marines. 'Tell Dino it'll cost him big. And we'll need some definite evidence that old Communists are behind this brutal attack on America's vital interests. No red dirt, no way we'll get it through Congress.'

'And the Brits are causing us a lot of grief,' said Staff. 'Your pal Warner can't put a blanket on his opposition and they're working a real head of steam about ANAPA. Some of the top lefties are talking about a capitalist plot to bleed the old country dry. We're the ugly Americans all over again, with dozens of political sewer rats and the usual dumb-dumbs lining up behind. Groom says play it long, and that smart Gurley dame reckons arbitration may still take the heat out of it. But the loonies are getting their poison on our breakfast TV, and our loonies in Congress are answering back. It could turn very nasty, Bill, and we need to have a game plan.'

Angeli watched breakfast TV himself. He liked the cooking, and the big blonde who fronted for ABC. He'd seen fifteen seconds of some wizened Brit with a Cockney accent standing in front of a fruit stall and mouthing off about the enemy within that same morning. 'Let's give Jeff Crew a call,' he said. 'Let's see if he can fly out from LA for Sunday lunch and a moment or two of business.'

Crew was an eight-stone midget Australian, but beautifully formed and – rumour naturally had it – wonderfully gay. He was also chief executive of News International, the old creaking giant of a media conglomerate. When Rupert Murdoch had died long ago (on the telephone to London, as it happened, so nobody realized for an hour that anything was wrong and then it was too late to resuscitate him), the empire had passed to the kids: stuttered, divided, flailed. Crew had started in Sydney, selling small ads for the *Herald*. A fixer of legendary competence. NI needed fixing when the call came. He had, by common consent, turned it back from disaster, sold the movie studios to the Filipinos, closed down the loss-making satellites, declared the digital revolution over and out. Wall Street loved him. They loved him because he was a man you could do business with. There wasn't much meat on the Crew back, but Angeli knew where to scratch it.

He helped himself to a few strips of cold guinea fowl and avocado as the room emptied, and the President sat alone, broodingly silent and troubled.

'I'm not here for the golf or the rodeo, I guess,' Crew said, extracting a tiny bone from his teeth. 'You want something, and News International has always been ready to serve a higher duty if that's ethically within our power. Rupert used to have that absolutely clear. When the chief calls, we jump. So here I am.'

No small-talk. Angeli had reckoned it would be that way.

'It's England,' he said. 'Your papers are beginning to be a pain in Uncle Sam's backside. They were pretty OK when we started ANAPA, they saw the point and they liked the Prosperity Area tag. But now they seem to think we're the devils incarnate, worse than the Euros ever were. See, Jeff, we don't want to dictate any line to you. We believe in a free press and the First Amendment deeper than anyone. But we have a duty to say when we aren't getting a fair shake, and that's all I'm telling you. Your British rags seem to think we're out to colonize them. To bury the old country in federal regulations. They think it's some kind of scam and they're hand in glove with Labour people who are so far left they're almost coming round the other side. Is that what you want, Jeff? Is that the NI mission to explain? Because it seems a damned funny mission to me.'

He knew Crew would assume they were bugged. He expected nothing but bridling caution. 'We don't run our papers on a leash, Mr President. We choose the finest journalists in our countries of operation and give them the independence to speak out. That was always the Murdoch way, and it's mine now. Of course, we'd find some accommodation if we could, sir. But this is principle.'

'Sure, Jeff,' Angeli said. 'Sure. I have no request, and if I have, I withdraw it. We shouldn't have asked you here and put you in this position – but I just wanted to get a beef off my chest. The other Rupert, this Rupert Warner guy, is one of the greatest living Englishmen, a man of true stature. He knows where his nation's trading destiny lies, and so do you, Jeff. It's all around us here, in the country which, as I understand, you want to adopt as your own. You love that country, just like me, Jeff. And I ask you, would we ever seek to dominate a partner? Would the land of Lincoln and Jefferson bully and connive for some narrow trading advantage? In my book, what your editors are saying about me and the British Prime Minister is a factual error, and I'm only using my rights here to point out that error of fact to you, old friend.'

Crew had a cup of coffee. He talked about the coming football season. He complained about the Japanese bid for NFL coverage. 'Hell, Bill, these Nips don't even speak English.' He went home. Missions possible, and understood.

It had gone well, Angeli thought. He gave Warner a call of elliptical comfort. 'Be strong, Rupert. Your friends here are with you. If we are staunch and true, as Roosevelt said, then we can never be vanquished. I think it would be best if this friend flew straight to London and confronted these liars who are costing you and your lovely wife so much sleep.'

This time there were two hundred reporters waiting and Airforce One taxied straight into the jaws of Heathrow.

'Mr President, is this a full-blown crisis? Will you be having an emergency summit with Prime Minister Warner?'

'Yes, Jonathan. Let's not hide the chickens in the coop here. I have flown over in emergency because I am seriously alarmed about some guys here who have nothing but ill will to the United States, folk who have never been prepared to see us as we truly are. These people, for their own ends, are imputing sinister motives to the administration I have the honour to lead, motives which I cannot and will not allow to pass without personal rebuttal. And I intend to be alongside my friend Rupert Warner, shoulder to shoulder, in order to fulfil that task.'

'Sir, sir, can you tell us a little more about these sinister motives?'

'Ladies and gentlemen, it's not for me to tell anything. I'm merely a reader of your fine British press. What is it your *Sun* reports today? Labour frontbencher in love-nest with IRA redhead. My God, and I thought you taught us English. I hope none of this is true. I have many dear friends in the British Labour Party. But if this man said half of the things your newspaper's tape-recording says, laughing at the great alliance our nations have formed, performing unnatural sexual acts while verbally denigrating the flag you and we hold dear, plotting and conniving to weaken the greatness of Britain by sowing seeds of distrust, then your friends across the Atlantic, sir, must be deeply concerned and alarmed. In a free country like this there is always freedom to criticize. But as I think your great London *Times* says this morning, "Honest criticism and honest analysis are the watchwords of democracy" – but honest is the word that must always come first. Thank you, guys. You have a pleasant day.'

When they got inside Downing Street Rupert poured him a malt and soda. 'That,' he said, 'was absolutely tremendous, Bill. Just the sort of thing you can say and I'd never find the words to get right. I think things are beginning to go our way, you know. The IRA thing is splendid. Labour can't defend it, so they're diving for cover. The Prosperity Area has many benefits, deep gratitude to the USA, natural hiccups at the start, opposition's duty to point them out. Puny stuff. And the *Sunday Times* had a belting story about the Huns being so alarmed about our success that they were briefing some of Forrest's key aides against us in secret. It couldn't be better. Heaven knows where all the dirt has come from, but suddenly our luck seems to have turned.'

'Really?' said the President. 'Well, I guess that's just the way the world rolls around. God bless independent journalists. Maybe we ought to cut this emergency crap short and you could take me for a few holes at Wentworth.'

Chapter Seven

Rupert sat for a few minutes at his bedroom table, red boxes open, then shoved them under the bed with a sigh and turned on the television. He found, increasingly, that he slept better against a descant of droning voices and flickering figures. Left to himself, in the still of the night, the mind twisted and turned incessantly. Had his mother, long, long ago, read bedtime stories to him? Was it just the stress that haunted him day after day, built into a pile of insomnia? In any case, it was jolly dangerous.

He had discovered himself, with horror, starting to drift away during long cabinet meetings. He was beginning to ration his Commons appearances to fifteen minutes here or there. One slump in front of the cameras and they'd have him mortally sick and close to resignation. Whereas he was merely a bit tired and a bit lonely. Jenny was in Italy again for the week raising money for a new outfit that had caught her fancy. Orphans Anonymous. The world's most neglected children, posing in a Naples ghetto with the Prime Minister's Lady. Was there another man buried out there somewhere under the spaghetti? He couldn't be sure. He'd happily concluded that she'd always chosen lovers who could never kiss and tell because they had as much to lose as she did. Nobody fitted that bill on the Naples swing. Unless it was Ponsonby, his overseas development minister? Surely not: Roger had come out two years ago, on a committee trip to Uganda, and he'd never thought of going back since. And Federico Ravanelli, down from the Vatican for the week? Check the small print. He was a cardinal. Even she couldn't do that. Could she? It was five hours till the BBC began to put out their dawn programmes for farmers, the infallible cure for sleeplessness. He looked at the screen. A very, very old film. *Logan's Run*, with Michael York and Jenny Agutter dashing round in what 1976 thought was the future – all one-piece sub-ski numbers and great steel doors.

Why, Rupert wondered, was the future nothing like Hollywood ever imagined it to be? Why was the future just a creeping accretion of the present? Red buses outside still stalled in a choked Whitehall. Men wore ties and shirts and charcoal suits. Women wore skirts that went up and down with the seasons. The London that stretched out before him across the river had the great Greenwich dome, of course, but that was over a quarter of a century old, and cracked and scratched where the kids had thrown bricks at it. An edifice without portfolio, waiting for the funds to knock it down. The children came from decaying tower blocks and walked down potholed streets to schools built seventy years before, their concrete sides bulging away from the wired windows. Overhead, fat-bodied jumbo jets carried ever more passengers to ever more places – but they looked, for all the world, much like the 747 in which Rupert had first flown to New York forty years before.

The electronics had changed, of course: instant messages, instant pictures, if you could remember which frigging button to push. But the people were the same, thinking the same things, dancing to the same tunes, trying to live their lives and fit in a spot of leadership around the side. It was people who'd started him in politics, people who still gave him a feeling of worth. He would have given anything for a family who responded. But not Jenny. And not his boys, lost somewhere in New Zealand and Australia, getting on with their own lives away from the press and from a mother whose lips had always curled when she touched them. It was left to him not just to survive but to set a course in a world where the maps seemed to have gone missing.

Had ANAPA, twenty months before, been a brilliant stroke

or a botch? Probably a bit of both. There was a first surge of optimism, and a continuing lift to the economy. Yet somehow it didn't feel quite right. You shouldn't have to rely on the White House pressing flesh and pulling strings every time some damned congressman began lording it over the Atlantic or playing up to the boys back home in the Tenth District. You shouldn't have to be constantly explaining that His Majesty's Government had made assorted representations to the Free Trade Commission, which would be duly considered when the Mexican swordfish issue was resolved. You shouldn't have to keep meeting the Guatemalan President in public, with cameras gobbling up every fishy grin. It was not a steady state. Give it another few years, with him pushing up daisies or the go-it-alone Democrats back in charge, and you could feel the European débâcle happening all over again. Why should he fear that? He was the bloody débâcle. But he had seen the people, talked to them, tried to buoy them up. And he really feared any next time.

Big Ben rang two o'clock. With a sigh, Rupert twiddled with the radio by his bed. No World Service worth talking of since Arthur Palmer's cuts as his Labour government began to turn up its toes. But the Voice of America was still droning on about Mark Twain. He turned the set so low that he couldn't hear the words, only the arid rhythm of them, pulled a pillow over his head and attempted sleep.

Polly Gurley was not sleeping. To the contrary. She was arched, naked, astride David J. Simmons Junior, enjoying her second noisy orgasm of the night. Her delicately muscled back twisted in pleasure, her small breasts bobbed in time with the squeals. 'Oh, God,' she said, when it was over, pressing herself down on him. 'Oh, God, it's been so long.'

'For me, too. Only twice in three years since Noreen walked out. And then I hated myself for it. Not like now.'

They had met on the 20.10 back from Brussels: nodding acquaintances. He was the lean, grizzled bureaucrat from

Houston, the head of the ANAPA secretariat in Curzon Street taking a foray into enemy territory with veal quotas on his mind. She was the minister he'd glimpsed occasionally on television. There was fog at the airport. Her private secretary, Morrison, had to be back in Brussels the next afternoon to pick up the leftover daughter of a leftover marriage. After half an hour, Polly had told him to go back to a city centre hotel and take the rest of the week off. Simmons was already in the departure lounge, pumping away at a mini-computer.

They made small-talk. She discussed bottled-water safety standards. (She was fed up with the Euro-water with Euro-chic that still slopped around British dinner tables when there was Chiltern or Saratoga Spring going spare.) He discussed veal, and how a native-born Texan could never come to terms with this thin white desecration of steak.

Still forty minutes to estimated take-off. They wandered over to the desolate trolley of a bar and drank Coca-Colas.

He knew her life history, memorized, with others, on the plane from the Washington briefings six months before. 'I'm a public servant, just like you used to be,' he said. 'A spear-carrier of a higher administration.' He didn't talk about that long evening with Angeli and the idea he'd sold in a sudden rush of intuition. He could not, for the life of him, remember whether she was married.

Polly took off her glasses and ran her finger unthinkingly along the top of her cheekbones, trying to soothe away the exhaustion. Politics was quite different, she said. 'Before, I was just a cog in a machine. I was a success if that machine functioned properly. But I thought I'd had enough of that. I thought I could run the machine better than the politicians, with their mandates and their evasions and their self-importance. Some hope! Now I'm in charge and they still expect me to take orders and give them the credit. I work harder. I've no private life. It was a bum swap.'

The words seemed odd and oddly passionate from a slim,

severe woman in a suit. He didn't know, for a second, whether to smile. Then he grinned and began to tell her hair-raising tales of Houston public life – including what happened to the Lieutenant Governor in the Equality Unit changing room. Polly relaxed. He told her about his lost wife, Noreen, and the Ghanaian diplomat she'd met at the Russian reception. There had been no kids, thank God. Just eighteen years chucked in the trash can. It had been the moment that he had had to get out of the States for a while, the transfer from Commerce to State. She told him nothing, for in many ways there was nothing to tell beyond a few fleeting liaisons long and far away, before her election.

As they climbed aboard the Boeing at last, a captain with a mincing accent apologized on the intercom. 'I'm so sorry, ladies and gentlemen,' he said, 'but little things have been going wrong here all night.' They grimaced at each other, then smiled. At Heathrow there was no ministerial car waiting. She phoned the Department. They had thought that because Morrison was staying she'd stayed too. Never mind, she said. A taxi would be easier now. 'Hey,' said Simmons, swinging her bag off the carousel. 'My car's in the lot. Why don't you let me run you home? It would be my pleasure.'

And here, in the most banal of ways, they were. Two lonely bodies too fatigued to care, enfolded in flesh. There was a glimmer of light through the blind. Simmons lay back and looked at her. This wasn't a one-night stand with one of the handful of passing bodies that had punctuated life since Noreen. He had known that from the first moments at the airport. She was so quick, so rampantly intelligent; but the fine lines of fatigue around her eyes lent that brilliance a hint of vulnerability. She offered the equality of partnership – and something more. He ran an index finger lightly across her forehead, kissed the bridge of her nose. God, what did this all feel like? He had almost forgotten through the years of hurt. It felt like love.

Outside the rain was bucketing down. Norman 'Shorty'

Maddox – Maddox of the *Mirror* – huddled into a doorway and waited. His luck had been lousy lately. Seven weeks without a picture on the front, his worst run ever. But perhaps all that was changing. He knew the secretary of state. It was part of the job. He didn't know the tall, limping man who had been helping her with her bag and with whom she had been so deep in conversation as they came through Customs. Maddox was coming back from Glasgow and longing for a half bottle of Scotch and a solid kip. But you didn't kick fortune in the teeth when it came knocking. He had climbed into a taxi as the tall guy's Ford swung out of the car park. Now it was just a question of waiting, and seeing.

Twenty-eight hours later the phone jerked Rupert awake. The report on the falling price of lamb, which had finally helped him nod off five minutes before, had still not finished. Welsh hill farmers were still complaining. Mold was still up in arms about something to do with mutton.

'Oh, all right,' said Rupert, glumly. 'It could have waited, but I suppose I might as well see it now.'

They had gone wild over the tale, five full pages of pictures in dark wet blue and dark wet grey. 'Prim Polly's Secret Tryst with US Mr Big. Top Trade Envoy's Night of Passion in Minister's Flat.' There was a kind of strip cartoon of the two kissing on the doorstep, her hair damp and dishevelled, her hand clamped tight to his back.

> Normally [said a leader on page 2] this paper would have no interest in what two mature and unfettered adults do in the seclusion of their homes. We are all entitled to privacy. But here, the girl with love in her eyes is Britain's young Secretary of State for Trade, the pivot of our new Atlantic relationship. And the affair she is having is with America's ANAPA mastermind in London. There can be no privacy to this. A nation, already alarmed about US entrapment,

demands the truth and the whole truth – from Pretty Polly, Devoted Dave, but most of all from Prime Minister Warner.

'I suppose,' Rupert said, 'that you'd better call her over pronto.'

No need. She was waiting outside.

The strategy, he had to admit, was all Polly's. She hadn't plucked it out of the air. It had taken a frenetic morning of talking and planning. Forrest helped absolutely as hoped. It was Wednesday with Prime Minister's Questions at three. Labour would, of course, be raising this grave and troubling matter with Warner that afternoon, the thin lips of opposition told the BBC. If there was no satisfactory resolution, he would be pressing for an emergency debate. 'Britain's national interest cannot be put in pawn to pillow-talkers.'

Rupert was at his most avuncular. The scarlet waistcoat lent a hint of Santa Claus. Wisdom and understanding oozed from him when Forrest did his Commons turn.

'Can I make three things clear to the Right Honourable Gentleman,' he said benignly. 'The United States of America is not an enemy of this country. It is our oldest and staunchest ally. Second, Mr David Simmons is not an agent for this ludicrously confected enemy of the benches opposite's imaginings. He is a public servant of a body that serves us all equally in one of the greatest trading pacts the world has known. He is no adversary. He is a discreet servant of the British people, as he is of the American people.

'And one more thing. Something the leader of the opposition may know too little about. I mean love, Mr Speaker.

'I talked most carefully over lunch today to my Right Honourable Friend, the Member for Leeds South-West, and Mr Simmons. They are both mature and certain of their views. Mr Simmons tells me that he has proposed marriage to Miss Gurley. She tells me that, with the greatest delight, she has accepted. I see nothing here for narrow carping – only a romance that, I hope, will warm even the desiccated hearts of the Members opposite.'

He beamed. A hundred yards away on College Green the lovers appeared suddenly for the press. Polly wore contact lenses and a soft blue shift. Her hair still hung loose. Simmons wore jeans and a loose brown jacket. There was a cornball air to him, a supple slowness. They kissed, several times, for the cameras.

'I ain't much of a hand with you gentlemen,' said Junior, with an easy shrug. 'My job's out of sight, tending the boiler. But I just wanna tell you I'm the happiest man alive. This fine lady here tells me she loves me. And I sure love her. Because something's quick, it don't mean it ain't true.

'Course I know there's a little bitty of a fuss. People who don't understand, asking all kind of questions. I don't want to cause no trouble. I told my boss this morning, if you want me to find another job, then I'm sorry, but I have no intention of bringing problems on your head, I'll abide by that decision. Meanwhile, gentlemen, I hope you'll understand that this lady and I have a lot of sorting out to do. It's Saturday at ten a.m. at Holborn Register Office. We hope and expect to see you all there.'

Polly said nothing. But she kissed him again, and smiled a last, all-consuming smile.

Jenny came back from Italy for the wedding, having paused in Rome to buy herself an outfit. Nevertheless, she seemed out of sorts. 'It was so bloody stupid at their age. Oh, I know you've turned it into a PR coup. I read the Gallup Poll on the plane. Give the voters something to smooch over and they'll turn turtle in a moment. But it was a silly, silly risk. I would have expected more of Miss Gurley.'

Rupert grunted. She was right, of course. Why, though, so spiky? Had Polly pulled off something his tight-buttoned façade of a wife secretly envied – the magnificent indiscretion you could get away with? There was something lurking there. You didn't always have to duck and weave. Sometimes the choice could be full-blooded.

By chance, Dave Simmons was thinking rather the same kind of thing as he waited in a tiny Chelsea restaurant for Polly's car to drop her off. From nothing to everything in three days flat. Was he mad? Probably. But did he feel instinctively, that boldness was their friend? Completely. He hadn't lived so close to the edge for decades on end. He felt almost light-headed. And, as she came through the door, clutching a pockmarked bulge of a briefcase, one idea suddenly chimed with another. There were times when everything came together. This seemed like one of them.

They had very little you could call a honeymoon. Simmons took a week's leave and trailed over to Strasbourg with Polly, carrying her bag in the shadows. There were two days of meetings – on semi-conductors – for which the Japanese were coming. She was the only one briefed. No escape. But then they hired a car and took a long weekend in Switzerland, buried anonymously, almost at random, in a routine white box of a hotel overlooking Lake Lucerne.

The Swiss asked no questions. The British tourists had long since departed for cheaper resting places. They made love, then lay on a warm, sheltered balcony, and drank the thin white local wine. The restaurant sent them up crisp fillets of pike with salad and another bottle. Small boats chugged across the darkening lake. Far on the slopes of the other bank, where villages hung, fireworks began to light the sky. The mountains were not high or lowering. They almost seemed to float in the darkness of the night.

For a while Dave talked politics. She sat up suddenly, all business, and went inside to sweep back her hair and get her glasses. She had never expected a conversation like this. It was a wild, idiotic notion: a total absurdity.

And yet something about the idea seemed to transfix her. Years of plodding round Whitehall had meant eyes to the ground. Don't dream great dreams, my dear, there are five-year plans to produce. She could be sharp, bursting with intelligence, but the job was really filling in the mosaics between the pillars. There must be more than this, she'd thought. If you could be a politician, you could propose while others disposed. The new career, the ministerial office and the late nights back from Brussels had never delivered that. She had been a cog, a small part of a machine that roared on regardless. But there was always a moment to break free. There must be a Rupert moment – the moment of difference. She had felt it in the heady excitement of the trade pact: not the damned detail, the idea. She had felt something stir as Rupert came to depend on her. He must have the key to the engine. And she felt it now, most passionately, as she looked into Dave's eyes, gleaming with excitement. For once, perhaps, there was a vision here that made sense to her and that bound her restlessness and her loves together in something she could believe in. How could you adore this easy, loping man and turn away from his big idea? It seemed suddenly to her as though destiny had her by the throat. Her life, his life, and now, almost naturally, a greater life together. And, oh, the difference to me.

'Why don't you feed it into your system?' she said, at last, with a coolness she did not feel. 'If it comes back wearing a medal, then we can wonder whether to salute it.'

Chapter Eight

Senator Mark H. Tate, submerged in leathers and a great green helmet, let his old Harley-Davidson idle over the iron bridge to Deer Isle. There were no secret service men on his tail, but there was no point pushing it either. He'd taken the back road out of Bangor and wound along the east bank of the Penobscot river, utterly relaxed on one of those warm Maine July days when there was still a cool breath to the breeze from the Atlantic. The traffic was tourist heavy in patches. Folks from New York heading towards Acadia Park and the tacky delights of Bar Harbor. Heaving trailers stuffed with dogs and snuffling kids. But Deer Isle barely rated on their map, a couple of dozy little towns tucked obscurely alongside Penobscot Bay. Sure, this was the season. The lobster deck out over the sea at Stonington opened right through the week. The genteel inns stuffed with antiques had full parking lots of Cadillacs and BMWs and Mercedes. The white wood postcard shops would order the *Boston Globe* for you, with a vague air of rural disapproval. Beyond that, though, the Isle people kept their counsel. Most of their year was snow and driving rain and grey isolation. They didn't see any great reason to change when the outside world came knocking.

Tate wheeled down the hill into Stonington, then left along the front to Oceanville. His summer house had a tiny bay to itself, with a jetty where the lobster boats came to call. The slate roof peeked out of the pine trees, but you could see only the red-brick solidity of the rest of the mock-Georgian pile as the path wound up to a small green plateau. He paused and looked out over the bay towards the Isle au Haut, where the furthest reaches of Acadia provided sand and seclusion for a million dollars and up. Three days of peace. Three days just resting and fishing and sunning with a few friends before his caravan reassembled and the last thrust towards the Philadelphia convention centre began.

Jeb, the oldest gardener in the East, raised a straw hat to him from the lawn. 'Afternoon, Mr President,' he said, with a cracked grin.

Tate found himself grinning back.

Coming home from Bournemouth Rupert snoozed in the back of the Daimler. The Institute of Directors – indeed, all institutes, all directors, and all speeches to them – tired him out. But it had gone well enough. The more the country whined about prices and profits and losing out, the more its directors, in their £2,000 suits and their shimmering silk ties, grew lyrical. Joe Public getting restive? Jolly good show, Prime Minister. You must be doing something right.

Jim Bannon, sitting bolt upright beside him, did not sleep. Inspector Bannon was a professional. He didn't always travel in the Prime Minister's car, but this time Hampshire, riven with flu, had been down to their last two motorcycle outriders and he wanted to be on board, instantly to hand. Bannon had been close to Rupert for twenty-five years now, ever since he'd been a young constable from Bridport, whose kids went to infants' school with Richard and Piers, and some yobs had tried to smash up the tea-tent on Sports Day. Rupert had noted the short, stocky copper who'd banged heads together and frogmarched the invaders, screaming and groaning, into the street. Ribs, unfortunately broken in the cause of duty, Your Worship. 'Have a drink,' he'd said. 'You deserve it.' And from that day on Bannon had been a friend and a reassurance. He never chatted about nothing. He could stay silent and watchful for hours. But if you spoke to him, the burr was of the West and of the country. He was the bodyguard of personal choice.

One more stop before another night of the red boxes. Ambassador Bonham was throwing a party for some aircraft builders from Seattle, come to dance on the grave of the last Airbus contracts. 'Another night of Boeing and scraping,' said Rupert bleakly. It was growing dark as they turned into Regent's Park and drove alongside the high steel fencing and thick hedgerows that cut off the residence from the world.

'Hey, slow down,' said Bannon, suddenly. The entrance gates were shut and he could see the white helmets of Marines bent behind the bars, guns trained in the arc-lights. At least two hundred kids were milling outside, shouting, throwing stones and bottles. Rupert saw banners flash in front of the car. 'Warner's the Yankee puppet.' 'Dollars – No Sense.' A brick thudded into the bonnet of the car.

'Don't fuck around,' Bannon howled at the driver. 'Foot down. Head down.' Dark shapes jumped for cover as the Daimler scythed through them.

'What on earth –?' said Rupert. There was a howl of police sirens from St John's Wood, a volley of shots as the Marines fired into the air.

Bannon straightened his tie and pulled out a tube of peppermints. 'One way it doesn't mean nothing, Rupert, sir,' he said. 'There are always a few Fascists around, stirring things up. A night in the cells and a kick in the groin will sort them out like always. But, you know, things aren't too happy. Like my missus says, "Are we Brits, or Europeans, or Yanks, or Guatemalans, or what? If we can't answer that question, it gives every thug in town a licence to keep asking it any way he likes." You can't have deference, I reckon, unless you know who you're supposed to be deferring to.'

Rupert looked out of the back window and saw the crowds breaking and running as more guns went off, scattering into the stretch of open land where the zoo had been. It wasn't the end of the world: it happened too often for that. But it was still a mess. He took a peppermint and hunched low among the softness of the leather.

The junior senator for Maine wrestled with his own leathers on the porch. He remained deep in thought. He had never, for a second, expected to get so far. New England wasn't fertile Republican territory. To be sure, the state had its full ration of elderly conservatives, but the state didn't count for much – too sparse, too peripheral, too lost in its own beauty, off the scene since Ed Muskie's weepy run for the White House more than half a century ago. Put Tate on the slate? Hardly. Some of the dimmer Washington pundits last year had jeered at the mere thought of his candidacy. Bangor? Didn't Canada begin at Kennebunkport? They called him the Cod Candidate.

And then the certainties of ignorance had started to fracture. Maybe the boy wonder, with his blond crop and clean jaw, looked only thirty-five. But he was forty-seven, in his third term, a committee charmer, only begetter of the North Atlantic Marine Protection Act. His speeches had a gritty, arrogant eloquence. Marti, his young wife, was a redhead from Baton Rouge with a swooping Southern accent and a plunge of cleavage. She took a great picture. His two kids might have walked straight off some Hollywood lot. He'd been the top Cornell history student of his year, and had founded Maine's biggest fish smokehouse a mile out of Buckport, where the discount shoppers arrived by the million. He was Mark One Smoked Salmon and Tuna. He'd played quarterback for the Green Bay Packers the year they won the Superbowl. A long way from DC? But so was the rest of America, and that America already knew Mark Tate.

Bill Angeli had not bothered much about his successor. Dan Grout, the Vice-President, was a sixty-five-year-old machine politico from Iowa, selected long ago after a decent show in his home caucuses, which had briefly made him a name in the land. But he was on his fourth heart by-pass already and the last caucus would be writing him off in a year or two. There were the usual governors, of course. A Croatian from New Jersey with an Adam's apple that undulated on television. A Native American from Wyoming, who wore a feather in the lapel of his Brooks Brothers suit. A Greek from Georgia, whose family built freeways. Tate was the only show in town that the Founding Fathers would have recognized. White and Anglo-Saxon, blue-eyed and fit, with a smile to make matrons heave. He came from fifth in a couple of weeks to win New Hampshire. Marti shook her boobs and tossed her red hair from her eyes, standing by her man from Fort Lauderdale to Memphis. He was the star of the South's Super Tuesday. He took Texas, then California, Washington and Oregon. He almost whipped the Croatian in New Jersey. Leading Candidate Tate, a few backroom deals away from Nominee Tate.

Was there a shadow somewhere? Perhaps. The commentators niggled at it. This, the *New Yorker* said wryly, would be 'the oil and water election'. Oil, as in olive; water, as in the creeks, bays and swiftly changing skies of Maine.

The Democrats were going to nominate a third-generation Mexican from Chicago. An astounding tale. Paddy Bordon's grandparents had been wetbacks. They'd worked their way up the coast of California, picking lemons and grapes, until they hit Castroville in the flattened armpit where the Salinas river ambles into Monterey Bay. And there, for decades, they picked artichokes, saved enough to buy an artichoke patch out on the Watsonville border to the north and to send Pedro and Maria Bordon to college in Santa Cruz. Pedro took a law degree and moved on, small firm by small firm, offer by offer, back across the East until he stopped at Gainesville, north of Fort Worth near the Oklahoma border, and fell in love with Juliana, whose parents owned El Taco Supreme a couple of miles down Route 82 towards Wichita Falls. There were enough Mexicans and Puerto Ricans – and Cubans, after the liberation – to keep him in business, and enough hungry children to make that necessary.

Pedro Junior and his three sisters were the stars of Franklin elementary school, bright and passionate. The Bordons sent their only son away to college in Fort Worth. He wanted to be an economist. Michigan State offered him the scholarship, and then a lecturing job. His first book – at twenty-eight – was called *After the Rust Belt*, a vivid critique of industrial investment policy. It sold 125,000 copies. His follow-up, *Reinventing America*, sold half a million, a Book of the Month Club Alternative Selection. The Autoworkers Union made him senior policy adviser.

The old Chicago Democratic machine, tired of too many mayors who were black but untalented, drew him in. Pedro Bordon became Paddy Bordon, a talent beyond ethnicity when the *Tribune* made fun of a St Patrick's Day speech which compared Zapata to Michael Collins. He embraced the joke. The Governor of Illinois liked to keep joking: it helped to defuse his cleverness, to turn him into a man of the people whose roots were both remarkable and inconspicuous. But he was still a Hispanic, a Latino, a spic and a greaseball in the saloon bars of Pennsylvania. They muttered about him in Memphis, Tennessee, and in Alabama. His aides tried to persuade the networks not to show him talking Spanish on occasional, necessary platforms.

The Bordon image needed constant spin. The contrast with a golden-haired WASP quarterback lay there in the open, an issue in waiting. What would Mark Tate make of that? The candidate made all the expected liberal noises with due fervour. 'When we got to the Superbowl, we didn't ask whether the fellows on our team were black or white, Latino or Lithuanian. We just asked whether they could work together to get that ball over the line.' But the pictures of Bordon in some of their ads had him in a sombrero, shaking Mexican hands in San Antonio.

Tate threw his leathers on the deck and swung his arms to dry off the blue T-shirt. Marti pushed open a bedroom window and gave him a wave. He waited outside to give her a kiss. There would, for sure, be one or two agents out there in the woods, keeping watch. They gossiped among themselves, even wrote tacky books from retirement. If you'd got a wife you loved, you might as well flaunt it.

'Where are the kids?'

'Out sailing,' she said, 'picnicking on Swans Island with the Jackson children. There were hundreds of seals around today.' They'd taken their camcorders for a nature project.

'It's you and me and the cook until supper. Then the crowds are out again.'

Tate sighed. It would not, by their standards, be a big party; just ten or twelve of the Deer Isle summer colony club, folks they'd known for years, normal folks to keep in touch with and fish with before they went back to Boston and New York and their corporation office. Normality. Did he feel like normality now?

'And Dave,' he said. 'Don't forget Dave and this new English politician wife of his.'

Good old Simmo from Texas had been his main running back at Cornell until he ruptured a knee against Stanford and hobbled out of the game for ever. But he and Tate had already been a bit of a legend then, instinctive partners of the long pass and room-mates for all the away games. They were still friends. Simmons might have disappeared into the depths of bureaucracy far away, but the Tates had tended him after the marriage went splat. He'd written a long letter to them about this wonder woman called Polly, and Tate had sussed her out with a few contacts at State. A formidable cookie. And now they were snatching a few days together – motoring down from Montreal to New York between conferences – and dropping in for dinner.

'They called from Benedicta,' said Marti. 'They guess they could be here around four, so I said come for tea.'

As they wound round the deserted bay, a man in a blue suit jumped out from behind a pine tree and pointed a Smith and Wesson at the windscreen.

Simmons braked the Buick gently, wound down the window and spat a small ball of chewing-gum into the ditch. 'Afternoon,' he said. 'Mr and Mrs Simmons, calling for tea with the Senator by prior arrangement. Have a good day.'

Tate and Marti had walked a little down the green slope to meet them. Tate examined the new wife, sliding out of the car. Interesting. Mid-thirties, he knew, but looking ten years younger in the shaded light of the drive. Blue linen shift dress with a white silk cardigan wrapped around her shoulders. Dark brown hair swinging. Dark, deep eyes and a wide, mobile mouth that, he reckoned, could be all pursed business one minute and break into laughter the next. But it was the way she moved that caught his attention. Very slim, but light and loose, not tight and scraggy. Like a natural athlete.

'Touch down,' he said to Simmons, as he clasped him by the shoulders.

'Love all,' said Simmons. 'We make do with a bit of tennis, these days. Though she can whip me when she makes me turn.'

They sat on the porch and chatted about the old days and the kids and etched tranquillity of Maine. No politics. Tate didn't start on that, and Polly veered away from any opening.

Marti was playing Mother Superior. 'Why don't we go for a stroll round the back lot?' she said to Polly. 'These old reprobates will only want to talk football and drink beer and be disgustingly male. If we walk back up the hill you can see right over to Bass Harbor. One time we even saw a whale.'

Polly felt rather as though she was being dragged away with the ladies after some repellent London dinner when the port and cigars and the dirty stories came out in the smoking room. But Marti was more instructing than asking, and it was a wonderful day. They set off together, Mrs Tate talking non-stop. Aspects of domesticity. Motherhood and apple pie. Mrs Simmons nodding gaily and striding out at her side.

'Let's go and sit on the jetty and throw rocks in the sea,' said Simmons, lighting a Chesterfield once Polly was out of sight. 'I don't want to wreck your weekend with heavy stuff, but I'll die if I don't get to chew a bit of election fat with you before we hit the barbecue.'

'The President doesn't really believe in much, you know,' said Tate, legs swinging over the water. 'He's got his chums and his ranches and his Library to get built. But he's just been playing out time for the last couple years since the ANAPA thing, taking it easy, keeping his little show on the road. The economy ain't great, but it ain't bad either. Folks aren't unhappy. They're just looking for something different. Bill made them feel good about themselves in that first term, and hopeful when the trade bloc grew. He's been drifting lately, though, and you can feel it in the wind.

'Are we a young country any longer? One way, that's good. We used to think the real young countries were out there in the Pacific, whipping the pants off us. And some of them still do. But democracy and Twenty-first Century Fox and Burger King have helped sort them out. They got their success and they wanted the freedom to go with it, and that knocked the hell out of their work ethic. Twenty years back, I reckoned China could have us for breakfast once those goddamn geriatrics in Beijing had gone to the great tea garden in the sky. But they've lost it. They've stopped toiling and started enjoying themselves. Corruption comes so much easier than competition. The question is what we do when we start stirring again.

'You don't know Bordon, do you? I tell you, he could be the guy. He makes his own hurdles and tells us to jump over them. He's like some glamour-boy aerobics teacher. We don't need to be fit because we're in some race. We need it because it makes us look good and feel good about ourselves. And that's powerful stuff. We've had decades of being told to shape up because some threat out there, some alien nation, was going to take us to the cleaners. We got fed up with running scared. We're ready to start moving again because we want to.

'We don't feel so good any longer. We're flabby. We got last night's bourbon coating our tongue. I'm going to take it in Philly because I'm a fresh face and I ain't got a pot-belly or a load of low-life friends in Vegas. But I don't quite know what the pitch is going to be yet.'

'Same as always,' said Simmons, snapping a twig and flicking the bits into the bay. 'The American dream? Family, endeavour, self-sufficiency, small government, low taxes, a Ford Excelsior in every garage, a TV in every bedroom, a computer in every toilet. Some things don't change.'

'Sure,' said Tate. 'But our tracking polls don't quite tab all that like they used to. We can do our Sons of the Pioneers stuff. Even Bordon will want to do it in his own way. From taco to big enchilada in three generations. This country isn't a melting-pot of ambition any longer, though. It's settling back into a whole row of different pots strung out along a shelf. Rich blacks, poor blacks, Chinese, Koreans, all those damn Pakistanis, Ethiopians, Yugos, and anyone who can speak Spanish. We're under the damnedest pressure from Puerto Rico. We keep telling those swarming spicos they'll never be a state if they don't use English as their one and only official lingo. We've been shutting that door on them for nearly forty years. But, my God, they're pushing again now – with truckloads of Latinos in every state hopping up and down demanding equal rights, hammering at the gates. One fine day those gates are going to come tumbling down.

'And that's only for starters. Once upon a time they'd come here and live together but want to break out, want to be part of something bigger. But we've lost some of that. We're becoming a nation of different nations – with their own radio and TV stations talking to themselves, not to each other. I was down in Portland last spring and took a wrong turn trying to get to the Hyatt. I couldn't find one damn man in the street who could tell me where to go in English. Non parla the lingo for two blocks – and that was Maine, for Chrissake! I sometimes wonder

93

where it will all end. We could wind up another minority in our own country unless we manage to get a grip on it.'

'In a way, I think that fits,' said Simmons. And staring out to sea, eyes intent, he began to outline his big idea. If the United States was adrift, so was the hulk they used to call Great Britain. 'I've got the feel of London,' he said. 'I walk the streets. I talk to the people in their pubs. And I go home to a wife with a brain I'd die for. And what I get from all that is simple. Here's a country that wants out, that doesn't know how to live with itself any more. They remember they were something once. Their television channels are still stuffed with the wars they won before any of us was born. But they're putrid at peace and it haunts the hell out of them.

'First they thought they were big enough and proud enough to make it on their own. Then we cut the slats out of them at Suez. So they signed up for Europe, and that was OK so long as we were all supposed to be lined up against the Russians. When the Evil Empire went kaput, though, the Brits slowly realized they hadn't got a role. They'd made it for a while playing our best friend across the Atlantic, the only country that could be a little bit European and a little bit American. Bridgehead Britain. With Moscow down the tubes, we didn't need that any longer. We went back to our ranch and tended our fields. All we wanted from Europe is that they didn't start any more damn wars so we had to send our boys over to die again sorting them out. We weren't interested in London. Frankly, we wished they'd just stop whining and get off our backs.

'So they finally got the message. Or most of them did. They stopped swinging around and signed up for one currency and eventually the biggest, most complicated damn federation on earth. End of story. The beginning of a new story. And then, darn it, they wobbled out of the whole thing again. They don't know who they are or where they are any longer. If there's a British Dream, it keeps falling out of bed. Give them a few more years and they'll start jumping out of ANAPA, destabilizing everything we've built. The young thugs are stirring it already, mugging tourists, torching burger bars, howling on about a land they don't remember, a land which never really existed. Is that sad, Mark? Is that tragic? Or is it opportunity knocking?'

Tate was sitting bolt upright, utterly still. 'Are you thinking what I'm thinking?' he said.

'Oh, sure. It's wild. It would be appallingly difficult to bring off. But, Jesus, if we managed it, the impetus would be amazing. And history would never forget you, Mark.'

Simmons took hold of himself and began to spell out his big ideas very slowly. A new State of the Union. No, maybe five new states. Six if you slipped in Puerto Rico and finally got that hump off your back. Upwards of 70 million new USA citizens, nearly 54 million of them white and European. 'It would give our economy the most tremendous charge. There would be something we could all focus on together again. And the balance of America, the balance you're so damned anxious about, that would be straightened out for a century or more. Leave things as they are and the Hispanics will be a majority before your grandkids are grown. When they were a clear minority, thirty years back, they learned our language because that was the American way. But lately, they're shrugging. What's the point learning, because we may be the masters now? We have to kill that assumption stone dead. Take this chance and there's the time to integrate, to teach the goddamn language, to get a grip. We'd be an English-speaking nation again.'

Tate was kicking his legs against the jetty. 'That's my dream,' he said. 'And, pardner, you may just have invented the all-time great way of making it come true.'

As Polly wound her way down the hill she could see the two dots on the jetty, locked together in conversation. Were they talking football, she wondered. Or had Dave unloaded his bomb?

'Hi,' he said, flushed with excitement as he met her on the

95

porch and kissed her lips. 'We're staying over, if that's OK. Mark and I want to chew things through in the morning, and you're invited.'

The first station wagon of the evening came round the bend. The first smoke from the barbecue began to drift through the trees.

She checked Warner's diary when she got back. There was nothing after eight thirty on Tuesday evening. She invited herself round.

Polly came, by design, in a soft beige shirt and slacks, hair swinging, contact lenses set. Dressed young, a little girlish. As she poured him a Scotch and sat beside him on the sofa, she might have been an attentive daughter.

'Look,' she said, at once. 'This is going to seem mad, really berserk. But I've got to run something by you. It's my idea. And I just can't let go of it until I see whether you think I'm off my head.'

Rupert seemed low and exhausted. The Party had turned as sour as usual in the dog days of July. The 2022 Committee had given him the full, griping works a couple of hours ago. Grizzling about a trade gap that had begun to turn cavernous in the spring when the Saudi tank deal had collapsed and slid off to Toulouse. Grizzling about a foul holiday season. The Italians and the French – with Brussels nodding away – had opened up twenty-three new airline routes from the Far East and subsidized them shamelessly. We'll pay your airport tax, for God's sake. Tourist figures were 23 per cent down year on year, and looking lousier by the week. The burger burnings were Cancellationville squared. There was yet another row about a Mexican computer company, which used child labour because it said the sharpest programming age was ten to twelve.

He barely listened as she started, then abruptly jogged himself awake. 'This isn't just mad, Polly. It's totally deranged. Are you saying we could become an American state – and that Tate wants to talk it over with me in secret? We can't all get a bed in the funny farm. There isn't an asylum big enough.'

She reached out and touched his hand. Of course, out of nowhere, that's what he was going to say. Perhaps he'd never say anything else. But she had rehearsed this moment – played it over and over again with Dave, swapping roles as they went.

'Let's take this one step at a time,' she said. 'See, we can put it on a big pad.' She pulled a thick felt pen from her bag.

Item. The Britain they both loved was in a cul-de-sac. Chasing a rainbow of identity that could never be found alone. ANAPA had been great for a while, but it wasn't definitive. Leave things another ten years and they could all fall down the hill again. Greatness wasn't words and history. Greatness was seeing a moment and grasping it.

Item. The America she knew so well had its own identity crisis. *Hasta mañana*, baby. Left to fester, it could as easily turn against Britain as continue to grin and bear our witterings and our thrashings. And what, pray, would we do then?

Item. There wasn't, she said insistently, any culture shock to get through once the history shock was over. 'We've always been a satellite state. We eat their food and wear their jeans. We like to vote first past the post, just like them, none of this continental PR muck. We drive the same cars, watch the same films, gossip over the same actresses falling out of the same closets. We simper when one of our people wins an Oscar. Most of our television might as well be beamed from Manhattan. How else can we fill up two hundred and fourteen channels? They own our newspapers, they treat us like doddering old retainers. We're like them, and we know it. What I'm saying is that we could become them.'

Item. 'And there are so many other problems this solves. Problems we can't seem to fix for ourselves.' Rupert wasn't given time to question her. 'Northern Ireland,' she said. 'We'll never really stop the killing for good and all while America pays the bill for the IRA guns and the blood. It will only come back again and again. But if Ulster gets its own chance to be a state of its own, a State of the Union, who on earth can see that pipeline staying open? The Prods can make Belfast as different as Salt Lake City – and there won't be any cause left for the Boston fund-raisers to work with. Who'd want to shoot themselves in the foot?'

Rupert scratched his chin. 'I don't see what Dublin does,' he said.

She grinned. 'Dublin gets the big question, too. We're asking the Irish, do you want to be proper Americans as well? No more fiddling and line-dancing for the coach parties from Kansas. Crunch time. We're in, so the Northern Protestants will have keeled over. You can't be loyal to something that isn't there any longer. That leaves the Catholics without a choice. And I'd reckon Dublin might have a great heart-searching, too. They used to be gung-ho in the early days when Brussels was papering the pavements with cash, but that's long gone. They've been net contributors to the EU budget for twenty-three of the last twenty-five years. Now, can they be Europe, while we're America? They'd have to think about walking out on Brussels. Christ, what a coup that would be. The Germans would be hopping.'

Rupert put his head to one side. 'Scotland?' he asked.

'Just the same,' said Polly. 'We all know devolution is a terrible game that the English will keep on losing. The Scots get their own parliament and raise some of their own taxes. But that's never enough. They always want more from London. And, of course, they're bloody canny. Labour gave them the Assembly long ago because they reckoned that would ditch the Nats. But, in fact, most of the time it's Labour who gets it in the neck. Scotland votes Labour for Westminster and Nat for Edinburgh. The screws are always on us. Dig a bit deeper, matey, or we'll go the whole independence hog. So we panic and try to buy them off. It's blackmail. But this calls their bluff. If they want to be independent, let them go. See what their beloved

Europe will make of them. But we're joining America, and they can be a state of their own, too. Are you coming, Jock? Have you bottled out? You and I both know that's exactly what they'll do.'

'Wales?'

'Same again,' she said. 'But much easier, less fuss. Tell them they can be like the Swedes in Minnesota, all the subsidized culture they want with none of the risk, and they'll bite your wrist off.'

'The King?'

'No problem. We've been trying to make the whole damned tribe of them more ordinary for decades. This puts the lid on the box for ever. Did you know there's a King of Hawaii?'

Rupert got to his feet and began to pace the carpet. 'It's still the sort of thing nutty professors come up with,' he said. 'I can see you've got all the angles sussed. Bloody clever-clever. But how on earth am I ever going to sell it to the Party, let alone the country? And whoever supposes that this Senator Tate can sell it to America?'

Polly didn't push it any further. 'Look,' she said, 'why don't you mull it over and have a private chat with Tate? After the convention he's coming to Europe for a weekend anyway. There's a speech in Paris to the Global Leadership Round Table, which he's going to use to get his foreign policy on the record for the networks. He could easily stop by and pay a courtesy call. You could even let Bordon's people know he'd be welcome too. Not that he'll come. Just talk it through with Mark. See for yourself.'

Rupert heaved his shoulders back. 'If you say so, Secretary of State. Mine is not to reason why. Mine, it seems, is just humbly to eat your American pie.'

He wasn't sure that he liked Tate. He hadn't liked the victory speech from Philadelphia as recorded for later analysis. There was a harshness to the man, a glint to the eyes. He'd said, 'I will,' sixty-three times in forty minutes. He's a doer, not a happener, Rupert thought. His basic distinction. Of course, he'd done a lot himself, but mostly it had just happened.

Still, this was, by prior calculation, a light-touch visit. The Senator was merely passing through because Marti wished to see a few old college friends. She chaired three children's charities in Maine, and Jenny, because they had a project for Chinese orphans operating out of Portland, had invited her round for a briefing at HQ. The Southern belle and the Dorset doll provided care for the cameras while their husbands had a sandwich lunch at Downing Street. Fifty minutes maximum. The confected air of boredom was lugubrious enough to carry conviction. Rupert had prepared to be bored himself.

But Tate was a salesman. He wore a loose grey Italian suit that smelt of money. He was vigorous, athletic and a flesh-presser. No small-talk. He shook Rupert's hand then held on to his shoulder, steering him towards the window. Down below, on Horseguards Parade, four guardsmen in busbies were performing a sweaty little parade.

'That's what I love about your country, Prime Minister,' said Tate. 'You're so good at irrelevant history. But I'm here, sir, to talk about your future.'

Rupert had thought he knew all of the arguments backwards. He had not realized, though, how hard the sell would be. He tried to tell the Senator about his dying father and about the Britain they'd left Europe to rediscover.

'Your Parachute Regiment and our Marines fought side by side in the Second World War,' said Tate. 'Your pa only got to his Falklands War because we made that invasion possible. I'm not talking here about some linkage that your people don't understand – Japs or Germans who'd cut your throat for a contract they wanted. I'm talking about the country that gave America birth, the old country, reclaiming its roots. This isn't a shotgun wedding. This is the love affair of three centuries finally getting its act together, for our mutual convenience.'

'I don't think I could persuade the voters of Britain, let alone the parties,' said Rupert. 'A plebiscite, a Statehood Act. It sounds like years in the salt mines. And I don't see why you think Americans would agree, either. You'd need an overwhelming majority in both Houses. Surely votes like that would be pretty impossible.'

'That's the curse of your country, Prime Minister. You always see what's difficult, not what's achievable. I tell you frankly, one of my heroes is Helmut Kohl, the old German Chancellor, the fellow who reunited Germany – to your cost, I reckon. Opportunity came knocking for Helmut, and opportunity don't knock twice. That great fat guy got out and did the business. He made the new Germany and then he dug the foundations of a new Europe single-handed, before you could say Wiener Schnitzel. He didn't prattle on about it couldn't be done, he went right out there and did it while your fine leaders stayed at home and sucked their thumbs. I did my major on Helmut Kohl, sir. And I tell you, if he'd seen a chance like this – a chance for two good buddies to lend each other strength – he wouldn't have paused for a second. If we want to do it, we can do it for sure.'

Rupert felt foolish and sheepish at the same time. He was used to taking orders from Americans: his not to question why, his simply to salute the flag. Here we go again. 'Well, perhaps,' he said. 'Of course, you're very persuasive and you have a lot of history in your travelling bag. But I still don't see how the mechanics would go.'

Tate picked up a sheet of paper from the desk and began scrawling the coming months on it. 'Easy,' he said. 'I can get the ball rolling tomorrow in Paris. Read my speech and read my lips. What are we to do with a world that sees the chance of reconciliation and of peace – but just spits in your eye? What are we to do in a world where tribal hatreds go on and on? Maybe you thought, once upon a time, that getting nation states together would be enough. Forget it. If you want order in this world, then the world has got to know what it's about, has got to have focus. And for that, my friend, you need an America that has all the toleration we can provide – but at heart is still the traditional America, the European America without European hang-ups that your guys brought us when they set sail from Plymouth. An orderly USA in an orderly world.'

'Isn't that precious close to racism, Senator?' asked Rupert, suddenly emboldened.

'You are just not listening, my friend. There isn't a racist bone in my body. My factory employs every colour and every creed in the universe. We pay 'em the same and treat 'em the same. My kids go to a mixed-race school. My wife works with little slitty-eyed yellow babies, just like your wife.

'I'm not talking race here. When Helmut Kohl pulled the Germans together again, that wasn't a race thing, it was a coherence thing. It's the same in America. Folks used to call us a melting-pot, and that seemed just fine. But now they say the pot doesn't function, that we're a hybrid society where communities have got to exist side by side. What I say is, let's give that hybrid mix a structure. Let's tell people we're an America that came, long ago, out of this broken-down old place, where our deepest beliefs were formed. So we're putting that structure of belief back together again. And don't forget that this is a two-way street. I keep hearing, on the best authority, that you're all a little low on self-esteem yourselves.'

Rupert felt adrift in the face of so much aggressive passion. He tacked for safer shores, the harbours of pragmatism and practicality experience had built for him. 'That's all very well, Senator. But you still aren't concentrating on what's possible. How am I going to persuade hundreds of elected politicians here – in my party and the Labour Party – just to roll over and cease to exist? A lot of the European resistance started in the Commons because we thought Brussels was handing out redundancy notices. This is that over again in spades.'

Tate shrugged with impatience. 'You think we haven't done

the details? You think we haven't worked on the transition? I've got plans a stack high. Your parliament is a national parliament, right? So everybody presently elected to it deserves a national salary and office allowance. They'd get full US Congress pay and conditions, and pensions, for as long as they got elected. Another forty thousand dollars a year, with all the pretty titty little research assistants you can hire. And when they're replaced, we'd still fix a state rate that would see them in clover. Cash up front. That goes for the Scots and the Welsh and the Irish, too. You're not going to tell me that's an offer without a hell of a lot of juice to it?

'But, hey, we can't do all this stuff in half an hour. You get two or three of your top honchos working at it and we'll let them compare notes. If we've got the beginnings of a deal, we can bolt it down. If we can't see a path, why, then, we can just walk away, nothing said. Meanwhile, I'm into mood music. And if you're with me, we can start singing the same hymn.'

'"O God, our help in ages past",' said Rupert.

Next morning he called in Polly and Robin Groom. It was a pretty way-out notion, he said. How did you buy the obliteration of your country from a retired footballer who hadn't been elected yet? But Downing Street life had taught him to rule nothing out until facts did the job for you. Perhaps there was something, even a tiny something, here that could give a lift to the national interest. He proposed a small top-secret working party from the Treasury and the Cabinet Office, to have the contacts and make the calculations. 'But no more than six people in all. Six sets of buttoned lips. And, obviously, I think Polly should chair it as my special representative.'

Groom, coming in from outside the loop, banged on for a moment about the Treasury's right of veto. But then he fell slowly silent. 'Maybe it's grandiose and crazy,' he said, 'but people said that about me when I built that first salmon lake in

Wolverhampton. Crazy, like a carp. I don't mind going through the motions. We'd all still be eating fish fingers if I did.'

Rupert ladled on the reassurance. That was easy. He needed it himself, perhaps most of all.

Sometimes, Jenny thought, God just tried to tell you things. There she'd been with the First Lady, cooing dutifully over kids' crayon scrawlings in some disgusting old East End social centre, new paint still sticky on the walls and bank sponsorship types tripping around with cups of China tea.

'What's your name, dear?'

'Ryan, Mum.'

'And what is this funny object on the left, Ryan?'

'Me dad's cock, Mum. Me dad's got a big cock.'

There was a mirthless gargle behind her. Her cheeks flushed, and she turned anxiously.

'Well,' said Michaelson, 'this sounds like the cock-up theory of history again.'

'My American Dream is the dream that generations, coming to this land, have dreamed,' said Paddy Bordon, as the first of the interactive TV debates got under way. 'My grandparents came here, worked every hour God sent cutting artichokes, and built a life of opportunity for themselves and their children. That is the essential dream. We need to renew the things that make it possible in the twenty-first century, to use all our resources to create new industries and to regenerate the mechanisms of our government. But I want that because I am still a dreamer. My America will still be that shining city on a hill, a magnet of endeavour for those who want to respond to it.'

The matron schoolteacher from Lebanon, New Hampshire, thanked him effusively and wondered if Senator Tate would disagree.

'No, ma'am,' said Tate. 'We all have the dream. When my forefathers came here, twelve generations ago, from Crewkerne, a quaint little market town in the west of England, they had just the same hopes for their future. They knew that folks from all over Europe were coming to join them, too. I don't question Candidate Bordon's attachment to the dream. What I question is whether the United States we all love doesn't need to draw breath, go back to the roots my forefathers helped grow, and define our national stance for the years to come.'

It was a great slice of luck. He'd had researchers going at it hammer and tongs for four weeks. He couldn't be sure that the Elias and Martha Tate who had married in Crewkerne Parish Church on 7 February 1812, were the E. and M. Tate who sailed to Boston five years later on the SS *Portadown*. But if he couldn't be sure, if all the cash and expertise he'd thrown at it had come up blank, what did it matter?

Rupert was in Blackpool again. Bloody conference, bloody town, bloody Metropole. And another bloody leader's speech. More sunlit uplands, more toil, more pilgrims with no evident sign of progress.

He'd asked Polly whether he might usefully plant a few seeds for the future so that the great god Consistency might be invoked as and when necessary. 'Go ahead,' she said, 'but don't make it too specific because we're miles away yet. See if you can get them to write a sort of deniable vision for you.'

He had had to work on the script himself. The Central Office writing team – an adman who specialized in soap powders and a hungry playwright of whom the National Theatre thought well – couldn't really be briefed specifically enough. 'I want to tap the well-springs of Empire,' Rupert said. 'Do me something that plonks the British way of things at the heart of what we call Western civilization. Plenty of adjectives and no jokes.'

Useless. 'This is like St Crispin's Day on a wet Friday in February,' he said glumly. Polly and Robin Groom sat up with him till three in the morning, eating drafts.

In the end he hurled away all the sub-Shakespeare. The hacks could do the routine stuff: the economy slowly recovering, the new hospitals and schools which, with restraint, might yet be included in the Budget. Growth next year could be 1.8 per cent, a full tenth of a point better than the year Labour left office.

'But this Britain, this Conservative Britain, is more than the failed efforts of our opponents,' he said magnanimously. 'This Conservative Britain is the Britain of adventure again.

'When you, the people, voted to leave the sapping, sickly embrace of the European Union – the Europe of officialdom – there were many who saw it as a desperate act of isolationism. A rejection of a world we found too complex, too frightening.

'Not so. I had the honour to help lead the campaign that brought you to that decision, and it has been my honour to lead you since. But I have never, for a moment, believed in the solitary confinement of nations. We are not the Albanians of seventy years ago. We have always given freely of our talent and our genius to a wider world that needs them. The father of a world family. And, ladies and gentlemen, that is why we are and always will be appreciated – not for some narrow line along some petty map but as a people participating in, shaping and counselling other countries that need that wisdom.

'Did you,' he asked, as casually as a question rehearsed six times before his bedroom mirror could be delivered, 'did you hear the young man who hopes to succeed my great and good friend Bill Angeli the other day? He sounds and looks very American. Unlike me.' Pause. Unbutton waistcoat. Run hand through hair. Wait for laugh. 'But, my friends, his family came from Crewkerne, only twelve miles from the farm that my father tended, the place I grew up. My father and his forefathers walked the same beaches, shopped in the same markets, attended the same country churches. We are peas from the same pod of Dorset life. We read Thomas Hardy and we shared his richness, his love of our land. Is that a love to be hedged in, hedged about, by rules and regulations, the familiar trappings of bureaucratic nationhood? Or is it an experience shared in the family?

'I bar no gates, pull up no drawbridges. The land my father adored, the heritage of us all, is a heritage we contribute to the people of this earth. The Americans, who succoured us within their great trading club, who rescued us from the direst crisis in two European wars, are not some alien nation. They are part of us as we are part of them. And it is in partnership that I find my pride.'

They rose and stamped their feet slightly more enthusiastically than usual.

'What on earth was all that about?' said Ferris of the *Telegraph* to Morris of the *Mail*.

'God alone knows. But they seemed to like it. Better get down to the briefing sharpish and hope that those who must be understood go at dictation pace.'

Polly wouldn't have let him stray so far if she'd been bleak about the way things were going. In fact, she was remarkably chipper, especially when Tate added Dave to his team – though Simmons was really playing sweeper, ferrying between the camps.

'Mark's got Germany on the brain,' Simmons said one night, as they lay in bed sipping de-caff and large Courvoisiers. 'He has this check-list of things Kohl got right and wrong.'

'Quite,' said Polly sourly. '*Deutschland über alles*. We have ways of making you utterly fed up with Leipzig public library *circa* nineteen ninety-one. We have had it up to here, if not there, with your little research lists. We want, how you say?, the big picture.'

Some detail mattered, but some seemed to her utterly irrelevant. 'I think the real trouble was ethical. The East Germans just came from a massively different environment. They weren't used to fending for themselves. Herr Ulbricht did that to them. The thought that you had to work hard – you, yourself – to get on, was beyond mass comprehension for thirty-five years. They merely waited for the safety net to get spread and pumped themselves up on steroids. And they weren't used to religion getting in on the act. Abortion was easy one side of the Wall, the other you had endless pastors denouncing works of a devil they didn't recognize. See? It wasn't the mechanics that caused the bother. It was what people had become used to. That's why this could all be a lot easier than anyone thinks.'

The TV in the corner was on Channel 201, screening the ABC evening news, coming direct to you from New York City. A Puerto Rican pineapple picker with a machete had gone wild over some juice contract and slaughtered five children in a Wendy's outside Tampa. Polly turned it off.

'My point. Crazed pineapple killer will be all over our break-fast news, as though Tampa was Taunton. There isn't a cultural divide, at least no more than there is between Vermont and New Mexico. Hollywood has filled in all the bits between. Of course, religion will be a problem because the English aren't much into that. The C of E is really just God Lite. But the Welsh and the Ulster Prods will roll over and kick their legs in the air once your Southern Baptists start pouring in. And even the sticky issues are half solved. Thank God we caught pro-Life fever from you twenty years ago. Though that was no accident, when you think about it. We're used to jumping to attention when Uncle Sam gets his agenda out. The East Germans only heard about the dream and caught glimpses of it. We know as much about America as we know about England. More, really. We've been watching real-life TV from American courts for decades and American hospitals spurting blood and American paedophiles breaking down on daytime telly. They're old gloves. We couldn't lose them if we wanted.'

Simmons put the brandy down, and his hands up in mock surrender. 'Sure. Of course. I understand, honey, even if Mark doesn't. The real lesson of Germany is just to do it, and sort out the loose ends later. Which is why this Transition Com-mission thing of yours is so damned brilliant.'

'Same era,' she said, with a mock flutter of the eyelids, 'differ-ent country. Johannesburg not Berlin.'

They had worked out a pound/dollar conversion formula a couple of weeks ago. There was a tedious hiatus before the US Treasury could get enough bills published, and nobody wanted a political hold-up: they all saw there had to be momentum.

'But why,' Polly had said, 'do we need to wait at all? Most of the world uses their local currency alongside dollars without a second thought. We did that ourselves for twelve months with sterling moving into the euro. If we can pin the pound at something easy, say one-fifty, there's no reason for any delay. Just phase away and send us every dollar you can print soonest.'

Something that had seemed hard, fast and intractable began to seem free, easy and flexible. 'Remember South Africa,' Polly had said, out of the blue. So they did. Enter the Transition Commission, mostly lawyers who could be relied on to decide nothing vexatious for months as long as they got paid and had the chance to sue later. They could set a target date for harmonization of legal systems and citizenship requirements. Meanwhile, under the Supreme Court, British justice could do its own thing and British passports could be deemed American until renewed. Nominated political leaders of the two countries – with the chairman of the TC holding the ring – would prepare a government harmonization blueprint for Westminster and Capitol Hill.

'If we do the deed first,' said Polly, 'all we need is an agreed forum for sorting out the problems later.'

'And don't forget incentives,' said Groom. 'Tax breaks for the first big companies to finish the process, free flights to Atlantic City for housewives who do their Christmas shopping in greenbacks – a Wonder Granny contest for senior citizens who get the hang of things soonest. I always say, give them the cash and they'll carry the bags home singing.'

They had begun to make rapid progress.

Jenny had nothing fixed that morning. She stayed in bed till ten, the new half-moon reading glasses perched on the end of her nose. He'd forgotten, of course. How on earth he'd managed that when the bloody date was up in establishment lights – *The Times*, page 27: 'Mrs Jenny Warner, wife of the Prime Minister, is forty-seven today' – was a mystery, as usual. Didn't they have people in this broken-down relic of a residence who were supposed to keep doting hubbies up to speed? She hadn't seen him for three days. Nothing unusual there. Nothing odd about his lousy memory, either. But even so, the lack of a card or a call or a bowl of flowers was faintly ominous. Had somebody told him about Michaelson? It had been nothing to her. The chairman of the Consolidated Westminster Bank and the PM's Lady, meeting again at some dredgy charity do and falling into a few weeks of lazy fornication, for old times' sake. Where was the harm in that? And who could possibly have known? They'd been boringly discreet.

Unless? Unless Michaelson himself had spilled the beans. He would know how to do it – and know, too, how much he could wound Warner. Bugger him, bugger, bugger, bugger him. He was a dossy lay anyway, with the kind of plump little belly they cooked in Lombard Street kitchens. She was getting fed up with older men.

Jenny washed her face and craned close to the mirror. Not bad. The skin was still tight enough, nipped and tucked by Harley Street's finest, and the delicate hint of a double chin seemed voluptuous rather than pendulous. There must be a firm young man around somewhere who would fancy a woman of experience. Juno seeks paycock for fun and games. And God rot power husbands who can't even send a card.

Chapter Nine

It was one of those campaigning days Tate had come to hate. Another Southern sweep. A breakfast press conference in Washington, then seven airport stops on the way down to New Orleans and the only mass rally on the schedule. Stop five: Augusta, Georgia. The plane taxied up to the terminal. A crowd of a couple of hundred or so flapped flags and star-spangleds. Be Great With Tate. The candidate and wife came down the steps, smiling and waving as though Augusta (or Birmingham, or Montgomery, or wherever they happened to be) was the centre of the universe. Cue the set four-minute yack of the day. Invite ten minutes or so of questions. Kiss a few babies. Kiss Marti. Smile. Head off.

He was weary already, bone shaken by too many short hops and too many bumps through too many clouds. Marti kept daubing on more paint with every runway. It was all necessary, he knew: you set national agendas morning and evening, but you had to make local agendas in between. And if you wanted the Deep South – with the lowest ratio of computer ownership anywhere – you had to hit the local TV stations and the local papers. Horse-and-buggy stuff. Look, I'm here! Look, I walk, talk, and say the word Georgia.

But something was wrong. The crowd was only a smattering along the tarmac edge. The press had their cameras in place, but no one manning them.

'I'll go see what's up,' said Janie, the six-foot blonde advance person they'd picked up in Charleston.

Tate waited by a crackling intercom for two minutes, then shrugged. 'Goddamnit. We keep losing time every shitty stop. It'll be carnival before we hit Bourbon Street. Let's go, go, go.'

As they came down the steps, a sudden swill of pressmen poured from the terminal door. Bunched microphones moved towards him like a frightened hedgehog.

'Senator, Senator, your reaction to the news, sir?'

'Your comment, Senator. Do you feel outrage or sorrow?'

Tate saw Janie running frantically up behind the crowd.

'Ladies and gentlemen,' he said, with exaggerated courtesy, 'I feel your distress most deeply. Please allow me time alone with my wife and staff. I shall be available to you again in a moment.'

What the hell was this? Washington HQ was supposed to monitor political news breaks every five minutes and be in instant touch. He could never be caught short. He was supposed to be omniscient.

'It's mayhem,' said Janie, as they huddled back inside the plane. 'A gang of Hispanics – probably Mexicans, but we can't be sure – attacked a garment warehouse in Hanna City, gunned down five guards and torched the building. What they didn't know was that there were thirty or so Guatemalan women in a back room having a union meeting. And they all got fried. The networks are going wild.'

'Why the hell –?' Tate began.

'It was one of those damned things. The team had been hyperactive all morning. They left a couple of girl volunteers to run the show while they grabbed a sandwich. I think the girls didn't know what was politics and what wasn't.'

'I don't have a clue about this Hanna City,' said Tate.

'It's just a suburb five miles out of Peoria,' said Janie. 'Zilch-town, Illinois.'

'But, my God, this will play in Peoria,' said the Senator.

Two minutes later he was back on the tarmac. 'You must

forgive me, ladies and gentlemen,' he said. 'We hadn't expected this appalling tragedy to break into our campaign. Marti and I are deeply shocked and our hearts go out to all the victims of this vile outrage. There are times, you know, where it gets kind of difficult to keep your bearings as an American citizen. This is sure one of those times.'

The first five questions were the usual stupid media stuff. 'How do you feel, Senator?' – as though more adjectives could heal the wound. But then some blessed stringer from NBC asked the one he'd been waiting for. 'Do you see this tragedy impacting on the presidential race, sir? You've made ethnic violence an issue. Will there be lessons here?'

'Why, Johnny,' said Tate, looking straight at the camera, 'I don't think incidents of this gravity are anything much to do with party politics. Seems to me, these days, they can happen anywhere – even in Mr Bordon's home state. My heart goes out to him, like it does to all the good people of Illinois. The question for me isn't what politicians can do. We don't have easy answers you can swallow like heartburn pills. The question is how, as ordinary folk, as citizens, as human beings, we tackle this stuff. I don't reckon that we can begin until we rediscover the shared values of the nation our founding fathers built. What was it Thomas Jefferson said? "I tremble for my country when I reflect that God is just." Johnny, I tremble for my country, which has strayed too far from Jefferson's road. Our God, the God we brought over long ago with us, who helped us build this land to a common ideal, is still just. But I fear we won't rediscover him until we set the American Way at the heart of all our endeavours.

'As you know, I'll be seeing Mr Bordon in a couple of days for our final debate. I hope very much to have a chance of talking these things through quietly with him, without any of you people looking in. He knows the kind of world that keeps unleashing these awful events on us intimately. If there is something we can do together to call a halt, then we should do it.

'Thank you all. You must forgive me now. I have a plane to catch and some quiet grieving to do with my family.'

Bordon blew it.

He was a brilliant fellow, silky strong on statistics, great at crafted passionate speeches. But, as Tate had always half thought, he was a technocrat first and a politician after.

Sir, these are your people. How do you feel?

'They aren't my people. They are Americans. I sorrow for them as I sorrow for all my fellow countrymen at a moment like this.'

Two of the gunmen, sir, are illegal wetback immigrants working, according to the FBI, for a Mexico City drug and protection cartel. Does that make a difference?

'Do not, please, make this a Mexican thing. There are millions of hard-working men and women from Mexico who will react in horror to what has happened.'

But, sir, you know Illinois and these communities well. You have friends there. Friends with big business connections in Mexico City. There must be some special perspective you can add?

'Why should I add anything? And what the hell are you saying? That we Spanish-speaking people are less law-abiding, less hard-working, more murderous than your great old Americans like – like Al Capone? Sure I've got feelings. I feel the police were a little damned slow to get there. I feel that that warehouse ought to have had a fire certificate. I feel that the Garment Workers Union would have done a good job if those poor women had been allowed to knock on its door sooner. I feel the wages they were getting – half the flat minimum Washington lays down, for a forty-eight-hour week – were an affront to women everywhere. I feel we've got to do everything we can to stop this thing happening again.'

Like tighter border controls, sir? Like rounding up the illegals and shipping them back?

'We have got to do everything we can.'

But aren't you on record as arguing for a review of border policy which is, and I quote you, sir, 'too often arbitrary and cruel in its operation'?

'We have to do everything we can. But, of course, we also have to keep a sense of perspective.'

What's perspective, sir, when Mexico City hoodlums are killing dozens of Hispanic women on our streets? Women, I may add, who in most cases didn't have the necessary paperwork to be working here anyway.

Bordon snapped, 'I'm not staying here for this. I don't intend to play border guards with you. We want to start talking about the economy again, about that national debt rising 2.8 per cent in the last fifteen calendar months.'

So you won't be taking up Senator Tate's invitation for bi-partisan talks on this issue?

'Mr Tate is as bi-partisan as a coyote with a dead chicken. I don't see anything to talk to him about.'

Three hours later, Peoria's white police chief said his men had been on the scene within sixty seconds. They had been tracking the extortion gang for weeks, with FBI assistance. The warehouse had a front-man, but it was owned by a Chihuahua syndicate. And, as they understood it from early testimony, the women had been meeting to protest that the local boss of the Garment Workers, a Puerto Rican, had been paid to keep their anger under wraps.

'Seems to me Mr Bordon has shot off from the lip a mite fast,' said Chief Davidson, a white-haired, white-skinned grandfather, who chewed baccy for the cameras. 'Course, I don't blame him. I know how it is when it's your own folks in the firing line. Things get kinda tribal out there. But I truly hope there'll be no more of these allegations about my men and our determination to see American justice prevail.'

'Senator Tate,' said the debate chairman, a cuddly old newscaster they called Grandpa Media, 'I must ask you briefly whether you have anything to say about the slayings in Hanna City?'

'No, I think I've said everything that I feel in my heart about reasserting the value system that founded this nation, sir. I'd have liked to discuss that with Mr Bordon, but I fully understand why he feels that inappropriate at this time. Beyond all the sympathy to all the relatives that my wife and I can offer, I don't think it sensible to go further at this time of mourning.'

'And you, Mr Bordon?'

'I agree, for once, with the Senator. I haven't anything to add.'

The polls had been too damned tight when they'd taken off for Augusta. Three days on, Tate had a seventeen-point lead – and it was rising.

There had been plenty of time to choreograph the revels in the Radisson ballroom, to mount the bunting and blow up the ten thousand red, white and blue balloons. A real elephant was chained on the lawn outside, waving his trunk for the cameras. The most beautiful people on the team (and a few models and film stars of appropriate credentials) were clustered tight in constant TV sight. The electronic scoreboard covered an entire wall, with interactive links to candidates across America.

It was a great night. The first heavy snows of November had swamped the Rockies: Chicago was suddenly ten degrees below zero. But Washington was warm and wet. You could get drunk early and stay high as the results poured in, a tidal wave of triumph. Tate was running at 67 per cent of the national vote. Bordon won Rhode Island, where there had been a nasty scandal about Republican funding, and Hawaii, which hadn't bought the Founding Fathers pitch. Even the Hispanic heartlands in Florida, Texas and California went Tate as the media screws tightened. So he wanted one nation. So OK, gringo. Who wants one law for the rich and nothing but blame for the poor suckers in the lemon groves?

They cheered themselves hoarse when Bill Angeli did the honours. 'Fellow Republicans, friends, please join in welcoming a great American and the next President of the United States, Senator Mark Tate.' Angeli, among much muttering, had sat this campaign out. The Tate camp had spent too much time badmouthing his record and snickering, behind hands, about the old campaign chests from Nevada. But he knew a victory when it kicked him in the stomach. He knew when to leap forward with one of those great bear-hugs. And Tate, the spin doctors had hinted, had something momentous to say.

He said it early. A tight, drafted paragraph of intent, meat in the schmaltz sandwich of success.

'My wife and I have learned many things from this campaign. But one thing above all. We have learned that we must reforge the consensus on which the old America depended, that we must reconstruct the heritage that my father brought to this great land centuries ago. Those ancient roots are our modern imperative, the roots of England and Scotland and Wales and Ireland – countries we all know well, but which have fallen too far to the periphery of our vision. Let me tell you this. It is my first task, and the core challenge for my first administration, to tend those roots and bind them into a new relationship of historic importance. My first visit beyond these shores will be to Prime Minister Warner in London. It is where I must start my journey.'

The briefers began interpreting in the far corner beyond the daiquiri stall. Give a little but not a lot. Don't be specific because it all depends on the Bath summit. But watch this space.

Dave Simmons, wearing an elephant cap, slid out of the ballroom, mobile phone clutched in his hand.

Rupert's statement was po-faced courtesy as diplomatic usual. Warmly congratulate the new President. Naturally glad to welcome him back to these shores. Looking forward eagerly to substantive discussions on a range of issues. But he allowed himself a little careful latitude at the press conference.

'If Mr Tate wishes to explore how the ties that bind us firm in a dangerous and treacherous world can be strengthened, then he will find a ready partner. Trade and culture are vital to us, but so is a sense of belonging, of a forum where our word is heard. I can't say what any new relationship would be. But I believe we are all ready to explore its possibilities with a full heart.'

We're there, Polly thought. A summit, a surprise, a State of the new Union. In two months they'd be through, if the momentum held.

Simmons scratched his backside as though the last horse had been riddled with fleas. 'Well,' he said, 'I guess the wagon train is rolling.'

PHASE TWO

Men must be taught as if you taught them not,
And things unknown proposed as things forgot.

ALEXANDER POPE

Then join in hand brave Americans all,
By uniting we stand, by dividing we fall.

JOHN DICKINSON

Chapter Ten

It was the first, much delayed day of spring. Polly glanced upwards at the bright haze of blue as she came out of number 10 and waved away the chauffeur. Five minutes' walk down Millbank would clear her head and lift her spirits.

The policemen at the iron gate were old friends. Their hands were folded, far away from the gunbelts. Sergeant Marchmont stood in the sun and tickled his chin with the butt of the sub-machine gun. 'Morning, madam. And a nice one it is, too.'

She nodded ritually. 'Have a nice day yourselves.' Golly, she thought, just two years in as the USA East and already we're drowning in niceness. Two years, and we're another town.

There was a commotion twenty yards towards Parliament Square, just by the State Department European Affairs hulk they'd carved out of the Foreign Office, with the Whitehall Hilton burgeoning from its back into St James's Park, covering the nearest duckpond with the spread of its atrium. An old woman had let her Pekinese foul the sidewalk. She hadn't got five hundred dollars for a fine, she was shouting at the attendant. Why wouldn't he take it in credit-card instalments? The words were lost, though, in the buzz of traffic stretching immobile from Vauxhall Bridge to Trafalgar Square. Hopeless. If there'd been shops, it would have been a shopping precinct by now, maybe with malls stretching up to Victoria. But the State Legislature's honoured electees needed their limos, so there was nothing to be done until the South Bank Parkway was built.

She walked briskly across Parliament Square, past the statues of Churchill and Angeli, glancing for a moment as the big cars swept the people's choices into New Palace Yard, hopping back on the kerb as a couple of the whining little electric buggies turned out of Lord North Street without looking. Too sodding full of environmental righteousness to care. Number 7 Millbank was only a minute away, hidden behind a great screen of bullet-proof glass. She waved her pass at the cop, who kept his hands on his gun.

'Congresswoman Gurley,' she said. 'I've just come from a meeting with Governor Groom that lasted longer than you were told. Senator Warner is expecting me.' The 51st State, duly anointed, was open for business.

Rupert's new office swept thirty yards in from the street and the trees that shielded the Thames. The inspection team from Capitol Hill had insisted on gutting the old building, installing an atrium and central courtyard where the innermost pile of MPs' office boxes used to be. Snyder, the chairman of the new Congressional Fitments sub-committee, had been horrified at what he'd found. 'You guys have to realize that there ain't no aura to a politician who lives in a cupboard,' he had said. 'You're dealing with the public who pay all our wages, and those folks expect us to look smart because we're supposed to be smarter than them. They don't like glitz, but they don't like coffee stains on the carpet either. We want some understated grandeur here. Now, I can understand why things have gone to pot in your parliament buildings, because they're history until some god-damn fusing kettle burns the whole lot down. But this stuff here is only refurbished garbage. We're making a statement about ourselves till things settle down. We can't have senators of the United States of America camping in trash cans.'

The windows out on to the atrium had the Persian blinds half closed, a shield against the small rainforest of plants that filled the courtyard. But Polly could glimpse Rupert at his desk across a swathe of deep green carpet. He was not different, but he was not quite the same. None of them was. The uncertain straggle of greying hair had turned into a fine plume of glowing white. The old waistcoats, with their bulges and wrinkles and oily patches were gone: one to Madame Tussaud's, the rest to Party funding auctions. He sat bolt upright. The tight blue suit hated slouching.

'My dear,' he said, standing up and stretching towards her as she padded across the carpet. 'My dear Polly. It's been too long.' The hand that grasped hers was firm and vigorous.

'Two months,' she said briskly. 'And one new image consultant.'

He blushed, and pushed at his hair in embarrassment so that it began to ruffle and protest. 'Mineral water? Coffee?'

'Double de-caff,' she said, and pulled one of the yellow padded chairs around to the side of his desk. She needed not be too structured when she talked to Warner. She needed to be able to lean and laugh and pop up to look over his shoulder.

For once, Polly had lost track of her own game plan through the milling months of the Sort-out. The bones of the script were clear enough. Keep moving fast, because delay was the father of second thoughts. Make sure there's a swill of a Harmonization Fund to plaster any problem in dollar bills. Eight billion, not including the atrium. Make sure that those who want something can get something. Neil Forrest wanted to survive and prosper. A nasty, ratty, gingery little man: the college lecturer who strung words together best when Arthur Palmer's sudden death had opened up another situation vacant at the top of the People's Party. But the Democratic Party couldn't be choosy: it needed every powerful recruit it could get. And Labour Party leaders had been flirting and simpering in its back parlours for decades, part of the furniture. The wonder of the notion, the magic of a transition between rather than at elections, was that democracy didn't need to get in the way. An America without by-elections was used to appointing the stop-gaps of Capitol Hill when somebody died. Well, Britain had died. There was a Labour senator to appoint as well as a Tory. Clever word, appoint. Knock the timetable around, give the bigwigs nearly four years slopping in the trough before they finished phasing in the voting systems. Leave the fattest till last.

Forrest had never waited in line. Would he take the Democratic whip? Of course. There was no clout without it. Could one thing lead to another? The Democratic and Labour Party of England was born over a single covert night at an American embassy safe-house in the avenues behind Kensington High Street. Deed done. A few of the stroppier old-timers – soaked in the anti-American rhetoric of ages – didn't like it. The leftover Liberals, who hadn't gone along with the merger twenty years before, made a scene until the broadcasters deemed them boring. And, of course, the Scots and the Welsh, still banging on about socialism, cut up rough, but they had their own fish to fry now. Meanwhile, though, the Leader was moving on. Senator Forrest, a pike in a bigger pond. His home office was one floor above on the Smith Square side of the atrium.

She and Dave had guessed that would happen. And they had guessed, in turn, that the Republican and Conservative Party of England would follow inevitably. More difficult, because still nationalist in ways that Labour could never quite follow, prone to sing 'Land of Hope and Glory' as though they meant it. Giving up country was a terrible hurdle. Giving up party as well seemed almost unthinkable – unless party warfare as usual decreed it. God bless Forrest. Never underestimate a left-winger when a main chance comes along. Warner and Groom had had just the opening to Conservatives they needed. We cannot, must not, allow our Labour enemies to steal a march on this, our great adventure. 'This is a bargain offer with a sell-by date,' said Groom. We must integrate, find common cause, with the Grand Old Party, whose thinking and traditions so closely mirror our own – no, have been so closely and affectionately modelled on ours.

'Damned clever,' said Warner. 'The patriotic thing to do is to scrap Great Britain.'

Bingo. The 2022 Committee took the cash. What was left of the Lords voted themselves parity with the Senate. The attorney general jumped at the seat on the Supreme Court they'd dangled. Groom opted for governor in transition and Himmler for the non-executive chairmanship of his old supermarket chain. 'A suspiciously big fish in a suspiciously smelly pond,' said the *FT* sourly. The earth moved in Cheltenham and Harrogate. Warner had always said that that moment would be the end of his journey. 'I'm old and I'm creaky, Pol. Time to get back to the farm and write the non-selling memoirs.' But there were too many dangerous years to go to the set dates with election destiny. Groom said he needed the time to bolt together a state machine that worked. Youth, drive, detail. 'It's vital to get all the right candy by the right checkouts. Get them sweet. Keep them sweet.'

Could Warner just walk away? Dave had taken Jenny to lunch at Quaglino's and chatted happily about the wonders of Washington social life. Polly had called evening after evening, talking balanced tickets, horses for courses, essential duties. Tate had picked up the hot line and spelled out necessary sacrifices. 'We aren't done yet, Rupert. You and I together have got to make this thing stick.' No contest in the end.

Polly herself had neither expected nor wanted any nomination. She'd seen transition as the moment for babies before it was too late. And maybe, Dave said slyly, a few million in consultancy fees on the side. But Groom had begged her to stay on. 'We have got to have people in Congress who don't make fools of themselves, Polly, who can keep on selling the deal like our profit margins depended on it. The bargain of every week. We're carving up Yorkshire so there's a natural district for you. Don't turn me down. Have a baby on Uncle Sam, if you must. Give the matrons something to coo about.'

So far, anyway, no dice: much copulation without procreation. She was having tests. Dave was having tests. Damn age, damn leaving it too long. She glanced out beyond Warner and saw a young couple in the garden by the Thames, playing with a baby in a pram and embracing.

The coffee arrived.

'How's Georgetown?' she asked.

'Oh, Jenny loves it,' said Warner. 'Highgate on the Potomac. A terrific relief after all those months in hotel rooms. It's a Cotswold manor house that got lost somewhere in *Gone With the Wind*. There are white pillars in the backyard. She wears great cotton dresses and ribbons for tea. Quite the Southern belle. Scarlett O'Warner.'

Sharper than usual, Polly thought. They rarely talked about Jenny, but here, without prompting, he was making bitter fun of her.

'She's there at the moment,' he said. 'Spending money. Redecorating. Building a new deck and a summer-house. Planning parties. I can't say I take to it much. Thank God our new masters, in their infinite wisdom, give us plenty of quality time in London so that we can wave the Stars and Stripes as required.'

Bitterness again. Warner had told the President he wouldn't be around in Washington much. 'I'm not elected, Mark. It would be quite wrong for me to jet in and deliver votes on issues that won't affect England till harmonization's over – long after I'm dead, if I have to keep climbing on a bloody plane every two days. Oh, I'll be there as needed, turning out on parade. But I think the main job is back in and around Westminster, making the odd speech, showing chaps that the world hasn't ended.'

Not what Jenny intended. She was a plump pig in a brand new jumbo pack of truffles. Occasional queen of the breakfast shows. Celebrity bedmate of the young interior designer who had turned the hall lime green. Forty-nine, and still at it like a thirty-year-old. And now she was moving closer to the edge, choosing lovers with nothing to lose, lovers who might one day kiss and tell, heedless as though there were too few tomorrows left. Rupert knew that disaster lay in wait, ready to happen. But what was there to say? What to do, after all those years of semi-detached silence?

'Well, at least you've got somewhere you can call home,' said Polly lightly. 'You should try my service apartment in the Baltimore. A bed, a freezer and a telephone. Who could ask for anything more, especially when your husband's stuck in South Kensington?'

Enough. She'd called because Groom sensed a crisis.

'It's the King,' said Polly. 'Robin has given up trying to handle him. Absolutely no sale and no sell-by date. I can't make sense of where he's coming from. Could you have a go for all of us?'

Jenny was beginning to growl with fury. Rupert's office in Washington was thinly, dozily staffed. A few kids on scholar-ships, a few dreary Foreign Office drop-outs from the end of embassy, gossiping, sneering, shuffling sheets of paper. The Senator, even when he left London, wasn't doing much, by design: he'd accumulated a team of no-hopers who couldn't do much if they tried. And she needed help.

Washington was parties: dinner parties, cocktail parties, lunch parties, tea parties. If you didn't party, you didn't get known. But if you didn't throw your own parties, nobody wanted to know you. They had to get out of that sickening suite at the Park Tower Plaza. They had to have a home, a base camp with a kitchen and a chef. Rupert, of course, wasn't interested. 'By all means sort it out if you feel you must.' She'd found the house singlehanded. Now she was trying to find the staff to run it.

The bloody office was no use. They were servants. They knew nothing about getting servants. They shrugged and said perhaps there was something useful on the Net. See here, DC Helping Hands, 1205 Leland Street, Bethesda. Domestic Assistants for Every Occasion.

The Lord helps those who help themselves. She trekked out to Bethesda, grinding down the Rockville Pike. She had interviewed three Costa Ricans, two Brazilians, four Mexicans, and Elena from Nicaragua, who spoke the most passable English. 'When I live with my boyfriend in Miami, I clean the flat every day. He like it clean for the crap.' The what? Oh, the crap game he was running. Where is he now? 'He guest of the government for four more years.' Hired.

So was Maria from El Salvador, who swore she'd been a sous-chef in the El Paso Hilton. 'I do good tamales, but I do great lobster soufflés like Señor Eescoffier he write.'

But where was the chauffeur-cum-gardener they'd promised? He'd been due for interview at three. It was four thirty and sliding. Egipane Engibono. The CV looked fine. Ex-farm labourer, from a village forty miles south of Addis Ababa. Ex-Washington cab driver. Clean licence. A second cousin of the Ethiopian ambassador. Perfect, except he hadn't turned up.

'He may have got the day wrong,' said the stringy blonde behind the desk. 'And his phone sounds like it's off the hook. But I'm sure he'll be very suitable if you can find him.'

'I'm not driving out here again when Venus elides with Mars,' Jenny snarled. 'The Pike is a nightmare. Which is why I want a chauffeur in the first place.'

The blonde thumbed the crumpled pink card and sniffed. 'He only lives three blocks away, down on Duke Street. Two minutes max. You could always try dropping by, if that's the way you feel.'

Duke Street was a litter of small shops and grimy, three-storey apartment buildings. She found number 37 between the washeteria and the Happy Guzzler liquor store. The door opened six inches, and two wide, glistening eyes shimmered from the dark.

'Mr Engibono?' said Jenny. 'I'm the lady you were going to see about a job.'

The door swung wide. God, he was beautiful. Broad shoulders, slim hips, a towel wrapped tight around his waist. She looked at the smooth, tapered chest, which seemed to shimmer in the sun, the restless muscles of the thighs. She looked into the eyes. 'When can you start?' she said.

The orange curtain on the first floor twitched back for a second. A hand held it, a blur of a face looked down and seemed to scowl. And then it was gone.

In one sense, the King didn't matter. The circus had moved to another town. A few decades earlier, the monarchy would have been a total spoiler. How, in the name of tabloid sanctity, could you bury the crowned head of Windsor in a republican grave? The old Queen would have reached for her hatpin. But there had been too much mess and peripheral misery for too long; and too much sudden death, buried with pomp but without compassion. Royal homes and marriages breaking up. Damaged kids from a damaged family picking up the baton and dropping it. One accident after another. And the detritus of failure stretched far across the world. The fat old Duchess lived in Beverly Hills, keeping semi-solvent on dogfood commercials. The Cape Town dissidents, carping and fornicating away. The young ex-Queen, who seemed to commute endlessly between the Florida Keys and Bermuda, beach bums piled on the deck of her yacht. A strew of talentless photographers and unemployed party addicts from the junior ranks wandering seedily through New York night-life. And His Majesty, the one with the current baton stuffed down his pants, deserted, alone, podgy, balding and the glum side of forty, rowed slowly towards the edge of public consciousness. Survival via Oblivion Avenue.

Rupert had never bothered about the ancestral weekly briefings. The King didn't listen. At one early meeting Rupert had talked for half an hour about the reshaping of the Western European Union after the winding up of NATO, and at the end found him snoring gently in his chair. Mostly he stayed on his farm near Truro, emerging only for mandatory monarch events and sleeping overnight in the flat at the southern tip of the Palace, which had been kept private when his father had shrugged and given the rest to the nation early in the century.

The Royal Clearances, they'd called it. Not quite your

Scandinavian bicycling bit, but acknowledgement, at last, that protocol was out of stock in a country where pumped-up council leaders from Darlington and Derby held the floor in the House of Lords. If you sounded the retreat, if you drew a new line, you might hope to regroup and hang on. But the line was a snare, not a shield. The royal flock, the copulaters old and new, learned no lessons. They merely carried on as before.

In the end, even the tabloids – bruised by too much tragedy – grew weary. A footballer brawling in a night-club was a bigger story than another wastrel princeling fondling a deb with her mouth open. But because they had retreated, because they had rolled up the rolling acres and handed them back, there was no easy political next step except abolition. And nobody had the energy for that. Anger had faded into inert disillusion. The King, and the rest of the dysfunctionals, were stowed at the back of a shelf. It had been one great boon of joining the States. 'Sure, you can keep him,' said Tate. 'Let him be a sort of historical monument wheeled out for pageants and things. My guys love that heritage pitch. We aren't joining up to wipe out your past. We want to wallow in it, to look through your palace windows. Why junk a tourist attraction when the Disney people would only want to build it again anyway?'

The light was burning in the little flat when Rupert's Cadillac turned into the inner yard. Bannon hopped out and opened the door for him. A couple of Marines on shared duty clicked their heels. A bored aide in a brown suit opened the door.

'Senator Warner, to see His Majesty,' said Rupert.

The King was standing by the window, hand twitching at its net curtain. He seemed older and more dispirited every time Rupert saw him. The hair had retreated early, and was now in full flight, revealing a lumpy pate that flowed without interruption down to a protruding nose and a pimple of a chin. Like some grotesque ski-jump. But there could be no jumping over the sag of shoulders pulled forward and down by a thick, round belly.

'Senator,' he said. 'I expect Groom sent you. But it won't do any good. I told him, "No sale – no bloody ring of the till." This pathetic regal corpse did a deal with you that gave us what we both want. A deal is a deal. This corpse has no intention of walking a centimetre beyond it.'

They sat down on the pink Queen Anne couch. 'Of course,' said Rupert, his voice growing grander and more avuncular, 'I have no right or expectation outside our agreement. You wouldn't expect me to say anything else in honour, sir. You could have caused upset when we were campaigning for statehood. But you caused none, and in turn we produced a list of core ceremonial duties that would be performed – which left reasonable scope for you to spend much of the year out of the public gaze. I may say, sir, that I understand that. Your wife had behaved appallingly. You were deeply affected and depressed. Both our advisers recommended a period of dignified silence. But there is a special situation here, sir.'

Special, Rupert thought, but not exactly unpredictable. States – in Europe as well as America – had always fought to suck funds back from the centre. That was the name of the federal game. We'd never made much of a fist of it. The bloody Treasury had spent the worst years of its life declining to put up the 'matching funds' Brussels insisted on – while a dawn chorus of second-rate politicians whined on about giving us our money back. And now we were dropping into exactly the same hole all over again.

It had been a mistake to prise the Irish out of the Union. Too damned neat for comfort. Sure, it had thrown the remnants of the IRA into terminal disarray. There wasn't a cause left, and there weren't any Yankee funds available to fight it with. But the mobs – the Republican mob and the Prod mob, the masters of the protection rackets, the gun and drug runners, the sainted keepers of the bordellos and deflowerers of Little Nellie Kelly – had simply carried on slaughtering each other as usual. It was what they'd always done, and the politics had long since become irrelevant. Which left plenty of time for Dublin's politicians to do what they were very good indeed at: blarney their way to the boodle.

They had taken over Boston for St Patrick's Day and painted the town bright green. They had bought one of the Twenty-first Century Fox TV channels for the day and filled it with famous Irish exiles – including a crooner from Cork who was big in Las Vegas – singing songs about bogs and peat and apple-cheeked girls who liked a tumble in the mud. The Governor, Treneman, had hired City Hall – 'where once the great Kennedy brothers had their first glimpse of politics' – and asked Mark Tate to open the first bottle and start the party. 'Sure with eyes like that, Mr President, your grandmother must have swum in the Liffey.' Tate declined to confirm any Irish lineage to add to the Dorset duo, but he had a good, clear baritone voice and sang 'Danny Boy' before the first commercial break. It was, said the *Washington Post*, an object lesson to all America. 'Eighty per cent slush and twenty per cent hard cash.' Translated as $3 billion in extra discretionary grants for the new Cork to Galway freeway when the Capitol Hill twistings were done.

That had been bad enough, but the Scots had picked up the tune in a trice. The Irish were using the techniques they'd learned in Brussels. The Scots – after decades of their own Edinburgh assembly screwing Whitehall via a succession of Nat chief ministers – knew what worked for them. A little harmless fear on the Quebec model. Governor Angus hadn't signed up with either the Republicans or the Democrats. He was hanging tactically loose. His scouts had found a Scottish enclave high up in the Santa Cruz mountains south of San Francisco, a hamlet called Bonny Doon, and, praise be, a reservoir called Loch Lomond. He organized the first united Highland Games, persuaded Vice-President Wilbur Galt to wear a kilt, and delivered a speech that somehow managed to mention William Wallace and George Wallace in a single sentence. 'The Campbells are coming. The need for justice for Scotland, inside or outside the United States, has never been more urgent or more passionately felt.'

Two point five billion dollars for the Aberdeen to Dundee freeway.

And England? 'We're still handing over tax dollars,' Groom complained. 'We're the biggest state of the union, but we haven't managed a single decent pay-back since we joined. No food stamps, let alone Green Shield stamps. We just stand on the edge of the party and cough apologetically.'

The King himself coughed. Rupert came back to business. 'You know, Your Majesty, how other states have been scooping up funding from Washington? You'll have seen about the Swansea ferry terminal this morning. It's a problem, and we need something really high profile to redress the balance, to remind Congress that England exists and would never say no to a spot of investment. And you know, too, that we've had an amazing stroke of luck.'

If you could call a fire luck. The popcorn-maker had short-circuited and spewed sparks into the balloon stall; the balloons had drifted, with flaming ribbons, into the flag-stand; and the blazing banner had lit the plastic grass in the Oakfield Coliseum, smoking and cracking the giant glass dome. Proper repairs would take six months. But the Superbowl had been scheduled there for next month. Groom had offered Wembley (home, among others, of the London Cardinals, once the St Louis and Phoenix Cardinals). ABC (with its new affiliate, the EBC) were ready to switch – but the game itself, Dallas and Denver again, wasn't rated much of a draw, and the pressure was on for added hoopla. Who would throw the opening ball? Tate was due in Japan for a rescheduled trade summit. Would they take Vice-President Galt instead? Boredom scored a home run. ABC's finest, sweating through the night, had come up with a Shakespearian pageant and starring role for the King of England in a crown.

'I don't call it luck,' said the King. 'I call it prostitution, and a complete severance of our contract. I am not going to demean myself, and what's left of my family, turning out for a football fancy-dress party.'

Rupert's game plan unfolded naturally. A moment of national crisis. A call to duty. A freeway that would bring Essex hypermarkets within seventy minutes of Sandringham. 'But naturally,' he said, 'we have to respect your right to refuse. Nobody can argue with that. And at least ABC seem to have a replacement lined up who's happy to play.'

'Oh,' said the King. 'I don't think Groom will be much of a stand-in for me.'

'Nor, to be fair, does he,' said Rupert. 'No, they've been on to the Queen. She'll have to cancel a lot of things in Bermuda to come, and she's asking seven hundred and fifty thousand dollars. But she'll wear her wedding dress and that Hapsburg tiara from the settlement. And her agent says she's happy to do pre-match and post-match interviews.'

His Majesty's Adam's apple wobbled vigorously up and down, appearing in the shaded light to rebound from the shrunken chin. He had been hopelessly in love with Samantha Milner-Monk when the foxhunting fall that had killed his brother made him monarch overnight, hopelessly in thrall to her golden bob, her tinkle of a laugh, and her screams of confected joy as he sank himself into her. So, she was a stockbroker's daughter, an air hostess who had made it to airline corporate relations. So what? Starched princesses from the finishing schools of Europe weren't the flavour of the century any longer. There were other dreams to re-create, other memories of touching and feeling. But Queen Sam ... It had never sounded right, and she had never, after that night with her bodyguard, made the slightest effort to play it right. Oh, she was still the little actress, still starring as wronged beauty with the chinless beast. Oh, that titter of derision still haunted his nights of sleepless miseries. A queen for all the country. It was a pity the country had turned out to be Grand Cayman.

'God rot it, Warner. Tell them that I'll be there. Ask a million and make sure everyone knows it will all go to charity.'

*

The 'new' Wembley Stadium, a temple of thanksgiving to lotteries everywhere, was more than two decades old now, and curiously dated in its heavy swirls and sweeps. It seemed, Rupert thought, like a giant blanket you peeped through to see what moved on the plastic pitch far below.

Show-time. Ninety thousand roaring people and ninety thousand waving flags. The massed bands of the Brigade of Guards, bearskins and the full kit, played Souza, and Rodgers and Hammerstein. The massed bands of the Marine Corps played Elgar and the Beatles. Two hundred blonde teenagers, half from Cambridge (Mass.) and half from Cambridge (Eng.), wove back and forth through the bands, kicking firm golden thighs and shaking firm youthful breasts.

The King had compromised on regalia. No crown, no ermine. But a royal coach, entering from the Willesden end, brought him to meet the players, and a black velvet cloak, wrapped around a Household Cavalry uniform, hid the protruding belly and danced around his shoulders, distracting eyes from the chin. As he walked along the stretching line of hulks and padding, he staggered a little, then smiled and recovered.

'It's a moment of moving symbolism, Jake,' said the ABC match commentator to the old pro who did the tactical summaries. 'This is our national game, and here's the monarch of England blessing it with his presence, just like good Queen Bess blessed bowls all those centuries ago. I think the people back home, you know, will see this as more than politicians getting together. This is the moment that says, "We're joined. Our game is their game. Our history will be their history."'

'Right,' said Jake. 'It's sure something to tell your kids about.' A gust of wind caught the royal cloak and raised it high for a second. 'Say, that's some sort of gale starting there,' he said. 'I don't reckon the Broncos will feel too happy kicking off into that.'

A large brunette from the Royal Opera sang 'The Starspangled Banner'. A large black soprano from the Met sang

'God Save the King'. His Majesty trudged up the long stone staircase to the open box and stood for a moment beside Rupert, waving with one hand and clutching his cloak with another, swaying slightly in the wind. Rupert thought he smelt the stench of whisky. Down below the Broncos kicked off and suddenly, from the Denver stand on the right, there was a great roar. The King swung round bemusedly, arm raised, and pitched downwards, cracking his head on the first stone step. He lay very still.

The fat wife of the president of the American Conference squeaked in alarm. But half the row were looking down on the pitch, and the din was all-enveloping. Latecomers hurrying to their seats clogged the gangway. The fat lady screamed.

Forty years before Rupert had done a first-aid course for farm managers. And sometimes, in winter, he had had to be his own vet, delivering sheep in the snow-drifts swept high when the north wind blew.

He bent by the King. Grey, cold face. Lips parted, eyes closed. The feeblest of pulses. Rupert bellowed for help, then swung the body on to its side, index finger struggling to prise the swallowed tongue free. 'Goddamnit, give me the gift of tongues.' Got it. The mouth began to move again. Keep him warm. Wrap my Burberry round him. Bellow for help again. SO bloody S.

Suddenly the King opened his eyes and put his hand to the great bleeding gash across his scalp. He began to retch and Rupert clutched him close, calming the convulsions. A camera was clicking somewhere. The first-aid team, fighting through the crowd that had stood to watch, took over. In five minutes the stretcher had gone. In thirty minutes a Palace spokesman said His Majesty was recovering well from an unfortunate fall. There was no reason for concern.

The Cowboys were ten points up at the end of the first quarter.

*

Shorty Maddox was not getting the best jobs any longer. There had been the unfortunate affair of the judge and the mystery redhead, who had turned out to be his daughter on a visit from Australia, and Shorty was being fed picture-desk scraps until the fuss died down. Even so, Royal Box stand duty was the tiniest straw. Nobody cared about Pimple Chin. The front page was bound to go to some cheerleader with a breast floating loose, or a twenty-five-stone linebacker making an obscene gesture at the crowd.

But safety first. He snapped away. And then there was a mêlée and a panic and a rush of bodies. Maddox began to concentrate.

Five Seconds From Death, Say Experts. Senator Saves Choking Sovereign. Quick-thinking Rupert Rescues the Monarchy.

And so on. The *Mirror* had six pages of pictures, a strip cartoon of crisis. There was a wonderfully sharp one of Rupert wiping his brow as the King stirred, and beaming with relief. Another of the King clasping his arm as though in profound thanks. Within six hours second rights on the Maddox collection had been syndicated all over the world.

Jenny was five seconds from what she judged would be a satisfactory climax with the pride of Ethiopia when the phone rang. He was not, she had discovered, a sensitive lover. Arched above her, that sensational black body streaming sweat, the noise at the back of his throat rising with the exertion, he attacked her as he had been attacking the thicket of brambles and berries at the bottom of the garden when she'd called him in. But he was magnificently fit, utterly dedicated: like a marathon runner trained at altitude. He was taking her as though the tape was in sight at last, pumping, pumping.

'Damn,' she said, stretched arms upwards to his shoulders, gripping to slow his dives and heaves. 'Damn. I forgot the answerphone. Get off me while I get rid of it.'

You needed to shove and steer Egi. He had almost no English, except for a few phrases he'd picked up driving a cab around

Washington last summer. 'Stop light,' said Jenny. 'No thru road.'

The bloody phone was still ringing. 'Is that the Warner residence? This is Tom McCullum of *Good Morning, America*. We wanted to talk to Mrs Warner about her husband, and what the Senator did for the King.'

It was the first of many calls. 'You're parked for the night,' Jenny told Egi, after five minutes, and he loped away to his cot in the garage. She had an inkling of what had happened from CBS and NBC. The CNN all-night interactive had some of Maddox's shots on screen with excited voice-overs from a lady billed as their European medical editor. 'See His Majesty's mouth fall open. Watch the skin tone begin to develop that greyish pallor all doctors fear. See the desperate search for the tongue. Without doubt, he can only have been minutes, if not seconds, from what might have been an irreversible condition.'

She got Rupert, groaning, out of bed, groping for his private line. 'You clever old thing, darling. Are you all right? You know that you're famous? Now, tell me everything.'

When he'd got home Rupert had had three stiff whiskies. HM was fine, the Palace had said. 'Though a little shaken naturally, the King is giving no cause for alarm and his doctors expect him to resume his normal schedule within a week. He thanks all those who have sent messages and particularly those who assisted him so speedily at the stadium.' The press, without at that stage having seen the Maddox portfolio, had treated Rupert as just another witness. 'I didn't do much,' he murmured, with a shrinking shrug. 'I just tried my best to help.' That was the only available quote when the pictures came out.

'What great British understatement,' said the editor at ABC. '"I didn't do much." Just saved the monarchy from a frigging black hole in history single-handed, that's all.'

It was six on a chilly London morning. Rupert, she thought, seemed blearily bemused as he took her through his two minutes of crisis. 'Look, honestly, Jen. I didn't do that much. I just happened to be there. I'm only glad he's not done anything serious.'

She took over. His dozy idiot of a press secretary would surely be calling him soon. 'I expect he'll have been blocking you off. The fool. But don't let him change course now. If you have to say something, just keep it short and sweet. I'll handle the rest. And the sooner you can get over here, the better.'

'Oh, right,' said Rupert. 'I love you.'

'Yes,' said Jenny. 'I suppose you could say that if they ask, too.'

She packed her blue suit and pink suit in a suitcase. Six interviews set over three hours. No point looking the same all morning. She wore her new yellow linen suit with a black silk scarf drawn tightly to hide the neck, but ends trailing lightly across the breasts. Jenny had done this sort of thing before, then watched herself over and over on the video. That bust was still a winner. If the hand occasionally strayed over it, stroking, twisting at a scarf, men ceased to listen to what she was saying exactly. They just took the best of the vibes.

'Egi,' she screamed. 'Get the sodding car out. We've got a lot to do.'

As soon as she got back Jenny watched all the videos. Not bad. Indeed, she thought, much better than that.

She'd crossed her legs at the wrong moment on NBC. Just as she was saying how Rupert never talked about his early life on the farms of Australia and Dorset. 'He's always been a man of action, a man of the soil. But it's been, well, private, between the two of us since we got into politics.' Damn, too much thick ankle waving around in the middle of the screen.

But ABC was perfect. 'I talked to him this morning and told him I loved him. In some ways, you know, he's so unworldly. The last thing he'll do is claim any credit for things like this. For Rupert, it's just duty.'

And CBS, she reckoned, was probably the pick of the bunch. She was into the cornflower blue suit by then, and it made her hair look blonder. 'Rupert and I love America, you know. It was the greatest thrill for him to be at one of your greatest sporting occasions, which is one of our great events now. England or Washington, we're at home. We feel part of something big. But you'll never persuade him to claim too much credit for himself over something like this. He's a courageous man but, if you'll forgive me, he's also a quiet man.'

Terrific. It had been right to change to the red scarf too.

Jenny threw open the window and let the chill of the wind cleanse her face. Outside in the street, a bulky man with a black spaniel tugged at the leash and walked into the park, not looking back.

She took the phone off the hook and wandered round to the back of the house where Egi was washing the Cadillac. Maria had gone to the mall with a week's shopping list. 'I think,' she said, 'that the road may be open again. Step on the gas.'

Chapter Eleven

Tate sat on the Deer Isle jetty in front of the house and flicked straws into the water. Dave Simmons walked down the lawn and squatted beside him. The bay and the sunlight and the gleam on the waves never changed.

'Four years,' said the President. 'Four years since we were here and it all began to happen. Only four more years to go, and then what? No more elections to fight. No more rubber chickens and TV crews camped by the gate. Nothing left to aim at. I'll be fifty-six, Dave, and I keep wondering what to do with the rest of my life. Is it the lecture circuit and the Presidential Library in Bangor kitted out with all my stuff from the White House, so that I'm a kind of stuffed dummy in a museum? Or do I go back to the beginnings? Smoke some fish, hope for some grandchildren, play at being an ordinary Joe again. That's what Marti wants, you know. She wants us to have our life back. And maybe she's right.'

Mark's changed, Simmons thought. Not just physically – a dozen or so extra pounds from all those burgers and fries working late in the Oval Office, hair thinning and scalp showing red from yesterday's boat trip in the blaze of summer. No, it's more than that. The edge to him is beginning to go, the ambition is running to seed. 'Hey, slow down, old friend,' he said. 'You haven't got those next four years yet. And this way you won't get them. Sure it looks easy rolling into the conventions. You're ten points up. The economy is getting a little on the hot side, but the Fed won't move interest rates much this side of

November. There ain't no wars and there ain't no crises. But Nate Plummer isn't Bordon. He's a cute guy, and a cute guy from Alabama. The Democrats never learn their lesson for long. When they put up fellows from the South who don't scare no one and say three hallelujahs before breakfast, they're always in with a shout. Then they go and spoil it, picking some labour hothead or a liberal like Bordon and it all goes to straight to blazes again.

'But don't,' he said, 'take your eye off Plummer. He was a damned smart governor, and he's a damned smart senator. He didn't just clean up in the primaries. He got the voters out. Go back and see how many Bordon polled in Wisconsin and Ohio last time. Nate puts twenty per cent on those figures. Make one slip, Mr President, sir, and you'll be building that Library of yours a mite ahead of schedule.'

Tate scratched the blister on his head and seemed to blush for a second. 'You're right, of course. I'm sitting back stroking my goddamn place in history again. And I know that's a mistake. The trouble is I'm surrounded by people on the team who are celebrating already. Hendrix and his Staff guys are so deep into the second-term bills they've barely given getting there a glance. The campaign committee is just going through the motions, spending cash and planning their memoirs. I need somebody in there to start kicking.' He paused and broke a straw. 'In fact, Dave, I reckon I need you. Help get me back safe and sound and you could be the new Hendrix if you want – really get dug in where the action is, make yourself a reputation you can live off while that sweet little English wife of yours cuts the Washington mustard.'

Simmons looked back towards the house. Polly and Marti were sitting on the porch, shelling beans and laughing together.

'Well,' he said, 'that sure serves me right for talking out of turn. Mind if I think on those things?'

Tate smiled suddenly. 'Sure,' he said, 'you've got at least twelve hours. And we've got supper with Vice-President Wilbur and the lovely Aileen to survive, starting, I reckon, any damn moment now.'

Three heavy black cars flying the stars and stripes emerged from the forest road at the end of the creek and moved up the hill towards the security post. The Galts had just happened to be vacationing at Kennebunkport and just happened to have asked themselves up for an informal photo-opportunity and ribs. Who said they weren't best friends with Mark and Marti? Who said the President thought his once and future running mate was a pain in the backside? Pass the corn-on-the-cob and smile like you're having a good time, for Chrissake.

Wilbur Richard Galt the Second was old, not new, Florida. Grandpa Galt had started building condominiums along the front at Daytona Beach after the Second World War and made a pile before Disney and package tours drained away the cash and the old folks coming down from the Bronx and Queens for the winter. He'd been savvy enough to move into office blocks in Jacksonville when land was still cheap, and far-sighted enough to buy Wilbur the First a state senatorship and then two terms as governor with a partying budget that floated on bourbon. That was how dynasties got founded. Wilbur Two didn't have to think twice about career choices. He was handsome, in a jowly way, with a smile you could switch on with a click of the fingers. He was no genius, but he could talk OK and shake hands and keep the punters happy and buy all the expert help he needed. The pros steered him straight into the House for three terms, and then the Senate. Why take risks with governing things, when things could go wrong? Tate had needed a fresh face and a Southern drawl on the ticket. Wil Galt, almost without breaking sweat, was the man.

Marti offered her cheek for a cautious kiss. He'd been drinking again. The gin and peppermint hit her together as he wrapped an arm around her shoulders and pulled her to him.

'Hey, this is great,' said Tate. 'You know Dave and Polly

Simmons, two of my oldest friends? You must have bumped into Dave around the White House some time.'

Galt shrugged. 'I've heard of you, of course. My folks give you a lot of credit for helping this fellow here shape up. But I can't say I think we've met. Mark will tell you. Vice-presidents don't see much of the action in this administration. We also serve who stand and wait in the outer office.'

Polly stopped herself wincing. This seedy Superman, with his six-foot pillow of a wife, had a curiously thin, high voice that quavered at the end of sentences. He sounded bitter and querulous wrapped into one.

'Aw, come on, Wil,' said Marti, chipping in. 'Mark always says you've been one of the rocks he clings to. A colleague and a friend. Why don't you folks come inside and have a drink?' She'd almost said 'another drink'. She linked arms with Aileen and marched up to the porch.

Galt hung back for a second and turned to Tate. 'Before we start relaxing, Mr President, I wonder if I might have a little private word about somethin' that's worrying the socks off me? It won't take but a minute.'

They wandered back down to the jetty. The sun was beginning to dip into the sea. The midges and horse-flies were heading up in clouds from the water's edge.

'Damn it,' said Tate. 'Let's go and have a cigar in the boat-house. The girls won't see and maybe we can give the frigging insects cancer before supper.'

Galt perched on the stern of a rowing boat and spat his cigar end into the bay. 'There's no nice way to say this,' he said, 'but I reckon I've got a problem. And I reckon it's got to be your problem too.'

Simmons heard them shouting from thirty yards away. They'd been gone for nearly an hour. Marti had cooked the steaks and piled them high on the side of the barbecue. Polly had unwrapped the silver foil on the corn-cobs. Aileen, flesh heaved into a tiny halter-neck top, was lying in the hammock, biting her nails. 'For God's sake,' said Marti. 'It'll be charred or it'll be chilled if those two don't come. Dave, why don't you try a little diplomacy down there? Tell Mark that he can have food or smoke-filled boat-houses, but he sure can't have both, and this little lady is asking him to choose.'

Simmons hovered on the jetty for a second, then coughed and pushed open the door. Tate was tense and pacing. Galt was squatting in the corner on a pile of ropes, red-faced and chewing lumps out of a second cigar.

'Don't tell me,' said Tate. 'You're the damned search party sent out to tell us it's face-feeding time. Well, bad news, bro. I lost my appetite. This fat worm has turned me off food and maybe politics, too.'

'I'll go,' said Simmons. 'Sorry, I didn't realize that you two were into something.'

'No.' Tate spun on his heel. 'Stay, stay. Welcome to the world you're going to help me through, come January. Welcome to motherfucker slobs getting their pecker in the works.'

Galt started to mutter, then slumped back among the ropes.

'This guy,' said Tate, 'this God-fearing, chapel-going, moralizing bastard, this louse one heartbeat away from the presidency of the good old US, this lump of 'gator crap from the Sunshine State, has got some titty-waving little blue-eyed girl in the club. And not any old butt-waggler. Not any piece of meat off the street who'd take a few bills and take a walk. No, the prize idiot here has knocked up a darling young slice of Cubano sausage who cheer-leads for Tampa Bay and whose uncle, if you goddamn please, is a Roman frigging Catholic frigging bishop. She's fifteen going on twenty-seven. She's under age. She's pregnant by Vice-President Supersperm here. And she don't believe in no fucking abortion. Otherwise,' said Tate, 'we're in great shape. Otherwise we can just wrap up four more years and get on with governing the country.'

'Mark,' said Simmons, 'I'm on your team, and you never said

it'd be easy. Why don't you and me and Wil here just calm down and go dig into those rib-eyes like nothing was causing any heartburn? Why don't Wil and his devoted wife drive back to Kennebunkport as though there's nothing more on their minds than a long weekend eating lobsters straight out the pot? And why don't I go down tomorrow with Polly for a little quiet meet with Mr Wilbur Galt the Second, while Aileen goes off to Bridgeport and shops till she drops? And why don't I see what the hell we can fix?'

He spat lengthily from the jetty and walked up the lawn to the house. The President and the Vice-President paused for a second, glared at each other, then slowly followed him.

They took the coast road down, winding through little towns and dozing white villages lined with antique shops. 'So damn tasteful it makes you ashamed to blow your nose,' said Simmons.

Polly offered to take him to the Wye valley one day. 'It makes all this look like a three-ring circus.'

Nobody, of course, had told the Galts about taste. Grandpa Wilbur had built Everglades North in 1952 on a patch of land one block back from the bay that one of his kitchen-unit suppliers had intended to keep for his retirement. Bankruptcy bopped that on the jaw. Old Galt didn't believe in architects. 'I read the Bible from beginning to end without finding mention of nary a one of those arty layabouts,' he said. 'If God had put architects on this earth for a purpose, he'd have told us so when that Samson guy started rocking the temple.' Grandpa Wilbur was his own inspiration. He went to the movies twice a week and made little sketches on a pad during the popcorn and ices intervals. One run of apartments in Daytona Beach came straight out of *The Big Sleep*. The big house in Florida was Manderley, with the conservatory from *The Little Sister*. He'd just seen a re-release of *Gone With the Wind* when Maine came up.

'Jesus,' said Simmons, as they drove through the pines and saw the white house a hundred yards ahead, across a carpet of a lawn that a Mexican in a red bandana was weeding on his hands and knees. 'Will you look at those pillars? It's Tara without none of the Selznick penny-pinching. Frankly, my dear, I don't give a shit.'

Polly laughed and fluttered her eyelids. They needed to relax. They'd stopped for scrambled eggs and hash browns at a diner and discussed the options. They knew this was going to be a miserable morning.

Galt had a butler called Arthur, who wore a beige jacket and a neat red bow-tie. 'The Vice-President is waiting for you in the summer house, sir.' Jeeves meets the Great Gatsby, Simmons thought.

The Veep was wearing a flat straw hat and smoking another cigar. 'Well,' he asked, tightly, 'what have the Brains Trust made of my little dilemma? Is that bastard Tate still chewing my backside off over somethin' that could have happened to any red-blooded male with a piece of ass who didn't offer no birth certificate before she opened her legs? I don't want morality. I want a nice easy way out.'

As they'd planned, Polly stepped forward. She flexed her chin and looked for his eyes. The accent was pure Cheltenham Ladies College. 'Spare us the Huey Long Memory Lane,' she said. 'I've spent half the night on the phone to Tampa. You know Jeannie Nash, the principal at Tampa High?'

Galt nodded silently.

'What you don't know is that she's one of my oldest friends. We were at Oxford together. Somerville. She's talked to Cindy. She's talked to the parents. She called on the Bishop at seven this morning. There's no way they're going to go quietly. The girl is hysterical and bitter. She was flattered when you started to paw her. She couldn't believe you'd strew your seed all over the beach. Her father wants to start a law-suit. Her mother is talking about the *Miami Herald*. I don't think there'd be a cat in hell's chance of keeping this under wraps without the Bishop.'

He was locked on to her now, neck reddening, tongue running automatically across thick lips.

'Here's the deal,' said Polly. 'It's what the Bishop thinks he can sell. No abortion, naturally. But money to have and keep the baby safe for life. Say five million dollars, with a million expenses on top for Mother Church. And not a word said – if they feel that you've done more than sign cheques, if they feel you've paid your other dues.'

'Which means packing up,' said Simmons. 'We engineer a little speculation about your future, talk of a life beyond politics, that sort of thing. Maybe a sabbatical from public service. Maybe more time with the family. And then, for the avoidance of doubt, you say, "Sure, it's true, I'm moving on, I won't be running again this time. It has been a privilege, a real privilege, to play such a vital role at the heart of America." But now there are so many good works you feel need undertaking in the great state of Florida.'

'You mean, God has reached out and called me back,' said Galt.

'I mean God has told you to get the hell out of here and bury your sordid little life as far away from the cameras as this country permits. Be clear, Mr Vice-President. The Bishop isn't seeking retribution. But he can't abide the thought of you running around smiling as though nothing had happened. He'll keep Cindy and his sister under wraps, convince them that this is the best way in the end. But he never wants to see your fat, grinning face again.'

'It looks,' said Galt, 'as though you've condemned me to a life sentence of just making money.'

'The story's crap,' said Tate. 'Such obvious crap. Who's going to believe that a greedy oaf like Galt has been touched by the Lord? There's bound to be every kind of speculation running round and round. It will never hold.'

Simmons shrugged. 'Maybe. Maybe not. But either way, you

acted decisively. You cleaned out the stables and, by golly, you put that little girl and her baby first. Your first instinct was to protect their privacy. I don't reckon that can do you any great harm as long as we make sure we're on top of the agenda.'

'The one thing that would be lethal,' said Polly, 'would be for anyone involved to talk abortion. Nate Plummer could get elected Pope if that happened. But there isn't a whiff of that here. We could say that you, personally, intervened to make sure it was never even discussed. When the going got rough, you chose Life.'

'Well, there's another matter of life after the death of the Vice-President,' said Tate, moodily. 'Seems to me we've got a fortnight to go before San Diego and a job vacancy to get filled pretty darned fast.'

They demanded country ham on rye sandwiches, coffee and a bottle of Wild Turkey. With a large side order of pencils and paper.

Chapter Twelve

Rupert was on vacation – and, more unusual than that, family vacation. Piers, his younger son, had two toddling children, a wife called Sandy, a home in Perth, Western Australia, and a small documentary film-making company, which managed to sell enough pretty ordinary shorts on Aboriginal culture, lizards of the outback and secrets of the Barrier Reef to keep ticking over. They'd just got a BBC2 commission for six mid-evening programmes on Australian wine-makers – provisionally entitled *Château Downunda* – which had arrived with twenty thousand dollars up front.

Holiday time. Piers, like brother Richard, had made almost a fetish of avoiding Mum and Dad. They'd hated politics; they'd loathed the gossip columns and the sneers when Richard had got thrown out of Sherborne for smoking pot; they had, in Australia and New Zealand, chosen obscurity – and, truth to tell, chosen to put as many miles between them and their parents as the globe made possible. But kids, you know: grandchildren. 'We ought to take them to meet the old folk while they're still cute,' Sandy had said. She was a plump, bouncy costume designer Piers had met in Sydney when he was filming the renovation of the Opera House.

'I suppose so, if you really want,' said Piers. His mother, he thought, was no great grandma. He'd never read an interview with Jenny that mentioned her sons, let alone wives and infants. But Sandy, in her wide-eyed way, punched him on the shoulder and passed the telephone. 'Aw, come on. They'll love the little darlings. It ain't natural to keep them apart.'

Senator Warner, to Piers's surprise, agreed. Mimsie was three, with curls and a slight lisp. Joey was fourteen months. Rupert had met them at Atlanta airport and Piers had driven the big hired station wagon, filled with bags and nappies and sweet, stinky smells, down the freeway to Brunswick and over the bridge to Jekyll Island. Jenny, she'd said, would join them at the weekend. She'd a lecture to give in Minneapolis on European approaches to Cultural Control. 'What on earth is the Twin Cities Social Dialogue Institute, for God's sake?' Rupert had asked, bad-temperedly. 'Three Swedish matrons and a soused herring. You knew Piers was coming weeks ago. Couldn't you catch a terminal illness or something?'

But she had merely shrugged and scowled. Of course, he knew she hated the thought of a week confronting her own mortality: the slim, tanned son who was already losing his hair, the loud, laughing wife, the children who might call her Gran in public. She had taken days before settling on Jekyll Island in a dusty-pink clapboard villa, looking out across the estuary, a hundred yards from the great white hulk of the club where, a hundred years before, New York's richest had come to play croquet on the clipped lawns, to see and be seen. It was a Radisson Resort now, ringed by pines and the sand bunkers of the golf courses that covered the island. But it was somewhere decent to swim and eat and amuse the kids as necessary, a sort of civilization. And the villa itself was shielded by a high hedge from the passing crowds. 'Piers and Sandy play a lot of golf,' Jenny said, 'though heaven knows why. I'll bring Florentina down from Washington to keep an eye on the kids and you can help her, if you want. As for me, after all the excitements, the last thing I want is broken nights and runny noses.'

In fact, of course, she'd be having a couple of hectically broken nights in Minneapolis with a college professor or a football coach. But so what? Suddenly, Rupert began to enjoy himself. He wore a purple shirt with sunflowers, orange shorts and a straw hat pulled tight over his eyes. Nobody gave him a second glance. He bought Mimsie and Joey chocolate-chip cookies at the Historic Area Village Shoppe and read them fairy stories at bedtime. Sandy took a photograph of Mimsie holding Pa's hand and smiling the sickliest of golden smiles. Rupert pretended to be embarrassed, then tucked it away in his wallet.

'You know,' said Sandy, on the Friday evening while they were sitting on the porch drinking jug Chardonnay and killing mosquitoes, 'this is turning out a real treat, Rupert. Their big, powerful gramps is a sweetheart, after all.'

And Rupert found his eyes watering. 'This is going to sound soppy, but it's the kind of life I haven't had for twenty years. There was ambition and things just driving on. I'd never expected to be a minister, let alone prime minister. I'd never expected to find myself propping up a seat in the Senate. It all happened somehow. But there was never a time when I could stop it happening, when I could be myself. Now, though, I'm almost at the end. A couple more years and it'll be Sun City or back to Dorset. A book to write maybe, a lot of reminiscing for supper clubs and television shows. But I need to get back to some roots. I think, in a way I didn't expect, that this holiday is telling me how to do it.'

He slapped his bare knee. Sandy couldn't tell whether it was a mosquito or a full stop to a conversation that had got out of hand.

It took Jenny four feeder flights and all Saturday before the taxi dropped her off. It was 78 degrees, even at dusk, and the air dripped humidity. She screamed for somebody to carry the bag. Nobody was home.

Suddenly Piers emerged from the shadow of the hedge at the side of the house. 'Hey, quiet, Mum,' he said. 'You don't want to wake the kids.'

She gave him a perfunctory kiss and complained of the head-ache that had first seemed to grip her skull in an iron glove at St Louis. 'Where's your damned father?'

'He's over having a drink at the club. He has a surprise visitor. Rather a good-looking younger woman.'

Jenny stopped and frowned.

'Polly Something-or-other. She phoned and flew down from Washington this afternoon.'

'Gurley,' said Jenny, with instant indifference. 'Have you got any aspirins in this expensive hole?'

There was a thick Persian carpet, Louis the Fifteenth replica chairs and a pianist playing Chopin. Polly, in a white shirt with the severe blue skirt from her congressional committee suit, was drinking mineral water. Rupert was on his second Johnnie Walker Black Label.

'You're joking,' he said thickly. 'I'm a poor old man. I've seen it all and done it all. I want a rest. I do not remotely want to be Vice-President of the United States. It's absurd. Either Tate's off his head or you are. Who, in this foreign country, would vote for an Englishman anyway? And not just any Englishman. A fat, balding buffer of an Englishman with sunburned knees.'

'Wrong question,' said Polly. 'There's a vacancy with nobody we can find to fill it half-way decently. Emergency. Who can give the ticket a bit of a lift, a bit of excitement, after the appalling Galt? We don't want another rich glamour-boy from Hicksville. We want gravitas. We want experience. We want to recall the triumphs of the first term and thrust them forward. And a touch of heroism, if that's available. It is you, Rupert. Mark and Dave and I spent a day on it. We fed every damned fact into the computer and then compared notes. It's you.'

'I don't have the energy any longer. I get tired, Polly. No, I am tired.'

'Fine. At last, a vice-president who doesn't moan about having nothing to do.'

'But finally I'm together with my family. There are grandchildren who might love me, and my own kids to get to know again.'

'Great. At least you won't be falling into some teenage floozy's pants, then.'

'No, I bring nothing to the party. I've never even been to San Diego. I don't know the party faithful and they don't know me.'

'They know you OK. You're the guy who gave the King of England the kiss of life – the one with that feisty little wife who's all over the talk shows. Look, Rupert. Mark has enemies, young people on the make from the South and West who want to get their oganization back, real conservatives and Bible bashers who'll knife you between prayers and who, sure as eggs, will want to sweep every trace of New England out of the stables once he's gone. Because Galt was one of them, but stupid, that kept the others at bay. But there's no chance of that happening now. Tate can't choose one of them for Veep, because there are at least two more who will turn poisonous. We've got to have a solution that keeps the future open for all of them so they have to toe the line. That means we need to choose someone entirely different. Someone who counts, who's worth a few votes. You can deliver some pretty vital states for us, Rupert – specially if you can find an Irish grandmother. Someone, though, who is no threat to the future, who'll go when Mark goes and let the succession wars take care of themselves.'

'It's still ridiculous,' said Rupert, heavily.

'No. Remember the rumour around that Plummer might go for Forrest? The Forrest boys were certainly plugging it pretty damned hard on the cocktail circuit last winter. Did you know that the Labour Party, as was, used to represent the finest traditions of the Democratic vision, that Attlee and FDR were brothers under the skin?'

'That would never have washed,' said Rupert. 'Once the Baptist TV preachers start digging Bevans and Benns out of the woodwork we'd have been back to Stalinism in fifteen seconds. Forrest has been around too long to play the white knight when those turds turn up the spotlight.'

'Of course, of course. We all know that. But even the chat

helped raise his profile – maybe enough to get him a job with a load of dough attached, if Plummer gets in. And the point is, it's great for England. It puts us square on the map, as a player that matters. You could do that, Rupert. Forrest can't, but you can. Mark and Dave don't count here. They're Americans. But you and I are English. We've come a hell of a way. But we still have our debts to pay.'

As he knew she would, Polly reached out with both hands and gave him a fleeting hug, the wise daughter seeking one more favour.

He sat very still.

'Hello,' said Jenny, walking across the lounge towards them. 'I finally got here and I want to go to bed. Or don't you care?'

Rupert got sheepishly to his feet. 'Sorry. Polly has just come down to say something amazing.'

She wanted to know what it was, of course. Bad move. He stumbled through the reasoning. Polly had to chip in and summarize, clinically efficient again.

'Well,' said Jenny, 'that makes sense. What on earth are you dithering about?' She turned away from him. 'Of course he'll do it. Tell Tate we'll both do it. And now can we get some sleep?'

Chapter Thirteen

Surprise, said Simmons. Surprise was vital. They had to keep this utterly under wraps. 'Give the weevils a sniff of the wood-work and we'll all be sawdust before breakfast.'

If there was secrecy, there was an easy spirit. Tate had the nomination in the bag. That meant the only drama from the convention would be his choice of Galt's replacement. No democracy there: the nominee's call. But the press had to get excited about something, so they'd want to set the pot boiling.

'You and Mrs Warner are on holiday, Senator. Stay there for a week, maybe with a few photo-ops for the grandchildren, if they take a good picture. Then go back to England for a few days and find some routine business to do. Naturally, you'll be turning up at San Diego. We'll schedule you a speaking slot on something boring – like foreign affairs – just at the edge of TV prime time, so that enough delegates get a chance to see the rabbit. There's a six o'clock gap on Tuesday before the party welcome for the Dallas Cowboys. If you stayed on stage and shook a few hands, that would remind folks of the Superbowl without slopping too much cream. Maybe we could factor in a few bars of "God Save the King".

'Meantime, Mark will be laying all kind of false trails. Huddles with Lloyd and Beaman and Crull and their ratpacks, setting one lot against another and keeping them all on heat. It won't do any of them any harm to have a few investigative journalists digging through their trash cans.'

Rupert put his hand over the telephone receiver for a moment and closed his eyes. He knew about charades. You couldn't be leader of the Conservative Party for long without the marketing men spinning their webs. But these were people who'd been to America to learn how it was done. Simmons had the professors on his team.

'So really I'm doing nothing.'

'No, wrong. Dead wrong, sir,' said Simmons. 'We'll be working like crazy, but right off the screen. I've booked Gloria Bradshaw into the club tomorrow. She'll come over and advise you both on a complete makeover. Hair, suits, camera angles, the works. We need you to look a little different. Less, well, less rumpled. Folks don't like to think that their vice-president has just tumbled out of bed. And Gloria reckons that Mrs Warner could lose a few pounds. She's a pretty woman and, with a little work, she could turn into an icon.

'Then Harris and Kraft will meet you in London. They're two of the brightest guys we got. They'll write your foreign speech, give it a bit of weight without it getting too interesting, and they'll take you through the acceptance segment. Remember, Senator, our TV fellows aren't keen on what you English like to think is content. They want ten seconds that sends a message. We got to get that message honed, and we got to make sure you can sell it when the interviews start.'

'The old man from the old country?' said Rupert suddenly.

'It ain't age,' said Simmons. 'It's experience. Summer and autumn – the great seasons for America reborn.'

Jenny was wearing a leotard for Gloria, who was stroking and prodding her, uttering small yelps of surprise.

'You are one fit lady,' she said. 'The cameras don't do you justice. Maybe the legs aren't great, but not many women your age get by without a trace of cellulite.'

She ran her hands up the thigh, and Jenny felt a tiny tingle in her groin. She had not been with another woman since high school, amateur fumblings in the dormitory where the giggling got in the way of the orgasm. Boys had always been so much more satisfactory.

But Gloria? Five ten, 130 pounds, California golden. It was her soft, long, slippery fingers that seemed to linger.

'The trouble is,' she said, circling the bedroom, 'your bosom and your shoulders. They dominate. If you were four inches taller, you'd carry it off. As it is, though, you're a neat ship always looking to capsize. Have you ever thought of plastic de-enhancement, going down from 34DD to, say, 34B? It's only a day in the clinic and the scars are gone in a fortnight. Not, I guess, that you'd be showing them off to too many politicians too quickly.'

Jenny brushed her fingers away from the left breast. 'Forget it,' she said. 'I've got through three and a half decades looking like this. I work out. I'm as firm as any woman I see in the gym. I am not going to turn all that into a phoney lump of sculptured meat at my age. If I diet, my neck goes. If I get cut, some bloody photographer will invent a mystery illness for me to suffer from. I'll do the hair and the face massages – but, otherwise, this is a clothes job only. Is that clear?'

'Well,' said Gloria, 'that's a denial of science. But let's see what azure and lemon, beautifully tailored, will do for you.'

Mimsie gave Grandpa a wet kiss at the airport. Rupert felt strangely resentful. For a few days he'd been a human being again. They'd built sandcastles and eaten stuffed stone-crabs at the shack on the pier. And now? God knows.

Joe Harris and Bobby Kraft had checked into a service flat just off Sloane Square, five minutes' walk from the Edwardian villa in Ebury Street that Rupert used when he was in London. It was one of those grey, blustery London days in early August. Rupert was wearing the Savile Row pinstripe in charcoal that Gloria had ordered for him. 'If you're English,' she'd said, 'you might as well make the best of it. We've got hicks from the Midwest in blue suits coming out of our ears. But once a hick, always a hick. You sound kind of aristocratic, you know. Like

Alec Guinness in *Star Wars*. I reckon that's the look to major on. Be superior.'

Harris was stubby and fat, with a crew-cut. Kraft was tall and thin, with hair waving wispily over his ears. Neither of them had seen thirty yet.

'We've spent forty-eight hours analysing every video of you we could find,' said Harris.

'We got every tic and every mannerism taped,' said Kraft. 'And we think we have a real problem.'

The two of them talked as one, sentence and sentence about, so that Rupert seemed instantly overwhelmed. 'You British used to think you were pretty sophisticated, but our researches show exactly the contrary,' said Harris.

'There were two traditional approaches,' said Kraft. 'One, like that Thatcher woman, where you managed to give her a new voice and a new style. We loved that, just like we thought Michaelson had been given an image that worked for him.'

'But you're from the other school, the one we call "Au Naturel",' said Kraft. 'You remember that old Major guy from the clips, parroting that he wunted this and wunted that. D-fuck-ing-saster. The brontosaurus as media star. And you are pretty much the same, Senator. Never use three words where three hundred will do. Showers of spittle when there's an S-bend in the peroration. Too many erms and let-me-make-this-clears. Who wants to make anything unclear, for Chrissake?'

'Let me make –' Rupert began angrily, then stopped. 'Look, this is imbecility. People here know me. I know myself. You're not going to be able to turn me into some David Niven movie character over the weekend. I just want a little assistance, a few pointers. And with civility, if that's possible.'

'Absolutely,' said Harris. 'We need to define you, not change you. And we think we've got that, what we like to call the essential thisness.'

'Try these key words,' said Kraft. 'Venerable – as in the universal father figure. Wise – as in the ways of the world.

Decisive – as in a man who has stood at the pivot of great events. Brave – as in I stopped the King of England coughing. Yet Human – as in somebody Joe Public can identify with, maybe enjoy a few drinks with in the golf-club bar. And here's the crux. Different – as in unexpected. Familiar – as in reassuring.'

'Perhaps,' Rupert ventured, 'it might be better to start with the Party platform and try to winnow that down to a few soundbites. If that's not an extraordinarily ordinary thing to do.'

Two days on he thought he had it licked. They had fished discs out of their suitcase constantly until an ancient episode of a 1970s series called *The Waltons* brought a pause.

'See,' said Harris, 'this Pa Walton is a Westerner with a face full of wrinkles and a jaw made for chewing. He's got grey hair, but he has authority with it. But he's a man of action, too. One moment relaxed and cuddling the kids, the next out shooting a grizzly. If you can catch that *relaxez-vous* and we can build the Superbowl drama around it, then there's one hell of a pitch.'

'An English Ronald Reagan who does rather than acts,' said Kraft.

'But don't get languid with it,' said Harris. 'Languid ain't relaxed. It's limp-wristed. It might go well in San Francisco, but it'll be damnation in Denver.'

Rupert had learned to stride rather than walk. He could rest his arms on his hips, standing legs slightly apart. The London haircut, with its blow-dried undulations, had vanished. 'Shorter, whiter, pivoting from the crown,' said Gloria. 'Action man with just a hint of the Marine Corps.' Before brushing his teeth each morning, he concentrated on a coiled stillness for the bathroom mirror. When Jenny came in to the loo, he moved close and put his left arm around her with a giant smile. 'Just practising,' he said.

She felt trapped, constantly monitored by aides weaving through issuing instructions. There was no chance to slide away and look up an old friend. She and Rupert were yoked together for the moment, partners in waiting.

Odd. They hadn't spent time like this for twenty years. Jenny fretted and snarled. Rupert took to following her around like a faithful, anxious dog. Did she have any feeling for him? Perhaps. She had spent her life trying to be separate, to build something of her own for she, surely, was the clever one. But now such separation seemed pointless. Some force, some outside element, had contrived to take hold of the bluff, bemused man she had married thirty years ago and make him the fulcrum of events that dwarfed them all.

'Why you? Why us?' she asked, one day, at breakfast. 'Would everything have happened anyway? Was it just luck that made you the man in the middle?'

He cracked his boiled egg and fiddled to strip off the fragments of shell that had fallen into the yolk, parking them one by one on the side of the plate, then noisily licking the sticky index finger. 'Dunno, old girl. It's what I often lie awake at night and wonder. Did we get out of Europe because of me? Or was I just the inevitable man on hand when the inevitable unwound? Was the choice we made afterwards so bloody obvious that somebody would have taken it willy-nilly? Or am I somehow the chosen leader at history's crossroads?' He cut the toast into slivers and began dipping them into the egg.

'Tell you what, though. If you look at the Europe we left, with Gross back for another four years and Paris sick to death of his little orders, then I reckon it was a lucky call. Michaelson used to reckon that three decades of integration would wipe away the past, but that's because he had no sense of it. There was always going to be a time when some German hotshot started throwing his weight around again. No, if you've got a better home, go to it. And I think we have the home the Lord intended us to make use of for his glorious et ceteras.'

*

He loved San Diego as surely as he hated Los Angeles. LA he knew from long ago. A prolonged stopover on that first trip to Australia, a choking swirl of freeways and flyblown streets where you kept glancing over your shoulder. It had not improved. The earthquake seven years ago, which had flattened Santa Monica, crumpling office blocks on to Wilshire and tipping the cliff down over the coast road, seemed somehow to have knocked the stuffing out of the place. Now, instead of being able to breathe as you drew closer to the Pacific, to see sky through the everlasting smog, there was increasing desolation. Winos still picked the debris from the wreckage of the beach-houses at Malibu. Kids camped out in their thousands along Venice Beach, a swill of sweat and filth and hash that made him think of the shanty towns around Johannesburg.

But the quake had barely displaced a hair of San Diego's blow-dried confidence. In the late nineties the city fathers had gone for hi-tech growth, companies with a bright idea starting up or starting over. They had left Silicon Valley for dead. Thirty-five per cent of all America's computing resource was stretched in gleaming offices along Coronado Bay. Young men and women arrived to make their fortune, paused, and left again with gold cards stocked for life. The average age of the population, he read, was thirty-five: the average IQ was 127. Was it all a little Fascist, cops with stun-guns parked on every alternate street corner? Perhaps. But Rupert felt safer here than he ever contrived in Dorchester on a Saturday night when the pubs closed.

They stayed ten miles north in La Jolla, opulence on a headland; with better shopping, Jenny said, than Knightsbridge. The English delegates were at the Hilton, five minutes away. Rupert took a suite at the Omni. And President Tate, of course, was staying at the Villa Crystal, wholesomely donated for the week by VidaTrax Electronics, Number One for Home Security. Tate had three days to wait out of sight, seeing only those he needed to see, preparing for the coronation. The King over the electrified fence, visited by large black cars with darkened windows sweeping swiftly through the gates.

They were not invited round. 'Why take the risk?' asked Tate, when he called. 'Polly has total heads of agreement. You've signed up for all the policies. We've swapped scripts. My staff guys know not to be too discreet when the Southern snakes come oiling round. It's asking too much for them to button up about a visit from you. Rumours get started that way. But how is the delightful Mrs Warner? I trust she's not feeling the strain of these endless jamborees. They can sure leave a body lacking its beauty sleep.' Amiable, meaningless, distanced.

'Of course, in any normal sense, he doesn't want you on his team,' Polly said. 'You won't be in there pumping around and chairing endless meetings. Mark sees you as a kind of trophy, a seal of approval, not a cog in the machine. He'll put you on the mantelshelf in the Oval Office and mostly forget you exist. Which is handy, because that's what I know you want too.'

'What a job! A pitcher of warm Scotch,' said Rupert.

The new convention centre was a great cocoon of glass beside the yacht marina, clear and sparkling so that visitors might walk over from the Hyatt and watch the delegates, like ants, crawling back and forth within their air-conditioned zones. Rupert spent two days at cocktail parties, drinking sparingly, wearing the designer creased suits and the brown shoes that needed scuffing every morning. His camouflage kit. Robin Groom took them both to dinner at the Coronado Hotel with the English delegates. 'Oh, Prime Minister,' simpered a plump lady from Torquay, with a floral hat and a developing bourbon habit. They slept a bit and watched the television relay pictures. Gloria called to supervise the final haircut and charcoal spongings. Harris, Kraft and a new young man called Papadopoulos sat in a row on the Omni sofa and insisted that Rupert had one last rehearsal.

'Show-time,' said Jenny. The chosen blue and yellow suit had vertical stripes 'for a real illusion of added height'. She felt like a curious tropical insect.

Nothing had quite prepared Rupert for the convention hall. A temple of illusions, he thought. For television by television. In the hotel bedroom it had seemed a vast, open auditorium filled with colour and banners and wildly cheering extras. But they'd done it with mirrors. The stage, rising from the centre of the hall at the flick of a button, was Las Vegas. A giant mirrored battleship prow, stretching towards it from the far wall, carried cameras and glass-box studios. The groundlings were stranded on either side, cut off from reality, linked only by a thin ribbon path under the ABC gun turret. 'Golly,' he said to Polly. 'Where are the politics?'

'Back home in your living room,' she said. 'I told you this wouldn't be Bournemouth.'

They parked Jenny in a small stand filled with wives and kids. 'Expect them to pan over to you when Rupert's speaking,' Papadopoulos said. 'Try to look kind of proud and feminine.' He held out his hand to help her to the seat. He was a slim, dark young man in a very white shirt. She steadied herself and held the hand for a second more than necessary. It was not withdrawn.

On stage, the Young America session was fifteen minutes from finish. A Jewish-Hispanic comedian, Enrico Dayan, who ran a TV talent contest called *Melting Pot*, had introduced what he said were the Cheerleaders of Hope, six girls kicking their legs and twirling batons while the band on the quarterdeck played 'Yankee Doodle Dandy'. 'And called it macaronee!' When the music stopped, they'd each stepped forward in turn. 'Give testimony,' Enrico howled. 'Testeemonee.'

The thin redhead from Abilene had been a coke addict until a Baptist minister had found her lying in the gutter and brought God to her life. The pudgy brunette from Pensacola had turned prostitute until the Mothers of America found her a job in a diner. 'Now I'm always sunny side up,' she vowed brightly.

A black girl from Baltimore had had, it seemed, two illegitimate babies before she was seventeen. 'But then I heard our President telling us all about welfare dependency and you know, my friends, I was inspired to take hold of my life.'

'And now,' said Dayan, 'now for a special occasion. We're privileged to have in our midst one of the truly towering statesmen of our era. Once Prime Minister of Great Britain and the man who put great expectations for his people back where they belong. The senior senator from London, England, the Right Honourable Rupert Warner, who will share his vision with us.'

Rupert came up from a small central lift just behind the red, white and blue podium. He blinked and tried to find his hips so that the hands could rest. 'My fellow Republicans,' he began, 'we are a fine and happy people, but we live in perilous times. For our world is full of challenges. There is the curse of famine in the dark continent of Africa. There is increasing disharmony among our allies in Europe. There is Russia, still struggling after decades of liberation from tyranny to find a settled state, and China enduring prolonged upheaval . . .' Nobody, he realized, was listening. The Alabama delegation on the left were jiggling their banners and singing Stephen Foster. The Delaware delegation on the right were walking out. A blanket buzz advanced and engulfed him. 'How much longer, my friends, can we alone be keepers of the global order? How much longer . . . root-and-branch UN reform . . . buzz . . . political mechanisms to echo our trading progress . . . buzz . . . less-fortunate nations weaned to responsibility . . . buzz . . . the stalwart example of a fine human being and an outstanding leader, President Mark Tate.'

He blinked and folded his arms. The Cowboys, in full kit, advanced from both wings of the stage. There was a swell of music. Elgar, he guessed. Maybe even they had thought the anthem too tacky. The lift took him down from sight.

*

'That was terrific,' said Polly.

'Yes, really great,' said Harris and Kraft together. 'You wowed them for sure.'

'But nobody was listening. I haven't felt such a prat since I did conjuring tricks at my kids' party and they threw sausage rolls at me.'

Polly gave him a brief hug. 'You stupid sausage. Listening isn't the point. Nobody comes here to listen. But the television was super. That moment when Jenny cried and dabbed her eyes was absolute theatre. She looked just radiant. There were seventy-three calls to the switchboard before you'd sat down.'

'We'll get her up with you and Mark and Marti for acceptance night,' said Harris. 'Meanwhile, there are the interviews from tomorrow at ten when we release the President's choice. We'd suggest she be with you for the first dozen or so, then maybe she can do her own rota through the afternoon. A lot of women out there are suddenly going to get damned interested in the both of you.'

Neil Forrest couldn't sleep. The junior senator for the great State of England was lying in bed in a Holiday Inn just outside Derby. Two in the morning. A grey day at the Young Democrats Summer School, Long Eaton, would be under way in six hours. A lecture on the Transatlantic Radical Tradition he'd given too many times before. His head ached. The three pints of brown ale for the photographers at Coalville Labour and Democratic Working Men's Club had been two pints too many. Christ, he was fed up with sucking round union branches getting pledges for Nate Plummer's fat funding people. Of course, on the surface, everything was fine while Congress ploughed in the development funds and Europe fumed on the sidelines. But Gross had turned into an ogre now, and that meant that Washington was keener on screwing him than keeping little old England floating high on a tide of dollars. Too many schemes were being deferred. The natives were beginning to get restless. Could Plummer use that? Probably: but it would need to be handled with super care. Tate and Warner had to be the villains, right-wingers who didn't care about broken promises. The last thing we need, Forrest thought, is some generalized English whinge that gets up American noses. Old Labour, New Labour, Caring Labour, Modern Labour – they'd squittered through every permutation under the sun, looking for a final resting-place. I can't afford that now. I've got to be loyal to the concept. Just disappointed about the implementation. I need my place on the team bench. It's the team players who get the prizes.

He was not averse to a little stirring. That was the way you got noticed. The brief flutter of speculation over his first meeting with Nate, the pictures on the porch in Montgomery, had been foolish but fun. Why not start thinking about something with a nice prize of a price tag attached? Secretary for Commerce, maybe, or Transport. Assistant Secretary of State for European Affairs would have constant headlines attached.

But he was going too fast. He was awake in this small plastic box of a room because of the TV pictures from San Diego. Why had they broken the song and dance for a pathetic four minutes from Warner, waffling on about global peacekeeping? More particularly, why had Jenny Warner been crying? Tears from the granite lady. Had Rupert contracted a brain tumour? No: she'd save the histrionics for the funeral. Something was up, something that set Forrest's thin ferret face in a frown. That silver perm, that unnaturally expensive tailored suit. It was a bizarre thought, but it niggled. He had Plummer's private-line number somewhere in his diary. Yip. One call couldn't hurt. Either it was wrong, in which case the guy who had nothing could lose nothing. But make the right call and who knows? You could wind up seriously influential.

Chapter Fourteen

Tate held the press conference at the Villa Crystal. The press were always more docile when they were suddenly favoured, allowed into an inner sanctum.

He, in turn, knew that he had to exude a feeling of power. This was a difficult call. It had to be delivered straight and stern. No first name mateyness and no long-winded questions. The President had decided. The President was in charge. Thank you, and good morning.

'Ladies and gentlemen. The greatest blow to me this year, as you know, was Vice-President Galt's news that he must put his family first and will not serve with me for another term in the White House. I don't need to tell you how much that decision has grieved me. Wil Galt is a treasured friend as well as a wonderful running mate. Marti and Aileen, Wil's lovely wife, were our constant companions, a team keeping their menfolk shoulder to shoulder for the challenges we faced.

'But all that, alas, is history. I have a new right hand to find for the years ahead. He couldn't be a man like Wil. Why settle for second best? So he had to be different. Gentlemen, he is different. The crowning achievement of my first four years, I believe, is the historic reconciliation of our great nation with its ancestors in England, Scotland, Wales, Ulster and Ireland. When the scholars, hundreds of years hence, come to look at our fusion, I'm convinced that one statesman above all – a man of personal courage and profound wisdom – will stand out in every book they write. I mean Senator Rupert Warner.

'Why waste that experience and intellect when we have it to hand? What would history make of that? Rupert, my old ally, confidant and guide, a new nation salutes you. Come run with me.'

Rupert had been waiting, sweating, outside the door. He pushed it open.

Nate Plummer was only forty-eight, but youth had never stopped on his doorstep. His hair had begun to thin before he was twenty. Now what remained hung limp around the periphery of a shiny skull. His belly pressed at the bottom button of his double-breasted suit. He was a good ol' boy and that foxy Southern persona had served him well.

Nothing about Nate seemed to threaten. Two terms as governor in Montgomery before he was thirty, three terms as congressman, two more as senator. He'd been around for ever, as worn and weathered as the old picket fence he leaned on for pictures. He was remarkable for his unremarkability. Before Plummer, Alabama had been Republican territory through the decades. He had succeeded at first because, in the rhetoric, he reached back to the time of the Wallaces long ago. 'George got some things wrong, my friends. Course he did. But he had his roots in this state – not in them big, bullying corporations coming down from the North, hiring our people then laying them off like they was corn husks. George knew what we could do for ourselves and how to put Alabama on the map. And that's my aim too. Show them damn Yankees what we can do.'

Governor Plummer did a great deal. The Ajaccio Chemical Company at East Brewton – 'so all their damn poisonous slop flows straight down the Escambia River flat into Florida'. Cap'n Crawfish's new prawnburger-manufacturing HQ at Orange beach. And – headline stuff – he sold Time-Warner the prime site at Pinto Island that Uncle Sam didn't need any longer for Hollywood South, the theme park developments that had begun to flatten Disney.

But he didn't just attract money: he spent it on roads and schools and hospitals. Twenty years of Plummer had made Alabama the tenth most prosperous state of the Union. Black literacy was 87 per cent. Unemployment was 3 per cent. The posters that plastered Birmingham already said, 'We done great with Nate.' His TV ads talked of 'the new Nate Society'.

'Hi, Neil, how you going? I just wanted to congratulate you soonest on your antennae, brother. That was some smart thinking. It seems to me we could get a little mutual business going here. I want to be president of this country and I know you want to do the best for your people.'

Forrest stifled an incipient simper.

'Now, this guy Warner,' said Plummer. 'You and him go back a long way, and I bet he ain't no Gandhi. The Pres, he seems to reckon that putting some doddery gentleman on the ticket will get the young wolves off his back. But here in Alabama we always say that you don't feed meat to wild dogs. You shoot them before they bite you. So I guess we can get the hounds yapping if this English gentleman turns out to be no gent after all.'

Forrest began a rapid thumbnail sketch, then paused, 'Look, Nate, this isn't for a phone call. I don't want to get into rumours down a line. Let's meet somewhere quiet at the weekend. I think I can be very useful to you.'

Fixed for downtown Atlanta on Saturday. Two senators passing through and chewing a little campaign fat. Plummer asked his backroom boys to get their electoral college figurings updated.

'We got six hundred and thirty-three votes in that college now and England has fifty-six of them. Roll in Scotland, Wales, Ireland and Ulster and that's ninety-five for a start, one hell of a lift-off. Them smart folks in the *New York Times* say choosing Rupert was a masterstroke. God, when has somebody called

Rupert been a master of anything? It's time to open the dog-food can, fellows, and begin spreading that gunk around.'

Bannon knocked at the bedroom door and brought his head gingerly into view. 'Well, sir, I just dropped in to say goodbye. It wouldn't do to disappear without a word after all these years.'

'What on earth are you talking about?' Rupert asked, rumpling the sheets on the bed with his arm as he turned. He had been eating a packet of digestive biscuits. He found Gloria's new training diet particularly irksome. Were the biscuits in sight? No, safely under his pyjamas.

Bannon stood before him, hands clasped. 'I thought you knew all about it, Mr Senator sir. Now you're the vice-presidential candidate, the secret service and the FBI take over. We country coppers get a bowl of soup and a one-way ticket home to Dorset and the missus.'

'Oh, no, you bloody well don't,' said Rupert, getting out of bed and beginning to pace. 'If you're out, I'm out. If I wanted a pack of Washington gorillas, that would be one thing. But I want you. We've been together now for twenty years and it doesn't seem a day too much.'

Bannon's lips screwed into a grin. 'Very heartening, sir. But if I might be so bold, couldn't you use some Brits and some Yanks for all this travelling? Two great forces joined for the common good, that sort of thing?'

'And I'm supposed to be the bleeding politician,' Rupert said.

Rupert's pinstripe was covered in confetti, tickertape and popcorn. It was sticky popcorn. He knew that he must wave and smile and hold Jenny's hand. He couldn't wipe himself off. But he felt ridiculous. They'd been standing side by side with the Tates for ten minutes and the hall was still raising the glass roof. In Bournemouth, long ago, he'd have raised a finger to his lips and expected the faithful to drop into silence. Standing for ovations wasn't good for their arthritis. San Diego, though, had clearly been in training. This was a multiple orgasm of enthusiasm.

The Warner speech had lasted all of ninety seconds. 'Tate is timed for twenty minutes,' Papadopoulos said. 'That's two commercial breaks wasted. If you want to be seen, get it in quick so they can try a double helping before the President. You're due four minutes of applause, and a quarter of that will still give the people at home a decent thrill.'

So he reworked one of his favourites. 'We Englishmen, through times immemorial, have known that we're coming home when we see the white cliffs of Dover, the great walls of chalk on which is written so much of our history. Today, my friends, those cliffs bear a new message for me. They say our home is your home, our dreams are your dreams. And there are new cliffs that we must climb together.'

Jenny had kissed him. It was, he thought, their first proper kiss for fifteen years – since Blackpool and a speech on family values no one else had wanted to give. 'And now,' said the boys in the booth together, 'stay with us for these messages.'

There were three editors at Forrest's breakfast table, and one exceptionally ancient peer ennobled by a long departed Labour government for his work in the marketing, promoting and co-ordinating of his masters and their obstreperous juniors. Once the feared Ray Sandlewood, shadowy monarch of the Cabinet Office, Minister for Menaces without Portfolio, now Lord Sandlewood of Powburn, columnist for the *Sunday Mirror* and puller of ancient strings. He had a long memory and a large computer diary, which he would pull out of his briefcase from time to time and with which he would hold communion.

'We're here about Warner,' said Forrest. 'Our friends from the South are interested in any facts, any memories, which the voting public might properly be informed of as they ponder a historic choice. Democracy, as they say, depends on full disclosure; and Warner has put himself under that spotlight.

'Now, I know you chaps were very laudably restrained during the crisis. So was I. We didn't want unproven allegations flying around when Warner got catapulted into Downing Street. We all knew where the national interest lay. We were shareholders in Great Britain Limited. But times have changed and so has our call to duty. It's our responsibility to make utterly certain that England isn't sullied by some skeleton that pops out of the cupboard and drags our name through the mud. If there are doubts about Rupert Warner then we must share them together now. In absolute and unattributable privacy, of course. This is a meeting that never happened.'

'It's always best to begin at the beginning,' said the *Mirror*. 'I'll get some of my top people digging around in Dorset, talking to the locals, trying to build the picture from the ground up.'

'The missing years are the Australian years,' said the *Star*. 'What did he do with himself on that cattle ranch? Was he shagging the local talent or kangaroos? And why are his kids so keen on keeping out of the limelight in Oz?'

'Perhaps there's more to that bust-up with Michaelson than we ever knew,' said the *New Observer*. 'They were so close one minute, peas in a pod, and then there were only snarls. Mikey's chaps kept hinting about a mental breakdown. We'll go back and rake them over.'

Sandlewood waved a dismissive hand. 'None of you will come up with anything. I did all this years ago. The man is no saint. Drinks too much under stress. Can't carry a brief in his head to stop his trousers falling down. But Warner is honest and painfully straight. He doesn't play around and he doesn't care about money. No, look to the lady – look to that tearful, loving little wife of his.'

'But she's a bloody God-spotter,' said the *Mirror*. 'So busy preaching at other folk about morality that she'd never have a moment to start straying on her own. Our cable channel hasn't ever recovered from what she and that stinking committee of hers did to it.'

Forrest poured himself another cup of coffee. 'Wait a minute. My old friend Lord Sandlewood isn't into wild theses, gentlemen. He always has a nugget buried down there somewhere.'

They all looked at the hooded eyes and the wet mouth sucking at the ill-fitting teeth. 'If I were you,' said his lordship, 'I'd buy Brian Carstairs a couple of bottles of claret some time and ask our washed-up wreck of an ex-foreign secretary what Joan used to do in his Arc.'

There was a week before the Democrats met in Atlanta, time at last for Warner and Tate to get together. They met in the Oval Office. The President sat behind his new teak monster of a desk. Rupert was waved to a spindly chair of uncertain age and fidgeted uncomfortably. He crossed his legs, then uncrossed them. This wasn't quite how he had imagined it. He remembered, uneasily, the days long ago when he would sit behind a desk and sadly inform squirming tenant smallholders that their rent was going up.

'OK, Senator,' said Tate. 'Dispositions first. You know Harris, Kraft and Nicky Papadopoulos. I suggest they stick with you for the ride. Gloria did a great job with your image. She's on the team, too, attached to Mrs Warner. Congresswoman Gurley will head up the Far Atlantic operation, liaising with Governor Groom's team and reporting direct to Simmons and the guys back here. You'll touch base with her every time you cross the pond, but bear in mind she's got a load of other fish to fry so she won't be able to steer you through everything. I'm sure you've got some fine young talent in your line-up already.'

Well, not exactly, Rupert was about to mutter. Young talent didn't tend to stick to a one-term senator with nothing to look forward to. But he bit his lip and crossed his legs.

'Now, strategy. You have only two things to target on. One is history. You're the embodiment of everything I've achieved in the last four years. The prime job is to remind folks of that, but gently.

'We've scheduled a whole load of campus appearances for you, with nicely sedated crowds of history students. The boys will write you a core speech and they'll top and tail it depending where you are. On no account get involved with campaign forums. It isn't seemly for a guy of your distinction to be wallowing around shouting the odds with run-of-the-mill pols. I want pictures of you arriving in town, nice shots of you using long words from the podium and a few mellow encounters with ordinary people as you leave. Papa Dop will provide the right ordinary people for you. Don't talk to nobody he hasn't approved.'

Rupert bridled. 'Look,' he said, 'I'm not some nutty professor escaped from Twilight City. I was, with respect, winning elections while you were still in college.'

Tate swept down his left hand, chopping at the air. 'That was when there was a Great in Britain. And, if you'll let me finish, I was going to say just that. Over the pond, you're the main man. There are a hell of a lot of votes there and we need every damned one of them, the way Plummer is running in the South and West. This is one crisp operator. Now, see . . .' and his voice had a touch of wheedle to it, 'I can't have you cannoning around here, mouthing off without knowing the people or where the Democrats are coming from, laying their elephant traps. Oh, I know they've been sweet as pie to you in the Senate so far when you've had time to turn up. There wasn't any point doing anything else, truth to tell. You weren't no threat. But now they'll be out to drag you down damn quickly, make you look an old idiot and me worse than that for picking you. So here you keep going on grooved lines. Harris and Kraft will tell you what to say. Just say it nicely and move on. But when we get to London or Glasgow, Senator, then the boot is on the other foot. You make the running and I read the script. Got it?'

'Absolutely,' said Rupert. 'We call it horses for courses.'

He saluted as he turned to go. Tate didn't smile.

'Can I have my own security guard along?'

'Sure, as long as our boys are on the bench, too. Remember, I said team-work.'

Carstairs was standing moodily on the terrace of the State Legislature overlooking the Thames. It was a sultry, lowering day, typical late August. Most of England was abroad or at the beaches. A few pleasure-boats chugged up and down the river, and he could hear the cackles of American matrons as the tour guides went through their weary routines. 'And over there on the left is what we used to call the Houses of Parliament, historic home of English democracy once threatened by the infamous Guy Fawkes and his Gunpowder Plot. Nowadays, of course, we'd set the FBI on him.'

He flicked the butt of his cigarette into the water. This was one of the few open spaces left in London where you could smoke – and then only when the Legislature was in recess, for which small mercy, minimal thanks. Christ, he felt like a drink. But there was no hard liquor on the premises now. Coffee, tea, spring water, Coke. Even Annie's Juice Bar was closed for the recess. Should he tramp back through the tunnel under the square to his office and slide a bottle of vodka out of the bottom cabinet? No. It was only four in the afternoon, a bare seventy minutes since his four-cocktail lunch. But, on the other hand, what the hell? Who cared about washed-up relics of governments past in countries past? Six years ago he'd still been His Majesty's Secretary of State for Foreign Affairs, a suitable case for bowing and scraping across the salons of the globe. Now he was just a thickening, balding state representative, dragging out the days to a November election he already reckoned was lost. And then? No House of Lords to feather enforced retirement any longer. He'd have to scrape a living from the lobbying companies that seemed to fill the office blocks in Victoria Street, peddling the illusion of influence to agricultural-machinery salesmen from Ohio hoping England was a quick buck.

'Brian,' said a voice at his elbow. 'Brian Carstairs. Golly, long time no see. What on earth are you doing all alone with your thoughts while our great former nation sleeps?'

She was, he thought bemusedly, quite beautiful: as tall as him, as black as he was white, with square shoulders pulled back, seemingly holding a formidable bosom in tight check, and a handspan of a waist. She wore a blue silk dress, fitted and belted. Her hair was cut short to the scalp, moulding the head, accentuating the high cheekbones and the wide mouth. Her teeth seemed to glint as she smiled.

'Do I . . . ?' he began, with a blush and a stutter. 'Sorry. I'm sure I should know you. I would remember. But I can't for the life of me quite . . .'

She threw back her head and laughed from the throat, her hand briefly clasping his arm as though to steady herself. 'My fault,' she said. 'You haven't seen me for ten years and I guess I was pretty different then. Do you recall Julie . . . Julie Ekpu, that sweet little Nigerian girl who was always around your house at weekends? Sarah's best friend in the sixth form at Westminster?'

He slapped his palm, exaggeratedly, to his forehead. 'Julie? That stick of a Julie with buck teeth and curly hair? The one with glasses who was always losing her books? Tell me it can't be true.'

She patted his shoulder and they leaned on the terrace together, her dress parting a little as the stonework pushed her breasts up and forward. He looked away, suddenly coughing.

'Yes, sir. I'm that Julie. Older, but not a lot wiser. And back in this new state of a country to make my name.'

How was Sarah? 'Married to a Frenchman with two kids now. Living in Toulouse. I don't see too much of her, I'm afraid. She blamed me when my marriage went down the pan. Too many long nights at the Foreign Office. But we still write and things at Christmas. What am I to tell her about you?'

She turned and somehow brushed lightly against him, then rolled her eyes and gave a brief jiggle at the hips. 'Me? Little me? Little Julie? I'm a grown-up girl with a master's from Columbia and two years writing Metro for the *Miami Herald*, back here to make my fortune, sir.'

She'd gone to the States when Shell posted her father there, she said. She'd thought she would stay for ever. 'But you know, Brian – can I call you Brian? You know, there's something about this place that kept bugging me. And when your *Mirror* paper in London came looking for black gals fitting all the positive criteria who might bring a little Stateside political expertise with them, well, that seemed an offer nobody in their right mind would refuse. I'm starting on contract next month. Meantime, I'm just wandering round these deserted old corridors, getting my bearings. It's just wonderful to find a face I know. And someone who can teach a girl so much.'

He had no pressing engagements, he said. Why didn't he give her the tour? Then maybe they could have a drink and a spot of supper. She teetered on high heels for a second as they came down the steps from the terrace and hung on to his arm, pressing against him, letting her breasts brush his jacket and chattering with a deep giggle at the back of her throat.

His mouth felt full of gravel; and somehow it seemed to rattle around inside his head when he moved. He was, where? On his own brown sofa in the little Paddington flat, grey light chinking in around the curtains. He was still in yesterday's suit. The waistcoat had worked loose and up, somehow threatening to throttle him. He could smell, then see, a slew of vomit on the carpet below.

What the hell had happened?

He pulled his right knee up under him and, hanging on to the end of the sofa, levered himself to his feet, staggering towards the curtains, drawing them, blinking.

Shower. A cold shower to swill away the fuzz. Coffee. Two sips and he was retching again. But he was beginning to remember. Julie. The eyes rolling in mock amazement as they had looked behind the Speaker's chair, the little yelps of enthusiasm as they'd trooped through the voting lobbies. And then the taxi to his club, the Carlton, with the champagne in the bar and the country members ogling this stunning creature from behind their newspapers. He'd felt great, back in command. Ready for a little food just down Pall Mall at Wilton's where they had finally begun to fly East Coast lobsters over on the day. Champagne cocktails, a bottle of Californian Chardonnay, two Cognacs.

'Well, sir,' she'd said, leaning towards him, 'I've told you all about what this girl's been doing with her young life. Why don't you catch me up on the political scene here? You must know Rupert Warner damned well after all those years together. What do his friends make of the next Vice-President of these United States?'

And he had told her, beginning to roll and to slur as more Cognacs arrived. About the bumbling glad-hander who had found himself prime minister, created by Broadbent and yours truly. About the years of drift and misery. About the moment that America reached out a hand and suddenly tightened it around his throat, throttling the political life out of Carstairs, casting him as driftwood on the beach of politics.

'Warner's a puppet for Groom and Gurley and that gang. They tell him what to do and he just goes along. He doesn't have friends. He has people, like me, who he uses for a while, then forgets.'

She held his wrist for a moment, bringing his head up so that she could look in his eyes. 'He sounds an ungrateful fool, Brian. Though, of course, folk say his wife's the clever one.'

What had happened then? He'd paid the bill and offered her one last drink. 'I've got an apartment in St John's Wood with a girlfriend from college,' she'd said. 'Perfect. Paddington's right on the way.'

And she had come up and found the bottle of bourbon in the cupboard under the stairs and asked him again about Jenny. 'She seems just so clever and loyal, and those causes she gets involved with – cleaning up TV and stuff – they're making her a real role model back in the States.'

He had laughed bitterly and attempted to put his arm around her shoulders, lurching as she swayed gracefully away. 'Well, little Julie. Let me tell you about that . . .'

Jenny insisted on her own schedule. 'I can't traipse around for weeks playing model wifey while Rupert delivers the same old history lesson to audiences of spotty students,' she told Papadopoulos at breakfast. It was just a week till the caravan started rolling. 'Oh, I'll do the first week up and down California. I'll hold his hand and look suitably adoring. But I want some events of my own. And I think that, most of the time, one or other of us ought to keep an eye on the English end. Give me Gloria and a gold card and let me work a separate team. Togetherness is such a putrid waste of time.'

He checked with Dave Simmons back at the ranch.

'Oh, God,' said Simmons, with a shrug. 'Let her do her own thing. If you don't, she'll eat you for dinner anyway. And Rupert is used to working on his own. I'll tell Polly to keep an eye out for her when she hits London. But she can handle herself well. At least, when anyone's looking.'

Papadopoulos went to find her in the garden, watching that black chauffeur of hers, stripped to the waist, wiping the big car down. 'Simmons says OK,' he said, 'but you've got to keep in touch every minute. And Polly will be Mother Superior as soon as you touch Heathrow.'

She scowled. Then, almost at the flick of some internal button, she flashed him a great, wide smile. 'If you get your wish,' she said, 'can I have one in return?'

Nice Greek boys had no answer to that. 'Sure,' said Papa. 'I suppose.'

'Then let's you and me go out for a delicious quiet lunch somewhere down the Potomac, and you can brief me with the right things to say till I'm running over with tact and tolerance.'

She called Egi. He put on his shirt and, with a dreamy smile, shifted the Cadillac into the driveway.

'Make it the Green Mansions Inn just off one ninety at Seneca,' she said. 'I'll call Rupert and let him know we're busy.' She turned to Egi. 'Maybe there's no point dragging you all that way, with so much of the back lot to get dug over. Papa will drive, won't you?'

Another great smile.

The Greek boy felt curiously wet under the armpits, puddles of sweat spreading across the crisp whiteness of his shirt.

Lord Sandlewood lunched at the Garrick Club: roast guinea fowl and sweet Savoy cabbage with caraway seeds. The cabbage made it more difficult than usual not to fart as he tottered up the winding staircase to the sitting rooms where coffee and Cognac might be served – each eruption of wind tugging the hood of his left eyelid upward in simulated surprise.

The editor of the *Mirror* was sitting in the corner, beneath a rather garish portrait of Mrs Siddons. 'Sorry, Ray,' he said, clambering to his feet. 'There's a development. I didn't want to call you on the phone, and it's a lousy drag out to Canary Wharf.'

'Well?' said his lordship.

'Well, I found just the girl for the job. Big juicy black piece from the *Miami Herald* by way of the *National Inquirer*. Better still, if you can credit it, a school chum of Carstairs' daughter. No need to make anything up. She could knock at the front door and go straight through. Which she did, in a fug of booze, waggling her boobs and keeping the recorder running.

'We've got him bang to rights, telling her about Mrs So-Saintly in graphic detail, even down to the yelps she'd give when she came. Very noisy lady, it seems.'

'My congratulations,' said Sandlewood, with a small forward bow. 'I am filled with admiration. Five years' chairing the Press

181

Standards Board gave me exceptional faith in your fine profession, my dear Roger.'

'But now we've got it, Ray, what do you want me to do with it? Run it tomorrow? "The Foreign Secretary and the PM's Wife: Days of Lust While Warner Spoke for Britain". That sort of stuff? Or do I feed it to the Tory tabloids, try to distract attention? Though it's a bloody good yarn to give away.'

Sandlewood sniffed. 'I'll talk to our ginger friend,' he said. 'But my strong advice just now would be to put the whole thing in your office safe and wait. It's too early in the race to gun Warner down yet. He's a shrewd bird. He might find a way of playing it for sympathy. And she'll say anything. One episode of passion before duty called. But she didn't do this once. She did it all the time. Warner is a serial cuckold.

'Let's spend a few days finding out who's shafting her now. If we can do that, and break it with Carstairs for the detail a couple of weeks from the polls, then we've got the killer punch bang on target.'

'Right,' said the Voice of the People. 'Julie has all the background she'll ever need. I'll put her on campaign assignment, following Mrs Warner every bed of the way. If there's a book in it at the end, fifty per cent royalties will have her uncrossing her legs with her tongue hanging out.'

Rupert had been with Harris and Kraft for five hours. He was hot and he was becoming despondent.

'Look, chaps,' he said at last, picking his jacket off the chair and walking determinedly to the door. 'Look, this simply isn't on. I am not Thomas Jefferson. I wouldn't know him if I met him in the street. All I know about Lincoln is that he got shot during some particularly beastly play – probably a drawing-room comedy by you two. I haven't read Edmund Burke. I used to think Descartes was the opposite of the *table d'hôte*. Please write something for me I can read with a bit of understanding, something I can answer questions about afterwards if they're asked. Harold Macmillan, dear old Maggie Thatcher, Willie Hague, George Bush and Gerry Ford. Yes, Ford. He was my kind of politician. He had a lot to teach us all.'

Jenny had eaten soft-shell crabs and grilled flounder with asparagus. They had drunk a bottle of Riesling.

'You'd better not drive for an hour,' she said. 'It's the most wonderful afternoon. Why don't we go for a stroll by the river? And maybe the tiniest of snoozes. All work and no play makes Papa a very dull Hellene.'

Chapter Fifteen

The governors of the proud new states of Scotland, Wales, Ulster and Ireland kept in constant touch. That was because, at root, they were all minnows in an English pond. 'And if we don't stick together, the carp eats us anyway,' as Treneman said, at their first, very quiet meeting at a lush Victorian hunting lodge overlooking Bantry Bay. 'Ballylickey Manor,' his invitation to the rest of them had proclaimed, 'where we need to decide how we'll bally well lick the old enemy.'

But that was six huddles away now and the leaders of the informal Eastern Atlantic Association of Small States were back in Scotland for the day at another five-star mansion, strolling together before dinner in the gardens of Ardanaiseig, watching the lazy waters of Loch Awe and the finger clouds stick at the top of Ben Cruachan.

'The question,' said Angus, 'is whether we can make any joint voting recommendation – and whether anyone would take the least notice of us if we did.'

That was always one difficulty. Bob Angus governed from Edinburgh – from the new Assembly buildings the English Treasury had so richly financed over a quarter of a century ago – and chaired the Scottish Democratic Party. Ivor Mills in Cardiff went along with everything he said. The pair, long ago, had been president and treasurer of the New Labour Students' Federation and had once, to their chagrin, discovered they'd slept with the same plump brunette from Sheffield at one pot-wreathed summer school in Bromsgrove. 'Nothing like a nasty morning in the clap clinic to make you brothers under the skin,' Mills had said, as they wiped their brows afterwards and headed for the pub.

But Fergus Treneman, for all his laughter and his sandy charm, had no Labour history. When the chips were down, was the Taoiseach of Fianna Fáil a Democrat or a Republican? 'Sure I'll join both and see which one can do me the most good,' he said with the broadest smiles. And the Reverend James Jeffreys – Iron Jimmy – hadn't known where to lead the declining rump of his Ulster Unionists after that. Belfast needed to see what Dublin did in order to do the opposite. It was hopeless if Dublin refused to choose.

'When in doubt,' said Treneman, 'issue a declaration. We could call it the Ardanaiseig Agenda. The people of our four great states express their united dismay at Washington's disregard of their investment needs, their anger at English dominance of the four old countries with their distinctive histories, and –'

'And are shocked, after recent discussions with their former European partners, to calculate that the GDP of their states have grown 1.4 per cent less than the average growth in the European Union?' said Mills.

'We can't play that card yet,' said Treneman. 'I've spent too damned long in Boston and the Wormy Apple this year throwing shamrocks at boardrooms. There'd be a backlash. It's a weapon, and we'd all better realize that. But we need to keep it under the bed for a while.'

'Right,' said Angus, wheeling back towards the house. 'A declaration. Deniable news of this meeting, upping the European ante a wee bit. And a joint trade mission to Washington and Berlin to examine future prospects for development – bureaucrats, a few tame businessmen, nothing official. How about that?'

'We'd need to go very gently,' said Treneman doubtfully.

'Nonsense,' said Jeffreys, so loudly that a couple of sparrows in the rose-bush ten yards away flew cheeping alarm into the sky. 'Fortune favours the brave. I shall write a sermon about it. We are all God's own people.'

He hovered, they knew, on the perpetual brink of self-parody, but he was smarter than he seemed. He needed to be, with a Catholic birth-rate that Belfast University reckoned would push his Prods into a minority box before the end of the decade.

'I don't think I could mount a matching sermon,' said Treneman. 'But if you must, I can't stop you.'

'Praise the Lord and pass his ammunition,' said Jeffreys. 'I've a date at the United Baptist Chapel, Atlanta, Georgia, this coming Sunday, just as the Democrats gather down the road and start turning on their holy televisions. What could be more God-given than that?'

Forrest liked to keep things modest. No point inviting predictable Sunday-paper tales about fat cats high on the Yankee hog. He parked his retinue of aides at a Ramada Inn twenty minutes from downtown and hailed a taxi up Peachtree to the brownstone bed-and-breakfast place he always used in Atlanta. Atriums made him dizzy.

Plummer's Georgia HQ was along Peachtree, too, a couple of miles south. The black Buick arrived, as arranged, at three.

'That glass of mint julep?' said the candidate, sweating on the back lawn, coat discarded, red braces heaving belly into line over the brim of dirty white slacks.

'Iced tea,' said Forrest. 'In this heat, I can't plot and drink liquor at the same time.'

There was a huge, shaking laugh, the braces squirming with effort.

Forrest ran tersely through the events of the week and played a minute or two of the Carstairs tape.

'That purty girl is some kind of fox,' said Plummer. 'I'm sure glad I didn't let her into my pants.'

Forrest began to explain that the clapped-out shit had been

too drunk to stand, let alone fornicate, but then he shrugged. What difference did it make? Julie Ekpu would probably have given Baldy a tumble if that was the name of his game. 'We think there's a lot more of this to be dug up yet. We think Madame Warner has the hots for any power guy she can hump without him dreaming of telling. Carstairs more or less said as much before he keeled over.'

'And Rupert?' Plummer asked. 'Does he play along with the little lady's tastes? Peep through the curtains when she's at it? Is the man who may stand a heartbeat from our presidency some sort of damned voyeur?'

'No such luck,' said Forrest. 'He has eyes but chooses not to see. Voyeurs don't pull blankets over their heads. All he seems to go to bed with, these days, is a hot-water bottle.'

Plummer spat a mint leaf on to the thick, coarse grass. 'Well, anyway, you got a real belter there, my friend. And it can only get better. Seems to me that my own choice for Veep ought to be everything this Limey and his rabbit of a wife ain't. A woman, a fine woman with kids and a happy marriage and a career we can all look up to.'

For a second Forrest felt his face slipping, peeling into chagrin around the edges.

Plummer laughed and wrapped an arm around his shoulders. 'Now don't you fret none, Senator. Old Nate looks after his friends, one way or another. I'm getting ever deeper in your debt, sir. But this is serious business and I've got the perfect bit of matching business just panting for my call.'

'He's taken the Santarini option,' said Papadopoulos, barging into Rupert's sitting room without a knock.

Rupert sat up blearily. 'The what option?'

'Elaine Santarini. Governor of New Jersey. Executive president of Macroword. Five kids by a TV sportscaster voted America's favourite hunk five years in a row, youngest of them only two weeks old. Blessed personally by the Pope on his last visit. She'll be breastfeeding her baby on the convention floor for sure. She always does. It's one of America's all-time most-loved pictures.'

Rupert lay back and scratched his nose. 'Good-oh. At least that's one thing even Tate can't expect me to do.'

Jenny was thrashing up and down the Tipper Gore Memorial Pool, 8002 Wisconsin Avenue, in a flaming temper she guessed might be menopausal. More fuel on the fire of her fury. The most immediate repository of it, the new bulky man in a black, buttoned suit, stood on the side of the pool, pursuing her with his eyes.

'I don't want to be followed by a bloody secret-service body-guard,' she'd said. 'I want a swim.'

'Sorry, ma'am, and I got my orders.' He wasn't in the least attractive. The stubble on his chin matched his jacket. The hair on his bulging forehead was greased back, thin against a reddened scalp. His lips seemed set somehow in a permanent snarl. People she knew, people who even wrote memoirs about it, had fallen in love with their bodyguards. But Dwight Schultz? It was a disgusting thought. She'd rather take Bannon and Mrs B for a *ménage à trois*. And while he stayed, she felt trapped – speared by those flat, fish eyes.

'Oh, my God, I'm so sorry.' She had ploughed headlong into another swimmer, bent head banged hard against brown body. They both stopped dead and paddled to the surface, mouthing apologies.

'That was my fault,' said Jenny. 'I just wasn't looking.'

'Nor was I,' said the black girl with a smile. 'That's men for you. You tell them goodbye and you can't look left or right for weeks.'

They both began laughing.

She was stunning, Jenny thought, young and lithe, with flesh that seemed to press outwards on her skin, giving it a sheen of health.

'I'm Julie,' said the girl, pushing out a hand. 'And don't tell me, I know who you are. I've seen so many pictures.'

Jenny looked over at Schultz, who had fallen back into the blank trance she loathed so vehemently. 'I'm still feeling just a little dizzy,' she said. 'Why don't you let me buy you a soda or something, so we can both make sure we're OK?'

They got out of the water together: the short blonde woman with the discreet muscles and the expensive tan, and the long black girl with the sway. They laughed again about something as they turned into the café, friends already.

Schultz let his fingers touch the gun on its holster beneath the dank armpit of his suit. He did not like the Warner woman. She was a hard bitch, since you asked. But she could be sweeter than rosebuds when she tried.

Rupert's first outing was Carmel Community College – the campaign computer's best shot at soft beginnings. They drove down from San Francisco, stopping twice along the way to talk to Mexican fruit-pickers hacking away in the melon fields.

'Delicious with country ham or a little port,' said Rupert, to a large man in a sombrero and flopping peasant shirt. They smiled uncomprehendingly for the cameras. 'Couldn't you find somebody who speaks English?' asked Jenny acidly.

'Much safer not. You can't programme what they'll say to the press if they get too much small-talk going.' Papadopoulos wagged a playful finger at her. 'Señor Tate, he say, "Give me a dialogue of the deaf and a good night's sleep any time."'

Carmel reminded her of Hampstead on the Pacific. They had Earl Grey and more pictures at an Olde English Tea House. Rupert complained loudly about the crumpets. 'Too sweet and too stodgy. Why can't they make decent pikelets over here, with holes the butter and jam can soak right through?'

Harris and Kraft moved in warning to his elbow. 'Not,' Rupert said quickly, 'that it isn't perfectly delicious in a way. It's just that nothing comes up to your blueberry muffins.'

As they walked to the college door Jenny took his arm. 'For God's sake, calm down and stop blathering,' she muttered. 'Read the script. Answer the questions they've arranged for ten minutes. Then out. This is not supposed to be difficult. This is –'

'I know,' said Rupert mournfully. 'This is net practice. Let's see if we can hit a few runs.'

'And don't use any of those bloody cricket metaphors,' she snapped.

Inside the white undulation of the hall, the students were quite as spotty as predicted. They were snickering and chewing gum and having trouble listening at the same time. Did the bank of cameras ranged at the back care about that? Surely not. If he delivered the couple of soundbites that Harris had taken him through five times last night, nobody would give a fig about the rest. The entire frigging campus could choke on its gum unremarked. But he still hated talking into a buzz of incomprehension and drifting attention.

Bite One: 'Once, men and women of your age fought, and died, to keep freedom safe on England's shores. Now we, and your great President, are freedom fused. Our future is your future.'

Bite Two: 'Not the old world and the new world, my friends, but one world, one dream, one more term of destiny.'

All this, he reflected sourly, in the first two minutes, so that the camera crews could pack up and move on early. He'd got another half-hour of Shakespeare and the corn laws and Winston Churchill – 'the towering leader in whose party footsteps I was privileged to follow' – to go, even before he reached Eisenhower. Oh, what the hell? Rupert thought. If nobody, inside or out, was listening now, why drone on?

'Look,' he said, pushing his notes to one side, 'maybe that's enough of fine phrases and high-flown notions. Why don't we just chat for a while?'

He did chunks of his Dorchester after-dinner-speech routine.

The Labour prime minister who'd lost his hairpiece on the airport tarmac in Brussels when a helicopter started up. The cabinet minister who'd got stuck in the loo half-way through their big budget meeting. 'I said, "Where's Harry? I know it's a tough target, but suicide before the coffee break seemed a bit OTT."' He nattered about Gross and the end of his union. 'We never really hit it off, you know. He'd bark something or other that I couldn't quite catch. I'd jump to attention without thinking. When it was all over I found myself marching out of the room. He thought I was taking the piss. But it was just seeing too many old war films on telly.'

They had long since stopped chewing, their hands sliding to their mouths and parking the globs of goo on the underside of their desks. They began to laugh, to rock and to stamp.

'So you see,' Rupert said, 'what's happened isn't all treaties and summits and men in overcoats shaking hands. It's chaps getting together, watching the same movies, eating the same food, drinking the same wine. Gross and I would never have hit it off. But your Wild Bill saw the chance to reach out a hand. And I took it. Now President Tate's pushing the whole thing forward, so that by the time your kids are in college, no one will ever think twice. History is really things just rolling along.'

Harris had scratched the skin off the scab on his nose, and a thin rivulet of blood seeped from it.

'That felt much better,' said Rupert. 'Perhaps I could always just get the formal garbage out of the way and then tell them a few tales. They seemed to like it.'

Kraft appeared to have his thin head buried in his long hands, like a pencil sticking from a plastic case.

'Well,' said Jenny, 'you certainly seem to have obliterated your own side. Tomorrow, perhaps, you could try obliterating the opposition.'

'Oh, right. The twin curse of liberalism and socialism,' said Rupert, cheerfully. 'I've got some quite good jokes about that.'

Julie Ekpu walked over from the press bench and moved close

to Jenny. 'That was really good fun,' she said. 'You must be terribly proud of him. If I could start the profile here, with you two together, it would be wonderful to tag along with you to England next week and watch you operating for him, but without him. If you see what I mean.'

Jenny nodded vaguely. She was a sensational-looking girl and she stood out in one or two of the group photographs, lent them a difference and, as Papadopoulos remarked, 'the extra ethnicity we're lacking'.

'Fine,' she said. 'Four days in Arizona and New Mexico and then we're splitting. He's got Oregon. I've got Fulham and Chelsea. By all means just come along. Too many makeovers wear a girl down. I'd be glad of the company.'

Polly was worried. No, more than that, almost despairing. 'This is just very nasty,' she told Simmons, when he called. 'I spent the whole of yesterday up in Leeds, beating round my own patch. I thought the mood was foul.'

They were, as expected, having second thoughts. Yorkshiremen muttering in their beer about foreigners; damned tourists in loud blazers crawling over the place as though they owned it and shouting, 'Isn't this cute?' in the street. 'Seems like they think they're bloody lords of the manor,' her agent had told her. 'Your average fellow don't like that. He reckons they're no better than they ought to be.' And then there was the economy, dipping off the boil because the Fed had got worried about interest rates; and the taps running dry because the cash from Internal Resources had gone missing somewhere east of Missouri; and old New Labour blowing cold.

'Forrest is playing every end against the middle,' she said. 'Christ, what a two-faced turd. One minute he's going on about broken promises and the vision that Mark has betrayed, the next he's getting at Rupert, feathering his nest in Washington and forgetting all about his roots. The Senator for South Kensington, he calls him, the man who wants to be vice-president for

Pimlico before he's finished. It's a terribly hard act to break down because it works on both levels. Either Rupert's some puffed-up grandee over the water, wallowing in the trough, in which case Forrest is the voice of England looking after its own. Or the whole thing is a kind of rotten joke, and your lot are just humouring Rupert, letting him wear putty medals and play the old fool while England gets the brush-off. And this, if you please, from the ginger toad you last spied sucking round Plummer in Atlanta, with all those big hugs and sickly grins.'

'Sounds pretty smart to me,' said Simmons. 'I never promised you politics was easy.' He paused. 'But, hey, honey, I miss you. This is turning into one hell of a ding-dong for me too. Seems to me, if there was anything else going wrong, I might slide over for a weekend and check it out in person.'

'Anything else?' said Polly. 'Well, you know about the Scots and the Welsh and the Irish because they've been doing it in your backyard, holding out their grubby palms and bleating for more. I know we predicted it. But these are still votes heading straight for Nate. And you know about Broadbent?'

'You mean that old Brit tub-thumper Rupert ditched years ago, along with Carstairs, after we sold him the good-time American religion? I know of him. I don't know what the barrel of lard has been doing, though.'

'You will tomorrow,' said Polly. 'How about running for President as the Independent candidate for the return of a Sovereign England? He's a fool and a windbag. The TV satire shows here dismantled him long since. But he's got a pile of funding from somewhere and he's bought himself a sack of headlines. "I Speak Out to Save the Country I Love." That sort of thing. Because nothing's going our way, he could be a nasty distraction – and that's before the big one.'

Even Simmons, feet on desk, shirt unbuttoned in the Washington heat, Budweiser sipped through a straw, was beginning to feel a churning in his stomach. 'You mean there's more? After Broadbent, it can only be the return of Dracula. Or Spiro Agnew.'

She gave a hollow laugh. 'Pretty close. I mean, if the word is right. The return of Michaelson. He's had a week in Europe, dining with Gross, oiling round the Elysée, pretending to be a banker building bridges and researching some paper for Chatham House. I had truly thought he was out of it, tail between legs. But the word is different. The word is, this speech is going to be a great big bomb, splattering anyone within a hundred miles.'

'Does Rupert know?'

'No. Jenny's expected any time for a few teas with the ladies and a round of daytime chat shows. But Rupert? The last time I saw him he was in Minneapolis doing his statesman stuff. Dave, I think it's a waste. Santarini was here on Thursday, talking about breastfeeding to a bunch of career women at the Savoy. In, out, a few quotes and a few photographs. Keep the media sisters hopping. They're playing it damned flexible, Dave. We're way off the pace and we need to get weaving.'

'I'll be over first flight on Saturday,' he said. 'And I'll talk to Papadopoulos about our boy. Come the hour, I hope to hell we can produce the man.'

Rupert was staying overnight at the Indiana Radisson, South Bend. The school speech was tomorrow at ten. The flight from Dakota, for imbecile reasons no imbecile seemed able to explain to him, had stayed stuck on the runway at Chicago O'Hare for three and a half hours. What he could see of South Bend, dark and sleeping apart from a few club lights along the strip, looked deeply unappealing. There wasn't even a bend on Main Street, looking south.

The suite at the Radi was thirty years old and thirty years scuffed, soiled and scarred by drunken salesmen puking and kicking lumps out of the furniture: a grey and green expanse of cheap wood and cheap nylon. Only Cokes and juices in the mini-bar, goddamnit. Rupert called down for two large Scotches and pottered off to run the bath.

The bell rang, he thought, with exhilarating speed. A short, round Cuban maid; a whole bottle of Johnnie Walker and ice clinking in a silver bucket. 'You want me to pour, sir?'

'Thank you very much. A double on as many rocks as you can fit in a glass, please.'

'You come long way? You very tired, very tense?'

He looked at her more intently. Black frizzy hair tied back in a red ribbon, rouge on plump cheeks, a body that had probably once turned heads all over Indiana now thickened into wildly improbable curves. Her breasts heaved as she trotted over to him, little legs pumping in a skirt that would have been too tight half a stone before.

'Is all right, sir?'

'Fine, Miss . . . ?'

'I called Florinda, Mr Wannabe Vice-President, sir. You tired. You relax good.'

She did not step back. She scrambled, puffing a little, to her knees and, to Rupert's bemusement, began unbuttoning his flies and rummaging around as though she'd lost a key in a deep pocket.

'What the –' He stepped backwards, wobbling alarm, spraying a slurp of Scotch on the sofa.

'No, no, Mr Wannabe,' she gurgled, crawling half upright towards him, stretching out her hands. 'No worry. Florinda, she give great blow job, very nice, very sexy. Just like she give to three presidents and two vice-presidents before when they come stay in South Bend. Mr Galt, he say, "Conchita, you got a wicked mouth on you. That the best damn blow I got in fifty states." And Beell, the great President when I was just a little girl starting out, he say, "You do this whenever a weary politician come through, honey. It sure gets the juice in the system running better than a hot bath and a big burger."'

Rupert turned desperately, one hand waving Scotch, the other stuffing shirt back in trousers, and ran for the door as she raced on her knees after him. 'Madam,' he said, with all the formality he could muster, 'Madam, kindly leave the room. It was kind of you to come and I appreciate your sense of tradition. But I am not one of your American presidents. I am English, Madam.'

It was then, with blessed precision, that Simmons put through his phone call.

Gross had had the Slovakian President all morning for the kind of talks about a new Volkswagen assembly line in Bratislava that made his jaw ache. Why were the Slovaks so bloody brass-necked, always insisting that Berlin could deliver the same goodies for them that Prague just went out and won?

'I am not the chairman of Volkswagen,' he'd said finally. 'I am a Bundeschancellor with too many of his own people out of work and a ten-point deficit in the opinion polls. You must begin to work your own miracles, Mr President.'

No use, of course. The bullet-headed man with the close crop and squint had merely leered at him and punched him on the shoulder. 'Well, Herr Gross, we shall see. But your sausage is no good. It gives my people stomach-ache. My scientists have found ball-bearing fragments in the liverwurst under laboratory conditions. This is not a political issue, Herr Chancellor. This is a question of health that no leader of his country can put to one side, a sacred trust for all Slovaks. The ban stays. The sausage mountain in our storage plant will not be released, I am afraid. Unless, of course, you give us good reason to examine all the facts again.'

Shit. He'd phone Fritz at VW in the afternoon and try twisting the prim bastard's arm. But the election was only six months away and too many of the snivelling pundits were writing him off already. Arms didn't twist for him like they used to.

Frieda came in with her message pad. 'President Peyerfitte's office were asking if there are developments, Chancellor. And Mr Michaelson wondered if you could call him back when you had a moment.'

'Fine,' said Gross. Here at least was his game, played to his rules. 'Get Michaelson first on the secure line. And tell Paris I hope to have news for them very soon.' It was, he thought, a gambit without snags. If it worked, there would be plaudits for him and confusion for his enemies. And if it failed? Who could, in any case, blame a world leader for trying? His State Department friends could make useful mischief with this.

As usual, Michaelson sounded metallic, distant down the line. 'A robot,' Frau Gross had called him after their dinner. 'But a beautifully programmed one.'

'You have the copy of my speech?' he asked. 'There are a few amendments. I think it best to make no specific references to Germany whatsoever, Chancellor. And certainly not to you personally. All the current research makes that of dubious utility. So everything is reworked in terms of France. Peyerfitte is a new man with good English and a nice sense of humour. He makes much of his days at the London School of Economics and his daughter – who, I'm told, may be considered pretty – is supposed to be the fiancée of a horticulturalist from Bath. In short, he seems the ideal catalyst. Any reaction to what I say should, I think, come exclusively from him.'

Gross clicked his teeth. This man, the washed-up ex-prime minister of a washed-up non-country, had taken his script and was writing him out of it. Typical effrontery. But still . . . 'So,' he said, 'how does it go now?'

'Oh, basically unchanged. I look at the history of the last decade. Of course, it cannot be altered. The people of England have spoken. But were they led too far too fast by desperate men who had contrived their own disasters? Did they foresee how Customs barriers at Dover, with all their bureaucracy, all their endless checkings, would halve trade between England and the Continent – and ruin the business of tourism on both sides of the Channel? Oh, we have our fellow Americans now, millions of them grubbing round our historical sites. But these planeloads from the Midwest do not spend enough money and do not appreciate the finer things of English life. They think of us as some dusty theme park. And, naturally, they don't go on to France or Spain or Italy in current circumstances. There is an animosity, a rivalry, which chills the air. There is no natural or easy movement, no congress of exchange or prosperity, between the peoples of Europe. What was Britain is not enough for the five states now – and those five isolated enclaves are insufficient reward for an America that must always play a greater role for Europe. I call it the imbalance of opportunities.'

'Yes,' said Gross impatiently. 'I have read all of this. Frankly, you forget that I helped write so much of it. But, please, how is the final suggestion now framed? Alain was extremely anxious that any response from him would be portrayed as interfering in your elections. He will not say anything if there is a risk of that.'

'No risk, I think,' said Michaelson, with the clipped petulance of old. 'My final call, and I quote directly, is for a fresh beginning with the next American president, whoever he be, because there is always a constant need for dialogue between the bastions of democracy. Could there be a revised relationship between the outposts of America and the Union, one based on more flexible trade and a return to the days of easy passage for citizens between the two blocs? Of course, with new thinking and revived goodwill. It is time, with experience, to put fruitful change back on the agenda.'

'So,' said Gross, 'there will be no reaction from my office to this speech. Merely that all ideas for progress receive automatic consideration. In Brussels, I have arranged for a few commissioners with good language skills to express a certain enthusiasm. But it is for the Elysée, and the Elysée alone, to propose the real possibility of joint talks once your voting is over.'

He paused and ticked the checklist on the desk in front of him. 'And then, of course, there is the question of Warner.'

'I've arranged a question from the floor after I finish,' Michaelson said quickly. His voice began to rehearse the precise phrases they'd talked of. 'Senator Warner has been at the heart of so much through the ten years of upheaval that, of course, it would be difficult to see him rebuilding the bridges which are necessary. I cannot disguise that he may be an impediment. But if he can acknowledge the errors, put so much of his rhetoric behind him, then I am sure that even he can be part of this future.'

'Very good,' said Gross. 'Very nice. If you'll excuse me, I must ring Peyerfitte. He will be back from luncheon now.'

Jenny had eaten a prawn mousse on the flight over which had made her feel slightly queasy. Heathrow was covered in thick, bumpy clouds. She closed her eyes for a second. One row behind her, Gloria and Julie sat together. They were still sleeping. Julie's head had fallen sideways, and rested lightly on Gloria's golden shoulder. Jenny could feel Schultz's eyes boring into her back. Her stomach ached; her neck ached.

There was the usual gaggle of pressmen waiting in the lounge. She was surprised to see Polly. 'My dear,' she said, 'surely this wasn't necessary. It's only little me come to open a few garden fêtes and visit a few hospitals. I know the way in from the airport perfectly well.'

Polly ran a hand through her thick crop of swinging hair and contrived a thin smile. 'Actually I'm here to meet Dave. He'll be in on TWA in ten minutes. So I thought you might appreciate a moment or two of briefing. Basically, we've got trouble. Michaelson is due to stir the pot tonight. Broadbent is making waves. Forrest is smirking everywhere you look because Tate's so far behind on Gallup. And Rupert's cancelled the whole Indiana and Ohio swing to get back here. You can put the kettle on around eight thirty, I think. Hubby will be a bit frazzled – and we're all going to have a heavy Sunday.'

The *Mail* and the *Express* had broken out of the line and began shouting at them. 'Mrs Warner! Mrs Warner! Can you tell us about your husband, please? Is there a crisis? Why did he leave a whole audience in South Bend just sitting there? Is there an illness you think you should tell us about?'

'Gentlemen,' said Jenny, firmly, 'there is no crisis and there is no illness. My dear husband was simply missing me, and there is a great deal of good he can do here. So we're going to spend a few days together doing it. Thank you. That will be all.'

Broadbent was no longer merely fat, he was grotesque. His jowls seemed to drape the sharp-starched white edges of his collar so that thin red lines traced across them when he moved his head. He levered himself out of the club chair, puffing, as Carstairs arrived. 'Brian, old son. Long time no chew the cud. How have you been? Not too well, I hear, and not too well treated either. Terrible shame. But maybe now we can get the old act back together – after all, we made Rupert Warner, so I'm sure we can break him if we put our minds to it.'

Carstairs grunted indeterminately. He had never liked Broadbent. A blowhard balloon wrapped in the flag. The man had never had to struggle for anything: the Broadbent Bank was one of the great high-street names and the Family Broadbent looked after its own, still scattering directorships among the sons and cousins of the inner core. That long tail of experience, half a column in *Who's Who*, had made him the inevitable Warner choice for the Treasury. But, truth to tell, he wasn't much good with figures. His only budget had been an abject shambles. He'd even knocked the water jug all over his notes, when he'd turned and caught the handle with his belly.

'I'm really out of things now, you know,' said Carstairs. 'Yesterday's man scratching a crust from the lobbyists and sweet-talking the sheikhs. I don't think I'd bring much to the party.'

'Nonsense,' said Broadbent, with an airy wave. 'We need you because we need every man jack of the crew who led us out of Europe on board – less Captain Warner, of course. That way we can claim to be the heirs of the great referendum, the founding

fathers of an independent Britain betrayed by fainthearts, sub-
verted by American ambition.'

'Isn't that, well, a bit backward-looking?' Carstairs asked.
'The same people who voted us out of Europe voted us into the
United States – and I can't see anybody overturning that.'

'Not overturning, distancing,' Broadbent said flatly, temper
beginning to fray. 'There's nothing ridiculous about changing
our minds and wanting out. Alaska's had a party pushing for
just that for years. But my backers and I don't think getting out
again is practical stuff, at least for the moment. We want the
special autonomy we're entitled to. We want to hang on to our
laws and our way of life. Congress can vote us grants for things,
of course they can. We deserve particular consideration. But tell
me, why should we be ploughing zillions into the Pentagon to
defend Honolulu lovelies, wearing nothing but a few flowers
around their fannies, from the beastly Chinese hordes? It doesn't
make sense and we'd do much better if we were allowed to look
after our own defence.' He leered at Carstairs, head to one side,
chins stacked like a filing cabinet. 'Softly, softly, makee monkey
of Uncle Sam, old boy. Five years of this stuff, and they'll be
paying us to bugger off.'

'Meanwhile,' Carstairs said sourly, 'who's paying you to get
this show on the road? I can't imagine the old gang sitting up
there on the fourteenth floor, signing cheques.'

'Perish even the thought, old son. No jolly need. Our young
pal Mujib's shelled out forty million on the quiet, and that's for
starters. The lad may not be Einstein, but he certainly lashes
the shekels around without so much as a blink or a bleat. Says
Grandad would have wanted it that way.'

Carstairs sat up straight and shouted for another drink. Mujib
was the third son of a Pakistani tennis star and his wife, the
daughter of an insanely rich Jewish detergent manufacturer and
market player who had, long ago, thrown money at all manner
of eccentric causes, laughing hysterically as they went West.
When he died, before the century turned, his billions had been

scattered among his wives and mistresses, but £750 million had found its way to the boy with the magnetic stare his mother and grandmother agreed reminded them of Gramps. The only Khan with a look of the past and a sense of the future, they said – maybe because an acutely acid stomach sometimes made him roll his eyes berserkly, too.

'Well,' said Carstairs, 'that's handy. We may not win, you and I. But I, sure as eggs, don't see how we can lose.'

Chapter Sixteen

The President of the United States took his fifteenth gulp of the morning, swilled the Cab round his mouth, and spat it into the fifteenth silver bowl. Cameras clicked for the fifteenth time.

'Hey, that's another delicious one,' said Tate. 'Raspberries, bilberries, and a real hint of rosemary hovering there in the background, exuding that spicy taste we love so much, imploding on the tongue.'

Crap, of course, he thought. He'd mugged it all up from two hours with the *Taste of Gracious Living* magazine on the flight over and a hectic call to the White House cellar master.

'Remember to talk berries, sir. It doesn't matter very much which berries, because most folk have swamped them in ice-cream before they ever get to finding the fruit. Any berry will do, so long as you spit it out and move on quick. And look as decisive as you can. If you start swopping taste-buds with those fellows, you could be there all day.'

They were working the Napa Valley together, he and Marti. Breakfast with the Methodist elders of Yountville to keep the AA lobby quiet, then sampling the harvest blessings of the Lord along the château trails. The Pres liked reds, according to his press secretary. He was doing the Cabs. The First Lady liked Chardonnay. She was glugging away a mile across the valley, prattling about apples and pears and melons as instructed. It was – what? – ten more stops till lunch in Calistoga and a snatched doze in the big car back to San Francisco. Christ, he hoped Marti was spitting it all out as instructed. He didn't want her snoring on the plane to Denver.

A hand tugged at his arm. 'If you could call a ten-minute break, Mr President, Simmons is calling urgent from London, England.'

The rear of the car, sound-proofed as well as bullet-proofed, let him sit back, close his eyes and hear Dave blowing his nose. 'That sounds a ring-ding of a cold, old friend.'

'And that's the least of my troubles, Mark. We just got the Peyerfitte text. I hadn't expected it till Sunday, but the Elysée has pulled a neat move. The Michaelson lecture is set for seven, and they've embargoed their response for that identical time. They'll make all the Sunday-paper editions with time to spare. Maximum exposure. I expect Plummer to respond any moment. His guys are well inside the loop. So we really need to say something pronto. Warner's here, but he's zonked, and this isn't his call anyway. Have you got an audience there we could use?'

When Tate got out of the car, he found a lawn and a Rodin statue and stood beside it. 'I want this to look as French as possible. Hands across the Gironde. One world of wine. Get a few of those pretty girls in their white aprons to come over and listen.

'My friends,' he said, when the cameras were running, 'the President of this great nation is always on call, and so it is this morning. Though I'd have wished to get to the Merlot first. But I must respond swiftly to events on the other side of the world, which raise questions about the territorial integrity of these United States and, in particular, our new states on the lip of Europe. The President of another proud nation, France, has just asked me publicly to negotiate a new relationship at that border. As I understand it, some kind of two-tier citizenship, which makes the English and the French more buddy-buddy again. And what do I say to that? I say sure, we'll talk. Sure, if there's something good for all the people of America, then you can depend on our sense of patriotism to follow through. But when you got two tiers, you also got a second class for some on the ride. And you won't find this administration letting no one play bureaucratic catch-up for any of our citizens. No, sir. Now, thank you all. There's work to be done.'

He could see Marti clambering out of the blue limo down the drive. She was staggering a little and her hair was awry.

'Let's get out of here,' said Tate.

The press secretary was briefing the *LA Times* and the *Washington Post*. 'I think the President took control there,' he said earnestly. 'Open-minded and flexible, but resolute too. He didn't say *non* and he didn't say *oui*.'

Polly had begged a ticket for the Michaelson lecture. It was a small cream hall with peeling paint and scuffed benches. The old Royal Institute of International Affairs had never had the money to match its name: the supermarket money which, only last March, had made it the Safeway School of Global Relations was still stuck at a check-out somewhere. She slid into a seat at the back, next to a wizened man in a grey suit who kept touching his long, aquiline nose.

'Ah, Miss Gurley. Come to see the enemy at close range?'

She nodded distantly. She'd thought Patrick Flint-Richards had gone to the great brasserie in the sky, buried in Provence with his FO generation of Brussels diners beneath a mildewed mound of *foie gras*.

The heat from the lights was already oppressive.

Michaelson came in from the side and did something she hadn't seen him do before. He took off his jacket and gestured to the hall. And he smiled.

In one sense, she reckoned, there were no surprises: delivered as text. But he had laboured long and hard over it. The details were all in place, the single sheet in the electronic passport that would set the English apart, the identity cards they could use in Europe. He wasn't just floating a notion. He was unveiling a plan. Whose? His? Possibly. But there was another dog somewhere, refusing to bark. And Michaelson was operating under new PR orders for sure. The discarded jacket lay casual, relaxed, on the chair beside him. There were self-deprecating little jokes. There were – of course, she should have twigged immediately – contact lenses instead of the steel-rimmed glasses. He'd been told one thing over and over: Don't be bitter. Be human, and concerned.

It was an occasion with a whiff of the Second Coming. Flint-Richards stood with the rest, slapping dank palm against palm.

Questions. Orchestrated, of course. The lady from the *Guardian* rose on cue. What about Warner?

Well, what about him? That had been rehearsed, too. But the new, easy Michaelson threw in a last half-joke for luck. 'I'm sorry, of course, that my old colleague can't be here tonight to tell us what he thinks. After all, I came to his speeches.'

Polly winced.

Julie padded round the Warners' kitchen, washing the smeary whisky glasses from the night before, tossing the heaped ashtray into the bin. Jenny had said nine thirty, but the house was barely stirring. Schultz had let her in, gestured disgustedly towards the debris, and sat down in the hall again, hand braced to bulging armpit.

Another bell, another groan, another shuffle. It was Papado-poulos: the gleaming shirt, the black slacks, a pink cotton sweater slung around his neck, the dark curl of hair. His skin had an olive glow and the smile hovered boyishly. He was gorgeous, she thought, if you liked them slim and soft. Was he gay? She'd seen nothing in his eyes to hint it. He looked women over. He was standing by the stove now, looking at her.

'Coffee?'

'De-caff. Mrs Warner was going to find me an hour or two this morning for the piece on the Dorchester years. You know, the young couple making a living from the land, the kids bonding with the animals. They want it for one of their glossy mags with uselessly long lead times. Not the master work. That comes later.'

There was a clatter on the stairs and a curse. Jenny was wearing a shapeless purple dressing gown. Her hair was uncombed and the face, smudged under the eyes, was still blotched from sleep. 'Oh, God,' she said. 'What sort of time is this to find a kitchen crowd on Sunday morning?'

She turned away from Papadopoulos and rummaged in the refrigerator for orange juice, suddenly talking too brightly. 'Poor Rupert's groaning around upstairs as though he doesn't know what day it is. Had we got some sort of meeting fixed? Last night was just such a haze when Polly came back with the papers.'

'You're cracking up, Jenny,' Papadopoulos said. 'Remember. Council of war at ten sharp. Harris and Kraft will be over with the drafts. Governor Groom joins us at eleven. There'll be a need to catch the lunch bulletins with something that gets our ball back in play.'

'Shit. I'll get him moving.'

She was somehow hunched so that he couldn't glimpse her properly, Julie saw. Head down, hand fiddling with the cord around the blowsy coat. She didn't want him to see her like this. These were not Warner terms. And he was grinning again, enjoying the embarrassment.

'It sounds as though we'd better fix another time for that talk,' Julie said. 'I'll go back to the paper and get on with some writing and call you this afternoon to see what's possible.'

The news room was pleasantly deserted, a tangle of wires and dirty plastic beakers from the night before with only a couple of engineers at the far end, fiddling with a broken terminal. She sat by the great window looking out over Docklands, early pleasure-boats plodding up the Thames, kids kicking a ball in Greenwich Park. When she called the editor was shaving.

'I just thought you'd like to know we're on to Number Two.

She's shagging Nick the wonder Greek, too. Give me a couple of weeks, and I'll give you a football team.'

Polly and Simmons sat side by side at the head of the table. Someone had to be in charge. The papers from the evening before were spread across it, with a new folder of polls delivered ten minutes earlier.

'Now,' said Simmons, 'time to take stock. There are six weeks and three days left. Nationally we're fifty-two/forty-eight down, but we reckon the electoral college stacks up worse than that. Plummer put on a good show in Atlanta. He don't talk like a liberal or look like a liberal. He don't frighten the horses none. He's going to take most of the South on our figures, but he's also promising enough juice to the unions and enough little bitty grants to our fine business corporations to keep them nodding along. That old boy is playing all the right tunes.

'But it gets worse. The Grand Old Party have had a lock on the presidency for twelve years. Folks want a change. Oh, they think Mark's done a decent job – better than Angeli, if you follow the leadership ratings in the right column. But the economy isn't winning him no applause, and there's what I call the Negative Change Factor beating away.'

Rupert coughed and raised a weary eyebrow.

'Shorthanding it,' Dave said. 'We're the party of no change, but we've changed a hell of a lot. Not least, the shape of this country. And the Democrats are the party of change, but Nate is promising four years of bedding down and resting up. We've got to get reassuring, which means telling the world that we're in charge and that there ain't no more upheavals down the pike. That's why the President wanted you on the ticket, Rupert. You kind of signal there's no more to come. But it all goes to pear-shaped if you turn out to be Mr Controversy.'

He waved a fist across the scatter of newsprint. 'Darn it. We need England. Without those fifty-six votes, I can't see where any majority's coming from. Even Ulster matters close to the wire. But Broadbent declaring may take ten per cent minimum. And this Michaelson stuff makes terrible waves back in Washington. It takes your old rows and dumps them straight on the President's doorstep. Fact is, on the telephone polls this morning, Plummer is whipping us here by twenty points. And that, my friends, is the Mississippi with the levees going splat.'

Polly looked at Rupert. He had that blank, sheepish look she remembered from the early days of ANAPA when he couldn't get the treaty straight. He was splashing out of his depth. His eyes, beseeching, had turned to her.

'Well,' he said eventually, 'it's an awful bind and no mistake. I don't know how we get out of it. But in the old days, Pol, you used to tell me to tackle one headache at a time.'

'And you know Broadbent,' she cut in quickly. 'Been there. Seen that off once already. Maybe that's where we start, Dave.'

'But the guy's a fat pygmy,' said Simmons. 'Taking him on won't cut any ice in Peoria.'

'Maybe. What do you call it in boxing – the bum of the month? There's always time to get the other fights in, though, if we can just win one fast to show that we know how. Come on, Rupert. Where do we start throwing leather?'

'Of course,' Rupert told the Sunday dragon lady on the *World at One*, Thelma the Tyrannosaurus Regina as they called her in the English Broadcasting Corporation. 'Of course I understand where Mr Broadbent is coming from. He was a good colleague with me in the early days after the vote when Britain stood alone again. He had a romantic attachment to our island history. And I respect that, naturally. I share it.'

The voice, as ever, was deepening, beginning somehow to croak with suppressed mirth.

'But let me be clear. The world moves on. Our world has moved on because the people of England have decided that we should join, as one, with the people of America. A great adventure. Now, there will be hardships, difficulties. There will always be would-be leaders who seek, at such times, to turn back the clock. To go round the country, stirring up apathy. It's at such a moment, such a turning-point, that our inner resolution must emerge, recalling the –'

'Surely, though, Prime Minister –' The dragon flamed, then purpled into a splutter of apology.

'I'm going out to see some friends. Rupert knows where I am. There's no need to come. This is my home town, where I live. I shall be quite safe.'

Schultz shrugged. 'If that's a formal instruction, ma'am.'

He passed her the old beige raincoat she was reaching for and draped it round her shoulders. He had unexpectedly slim hands, she thought, long, supple fingers sprouting from that tub of a body. She wrapped a silk scarf around her head. The nights were drawing in fast. Broadbent's Croydon rally must have finished at seven. She guessed there would be minimal lingering over the majesty of his rhetoric.

The taxi dropped her at Paddington station, five streets away from the whitewashed Victorian terrace. Better to walk the rest of the way and see if the window in the flat was lit.

As she turned the corner, the light flashed on and an unseen hand pulled the curtain shut. Would he be alone? Of course. He was always alone these days. She pressed the bell and his voice, slurred as expected, crackled over the intercom.

'It's Jenny,' she said. 'I thought I'd pay you a visit.'

He met her at the top of the stairs, more haggard than she remembered, red striped shirt unbuttoned, tie hanging loose around his neck. 'Well,' said Carstairs, 'this is a totally unexpected honour. Would it be seemly' – he dwelt on the word, staggering for a second – 'would it be seemly to offer the Senator's lady a drink?'

'No,' Jenny said. 'But I'll have one anyway.'

The flat was a scruffy shambles, breakfast pots still on the table, papers strewn on the floor, a pair of socks lying by his bedroom door.

'You're not looking after yourself.'

He poured her a Scotch and wove his way into the kitchen to find water. She could see breakfast cereal littered across the floor. It grated as he walked, flat-footed, to the sink.

'OK. I know this isn't a social visit. You don't, I assume, want me for my body. But what has this decrepit, addled brain to offer the lady of the night?'

Jenny had heard about his bitterness, and in her mind she had expected a moment like this, planned the possibilities. Would he be best kicked, like a wounded dog? Or should she somehow reach out to him physically again? Wham, bang, was there something else, ma'am?

Instead she clinked glasses and brushed her hand ephemerally, almost accidentally, against his arm. 'Cheers. Good health and good memories.'

Pause. 'Brian,' she said, 'I don't want anything from you. Except to know that you are all right. I just wanted to ask you a question. Perhaps you want to get back at Rupert for what happened?'

He started to shake his head, but she raised her index finger and put it to his lips. 'Perhaps, perhaps not. I wouldn't blame you either way. But why Broadbent, for heaven's sake? Why that ludicrous bullfrog? The whole thing is bound to go to sick and tears. He oozes fat – and that horrid, slimy patriotism only cartoonists can make anything of. His sums don't add up. People remember that from the last time. President Broadbent? It's a joke, Brian. About nothing but mischief, headlines for a few days until the money runs out.'

Her hand brushed his again.

'My question. Why waste what you've got left on that?'

He babbled, the cadences slipping, bumping into each other, emotion stirring from the bottom of a glass. 'Oh, it's not about Rupert. Nothing about him. Jammy bastard. So he had the luck, so fine. Not about you, either. We had good sex for a few years. What else? A laugh now and then, but we both knew it wasn't going anywhere. You had plenty of others on the side. I would, too, if anybody had offered.

'No, I'm with Broadbent, Mrs Senator, because he asked me. Don't get asked any more. Sit on platforms, make speeches, hear some applause again. Why not, if it gives me a kick? And you're wrong about one thing. Money won't run out. There's lots and lots of money every time that podgy little Paki opens Grandpa's wallet . . .'

Mujib? she thought. Mujib is funding all this?

Jenny took the glass from his hand and gave him a hard, efficient hug. Stepped back. Maintained eye contact. 'Poor Brian. Poor, poor Brian. I hadn't realized how desperate things were. It seemed so personal, so angry, but now it all makes sense. Rupert is going to dismantle Broadbent, you know, with the whole of the White House behind him. Try not to get hurt.'

His face broke into a sloppy, lopsided smile.

'I must go,' she said. 'You never know these days who'll be following you. They're always on my back. Take care. Be in touch if I can help.'

She began to speak very slowly, very clearly, as though dictating to a befuddled secretary. 'And all of this is on our usual terms. Another meeting that didn't happen. Secrets.'

'Of course,' he said. 'Not a word to anyone in the world.'

But his eyes slid away from her, and she felt a sudden chill of apprehension. He's a gabby drunk, now, Jenny thought. I have his Mujib secret to carry away. And what secrets of mine has he poured into the ear of some passing companion, some girl who would flatter his memory by listening?

She walked to Paddington station, hunting a taxi. She did not see the man in the raincoat padding in her wake.

Plummer had proclaimed Monday a day of rest. It had been a hectic but entirely satisfactory weekend. His Chicago rally had whipped up a storm. His tribute to Paddy Bordon – 'a true patriot and a fine American traduced by Mark Tate and those seven dwarf spin doctors of his' – had had the hall on its feet, though Bordon, of course, had been told to keep well away. Nate Plummer's men didn't want pictures to go with the words. We're warm human beings, they said. You've got to salute the cleverdick Latino in front of his own folks. But the guy was a failure. Make sure he doesn't go anywhere near a TV camera.

The news of England was great, too. Forrest was on the line, chuckling over the latest polls. 'They're trying to get it together, telling the press that there's plenty of time for the issues to come through. But Warner's going to lose weeks trying to deal with Broadbent, if he can. They can't begin to focus on you yet. And Tate will have to stick out of it for a while because the moment he moves in they hit him with the French connection all over again.'

Plummer ate while he rested. Lunch on the back porch with Jeff Crew. Every candidate's ritual worship at the shrine of News Corp.

'Your people are taking more stick from the Chinks,' he told Crew, waving a spare rib like a baseball bat. 'You need an administration in this country that'll stand up behind you and tell them Orientals where to put their chop suey, messing with our TV stations and fine newspapers bringing them the words of freedom.'

Crew sliced a tomato, very slowly, into fifteen slivers. 'We could certainly do with some help,' he said, trapping a single Bay shrimp in tomato with a spear from the silver fork. 'But it would need to be quiet, discreet. I don't think any of us can be seen to be shouting at our Chinese friends, these days. We want access, they want access. And maybe we could go a little easier on this endless dirge about human rights. Different societies have different ways with self-discipline.'

'Course,' said Plummer, dabbing his lips. 'It ain't a question of posturing, it's a question of resolve when push comes to shove. And what I'm saying to you is, any administration I headed would certainly have that resolve in plenty. If it was our friends who were getting it in the neck.'

'I think we understand each other,' Crew said. He understood which way this election was heading. He understood the importance of calling it right, of getting aboard the winning campaign. The Words of Murdoch were enshrined in a little wooden frame on his desk: 'Don't get mad – get on board.'

Three shrimps later he took his leave. It was almost time for tea. Plummer dozed a while until a violent snore woke him with a start. The front-door bell was ringing again. Next, please.

Jeffreys was wearing a lime green linen suit, trousers wrinkled deep around his crotch, sweat beginning to stain the armpits. Alabama was his idea of hell. If the good Lord had intended people to live in hot-houses, he wouldn't have given Belfast its driving rain and wind chasing in from the sea.

'Seems to me you could handle a pitcher of iced tea,' said Plummer. There were wicker chairs in the garden under a slung canvas awning, and a tall black man to carry the tray. 'My folks heard you at the Tabernacle in Memphis yesterday, sir,' said Plummer. 'They brought me a tape. And, I have to say, you preach one wing-ding of a sermon. All them fires of hell burning, just like my daddy used to tell me. We don't hear too much of that now in this godless country of ours. Rot set in when preachers started going to college rather than communing with the Lord.'

Jeffreys grew red. 'You may not know that I have American qualifications, Senator. A doctorate in theology from the Henry J. Wilks Baptist University, Tuscaloosa. *Summa cum laude*.'

'Don't know of it myself,' said Plummer, swinging his legs. 'But if that's where they taught you about hellfire, sir, then I'll surely put it top of my list.'

Did this puddle of sweat talk politics? he wondered. He wasn't too sure.

'Which party did this brimstone belong to, Nate?'

'Only got one teensy-weensy bit of business with you, Reverend, just one thing it was neighbourly to say straight out with you passing through. I reckon you don't think too much of us Democrats, do you? Reckon we're all called Kennedy and live in Boston and wave incense at Dublin three times a day before we have our grits.

'I just want to say, sir, that that ain't so. We Southerners know a man of conviction with a long memory when he sits on our lawn. You got your battle of the Boyne. We got Mason-Dixon. I don't have no dues to pay in Boston any longer. Those northern liberals have got nowhere else to go. Meantime, President Tate is sucking up to the Irish, promising them all the troughing they lost when he suckered them out of Europe.

'Now, I can't compete with those promises, Reverend. When God hears my prayers every evening, he says, "Nate, if you're going to win, win straight. Treat all the people the same, just like I would if I was down with you, not sitting on some cloud somewhere." And that's my message for you, sir, my message from God. Your folk will get a fair deal from Nate Plummer, no Papist twistings, no whispered confessions, and there's my hand on it.'

'It's been a revelation to share these moments with you, Senator,' said Jeffreys. 'And maybe the Lord would like me to mention the meat-canning factory my flock in Fermanagh remind me of in their own prayers each day.'

Simmons was flying back to Washington that evening. Rupert was due in Idaho on Wednesday. No way out. He couldn't cancel anything else. It would look too much like panic. Polly sat silent as they talked. Jenny came in without knocking.

'A little bird brings big tidings,' she said. 'I know where Broadbent is getting his campaign money from. That slug Mujib. The rich young idiot who bankrolled the *jihad* in Jammu and the Moldavan referendum is paving Broadbent's path back to a Great Britain with hundred-pound notes his dad left in a bank vault in Vaduz. Some bulldog! Land of Lahore hope and Guadalajara glory. We'll have a field day when the press get hold of it.'

'Are you sure?' said Simmons, leaning back. 'Sure enough to get some briefings scheduled?'

'Right on the button,' she said. 'But I wouldn't want this coming back to us too directly. The source is an old chum and I don't want to get him shredded – so it isn't something for a mass session. Let's feed it to one trustie and let her work it up off her own back while we plough on as normal.'

'Her?' asked Simmons. 'You mean Sue Hodkin in New York?'

'Well,' said Jenny, 'I was rather thinking of Julie.'

Chapter Seventeen

It was time, Gross thought, to turn the screw. The Americans had had four days to get their response to Peyerfitte right; instead they'd clung to the crudities Tate had mouthed from some second-class vineyard. That might seem enough in the teeth of an election crisis, a few insults, a little blustering. But the French President was a remarkable television operator, full of warmth, charm and the kind of earnest sincerity that melted hearts, particularly female ones. After the Sorbonne, he'd acted in a few B movies, always playing the young lover, and a TV series called *Pepe En Amour*, which ran for a couple of seasons until the greybeards of Gaullism recruited him to their platforms and made him mayor of Soissons. Now he was the architect of *Le Gaullisme nouveau*, which Gross embraced with enthusiasm. He'd no time for the doddery socialists that France kept electing, wittering about jobs for all and free hay for anyone who called himself a farmer. When the lorry drivers started their juggernauts rolling they just lay down in the road. They weren't proper socialists in Gross's view; they were feeble sentimentalists who had provided constant irritation through his years in the Chancellery. Peyerfitte, thank God, was a modern man with moderately rigorous ideas about welfare reform. A Frenchman he could do business with, and who was already doing British business for him.

They had their second meeting scheduled for that Wednesday; and Gross, leaving nothing to chance, had suggested the Château des Alliés near Verdun, an obscure government-hospitality establishment among the war graves of the last century. 'It has the touch of penance the British like,' he told Peyerfitte. 'None of us think about the First World War. We might as well get up in the morning remembering Agincourt. But the British like to recall these things, and it gives their journalists reasons to use the adjectives they relish so much, which in turn means that they will be there in numbers for our little conversation.'

And there was, indeed, an audience of over a hundred, shivering around the summer house in the château grounds, drinking coffee, interviewing a few passing locals for colour – and waiting. The timetable had been oiled, undramatic. Two hours in the morning. Lunch. Two hours in the afternoon and the briefest of press conferences. It must all be over by four thirty. The Bundeschancellor, they'd been told, had a binding speaking engagement back in Berlin at nine. But now it was well past six, with the wind from the east stripping leaves from the chestnut trees and piling them against the red-brick walls of the garden. Half an hour more. The light was fading. They watched as the curtains in the first-floor conference room were drawn.

The chapel clock rang seven and there was a scurry of movement in the dusk, a roaring of engines. The two German embassy Mercedes raced through suddenly open gates and were gone. Peyerfitte remained on the steps of the château with Juste, his chief spokesman. The President's tie was a little off centre, his hair uncombed, his face white and strained.

'I have nothing substantive to say at this stage.' The words came flatly. 'The Chancellor and I had a useful exchange of views. I look forward to resuming that dialogue at some future juncture. Monsieur Juste will give you such further information as you may need. *Vive la France*.'

He turned back into the house and the correspondent of the *Washington Post* called out to him, 'Hey, Mr President, did you guys have a row or something?'

Peyerfitte swung back for a second and gave a shrug; not just any old shrug, but one that jerked arms and mouth and eyebrows upwards together. An expansive, self-explanatory shrug. The cameras flashed simultaneously. That was the picture.

Juste had nothing as vivid to offer. 'The two leaders enjoyed a wide exchange of views. There was a broad measure of agreement, although one matter remains for resolution. The President is confident that, with better German understanding of the French position, our normal harmony can be restored.'

The *Figaro* reporter had his own sources. 'Gross just walked out,' he told the pack, over Pernods at the café in the square. 'He wanted no concession made to the English. He called it French weakness, which the Americans would use against us. But I am told that our president did not flinch. He believes that the French national interest dictates specific border relaxations. Now the Chancellor has told him that the Germans will veto any movement whatsoever.'

The story, of course, wrote itself. 'Brutal Berlin Shoots Down French Dove. Gross tells Peyerfitte: Freeze out the English, or else.' The editorial writers operated in predictable chorus. 'Who,' asked the *Telegraph*, 'does this latterday German autocrat think he is? The French plan is not perfect, but it recognizes the need for better cross-Channel relations, and whatever President Tate may claim, that must be in the interests of all who live in the British Isles. Stick to your guns, Monsieur Peyerfitte, and you will not find the English people ungrateful.'

Gross put his feet on the desk when the papers arrived and smiled a thin smirk.

Rupert looked out mournfully over the flatlands of Iowa as the plane made its turn into the new concrete stretch of Black Hawk County Airport. The prairies, he'd decided, made him homesick. Alien in their nothingness. O Lord, give me sea and mountains, not corn and creeks and desultory clumps of woodland. And men in jeans chewing gum.

'Remember, even the hogs have a vote,' said Kraft. 'And try to be a bit effusive. Waterloo is as good as it gets around here.

They have a hockey team and a symphony orchestra and a university and a dog track. It's last stop Cultureville USA till you hit Seattle.'

Harris hadn't used a pin when he'd picked Waterloo. For one thing, the name of the place had a few pleasing echoes. For another, the Hanna Memorial Lecture – named after the first settler at this ford on the Cedar River – carried prestige far beyond the state borders. Folks from Wisconsin and Nebraska bussed in for it every year, for high tea and high thoughts. There was a bust of Jimmy Carter, the first lecturer after endowment, on the side of the stage in the brick hulk of the university hall, his bronze face transfixed in a chimpanzee grin.

'A truly wonderful likeness,' said Rupert, and posed beside the monster metallic peanut, running his fingers gingerly through the sharp crinkles of its hair.

The lights went down. 'I know,' he began, 'that the Hannas called this Prairie Rapids City when their wagon train stopped so long ago and found this Promised Land. But I have to congratulate them on their wise and evocative change of mind.' Rupert had to laugh at his own joke. Nobody else had managed even a gurgle. Hell's teeth, this was going to be a stinker. He'd better do the gritty bit for the cameras first, then try to warm them up with a few of his yarns. He couldn't launch straight into the pages of detail on settler patterns from the prairies to the steppes that Harris and a tubby girl researcher in unsuitable pink shorts had concocted for him. That was right off the practical agenda.

'Joking aside,' he said, 'there is one thing I should say about relations between my country, the United States, and the country of Napoleon, France. Like your president, I welcome the new government in Paris's wish for a fresh and more flexible start after the bitterness of the last few years. My friend Mark Tate was right, from the outset, to stress that there could be no deal, no arrangement, that would artificially disadvantage the other citizens of this great land. And right, too, to insist that the

European Union as a whole make its enthusiasm for such flexibility clear.

'But he and I are no Gradgrinds in a bunker. We are enthusiastic seekers after the better life, like the Hannas of Iowa long ago. We have a duty to explore and talk. Which is why, ladies and gentlemen, I am able to announce this very night that Secretary of State Rogerson will be flying to France at the earliest opportunity to bring back what I dearly wish may be a full package of hope and of opportunity.'

There, now! Had that kicked the wretched ball into touch – at least while they had time to regroup?

When he heard the clip on the morning news, Michaelson pottered downstairs and made himself a cup of Colombian coffee, topped with a splash of double cream. By his lights, that was celebration.

They'd spent, at last, the promised hour talking about old Dorset times, gossiping and drinking coffee over Jenny's kitchen table.

How did you first meet Rupert?

'I was duty receptionist, just for a day, at Porter and Price in Dorchester. They were the biggest feed, seed and fertilizer suppliers in the area. My friend Sandra, who usually sat there, had flu. I was seventeen and polishing my nails when someone coughed. And I looked up and it was this big man, really mature, a dozen years older than me at least with a white streak at his temple. I could feel myself coming out in bumps, because our eyes had somehow locked.'

What did he say?

'Oh, nothing at all romantic, I'm afraid. Something like "Do you know where Mr Price left the two sacks of Xylonplus for my pigs?" But he was stammering a bit and I said, "Name, please." And he said, "Warner, Rupert Warner." So I smiled. I knew that name because Daddy was always talking about it after Country

221

Landowners' meetings. It would be young Rupert this or young Rupert that. And Daddy was also treasurer of the local Conservatives and I knew he had Rupert in his sights there too.'

So you clicked from the start?

'Not really. I thought there was something wonderful about him, but he was very much the older man and I was still hanging out with the boys from the technical college. I had a boyfriend called Gary, who mended motorbikes and used to take me to dances in Weymouth at weekends. But then one day I was typing something in the Conservative Club and there was Rupert again and he said, "I know this is an awful cheek, and please feel free to say no, but I was wondering whether you might like to come to the Northcott Theatre with me next week. It's only *Private Lives*, but if you haven't seen it before, you might like it. And perhaps we could have a spot of supper on the way home from Exeter?" So I said yes straight off and that was that. Six months later we were married and Richard arrived on my twentieth birthday.'

You were terribly young for marriage and a family.

'Yes, much too young in a way. I'd got my A levels and was applying to all sorts of universities, but I wanted a year off from books and things. And, frankly, I was keener on Gary's bike than I was at ploughing away through more Spenser or Marlowe just then, thank you very much. So I dropped out and Rupert dropped in. That was how it was. From Yamahas to nappies in eighteen months flat.'

You don't, with respect, sound anything like the feminist role model you've become?

'I was very young. In a sense, I lived my life a different way round. I was a wife and mother first, then I became something else.'

Jenny stood up and switched off the recorder.

'Can we take a coffee break?' she asked brightly. 'There's something I'd appreciate a brief chat about.'

She told Julie about Mujib and the money. 'He's a devil

with more cash than sense. This whole Broadbent thing is his creation.'

Julie smoothed the short skirt over her thighs. 'You got evidence for this?'

'The best. I heard it straight from the heart of Broadbent's camp. I know it's right. The person who told me, an old friend, he wouldn't have invented it. And, anyway, he was too sloshed to invent anything.'

'Will he testify?'

'No. He shouldn't be identified specifically. But that can't be a problem. This is absolutely straight up. Forty million dollars from some sub-continental slush fund keeping John Bull in business. If you write it, they can't deny it.'

She paused and stirred the coffee.

'We're giving it to you because we all rate you. We want to help. This is the scoop of the election, and we think it should be your scoop.'

Julie did not go back to the office. She sat for twenty minutes at a brasserie in the King's Road, drinking half a bottle of acid red Burgundy at an outside table in the autumn sun, head bent into notebook, oblivious of the men who walked by and paused, swinging on their heels, to examine her.

This all came from Carstairs. Of course it did. Who else would be drunk enough to shop himself to an old mistress and, he hoped, a future one? But now she had two stories and two paymasters. She had to place a bet. Stick with the *Mirror*, dish the dirt on Jenny – and she'd be made. If the scam worked and Plummer won. But what if things went awry? She was operating on the edge, not yet even a member of the *Mirror* staff. She could be junked and disavowed in a trice. A hungry, horny woman freelance with too little English experience simply pushing too hard, old boy. Well, we can't have that, can we? Just pack her off home to bed. I'm sure she'll make some lucky chap very happy.

There was nil loyalty in this game. On the other hand, if she played along with Jenny, and Warner and Tate made it to the White House, well, then, here would be one smart, sassy lady with a whole lot to look forward to.

She got up and hailed a cab. Mujib, as every gossip columnist knew, kept a permanent penthouse suite at the Royal Garden. Let's see if she could get a delicate foot – and as much leg as possible – in his door.

The world had changed: there was no more Britain and no more Labour Party. But some things, as September turned to October, did not change. Whatever the name of the party, in whatever the country, there was always a conference for the faithful. This year, Blackpool was back in favour.

Forrest sat moodily in a window-seat on the Accelerated Passenger Vehicle as it ground to its fifth unexplained halt of the journey and examined the grimy platform of Stafford Station. A litter of sweet wrappings; a huddle of dossers on the bench by the café; a moon-faced kid in a leather jacket peeing on the graffiti-covered old statue of Lord Branson behind the left luggage.

It would be his thirtieth conference: as assistant chief organizer of students for New Labour and New Britain; as a press officer at Millbank; as special adviser on presentational matters to the Deputy Prime Minister; as founding chairman of the College Lecturers Association; as MP for Rugeley, secretary of the Reclaim Socialist Values Alliance, right-hand man for Arthur Palmer. Not many laughs there, he thought morosely. And now it was going to be a totally lousy week, as usual. The organizers at the back of the stage white-faced if a word out of place from some unreconstructed idiot gave the GOP press a headline; the rank-and-file, in their cheap cardigans and shark-tooth sports jackets, muttering in the bars and passing interminable motions. Who needed a bloody apology for a rally four weeks from voting day? They should be out on the doorsteps, not boozing and plotting in cheap hotel lounges.

'Pretty nice springboard,' Plummer had said. 'Nothing like a setpiece on expenses to get the gentlemen of the press out in force.' But he could afford to be relaxed: he wasn't coming within six thousand miles of Blackpool – except by satellite to a giant conference screen. Forrest was stuck plumb in the middle, conducting the hairy multitudes with a stick of rock. The rest of the gang had about as much charisma as one of those jellyfish washed up on the town's oily waste of beaches. They could mutter and plot behind his back, organize little rebellions to get their names in the papers. But they carried no burdens. If there was going to be a stand-out speech, he would have to make it himself. 'We are all in need, brothers, and we all need Democratic Labour.' No wonder poor Palmer had keeled over in mid-flow seven years ago. Clutched his chest in the second minute of his peroration then pitched forward, knocking all the state-of-the-art prompter kit into the hole where the electric organ used to be. Fifty thousand pounds' worth of investment and one saintly politician wiped out at a stroke. Arthur was dead before he hit the ground.

The lost leader, half Roosevelt, half Gandhi. The squat saint of modern socialism putting Yorkshire guts back into a party after the decades of smarmy technocracy. Forrest always had to wheel out the adjectives as Conference did its minute remembrance. 'A giant intellect, a giant of a human being. Without him, my friends, we would be nothing, still wandering without roots from one set of so-called pragmatics to the next, still operating without a compass. Arthur Palmer, you gave us back our bearings. We salute you. We stand for a minute, silent.' Thank you and goodnight.

'Well,' said a voice in Forrest's ear, 'slow trains make strange bedfellows. Good afternoon to you, too.'

He knew before he turned. It was Michaelson.

'Get on the wrong platform or something?' Forrest said, half pleased to see anybody who'd rescue him from trying to structure this wretched speech.

'More like the wrong country. At least some trains were on time when Virgin were running it. You travelled hopefully. You knew you might arrive. Expecting the Americans to run this railroad when Lord B's heirs and successors bailed out was always daft. First they closed down their own, and now they're wrecking what's left of ours.'

The APV juddered into life again and moved a hundred yards down the track before resting again beside a large sign with an arrow pointing north. 'Crewe: five minutes.'

'Where were you trying to go?' Forrest asked.

'Changing times.' Michaelson gave a brief, mirthless smile. 'Same place as you. I'm the latest speaking recruit at your conference. Oh, don't worry. I won't come within a mile of the Winter Gardens. It's the fringe of the fringe on the South Pier. Something called the Labour Europe Understanding Group. They only rang last week and wondered whether I could push my Chatham House stuff a bit further for them.'

And so they began to discuss the Peyerfitte proposals.

'Tate's all over the place,' said Forrest, 'and Warner is stuck playing for time. Of course, none of us can get in too deep, too quickly. But I've never thought that that bloody referendum ruled out reasonable relations and I can't for the life of me see why some easing deal would be impossible.'

'What about Plummer?' Michaelson asked.

'He looks like a hick from the sticks, but that's one of the world's great acts. I think if a risk-free chance to get involved came up, something that hurt the President and showed he could get his mind round international relations, then there'd be a real push over the parapet. We're on a roll, but that's the trouble with momentum – you've got to keep rolling.'

For a second the train seemed to take the hint, then subsided.

'We're both grown-up people,' Michaelson said. 'I'm not into party politics any longer. I have the luxury of saying what I believe and working for it. If Plummer can deliver something, then good luck to him. And, of course, I have connections elsewhere too. Should I feel free to give you a private call if the time is right?'

'You can always find me,' said Forrest. Precisely who, he wondered, were these elsewhere fellows? And what time, with what message, would they dream of deeming right?

Warner had wriggled on a breakfast TV couch for ten minutes while a blank blonde read patball questions to him. 'Sir, are you pro-Life?'

'My dear, I believe that life matters deeply to us all.'

'Sir, are you religious?'

'My dear, I belong to the Church of England.'

'And finally, Senator, what would your secret dream for the new England be?'

'Freedom, prosperity, and a cricket bat in every cupboard throughout America.'

Christ, why bother to get up at ungodly hours for this kind of pap? But at least he'd given himself a light day. Nothing scheduled, by insistent request, until the Plymouth rally in the evening. 'I want to call in on Dorset and see the family for a few hours,' he had told Papadopoulos. 'Try and keep the guard dogs down to the minimum. This isn't on any schedule and there won't be mad terrorists behind the bushes. I just need a little time to myself. See you on the Hoe at seven thirty.'

The car drove slowly past Hatty's house. The grey pebbledash was more stained than he remembered, damp blotches hanging like bloated fruit below the window-frames. The yard was still strewn with rusted vans. A scrawny Alsatian on a chain barked as they went by. He had not come to see his sister. There was too much unfathomable bitterness there. She'd said some grisly things to the press when he first became prime minister. One *Telegraph* interview in particular. 'Oh, you could depend on Rupert, all right. When his father was dying you could depend on him sloping back to London and leaving somebody else to clean up the mess.' Now they just sent terse Christmas cards, names scrawled beneath the printed message. Season's Greetings – from Rupert and Jenny.

'Turn right at the end, down to the sea,' he said. Through the sparse bungalows and boarded holiday flats of West Bexington, down to the car park by the edge of the steep, pebbled beach. There was the usual strong wind of October beating off the sea, flecked with rain.

'I'm going to walk along the coast to Abbotsbury,' Rupert said. 'Meet me at the church in a couple of hours.' Bannon and Schultz, little and large, hunched in trenchcoats, got out of the second car, waited as he set out along the puddled track, then plodded a hundred yards behind.

He had not walked the old path for five years. The last time in a different country called Great Britain. Could you tell? The caravans in the field by the white house were bigger, ballooning in chrome. Seth Yates and a bank loan must be trying to find a new market. And the signs along the way were somehow alien, more peremptory. 'No dogs without leads. No fouling. No littering. $500 and upwards fines.' He reached for a toffee in his coat pocket, unwrapped it, then began automatically to flick the ball of paper into the long grass. No. Rupert looked guiltily back at the pair in the distance. They paused and watched him. Bannon was a tidiness freak. Schultz seemed to be glaring into the nether distance. He stuffed the paper back in the top of the packet and turned up his collar.

The churchyard, as he knew, would be wettest and coldest of all. The grave was where? Yes, top left, at the corner of the stone wall nearest to the path down to the village. There were more graves here than he remembered, one with fresh soil and a pile of roses from which the petals had barely fallen. But there was nothing where his father lay, just a small concrete urn with a puddle of water at the bottom. Hatty didn't care for expensive sentimentality.

He stood at the foot of the grave and, for some reason he couldn't explain, took off his pork-pie of a hat, so that the clipped white hair was suddenly lank, wind smeared across his forehead. 'Hello, Dad,' he said. 'I was just popping by. It's been so long and I thought you'd like me to explain. You see, this all started with you. I never know what you'd think of it.'

Schultz, in his beige coat, huddled deeper to the side of the church. 'He's been there for twenty minutes, talking to himself. The guy must be off his head. We'll all be dead of pneumonia by lunch.'

Bannon lit a cigarette in the doorway, puffed three times then stubbed it out on a gravestone and dropped the butt neatly into the envelope he kept ready in his pocket. 'He's always been like this,' he said. 'His father matters to him, and sometimes I think he's lucky. Anyway, he's coming now.'

'We'll go into Dorchester and have a pint and a ploughman's at the Mayor of Casterbridge,' Rupert told the driver waiting under the walnut trees. 'It's just across from the *Echo*. Never hurts to have a cameraman close, I always say.'

'I don't feel right about this any longer,' said Papadopoulos.

'That's funny,' said Jenny. 'Thirty seconds ago you sounded pretty right to me.'

He stood up and pulled a towel around his waist. She rolled over on the bed and raised her head to look up at him, her bare breasts brushing against the crumpled sheets.

'It's just that now I keep thinking of Rupert when we're doing it, wondering where he is, wondering if he knows and what he'd say. I've just got too close to everything. I want to back off for a while. Try to sort myself out.'

'Right,' said Jenny, pulling the red dressing gown around her. 'What is it that I'm supposed to say? Don't call me. I'll call you.'

It was time to end it anyway, she thought. It had become too easy and too convenient. Lacking something. Lacking danger.

Chapter Eighteen

Julie had always lived on the brink, always thrust back on herself. You couldn't be a child in Lagos without learning to cope with that pressure. Your father was away at an oilfield somewhere. Your mother had five kids, and no amount of servants or gates shut against the raucous, vicious world outside could shield you from it. When the car that took her to nursery school stopped at the lights, or because of some new hole in the thin, molten tarmac of the road, boys selling cigarettes or paper handkerchiefs would knock at the windows and the little girl, wide-eyed, would huddle in a corner, praying that the ride was over. There were two things she could do. Live in a nervous terror, or take control. She grew tall quickly. She became a leader. And the Shell postings – to London and then to New York – gradually strengthened her sense of self. She had to make new friends. There was a knack to that. When her father died suddenly, one hot morning in Houston, one minute smiling at his desk, the next prone on the purple carpet she'd helped him choose, there was a choice that was no choice. Back to Lagos and her extended family – the aunts, the uncles, the tribal elders? Or stay and survive? Julie was a survivor.

Storming the Mujib citadel direct, she'd realized on the long lift ride to the penthouse, stopping constantly as fleshy American families struggled in or out with their baggage, was quixotic nonsense. Why should anyone let her in? There must be a better way. She returned to the lobby and begged a sheet of paper from a surly clerk, who looked at her legs and her bright green shirt and automatically, she knew, thought her one of the prostitutes who wandered through the lobbies touting for business.

The Westminster accent submerged the light cadences she'd acquired around the Florida Keys. Another cucumber sandwich, Lady Bracknell?

'I'd be awfully obliged if I could leave this for Mr Khan,' she said. 'Thank you so much.'

He handled it gingerly, with distaste. Like discarding a used condom, she thought. But it was in the system now. 'I know about the way you're funding Broadbent. $40 million is a lot of money. If you'd like to talk about it in total privacy, leave a message with a time and a place.' She had scribbled in the number of a Lebanese banker's Kensington flat. She knew he was in Turkey for a fortnight, getting some loans together. When, briefly, they'd shared a few nights together again last month, she'd taken care to get his answer-machine pin code.

She spent the afternoon at Canary Wharf, fiddling with the piece about Jenny, then dialled to see if any fish had bitten.

The voice, crackling after the bleep, was curiously mannered, Eton with a hint of Wooster. 'Mrs Broadbent, dear lady. Always happy to meet you again. Shall we say lunch tomorrow, at my place, not yours?'

There was nothing to cheer Tate in the polls. The Plummer lead, four weeks to go, had stretched to five points nationally. In England, that was twelve points. The Democrats were back in charge of the South, and California looked increasingly uncertain.

'He's so damned smart,' Simmons said, at the morning briefing. 'He doesn't take chances. He could have gone to Blackpool, but he stays home and makes waves with videos of Windsor Castle and Hyannisport. "I am a man of history in a new nation of history." He can't get away with the Big Daddy mush face to face. If you could pin him on the spot anywhere from Sacramento to Sheffield he'd look like a goddamn parody.'

231

'But he keeps on hitting and running,' said Tate sourly. 'If I can't tag him in the debates, we have to face facts: we're in real trouble. And I won't be able to lay a finger on him when all the shit is about my administration, my record, my economy. That has just got to be turned round, and turned before Baltimore on Tuesday.' He scowled. 'And what the hell is Warner doing? Has that Broadbent guy been trashed yet? Why does that blubber frog keep arriving on my screen playing to the English gallery and winding me up? Goddamnit, Dave, I want some action.'

Simmons could feel a flush on his cheeks. 'We're stretched,' he said. 'And we can't deliver to any kind of schedule. There's a line on Broadbent could sink him fast. But it ain't ready for winding in yet. We may have to pull rank on Peyerfitte – offer him a summit after your re-election or something and try to keep the ball in the stands. You got your Dublin speech on Saturday. You could use that to lower a few lids. But there's no point getting uppity with people who are working their guts out for you, Mark. This is one tight bind. If Baltimore can't deliver, then LA or Dallas will have to. And you haven't even mentioned the one that keeps me tossing at night.'

Tate was calmer, and his face was whiter. 'Which is?'

'Which is Boston a week on Tuesday. The vice-presidential debate we've all been hoping we could find an excuse to cop out from. Madame Santarini and her glugging infant versus Rupert the bumbling Brit. On present form, we've got to go through with it. They'd eat us if we pulled out. But that's one evening I reckon none of us will be going to the movies.'

When Julie rang a woman opened the door. She was short, with cropped black hair, and stout, poured into a curious pill-box of a uniform. She wore white gloves and a leer.

'Broadbent,' said Julie. 'I think Mr Khan is expecting me.'

She was deposited in the first room down the hall. It was small, but stuffed with furniture. She squeezed past the oak desk, with its gold telephone, and the teak coffee table strewn with glossy magazines. The sofa, candy-striped in cream and royal blue, was low and soft, only six inches off the ground. Her skirt rode alarmingly high on her thighs when she sat on it. She swung round with her right knee and crawled upright.

The bullet crop appeared round the door again. 'Sir will see you now, Miss Broadbent. He asks whether I can get you a drink?'

Julie didn't think so, thank you. She had a rule: never take a glass before you know whether the natives are friendly.

She had seen pictures of Mujib. They didn't tell the story.

He was, she knew, just twenty-seven. The hair, swept back, had grey flecks at the temples. The body, in a cricket blazer, was soft, a swelling belly pressing against polished brass buttons. The nose was hooked and brown eyes darted disconcertingly. But it was the skin she had never expected: smooth and sheeny, almost translucent. It made him seem like a little boy atop a body assembled from bits in a tool-shed.

'So, good morning. You are not at all what I expected, Miss . . .'

'Ekpu,' Julie said quickly. There was no point in silly games. He had seen her. Others would put a name to her within minutes. 'I'm a journalist working on the election. For the *Mirror*. One of my sources told me you were funding Broadbent. They gave me a lot of detail. It is obviously a story and I think I could have written it anyway. But the fairest thing seemed to be to put it to you and see what your motives were. You've paid out millions to institutes and electoral trusts, but never to a political movement like this. I know your grandfather tried politics, but he failed pretty ignominiously. What makes you think you can succeed?'

She had seen only the skin, not the room. Now she glanced round. It was five times the size of the antechamber with a window covering the entire wall on the left. Nannies pushed prams through the leaves of Kensington Gardens far below. An orange kite hovered against the sky. That was the only hint of space, though. The oak panelling was lush, dark and oppressive. Pictures in gilt frames bore in on her. Two Renoirs, a Monet, a brooding court scene by Velasquez looming above a sideboard with candelabra. It was a cave. He was Aladdin. The eyes of the powder-white boy prince in the Velasquez were blue and staring. They seemed to follow her.

'Come and relax. Have some lunch. We need to understand each other.'

She sat, gingerly, at the table near the window. He began to speak in a torrent of words, sentences unfinished, his mind skipping back and forth so that she could barely follow the drift.

'I never knew my grandfather, but he had a dream, a dream that lives. He made money from trade. Trade in the world. Trade in food, trade in currencies. But everywhere he went, he saw that the world was different peoples in different lands with different heritages. That was the world that worked. And he saw other men, ruthless people of power with no imagination, seeking to erase that world – to turn it into one vast corporation for their own enrichment. He knew they had to be stopped. When he died, my mother chose me, and me alone, to carry on that crusade.'

'Not your father?' Julie said.

He tapped the tiny silver gong on the left of the table. 'My father was a sportsman who loved his own people, not a politician. He saw only the evil of corruption all around him and he fought it till the great umpire on high called time. But he could not see where that corruption came from, far beyond the borders of our sub-continent. He was a good man of limited vision and he could make no connections.'

Two plates of asparagus tips appeared silently before them.

'When I was a boy, maybe ten, my father took us to Wimbledon, to the tennis. Grandfather had bought us seats behind the Royal Box. At that time I knew nothing of such things. I knew the house in Rawalpindi, the villa in Lahore, the ranch in

Argentina we would sometimes visit. All of them hot and dusty, crowded with chaos, beggars with hands outstretched.

'But Wimbledon was something new, beyond any expectation. It was organized by men in uniforms, beautifully organized, drilling children with a flick of the finger, not throwing stones after them in the street.' The uniform poured them a glass of Riesling. 'Women in wonderful dresses queued for strawberries and applauded girls with golden legs when they hit the ball over the net. There was something about it, something ordered, something certain, which made me feel that the human race did not have to be broken and poor and disorganized. And when the old King came in, with his lady, the consort with the teeth, and they all stood up, applauding, then the message for me was inescapable. I could never forget it. My real world was England and everything that had made it. I loathed the bureaucrats and the loud Americans, with their crude beliefs and intolerances. I despised the Germans, strutting as though they owned the earth. And the slimy Italians, the *petit bourgeois* French, the appalling Belgians with their fried potatoes and boils. My grandfather in death has lifted the blindfolds on my life. If all the people of the world could live like this, I thought, if we could make a Wimbledon of it, then mankind was safe.'

'This?' said Julie.

His hand swept across the window at his side. 'This grace. This order. This England.'

He talked of Broadbent when the lamb chops came.

She talked of Lagos over the wild strawberries, of the grime and the maimed limbs and the palms that must always be crossed. And she smiled and locked his darting eyes.

'This has been such a privilege,' she said. 'I never guessed we would have so much in common. You're not at all what I expected.'

Jenny sat in her darkening living room and drew the curtains. The chill was back in the air. She could hear someone – Schultz, probably – coughing down the corridor. Rupert was in Florida with Bannon for forty-eight hours, addressing two senior citizens' conventions. Research, apparently, had identified some pensioner empathy with him that the White House considered useful. But he'd be back on Thursday, ready to flip down to Brighton for thirty-six hours and the truncated Republican Tory conference that Central Office insisted was necessary. 'No debates,' Governor Groom had decreed. 'Give them a basket and a smile and a stick of candy when they come through the door. We need plenty of speeches from people who'll get twenty seconds' air time.' Currently these included the director of Covent Garden Opera, a thirty-seven-year-old ex-showgirl, who had made four billion from a chain of safe-sex shops, and a teenager with glasses, who'd just got a double first in mathematics and creative statistical theory at Oxford, where he had also been president of the Young Republicans. And, of course, Rupert.

She'd spent the day opening a crèche in Bristol and touring an old people's home in Norwood. Deathly, deathly boring. The baby she'd picked up to cuddle for the cameras had been sick on her yellow suit; the woman who was supposed to be 102 had kept calling her Mrs Thatcher. She felt restless and itchy.

Julie sat in the *Mirror* editor's office. He was growling at her. Getting Carstairs on tape had been good work. Spotting Papadopoulos was very smart. They might confront him when he turned up at Brighton with Warner, try to shake the truth out of him. But it wasn't the story they'd hoped for yet. 'Mrs W has been putting it about for years. We need a list. We need something we can call a dossier. You're in on the ground floor of this, in and out of the house every day. But when we bleep you, you don't call back. There's a deadline we all agree on. The morning of Warner's debate with Santarini. Maximum impact, Julie, and that is six days off. Resources I can give you. But this is your beat, and it's your future.'

No, a voice in her head seemed to scream. There are two

beats and two futures. Did it have to be one or the other?

'OK,' she said. 'Don't take it out on me because your boys at the Washington end have come up scratching themselves. I didn't send the maids to Puerto Rico – or the chauffeur on holiday in bloody Addis Ababa. What we've got so far is what I've got. I'm working my butt off.'

'Oh, I don't know,' said the editor. 'There still seems plenty of it left to me.'

She got up and sashayed out of the door, raising two fingers. Who needed sexist crap from middle-aged white journos with eczema and halitosis?

Tate hugged Marti and ran his fingers through her tumble of red hair. An affectionate, private moment, shared with a crowd of twenty-five thousand.

'You know this little girl?' he said. 'My sweetheart. The mother of my children. When we met twenty years ago at that Lyle Lovett concert just a few miles from her folks' home in Memphis, I asked her the question we all ask our loved ones. "Honey, what's your name?" And she looked me in the eye and smiled, with that dimple you can still see here on her chin. "It's Marti," she said, "Marti O'Rourke."

'Now that's a great name for a Southern belle, ladies and gentlemen. After Scarlett O'Hara, I can't think of a better one. But, folks, my gal isn't something out of a book with a steamy cover. She's got roots as long as those lovely legs of hers. I want you to know that the O'Rourkes came to Memphis from Galway a century ago. They upped and left Ireland five weeks after Great-great grandpappy Billy O'Rourke was killed in the Easter Rising, shot down in his own potato patch. And that's why the woman he loved, the mother of his ten children, Megan O'Rourke, came to be buried deep in the soil of Tennessee. So you see, in turn, my friends, this is coming home for her, and for our kids. And just watch her Irish eyes smiling.'

An exhaustive computer trawl had failed to discover any

remnant of the Dorset Tates who had paused, let alone lived, in Ireland. 'If you're anything at all, Mr President, you're English,' the heritage expert intoned. 'But we can find seventy-three traceable ancestors of your wife, living in fifteen electoral districts.'

'That will have to do.'

And it was doing very nicely. Plummer seemed to have come from nowhere. He couldn't find any family before 1943. Rumour, gently fanned through the seedier tabloids, said that his great-grandma was an Australian nurse who had got banged up in Biloxi by a naval rating on furlough. The Tate briefers made him a Polish chef, vanished without trace after a food-poisoning scare in the Bronx five years later. There was a possible trace to a paedophile called Wiborski, who served ten years in a Detroit prison a decade later, but 'in fairness', as they put it, the Christian names didn't tally and the child molester appeared to have shrunk three inches with age. The Plummer spinners had found a second lieutenant who served with John F. Kennedy and whose golden head was last sighted sinking in mid-Pacific after a kamikaze attack. But since they didn't acknowledge that the candidate was a bastard three times removed, they couldn't make anything very useful of it.

Meanwhile, Heidi Plummer was a Bavarian from Cincinnati. Apparently, she cooked beautiful dumplings. She was not scheduled to visit Ireland during the campaign.

'Marti learned on her mother's knee of the sacrifices in blood that family made in their quest for freedom,' Tate declaimed, eyes raised to the arc-lights. 'Their suffering humbles us all. And it fills me with a passion not just to keep the peace on this blessed island, but to work ceaselessly for a lasting prosperity that gives a new generation compensation for the ordeals of the past.'

Governor Treneman, who knew a promise with a cheque attached when he heard it, cued in the fiddlers and the dancing girls in the green smocks. He began to walk the stage waving his hands, conducting the roars of pre-emptive gratitude as they eddied down the Liffey.

She did what she always did when a story got impenetrable. She went, very slowly, through her notes. She listened to the tapes, pausing from time to time, jotting on a separate pad. Then she poured herself a glass of red wine and did it all over again. The Carstairs stuff was terrific, though she'd have to check where she was on privacy. Before they started turning English law into Americana, she'd have been up before the beak in ten seconds flat. The judges had been high on privacy for twenty years now, ever since Hague v. the *Sun* and the Protection of Personal Information Act that followed it. One silly tale about premature hair loss, and the edifice of the state had finally descended. But that was then – and this was now, with the First Amendment and new sleaze sheets piled high on supermarket shelves. Carstairs had fornicated under one jurisdiction and yacked about it under another. If some politician blew the gaffe in the middle of an election, maybe nobody would stop to worry. But if it was her story with her byline, it was her neck if things got rough. Check, she wrote. Then suddenly stopped the tape and rewound for ten seconds.

Carstairs had been telling her about Jenny, slurring, weaving, but emptying his bilges at last. 'He was downstairs in conference. We could see him on the box. And then she said, "Christ, get out of here. They're breaking for tea – or something." I was scrabbling round for my trousers and you could watch Warner heading our way. Pathetic. That was really the end of it, a bloody farce . . .' The voice dropped and the tape buzzed. He'd got up, she thought, and gone to find another Scotch. Yes. He's tripped against the coffee table and banged his knee. 'Shit, shit, shit.' But he'd said something else, stumbling with his back to her. 'The damned cow. Probably thought she was humming it with me after old Sykesy. Shop people braying habits.'

What the hell . . . ? Julie turned up the volume and played the seconds over and over. Not 'humming', slumming. Not 'shop people', top people. Not 'habits', rabbits. And not, not, not 'Sykesy'. He'd meant Mikey.

Even though the cash was a few grand short of a load, Michaelson loved Triscam Securities. They knew how to look after a non-executive chairman. He had a Rolls and two secretaries (the pretty one with blonde curls and the efficient one with crooked teeth) in an office the size of a tennis court slap over the Thames. He did all his political stuff and his other directorships from here. Unlike the bank, they didn't seem to mind. And he could look along the river as far as Whitehall, see the grey roof of Downing Street nestling in the shadow of the old Foreign Office. He could feel he'd gone up in the world.

'That journalist you said you'd talk to is here,' said the pretty one, when he arrived.

'But remember, you've only got fifteen minutes,' said the efficient one.

Through the open door he could see six feet of sinuous blackness twisting in a sparse yellow dress with a ripple of bare shoulder.

'Right,' he said. 'I'll do the post later.'

Julie had not known which role would work. The wide-eyed girl, awed and giggling in the presence of the mighty, unaware of white silk panties flashing beyond the stretch of thigh? No. He didn't look remotely fatherly. He looked chill and pursed. She crossed her legs and lowered her voice an octave so that it became a curious gurgle, as though always on the point of laughter. She had to be his equal. He would have to come to her.

'I'm grateful,' she said. 'This won't take long. I'm doing a profile of Jenny Warner and I need to talk to people who know her well. You must have seen a lot of the cabinet wives when you were at number ten and I wondered whether you had any special remembrances or anecdotes I could use. I realize you and Mr Warner don't get on, but this isn't a political piece.'

There was something in the way she said 'political' – running it round her tongue, tossing it on her lips like a salad – that made Michaelson feel suddenly on edge. He took off his glasses and began cleaning them with the corner of a blue silk handkerchief.

'I'm sorry, Miss . . .' he glanced down '. . . Miss Ekpu. Of course I saw the wives from time to time, but usually at official functions. I don't think I have anything your readers would find very riveting.'

She smiled and moved her chair a centimetre closer to his desk. 'I'm sure you're right, but could I just mention a few things to see if they jog your memory?'

There was a knock at the door and the pretty one mimed apology. 'Sorry, sir. Marketing have come to collect the Cardiff speech and the numbering seems to have gone wrong. They want to distribute it by lunch and they wonder if you could help them sort things out. We wouldn't have interrupted, but it seems urgent.'

'Well, let's be quick about it,' he said. Julie got up.

'It would be easier outside, sir,' the PA said. 'We've all the sheets laid out on the boardroom table.'

Julie sat down again.

'Forgive me,' said Michaelson. 'I'll only be a minute or two.' He began a rasping mutter of complaint at the good fairy, who seemed to wilt as he reached the door. He shut it behind him.

When she was at college, Julie had wondered uncertainly whether there was any career – apart, perhaps, from prostitution – for which nature had kitted her out. Then she had found herself rummaging through lockers, listening to conversations around corners, instinctively reading other girls' letters over their shoulders. Why? she had asked herself. Do I feel guilty? No. What if I get caught? I won't be. It's just how I am, a curious cat. I'm a journalist.

She stood up instinctively and leaned over his desk. The diary was open. Cardiff, Bognor, Triscam executive. And on Thursday evening, in his own pencil scrawl: 'JW: 9.30. Home.'

The red message button was flashing on the smallest of the phones. His private line? I'm mad, she thought, and pressed Play.

'*Guten morgen*,' said a flat, thin voice she was sure she recognized. 'Our Gallic friend is scheduled for fall-out this afternoon. We need to agree the text. Call me.'

She switched off her own recorder, sat down and opened her pad.

'Well, now,' said Michaelson. 'Where were we? I think of her being very upset at Rupert's father's funeral, crying for minutes on end, snuffling into her handbag. We were all genuinely touched. It wasn't expected, I suppose, that someone so assured, so in control, could feel so much, to be honest, for rather a difficult old boy.'

Tate was walking alone in the Rose Garden, smoking a Camel. He'd given up, at least officially. Last week, in Delaware, they'd sentenced a sixty-five-year-old market stallholder to three years' jail for smoking in a public place. But he, the press said, was an unLucky Striker. Nevertheless, the President had declined his attorney's plea to become involved and the networks' demand for a quote. He cupped the cigarette in his hand and glanced upwards. One camera on one helicopter could puff him away.

And Baltimore had been a bust. He hadn't, the *Post* reckoned, laid a glove on Plummer; and the fact that Plummer had nowhere got the better of him didn't seem to matter. It was the President who was trailing. It was Tate who needed to win. Maybe he would have, if they'd been together on the same stage with one audience. But Angeli, like the two presidents before him, had wanted anodyne contests where no blood flowed. Contact free; content free; risk free. Put the candidates in scattered sterile boxes somewhere, shielded by a nervous referee – and make sure Joe Public doesn't get an elbow within a thousand miles of the action. Angeli had debated in Austin, Texas, on his last outing, with the Democrat in Denver and the panellists in Vermont. Whenever there was anything tricky, he'd waved his earpiece and damned it for dead. At least Tate had got them back in one building. But Plummer was cute. You couldn't pin him with a remote button. You had to see the whites of his eyes.

Simmons came loping over the grass. 'Sorry, Mark,' he said. 'More crap. They threw Rogerson out of the Elysée today. He was due three hours with Simonet, but he got three minutes. And Peyerfitte is on TV now, going apeshit.' He pushed the tiny monitor into Tate's hands and there, indeed, was the President of France, two inches tall.

'We sought to negotiate in good faith, my friends. We reached out the hand of reconciliation and of common sense. But the American secretary did not come to negotiate. He came to dictate and to use our concern for our relations with England as a stick to beat us with. Ladies and gentlemen, that is not acceptable. France is a proud and independent nation. We are not some appendage of the great gods who live in Washington.'

Tate spat in a rose-bush. 'Damnit, I told Bob Rogerson to go easy. Talk softly and carry a big bowl of crap. And Bob's no dummy. He knew that. We were stringing them along. What the hell's going on here?'

'Something stinky,' said Simmons.

CNN had cut away back to Washington and Connie Wan was anchoring as though the Third World War had started at last.

'So, a dramatic outburst from the French President, alleging bad faith and cynicism from the Tate administration. Cy Gunter at the White House, what have Tate's people got to say to that?'

'Sweet nothing, Connie. There is no reaction from the Oval Office. Officially, the President is only just being informed. Unofficially, as one aide puts it, "The frog just shat on our patch." We'll have more for you the moment the White House gets its act together.'

'Thanks, Bob. And from Birmingham, Alabama, we've got Democratic candidate Nate Plummer standing by. Senator Plummer, these are worrying times for the American image abroad. Your thoughts, please.'

'Well, heck, Connie. I just watched Mr Pairofeet and I'm deeply concerned for the people of this country. Seems to me that President Tate is just playing fast and loose with all our futures, going around stirring up some natural allies to get a few cheap cheers from the gallery. If Paris is sincere, we ought to be exploring that with an open heart and an open mind. We can't afford no posturing. That's why, on behalf of the Democratic Party and all our citizens, I'm phoning my own special envoy, former Prime Minister Michaelson of Great Britain that was, as soon as we're finished here, and asking him to go to France on my behalf to see what we, the administration in waiting, can do to repair this damaging whole darned situation.'

Tate dropped the TV on the ground and stamped on it. 'It's a fix,' he said. 'It's a motherfucker of a set-up.'

Julie had been on her way to the coffee machine in Canary Wharf when she saw the crowd watching the television. In thirty seconds she knew who was setting up whom.

His London flat was in Yeoman's Row, a thin canyon of opulence stretching back from the Brompton Road. She arrived with fifteen minutes to spare and stood, huddled back, in the doorway of an old, bankrupt brasserie. The taxi arrived at nine. At nine five the lights on the fourth floor went out. It was ten thirty-five before the woman in the raincoat and headscarf reappeared.

'Well,' said Julie, stepping out beneath the street-lamp, 'what a tiny village this big city is. Or are we both interested in the same man, honey, the same ex-prime minister?'

Jenny pulled the scarf back from her face. It was yellow. 'I can explain,' she said.

'You don't need to. You see, I know. I reckon I know all

about you – with pictures.' She twirled the tiny camera from a string wrapped around her wrist. 'I think you and I deserve a conversation. And maybe something more.'

They walked side by side for a few minutes towards South Kensington and found a dark bar with a booth at the back.

'It was business,' Jenny said thickly.

'You do a lot of business, dear. With Brian Carstairs and Nicky Papadopoulos and Curtis Michaelson and . . . Well, let's not bother about the whole list. It's a bigger cast than the National Theatre and there's no point overegging the omelette.'

'It was Brian, wasn't it?' said Jenny. 'I thought that stupid sot had blabbed to somebody. I didn't guess it was you.'

Julie was ravenous. The burger and fries had arrived and a smear of onion hung from her chin. She wiped it away with exaggerated neatness. 'I'm not into sources,' she said. 'I'm into a deal. You were with Michaelson for the same reason you were always with him. It's the danger that turns you on. Little Miss Goody Two Shoes hanging from the chandeliers. That's the story I was sent to get, and I got it. You took a left down a No Entry, honey. My guys back at the *Mirror*, and the guys who are pulling their strings, they're going to kiss my ass.'

She selected a single sliver of fry and bit through with a click of teeth, as though decapitating it. 'But maybe I don't want them kissing nothing. Maybe I think they're a posse of shites and maybe I like you and that lovely old cuckold who might be heading for a home up Massachusetts Avenue. Powerful friends can be powerfully grateful. Maybe we can still get together.'

Jenny sipped her vodka. 'I never knew quite why I liked you,' she said. 'But now I think I do. You remind me of me.'

Chapter Nineteen

Polly and Groom were sitting in the Chairman's Room in Central Office with tracking poll spreadsheets littering the carpet. The room, like much else in Smith Square, was a heritage site. Tourists in the summer dog-days could take guided patrols through the old edifices of politics past – lean from the same window that Mrs Thatcher had used for her victory wave in 1987 with a video and audio commentary, tour the Major bunker and the Warner war room. The wall of pictures at Polly's back was filled with portraits of party chairmen: Brooke and Fowler and two Parkinsons, arrayed as though in some transplanted Versailles. It was generally considered a very satisfactory five-dollar tour, though qualified guides were becoming ever more difficult to find. There had been an embarrassing correspondence in *The Times* when one, a South African exchange student, had persistently confused Mawhinney and Gummer before a visiting delegation from Botswana.

But in elections the whole building was closed off and the apparatus spread like bindweed. A screen on every desk and a half-eaten chicken sandwich in every drawer, as Polly told her staff when the campaign began.

'Issue wise,' said the Governor, 'we're beginning to make a few tracks. No sale yet, but a few down payments. See how law and order has swung since my fact-finding trip to Texas. The death-penalty pledge was worth ten points and Forrest clearly got it wrong. "Say No to Death Row." That was a gift to the ad boys. Give Plummer enough rope and he'll hang us all.'

Polly wrinkled her nose. 'I'd rather we were doing better on health,' she said. 'Enhanced Medicare is just such a useless pitch. The voters are used to student loans, but operation loans you pay for when you go back to work – that was always going to be a bit of a bummer. You're right over-all, though. There's a balancing out – except where we need it. People still expect us to lose. They're set on change and they simply refuse to think about the consequences. Nobody likes Tate much and he's not begun to puncture that cuddly-uncle stuff Plummer does so well. And Rupert's hopelessly stretched – you can't do Kansas City and Carlisle properly, you've got to find a way of concentrating attention.'

The phone rang and she broke away for thirty seconds.

'I'm off,' she said. 'Foxy is suddenly howling for attention and she says it's urgent.'

Groom put an index finger to his head and mimed pulling a trigger.

Neither of them were founder members of the Jenny Warner Appreciation Society.

She was with Gloria in the Draycott Place bedroom, face caked in cleansing cream, when Polly arrived. She did not wipe it off. The mask, she thought, would be some kind of protection.

'Let's be frank at last,' she said. 'We don't like each other much, do we? You think I'm a bitch. I think you're a clever girl who moons round my husband too much. But we are both, in a way, saddled with him. We have to go along for the ride. Now, I have one or two bits of information that could help us all. But they can't come from me and I can't tell you how I got them. Is that a promise?'

Polly nodded dumbly.

'Item One. There's an article I thought we might arrange to get published.'

It was a thousand words or so long, on three neatly anonymous pages. The heading said, 'Debts, Across the Decades: An

Interview with Mujib Khan, Benefactor Supreme, by H. J. Abana.'

The prose, Polly thought, seemed merely gushing. 'The quiet, unassuming grandson of a great man . . . a shrewd intelligence locked in a cocoon of shyness . . . the Sportsman's Hospital in Peshawar, funded to honour a family memory . . . the rebuilding of Stonehenge . . . the Alamo Foundation . . . a modest intensity and a passion for restoration.'

'It's pretty fair turge,' she said bemusedly.

'Try the top of page three.'

The paragraphs were lightly underlined in pencil.

'And what, I asked him, was his new great project? "Oh, the England that is always in my thoughts and an election which will chart its future."

'He talked of former Chancellor Broadbent and his drive to lift what he sees as an "alien yoke" from the land of Shakespeare and Trollope. "A great nation buried in fear and a great man ready to set it free, a St George poised to slay the dragon."

'But could such a lonely crusader ever break through against the forces of the big parties arrayed against him? His eyes flashed with commitment as he looked at me. "I have given him forty million dollars for his wonderful fight. I shall give him more, whatever he needs to succeed. Mr Broadbent is my friend. He must lack for nothing."'

Polly sucked at the air. 'Christ,' she said. 'If this is true, we've got them cold.'

'Oh, it's true, all right. I have the tape. And Item Two's on tape as well.'

Jenny played the clipped sentences of Gross once, then again. 'There's a date and time,' she said, 'four hours before Peyerfitte threw Rogerson into the street. And there are certificates of authentication from the best three experts I could find. They'll swear in court that that's our chum the Bundeschancellor and nobody else. So, we've two grenades in one handbag, my dear. I was wondering how we should pull out the pins.'

*

248

The editor of the *Austin Bugle* was an Army chum of Simmons'. They'd served together in the Marine Corps, mopping up with the French Foreign Legion when the Sons of the Sandinistas had tried to storm St Bart's and held twenty American millionaires hostage in a compound at the Hotel Toiny. Dave had got a chunk of shrapnel in his knee. The editor had got food poisoning from some leftover lobster. They found themselves in adjacent beds in the Anse de Toiny Beach Hospital. They were mates for life.

'That article you sent,' said the editor doubtfully, 'it's not much of a read. I mean, this Khan guy ain't exactly big here down on the Gulf.'

'I'm not asking you to put it on the goddamned front page,' Simmons said. 'It's a feature. Stick it away on page ninety-seven with the shopping news and cheesecake recipes. I just want to encourage the author, bring young talent along, that sort of thing. It would mean so much to her to get something in print.'

'Well,' said the editor, 'I don't suppose it'd hurt.'

'And not a word about me, old friend. I just wouldn't like to turn out the public Good Samaritan in this.'

'You mean you still haven't told Mark?' Polly asked.

'Nope,' said Simmons. 'He's got LA tomorrow and he's all fired up for it. If I start feeding him little tales about the mysterious Mrs W and her unmentionable pals, he'll take his eye off the ball. We've got to start tagging Plummer head to head, whittle him back on the things folks care about. Then splat! We can start spreading the shit.'

Polly looked at him, greyer, more grizzled, the limp more pronounced, the strain around the eyes wiping away the relaxation he strove so hard to maintain. This was our idea, his and mine, she thought. We did it together, and now we must finish it together. We started with two nations and two problems and we made them one. And we became one at the same time.

She reached and ran her fingers across the furrows on his brow.

'See, I keep telling you, sugar,' said Simmons, barely seeming to notice, 'you win when you've got one damned thing following another. That's what we country folks call the Big Mo, honey.'

She had flown to Washington for the day: to be accurate, for four hours. She looked out of the window through a mist of rain and saw the leaves piling the Georgetown streets. 'Since we're on the subject, sir,' she said, 'how's about a Little Mo?'

Three in the morning. Jenny was watching the Tate and Nate Show, episode two. Rupert wouldn't be back from Derry before ten, and a long day of Harris and Kraft rehearsing him for the Boston debate. 'Funny trip,' he'd said, when he called. 'Whole afternoon sucking up to the Nats now that Jeffreys has done the contrary thing. They asked me if I'd lay a wreath on Gerry Adams's grave. Said I'd prefer tea and a bun somewhere else, if that was all the same by them.'

Tate seemed to be doing better this time. And Plummer looked a bit subdued. They'd started on state sales taxes. 'Let us put this in perspective, Senator. It's a question of degree, not principle. But where do you stand on your party in Scotland's policy? Do you endorse their last raft of tax rises? Or do you think that they went too far, killing jobs and initiative? For, Mr Plummer, if you think the latter, then why are you promising them bigger federal hand-outs if you should ever come to power? I reckon you must think all good Democratic states can load up their taxing on honest citizens and get a round of applause.'

There was stumble and a mutter outside her door. She pulled the strings of her nightdress tighter. 'Who's there?'

'I'm sorry, ma'am. It's only me, Gloria. I left my pills in my coat downstairs. I didn't mean to wake you.'

They had been trying dresses for the Boston trip late after supper and Jenny had suggested the stop over. 'There's no point trekking back to that hotel when we've got to get moving again at eight.'

'Come in for a second and see how Tate's doing. I think we're scoring a few shots,' she said now.

Gloria was wearing a grey T-shirt. The blonde hair was frizzed from sleep and bobbed chaotically as she walked. The long golden legs moved uncertainly over towards the bed.

'It ain't a question of approve or repudiate, Mr President,' Plummer was saying. 'It's a question of the resources needed to help folks pay for a better life.'

Gloria sat beside her on the quilt.

What the hell? Jenny thought. She'd run out of men: drunken men, manipulating men, nervous men, stupid men. She ran her fingers very slowly along the stretch of Gloria's calf, pausing, stroking, then up the taut expanse of thigh.

Tate was back on the attack. 'The Senator has to be clear one way or the other. Leadership isn't about trimming. Leadership isn't having it both ways. Leaders have to choose.'

'Oh,' Jenny murmured. 'I'm not sure about that.'

Sandlewood could feel the ache in his bladder again, the prostate problem his doctor said would kill him within twelve months unless something else went first. He squirmed in the deep leather of the Garrick Club chair.

'So, this is the day,' he said.

The *Mirror* editor looked down at the bag of bones and the green parchment skin, trying to wipe the repugnance from his face. 'Got to be. Our friend here is calling the shots.'

Forrest slapped the arm of the sofa. 'No question. We need to hit Warner hours before his debate, so he hasn't time for damage limitation. Then Santarini can do the full moral bit – sympathy, restraint, but shock deep down for a family betrayed. It's her A1 script. She doesn't need to be told. Just naturally she'll make the poor old dud look like a fool.'

The editor had spent the morning with Julie, working on her

intro. It was good enough now, in his opinion, though still longer on adjectives than the killer facts he'd hoped for. The house lawyer, to be frank, had been a bore. An 'amazing chronicle' of infidelity involving the Senator's wife in affairs with his senior colleagues and aides was, at the margins, OK – if they could count on no instant writs. But mentioning Papadopoulos by name without putting it to him was dangerous, and the account of the night visit to Michaelson brimming with risk. 'Carstairs, yes,' said the eagle, ticking the text. 'The quotes carry it. But the others have got to be Mr X and Mr Y. You can say you're protecting their privacy.'

Forrest laughed. 'Thank God for our responsible press,' he said. 'And, anyway, this will do the trick. She won't be able to laugh off Carstairs. That quote about the kitchen table at Chequers is classic. It's when the bread knife falls on the floor that breaks me up.'

'Just one snag,' said the editor. 'We have to go to her for a quote. Normally we'd do that around eight tonight, just before the edition goes, so she can't try any legal hanky-panky. But they're flying to Boston at seven. We'll have to risk an approach around five before she heads for the airport.'

'That's your business,' said Sandlewood. 'I can't see it can be a problem. You don't find judges hanging around their chambers much after tea-time. But if you're worried, maybe we could all join in the fun?'

'Why not?' said the editor. 'You're both invited. I'll fix the management's back elevator for you and a key to the chairman's office. A seat in the stalls for one thrill-packed night only.'

They were listening to the intercom when the night news editor did her stuff.

'Mrs Warner. My name is Myra Smedley from the *Mirror*. We're running a story tonight about your love affairs with Mr Carstairs, Mr Papadopoulos and Mr Michaelson. Please don't deny anything. We have the proof. Our lawyers are fully satisfied.

I know you're just about to leave the country, but my editor thought, in fairness, that we should ask you for a comment.'

There was not even an intake of breath. 'Do thank your editor most warmly,' said Jenny, 'but I'm not going anywhere. I'm downstairs in the car park. Indeed, I watched Lord Sandlewood and Mr Forrest go up to his floor only twenty minutes ago. Would you be so kind as to let them all know that I am on my way up?'

Forrest's eyes were staring; a thin dribble of saliva edged from the corner of Sandlewood's mouth. 'She's coming to plead with us,' he said. 'I suspect it will all be rather entertaining – and most satisfactory.'

'Better get a snapper in,' said the editor. 'This looks like a photo-opportunity.'

'Gentlemen,' Jenny said, bustling through the door, bosom puffed in attack formation, 'how nice to find you together.'

She was wearing a royal blue coat of spun silk with a red pill-box hat and a white scarf. There was a single star on the hat and a matching star on the left hem of the skirt. It had been specially designed for Boston airport.

'I'm not going into details of what you've been doing. But I have them. I can prove them if necessary. I just wanted to use the best arguments I have not to make them public in a manner we could all regret.'

Her shoulder bag, of course, was red, white and blue. She delved inside it and tossed a handful of photographs on the table.

The editor picked them up, looked and passed them on. Nobody spoke.

'Quite,' she said. 'It's another of my little romances I'd not wish made too much of. It only lasted for three months or so. But we were very happy for a while. See the one in the boat? That was Lake Windermere, just before the conference in Blackpool when he abolished the national executive committee. And the one with the gondola. How about the Venice Socialist International,

Neil? Were you there? I can't remember. But he made such a good speech.'

Sandlewood picked up the photographs and tapped them together, as though they were a pack of cards. 'I thought Arthur Palmer told me everything,' he said. 'He never told me about you.'

'Well, that can't be helped, can it?' she said gaily. 'Into every life a little relevant information must eventually fall. I didn't betray him. He didn't betray me. What business was it of anyone else's? But let me make a wild guess. You intend to make me look a whore and a hypocrite, having it off with Rupert's colleagues wherever and whenever they chose to pull their pants down. O.K. I'm not the Virgin Mary. I am what I am. But, gentlemen, this has nothing to do with politics. You think you have me in a corner. Fine. Then I have nothing to lose. But the sodding Labour Party isn't going to keep its patron saint and his holy tales of Accrington intact. We made love in the back of his Rover in Hindle. We put the sex back into socialism. And, if you want to see his memory turned over, if you want Mary Palmer made a laughing stock, blubbing away on some lousy newscast, sniggered over on every flyblown talk show, then just go ahead. Try me. But don't reckon on winning.'

She turned and walked to the door, then turned again. 'Keep the pictures,' she said. 'I've plenty more.'

They sat silent for a moment. The editor got up from his desk and walked round to face Forrest. 'It's edition time,' he said. 'I've got five pages of background in my queue. What do you want me to do?'

'Sit down, you silly little man,' said Sandlewood, hissing as the wind from his stomach whistled through his teeth.

The wizened gnome of a staff photographer, hovering by the bookcase, coughed as though to signal his continuing presence. 'Will there be anything more, gentlemen?' asked Shorty Maddox, grinning through battered teeth. 'Do you fancy a few mug-shots?'

*

Polly flew to Boston with them. It seemed the surest way. Jenny sat at the back of first class with an eye mask and a large Martell, Schultz across the gangway reading a battered paperback edition of *1984*. Polly went over things with Rupert, and over again, till he nodded. 'Got it. By Christ, I think I've got it.'

When they landed, Groom had been holding his London press conference for twenty minutes. He had flourished his copy of the *Austin Bugle* and read his script. He was horrified to discover such astounding news about foreign funding of an English campaign in, of all places, a Texas newspaper. He was shocked when a tape transcript, delivered by loyal party workers in Austin, showed no dubiety and no misquotations. Mr Khan was proud to be feeding $40 million from his bank accounts in Dubai and Zurich to allow Broadbent to play Johnny Patriot. Well, foreigners did not know our ways. 'But, Mr Broadbent, you're no foreigner. You want to get your fingers on our cash registers. And to cover such funding in secret shame reveals you as a hollow politician, pursuing an unscrupulous cause.'

The agency boys were waiting for Rupert in the airport lobby.

'I'm both angry and distressed,' he said. 'I worked with Broadbent and Brian Carstairs for several years. I took them to be real loyalists, toiling with me in the best interests of the English people – and now that the English people are the American people, I believed such patriotism endured. Alas, the facts confound my hopes. The Governor of England is not the Governor of Pakistan. We are electing a president and vice-president of the United States, not the United Arab Emirates. Of necessity, I call on Mr Broadbent to renounce such tainted gifts and to pledge his loyalty to the one flag that matters most to us all, the Star-Spangled Banner.'

'What's Mr Toad saying now?' Polly asked a man from Reuters.

'Sweet zilcho. His campaign team have called in the auditors. They say they can't comment until they receive a full report, which needs time to gather all the blah and set it in blah-blah context.'

'Great,' said Polly. 'One more down, and one to go.'

Crew reached across the pine canyon of his desk and picked up the phone. The consultants had been clear enough. 'A small man needs a small desk. It's the reduced disparity syndrome,' the bossy redhead from Vassar insisted.

'No,' Crew had replied. 'Little men like big things around them, sugar. Would you like to see some of my big things?' He'd grinned and reached for the top button of his pants. She had fled, squeaking.

He called London. 'Walter. Pass it on to the others. They're not to go overboard for Plummer at the end. Repeat, not. No, I know what I said. I'm not saying that now. Are we backing Tate, then? No, Walter, we're backing ourselves.'

Harris and Kraft had been smart, Rupert thought. They'd steered the Veep debate away from TV studios and coated it in history. This wasn't the Quincy Market he remembered from his boyhood, a riot of T-shirts and tourist trash. Now, the stalls sold terminals and modems and the whole damned electronic thing. Whether you came from Shanghai or Salt Lake City, you could wander from counter to counter – calling home, seeing Mom cook dinner in her kitchen, accessing the world. The banner waved in the breeze off the Charles river. Bill Gates Memorial Park, Boston's Biggest Net Asset. But at least Faneuil Hall still stood stiffly aside.

'We want the Old State House,' Harris had said. 'We want you for a photo-op on the balcony where they read the Declaration of Independence. That way you can resonate.'

'And,' said Kraft, 'the hall is just perfect. You sit slap in the Cradle of Liberty, paying tribute to all the founding fathers. That way you can wave your hands about.'

'Get the symbolism,' said Harris. 'The ultimate reconciliation in the bosom of the American Revolution. You're not saying sorry, you're saying things have moved on. And it don't matter that you're a bit long in the tooth. Our focus groups reckon that might be an advantage here.'

'Not to mention,' said Kraft, 'that the stage is bound to give Santarini the shakes. She'll be so high up that anyone in the first three rows can see her panties. The body language implications are all A1.'

It was, though he said it himself, going splendidly. He felt wonderfully relaxed. The old hall reminded him a little of the Athenaeum in Pall Mall, green and grand and fixed in time. When he opened, it was like an after-dinner speech without the port. Santarini sat hunched with her hands on her knees. The red dress was an awful mistake. On the monitors she looked like the Italian flag. And, in these surroundings, she didn't sound right either: shrill and grating, complaining that hubby was late home from the country club again, that the chicken had died waiting in the pot. 'What's more,' she chafed, 'President Plummer and I will bring you more than prosperity at home. We'll bring you peace abroad. Not just a peace where our boys, our great American soldiers, aren't shot at or spat at in every third-rate nation on this earth, but a diplomatic peace, too. We believe in working with allies, not roughing them up. We shall repair the bridges with France so crudely destroyed by President Tate and Senator Warner. Ex-Prime Minister Michaelson, on our behalf, has travelled to Paris, France. His personal report, delivered today, sees no reason why a fresh start should not bring dividends to Americans and French alike.'

Rupert coughed and reached inside his waistcoat pocket. 'I hesitate to disillusion Senator Santarini,' he said, with all the exaggerated humility he could muster, 'and I have no wish to be the spectre at this feast of inexperienced aspiration. But could I just ask my young opponent what she thinks of this?'

He produced a tiny recorder. He played the curt gutturals of

Gross. She joined her hands beneath the knee and pulled them towards her, retreating briefly into some womb of certainty.

'I'm afraid,' Rupert said, 'that there we hear the Bundeschancellor issuing instructions to Candidate Plummer's so-special envoy a few brief hours before the French President and co-conspirator publicly humiliated Secretary of State Rogerson, a fine servant of this great country. I am afraid, and can prove, that we have all been the victims of what can only be described as a plot by outside powers to interfere in this election and covertly to suborn the American people. Now, dear me, we can't have that, can we? We need men and women who know the ways of the world to protect us from such tawdry manipulation. Don't you agree, Senator?'

Her face had changed to match her dress.

Suddenly, at the back of the hall, a baby began to cry.

Chapter Twenty

Tate had wanted them to be in Washington on election night.
'Win or lose, we ought to be there together. If we go down, it'll
look like we're hiding. If we win, the media will want one big
happy family.'

'No,' said Polly. 'I'll have to be in Leeds, through the day at
least. And Rupert must be over here. It won't feel right otherwise.' Simmons understood: he fought her corner.

So Rupert spent a day choked with roots and photo-
opportunities. The morning was Mountsorrel, a grim Leicester
commuter village hacked apart by old granite mines, five miles
north of Birstall. His grandparents and a clutch of Warners were
buried there in a cemetery that stretched back from the road
and edged gently up a green hillside.

He left Bannon and Schultz hunched in the crematorium
doorway and walked slowly up the hill to the patch on the left
where the graves clustered in a forest of crosses, and posed
against the skyline. Then he headed, for a while, into the fields
beyond, a solitary figure walking to the very edge of the granite
slurry. It was an eight-column job.

In the afternoon Jenny joined him. They had tea at Abbotsbury
Tropical Gardens, shivering in the cold, and a moderately happy
hour at the Mayor of Casterbridge with assorted yokels as
the cameras flashed. Then Chelsea as the long night began.
'Vice-Presidential Candidate Warner spent the evening at
home with his wife,' Independent Television News reported.
'They ate carrot soup and beans on toast on a tray. It is, the

Senator told us, a time for modest meals and for modest reflection.'

Two in the morning. The exit polls were winding down, the results emerging. Plummer took New Hampshire and Vermont. But Tate took Florida. Plummer had Alabama, of course. Tate, beyond expectation, had Mississippi and Tennessee. Then Ireland. Then, by a majority of ten thousand, Ulster. 'Truly amazing,' said the EBC anchorman. 'That's the first time they've agreed about anything in three hundred years.'

'More than that,' said the political editor. 'It's the moment London has been waiting for over centuries. There aren't enough Protestants to deliver any longer. The Catholic birth-rate would seem to make them the majority rulers now. You could say the Irish problem has turned over and gone to sleep.'

Two thousand irate callers had jammed the switchboards within sixty seconds.

Rupert poured himself a last Glenlivet.

'Let's get down to the Hilton,' he said. 'I think we're going to do it. I can smell it in the wind.'

'Of course,' said Jenny. 'Once the tide turned, I knew you'd come through. Whatever Tate says, this is your victory. He should be down on his knees thanking you.'

'Us,' said Rupert elliptically.

Plummer put his fingers in braces and wandered on to the porch. The cameras were like fireflies clustered in the black Alabama night. 'My friends,' he said, 'this may strike you as pretty darned peculiar with only twenty per cent of the votes in. Nevertheless, here's one good Southern boy who knows when the barrel's running dry. We came near, but not near enough. What pulled us down? Unforeseen circumstances. Can't do nothing about them, cos you can't foresee them. So I'm conceding. Might as well get a decent sleep for you all tonight rather than hanging round pretending and looking brave. I wish President Tate and that tricky old Englishman everything they wish me, and then some. The President's reward will be four more years in the Oval Office. Mine will be in heaven.

'Thank you. The Lord bless you. And stick around and keep the faith. You never know, you might see me next time.'

He pulled the braces forward, then let them go with a hollow thwack on the rippling expanse of his belly.

Jenny turned off the set. 'It's time to go down to the ballroom,' she said. 'Brush your hair, tuck your shirt into your trousers and try not to look so damned exhausted.'

Rupert opened his flies and wriggled uncomfortably, tugging the bulge of the shirt below sea level. Where, suddenly, had all the old enemies gone?

Broadbent to oblivion. Two per cent of the English vote. That was the Europe argument buried. Forrest to a struggle for survival. There was enough evidence to tie him in with Michaelson. Weeks ago the affable Mr Crew's *News of the World* had snapped them deep in conversation on some railway train or other. What had they been talking about? Forrest couldn't explain. And Gross? The Germans, it seemed, had a sense of humour after all. They were laughing at him. He scowled and he snarled, but they laughed as his fingers stuck in the cookie jar: they laughed and laughed as his ratings tumbled. He was not long for this political life.

'God smiled on us,' Rupert said. 'Heaven alone knows where those tapes came from. It was magic.'

She pushed him through the door and down the long hallway to the great room of revelry.

Tate's speech was longer than Plummer's, and rather sourer. They watched it on the giant screen in the ballroom, so that the once and continuing President loomed over them, five metres high.

He was glad, Tate said, that a hollow candidate leading a hollow campaign had thrown in the towel so fast. 'I guess he had to get out of town before folks caught up with him.' He was pleased to be back in the White House for four more glorious years. 'I want to finish what I started and I'm glad you recognized that was necessary.' He was looking forward to business as usual. 'Fact is, I just fought my last election. I don't have to worry about that stuff any longer. I can get on with serving the people of this great nation full time.'

There were, and Polly was counting, just two mentions of Rupert. But always as though he were some appendage, as in 'Tate–Warner believes in making sure that the workers work.' And she didn't catch a word of thanks or a sniff of a tribute. At the edge of the big screen, she could see Dave looking at his boots.

'Some bloody big ego all of a sudden,' she muttered to Jenny. 'I'd hoped he'd be a bit inclusive. You'd suppose that Boston hadn't happened. Or the other thing.'

Jenny laughed thinly. 'No surprise,' she said. 'Rupert always thought we were just a means to an end. And he doesn't mind that. He knows we're on the celebrity circuit for a while, and nothing else. Tate drew up a pretty tight prenuptial contract.'

There was a cheer and Rupert, face red, puffing gently, climbed on to the stage. He thanked the campaign managers, the team, the family. 'But most of all,' he said, 'I want to thank you, the people of these islands. We are inveterate adventurers. For centuries we sailed the world, discovered the world – setting our flag and our civilization ashore wherever the ships found land. Now, another great adventure is nearing its end. Now, a different flag is planted. And, as my captaincy is sealed in history, new sailors with new spirit must begin to take the helm.'

Polly found a tear trickling down her cheek, and wiped it away almost angrily. Gloria, bronze flesh straining free from minute black dress, teetered to the middle of the dance floor, waved to the band and began to dance. She put her hands on Papadopoulos's back and propelled him forward. He tagged Harris and Kraft and Schultz, and within thirty seconds there was a caterpillar of celebration jolting around the room. Jenny joined in behind Gloria. Rupert stood on the stage and flapped his hands together in genteel approval.

Suddenly Polly felt a little faint. She leaned back against the trestle table piled high with champagne bottles and looked up towards the screen again. Tate had disappeared somewhere, working the crowd.

Dave stood alone in vision, looking out towards her. We've done it, she thought. I'm not a nanny and a nurse any longer. Nor a favourite daughter. Maybe I can begin to get on with the rest of my life?

The last suitcase lay open on the bed. Jenny pulled out the top drawer of her dressing table and carried it over, pouring the pile of panties and brassières on top of the dressing gowns and nightdresses. Julie stood by the window, face turned politely away from the squalor.

'Well?' Jenny said, fishing a bra from under a pillow. 'It's a good offer with great prospects. Press secretary to the Vice-President's wife. Eighty thousand dollars a year, all the free lunches you can eat and a contacts book to die for. And I can't imagine the *Mirror* will be back with a big bid.'

Julie watched the black cars changing shifts in the street below. Bannon was taking a couple of days at home in Dorset; Schultz, white skull gleaming beneath the thin, oily streaks of hair, was back on watch.

'Thanks a lot,' she said. 'But, no, I won't be coming. In fact, I'll be getting married.'

Jenny turned wide-eyed. 'My dear,' she said, 'this is so sudden and, frankly, so unexpected. Congratulations. Anyone I know?'

'Sort of,' Julie said. 'He's a lovely, trusting man. Like Rupert, I suppose. Though not as bright. He thinks we're perfect together and that we'll make a wonderful team.'

'Heavens, it doesn't sound much of a love match. He must be very rich, darling.'

Julie smiled her widest smile. 'Meet the first Mrs Mujib Khan,' she said.

'I do solemnly swear that I will faithfully execute the Office of President of the United States. . .'

It was noon on 20 January and flurries of snow mounted desultory attacks on the western walls of the Capitol Building. Tate seemed hunched somehow inside his grey mohair coat, hand raised in surrender more than affirmation.

Rupert edged further behind him, out of the Arctic wind. The families were at the back. Mimsie, in a powder-blue parka, kept chattering and smiling, flashing her braces and giggling when the cameras clicked. The governors sat shivering at the side: Treneman smiling, Jeffreys glowering, Angus and Mills lost in their own thoughts, another loser backed too hard, another stretch of bridges scheduled for rebuilding. The crowd in blacks and browns, with only a few flags waving, stretched as far down the hill as the eye could see. It was, the forecasters had said, the coldest Inauguration Day in recorded history, with a 95 per cent chance of blizzard conditions.

'Jesus,' said Tate, swinging round from preserving, protecting and defending, 'if I'd have known about this motherfucking freeze-out, I might have stayed in Maine.'

Rupert's nose began to run again.

At the back of the podium, Polly wrapped a second scarf around the neck of the small, grey woman who sat beside her and squeezed her hand.

'Well, Mum, you said you wanted a difference.'

The fingers on the hand she held began to drum insistently. 'Yes, dear. But how long is this going on? It's perishing, and my stomach's playing up something awful. If I don't eat something every three hours, there's the devil to pay.'

Some things, Polly thought, would never be different.

*

She was furious. She took a step towards him and seized his shoulders as though to shake his head loose. 'What do you mean, new offices?' she said.

'I mean, the ones at the back of the press complex I've been given while the old ones are refurbished,' Warner said patiently. 'It's perfectly simple. The plaster was rotten, they said. The pictures of the Navy secretaries kept falling on the floor. Would I mind moving? How could I refuse? The Pierre Salinger suite is quite comfortable enough, and they have absolutely promised they'll clean the carpet.'

'How are we supposed to entertain the President of Mali in a grubby little box with coffee-stains all over the desk?' Jenny howled. 'And when the bloody hell will the sodding refurbishment be finished?'

Rupert shuffled backwards. 'There isn't exactly a date. It's all wrapped up in a White House funding package that Congress hasn't cleared yet. And Dave says anyway that Mark may want the suite for his Food Hygiene Task Force if the Reafforestation Task Force hasn't shouted "Timber!" by Christmas. He thinks maybe I'd be better staying where I am. It's really quite ample, you know. Not as though I'd got a vast staff or anything.'

He was out at Dulles, waiting for the plane from Mali. Three hours late, they said. Traffic congestion over Jamaica.

She had gone back to Georgetown. 'I'll check on the pipes,' she said. 'Nothing freezes in Puerto Rico and Maria's so bloody stupid anyway.' She took Gloria. 'We can work on the wardrobe for Paraguay,' she said loudly. 'I don't want anything too flashy if they're all wearing ponchos.'

Gloria undressed quickly and leaped under the duvet, goose-pimples puckering across her buttocks. Jenny scattered the panties and slips across the floor. She touched an upright nipple with her index finger and wiggled it cautiously, waiting until the implants began to wash back and forth in a contrary direction so that Gloria's breasts seemed a tide of pleasure on the turn. 'We've ninety minutes at least,' she said, raising her watch. 'Let's take our time.'

The man in the black car outside turned up the heater and reached for his headphones.

Chapter Twenty-one

It was six in the morning, and the sun was already strong enough
to begin etching the canyons and buttes and creeks in shadow.
The Utah sky bore no trace of cloud. The air carried an early
bite of chill, but soon that would be gone.

Bill Angeli had been awake for two hours. He had never
needed sleep; now it passed him by with barely a nod. He thought
of the library in St George that would be opened next week,
his papers, his effigies, the transmuted Oval Office where his
memory might work for ever before threading crowds of school-
children. A great day coming. His return to the sun, with the
magazines and bulletins full of his face and his record once
more. He missed that searchlight of attention. Opening rodeos,
playing rounds of charity golf, after-dinner speeches on the Elk,
Moose and Rotary circuits, long evenings drinking bourbon
with Tug Bonham or working on his autobiography with a thin
girl ghost writer from Denver who insisted on calling him sir
. . . What did it all amount to? Just a leftover life to kill.

Angeli got up and pulled on a thick woollen shirt. The ranch
was barely stirring. Sturgess, his bored bull of a security detail,
still slept, curtains drawn, in the little room over the stables. He
left him a note, as he often did, climbed into the Jeep and eased
it quietly out of the yard. Gone to Zion. Back in a couple of
hours.

The road wound through the foothills then turned sharply
towards the mountain range. He passed the ranger station and
waved to Cy, standing pensive by a water fountain, sucking a

straw. This was not the month of the crowds. A handful of campers were out, washing in the river, wiping away the bleary remnants of the night before. A pair of rock climbers stirred high on the yellow canyon walls.

He parked where the valley suddenly turned to a winding slit and wandered through the last trees before Zion closed around him. The snows were melting. The waters were high and foaming.

Angeli stood on the thin ribbon of rock looking down. It was his favourite place in all the world, where he had come sixty years before, with Ted and Maurice and Franco, the kids from the mall; off the leash, bathed in their own imagination. They'd splashed and laughed and swapped grubby pictures and masturbated together. Their world was the enjoyment of innocence.

He looked up to the sky and put his right hand to his left arm.

Suddenly the pain gripped him, bands of hot wire pulled viciously tight across his chest. There was no time to cry, no time to think: just pain wrenching him apart. He pitched forward into the river, dashed face down in the foam, and was carried from sight, body tossed from rock to rock.

It was almost noon when the sweating man in the green check shirt and the two little boys who trailed behind him walked up from the valley and paused at the mouth of the canyon.

'Daddy, I'm so thirsty,' wailed the four-year-old. 'I wanna Pepsi or I ain't going a step.'

'Yeah,' said the six-year-old. 'You didn't say it was going to be hot, like baking.'

This was not the call of the wild he'd intended. 'In the wilderness,' the man said, 'you drink water or you don't drink at all.'

He left the narrow path and headed through the green marsh of meadowland to where the river ran, pulled a tin cup from his knapsack, bent to scoop it full. And there below, looking up at him from the water, was a face he had seen a thousand times, but now battered and bleeding, the mouth of death open, choked full of weeds.

'This is bizarre,' said the man in the green check. 'This is goddamn stinking eerie. Boys, go run back to the ranger station and tell them to come quick. Your daddy's found the President – just like he found the President's old pa ten years back, when he was pumping gas.'

The memorial library was white marble with Grecian pillars. 'No use not telling folks where it's at,' the architect had said. He'd made his name in casinos, and Vegas money had paid for the pillars anyway.

St George sprawled up a valley from the Interstate, fringed by a low range of hills. Angeli had wanted a site within reach of the old deli and the restaurant. 'You ought to be able to see where it all began.' And, lo, the Western Dream motel, with two swimming-pools and a tennis court, went bankrupt, leaving five acres sloping down towards the edge of the shopping centre. They built walls, planted lush lawns, bought fountains. They cut and watered a green slice in the scatter of rocks and shacks and bars.

You could stand on the front steps and look north to the mountains, its outcrops red sentinels on constant duty. You could look down to the ants and their chrome carriages fuming along the main drag. Tate looked down. 'And there, my friends, one of the great presidents in American history began to realize his own dreams, scattering cheese on the pizzas his father baked, making the meatballs for the spaghetti his mother mixed with her own hands – but always, as so many dreamers have, turning his eyes to the stars and to the opportunity of public service.'

Harris had written this speech. Turnbull, the number one presidential speechwriter, had developed post-electoral ulcers. Rupert shuffled uneasily, hands clasped behind back. He hadn't enjoyed the Mormon bit of the funeral. It had been frankly gamey: too much emotion smothered by sullen preachers with blond hair and square jaws. Had Angeli been remotely religious? The man had sworn like a trooper when Rupert, long ago, had poured the Scotch. And the stories since his wife had died, of the slinking trips to the whorehouses of Nevada, were too constant for comfort. 'That Wild Bill, he'd fuck a cow if it turned his back on him.' Rupert had only been making polite conversation as the coffin had been lowered into the grave. He'd supposed the frail, grey-haired woman at his side was some kind of relative.

'Naw, I kept the Rooster Ranch for thirty years. After he quit, Bill was my top customer of all time, most bangs and most bucks. We got his old Amex card engraved in a frame over the water bed. It's a half-price night in his memory, starting at five, if you want to stop by.'

Tate was winding up. 'This is the land that our hero, President Angeli, would have loved. Laid to rest where he can see the big sky for ever and be remembered as the big man from the West who always gave his best for the people who loved him. Let's pause for a minute, my fellow Americans. Let us honour our fellow American.'

ITN and EBC were taking this live. Robin Groom had announced he'd be looking at TV monopoly legislation in a state-wide context. Such announcements, he'd further suggested, arrived inextricably bound to their readiness to cover great national events. Like presidential funerals. Like showpieces for Vice-President Warner. 'When you've got the goods, you put them in the shop window.'

'But will Rupert be speaking?' the editor-in-chief of ITN had quavered.

'I'll make sure that he does,' said Groom.

Rupert buttoned his suit jacket and stepped forward. 'I add my tribute with special grief and special good wishes from the citizens of the country we used to call Great Britain,' he said. 'For it was the vision of Bill Angeli that set us out on the great trek, that filled our wagons and fed our horses. He came at our hour of need. He offered the hand of friendship. He forged the moral bond that now unites us in one America, a land of Christian fellowship and Christian values.'

Harris had written this one, too. The latest research had shown family values on the up again, running two on the basic issue count.

'Bill Angeli,' Rupert said, 'was a human being of value with values he shared among us all. He, like so many before, saw a dream on a mountain top. He burnished it with his own deep beliefs, his own moral strengths, his pure love. Like your president, I shall remember him.'

It was already eleven in the morning and the sun was high. He could feel a stream of sweat flowing down his back, his shirt sodden and clinging. There was a ripple of applause. He stepped back alongside Jenny.

And then one of the security guards – what was his name? The heavy, rawboned one in the dark suit . . . Schultz? – walked from the side of the steps, from the shadow of the pillars. He seemed to stagger, tugging at something beneath his arm, wrestling and cursing. It was a gun. He had a gun in his hand. It was pointing towards them. The steel snout glinted in the sun. Time froze in bemusement, seconds stretched into slow motion.

Tate, eyes bent in reverence, had seen nothing. He stepped forward suddenly, poised to read the final sentences and cue the Last Post. Schultz was shooting. Three thick, dulled shots one after the other. They lifted Tate in the air and hurled him down the steps.

Where was Bannon? There, coming from behind, head down, groping under his armpit, too, scattering pencils and combs on the floor. Now he had a gun in his hand, too. Schultz was blown backwards. The top of his head became a fountain of blood, spraying the marble of the pillar. Suddenly everything had changed.

The steps of the library, glistening white criss-crossed with crimson, looked for all the world like the stage of a Greek theatre at the end of a prolonged tragedy. Oedipus wrecked.

They had retreated, eerily, to Angeli's transplant of an Oval Office. Marti was silent, shivering in horror. Rupert sat at the big desk, his head in his hands, immobile. Jenny, twitching at her canary-yellow suit, hand scratching automatically at a stain of blood below her breast, stood by the window, looking down towards the Chinese laundry at the bottom of the hill. A cloud of steam rose from it and drifted towards the second-hand tyre store. Outside the door there was a wail of secretaries weeping.

Tate's body was gone, helicoptered away to Los Angeles and FBI HQ West. The corpse of Schultz lay where the bullets had left it, flung six feet across the stage, shielded by screens from the silent crowds who filled the foot of the hillside.

'Oh, Christ,' said Rupert, 'oh, Jesus, Jesus Christ.'

Marti stood up. 'I'm going to Washington,' she said. 'The kids will be coming back from school. Somebody has to be there. Can I keep them in the White House for a few days till we can find somewhere else? There's no point going back to Maine till the summer. They've exams and friends and sleep-out parties, the usual silly things.'

'For heaven's sake,' Rupert said, 'it's your home. Have it for as long as you need it. And if you want somewhere to hang a hat afterwards, there's my Georgetown place with nobody but a maid in it. Just help yourself. Don't even ask.'

He gave her a huge, clumsy hug. Her makeup was matt perfection, as though the pain had set. His face was still stained with tears.

She left, her coat collar pulled high, sunglasses hiding the dry eyes.

'Mr President,' said the First Lady. 'Have you thought about it? Mr President.' There seemed to be a flicker of mockery in her voice.

Rupert walked over to her and they stood by the window. 'Don't say that,' he said. 'I know less than nothing about this damned country. I'm the sucker who got left with the toffee apple when the music stopped. We've both got a hell of a lot of thinking to do.'

He was sworn in that night in the real Oval Office. No cameras, he'd said, just let them know it's happening. Then sixty seconds of radio, so they can't see my face. So I can say that I'm saddened and awed and humbled, and will need to draw my strength from them, and that we shall all mourn quietly for a while.

'You'll need a photo-call somewhere,' Jenny said. 'They'll want today pictures – otherwise it will be all Tate. And you, my dear, are the future.'

Mansfield and Macdonald spent six hours in Schultz's lodgings. A room, a single bed and a microwave in a grimy apartment block down a Bethesda mean-street. The man had nothing and had left nothing, except the stench of cheap cologne and three more black suits in a cupboard with a broken hinge.

There was a box file under the white shirts on the cupboard shelf. They tipped it on to the bed. He'd sat for day after day scrawling in red ink on sheets of paper.

> The Egg of Life is cracked for ever, the scrambling of my hopes . . . You took that scared shell of beauty and turned it over easy . . . Now the Yolks of Fornication are death . . . God can see you, God will revenge you . . . The taint will taint us all . . . I followed and I heard you cry havoc, the end of the nation, writhing in the Sweat of Evil, eating from the pan of Lust and Destruction, addling in the fried slop of your Sanctimony. May the omelette of retribution Poach and Boil you in Hell.

The words grew weary as they turned the pages. Copulation. Betrayal. Decline. Revenge in the Name of the Sweet Lord.

Agent Mansfield carefully reloaded the box, fitting leaf upon leaf.

Behind the trash can in the kitchen, they found a bundle of gay porn mags, the bodies covered again in red ink. There were seventy-three Gideon bibles stacked in the toilet.

'He must have taken them from every hotel he stopped in,' said Macdonald. 'Laid there on the bed with his little red pen and his filth, then reached for the testaments.'

Mansfield shrugged. 'It's fruitcake time. It's goddamn religious fruitcake time, with an extra helping of nuts.'

They had the sketch of the library steps on the table in front of them.

'I'd just finished,' Rupert said. 'You can see me look left on the video as I step back. You see, I thought I saw something moving towards me. Then Mark was forward in one second, and the next second he was dead. Schultz didn't say a word. He just shot the President.'

Mansfield dealt out copies of the red-ink ravings as though they were cards.

'And you don't have any idea of why he should have written this?'

'Absolutely none. Mark and his wife had an ideal marriage. They barely knew Schultz. He'd been with me and my wife for a few weeks, but he never said anything much. He was just part of the detail, there or not there. All this must have come out of his head.'

Jenny fingered the sheets and looked again at the words. 'The adulterers shall burn in agony . . . The gold is brass, the cries of the creatures turn to dust . . . Sweet, stinking coupling in the eye of Jehovah, the sickly musk of Delilah . . . I am Samson and I stand beneath your temple, rocking it.' Some of the sketches down the side left her sick with revulsion: giant eggs broken open, snakes slithering from them on to the floor. 'There's nothing to add, really,' she said. 'He never talked. He followed

Rupert and me wherever we went. That was just what he did. Why on earth he'd want to kill the President I absolutely can't know. Except to think, like everyone else, that he was demented.'

Macdonald nodded. 'It's not what the conspiracy theorists will want to hear. We'll have nutcases ranting on about this till Doomsday and commissions turning over every stone, but the truth is just so damned banal. I reckon the Department shrinks screwed up big-time. Truth is, he was just a maniac with a gun and the system didn't pick him up.'

The advantage of the White House, Jenny thought, was that the First Lady had an entire dressing suite to herself. Vital, because otherwise they'd have nowhere to hide, nowhere to turn. The security was choking now. She couldn't go anywhere without the bloody posse. But she could stay in for a massage.

Gloria ran her fingers slowly across the nape of Jenny's neck, then turned her on to her belly, straddling across the buttocks and delving.

'You know,' Jenny said, her thighs beginning to convulse, 'we have the biggest secret in the world together.'

Gloria stopped and scratched her nose. Jenny reached for the hands and pulled them down again.

'I can't prove it, and probably nobody can ever prove anything. But Schultz didn't intend to assassinate Tate. I've looked at the tapes over and over. Mark moved into the line of fire too quickly. Before he did that, the gun was pointing between Rupert and me. I think it was me he wanted to kill. The President, you see, just got in the way. What was all that egg stuff in his notebooks? It didn't make any sense. But I know Duke Street, Bethesda. I was there when I hired my dear departed chauffeur. Yes, Egi. I'm sure he swung both ways. He'd swing anything, if you paid him enough. And there was someone there upstairs in the apartment when I hired him, someone he was living with – maybe the someone who kept spying on me and then got himself a job under our noses. I'd broken up the *ménage*. He was totally off his trolley. Could I be allowed to get away with it, and then move on?

'You're Delilah. It's that ghastly Japanese perfume you use to get me going. Schultz was always in the bedroom. He'd have seen it. And it was his job to watch us. He must have boiled over inside. When Rupert started talking about "moral strength" I think something just went snap.'

Gloria's eyes were wide with fear.

'But, of course, it's only a theory,' Jenny said. 'And even a whisper of it would destroy us both, wouldn't it?'

Gloria nodded.

'Dear Egi is safely back in Addis, and he isn't coming back. I never got round to registering him with the agency. What was the point? And, anyway, he was supposed to be parked somewhere on the Ethiopian embassy pay-roll. There isn't any evidence at all, unless you're a magician who can make something out of bugger-all. And we don't believe in magic, do we, love?'

Jenny reached into a cotton-wrap pocket and held a pinhead of metal in her fingers, waving it carefully under Gloria's nose. 'Standard issue CIA bug. I found it in Georgetown yesterday, where the bedpost ends. Somebody knew, somebody heard. Let's hope it was Schultz, my dear, because otherwise we could all be in the shit – especially if you ever let that pretty little mouth of yours start flapping.'

Gloria said nothing.

'Now, darling, take off that great floppy of a T-shirt. Let's concentrate on things we can do something about.'

The road from Bole airport into Addis was chaos as always. Ancient lorries listing to starboard under the weight of cows or sheep or people. Bicycles weaving back and forth through the jam. Tall, swaying women with bundles on their heads stalking the footpaths. Beyond the office blocks, the mud and wattle homes of centuries stretched up the tentacled slopes of Mount Entoto.

Yet the little shopping centres you could pass and see from the airport bus were sprucely painted in creams and pinks. The dry-cleaners, the bread shops, the baggage stores hung deep in leather. And there, just there on the left, the newest front on the block, gleaming in the sun. Antebellum Ababa. 'White House Motors. Chauffeur-driven excursions. Driving instruction. All services. President and Chief Executive: E. Engibono BA.' Was that him, stripped to the waist, polishing the golden Mercedes in the forecourt and pausing occasionally to turn his wide eyes towards the women tourists as they stopped and stared?

The two secretaries from Mannheim, beginning their great adventure, wound the bus window down and waved to him.

'Do you do the Blue Nile?' shouted Trudi.

'Lady,' said the Chief Executive, 'I do anything you like.'

They had eaten together in Rupert's dining room. Tomato soup and steak and kidney pie with peas and boiled potato. 'I've had it with fried chicken,' the President said. 'And I never want to see another seared tuna as long as I live.' They had hired the deputy chef at the Athenaeum on contract. 'Remember, watery cabbage and Yorkshire pudding are as American now as grits. Bring on the tapioca with strawberry jam.'

Polly barely touched her food. 'It's not the cooking,' she said, 'though it could be. I have some news.'

Simmons grinned. 'No, we have some news.'

They called for a bottle of Napa Valley Mumm. 'Mumm by name and Mum by celebration,' said Rupert elaborately.

Jenny sat beside him on the sofa. 'Here's to us,' she said. 'We four. We were there at the beginning. This has been our story.'

Rupert was suddenly crying again. He had taken off his tie and jacket, and his stomach swelled over his trousers. He was a great, heaving shambles of a man.

'And one more toast,' Polly said. 'To Rupert. A friend for history.'

The President wiped his eyes. 'When I look back,' he said, 'I see nothing of inevitability to any of this. You can stand by the seashore on Chesil Beach and hurl a stick into the sea for your dog and know that, no matter how hard you throw, the waves will bring it back and leave it on the strand. There was never a moment of such certainty here. I never guessed what would happen next.

'But somehow, somewhere, there was always a tide to events. We couldn't settle in Europe. They aren't like us. Our eyes and our hearts were always looking further afield, or turning in on ourselves. My father was right. We could rip up our past. But he didn't have to live with our future.

'What happened? Events happened. And the funny thing, you know, the thing that haunts me, is that they had a momentum of their own. Once we began to move there was never a chance to turn back. It was as though someone was guiding us.'

Polly put her hand on his.

'So here I am. President of a country I barely know that speaks twenty-five languages I can't understand a word of, mouthing slush about frontiers and families because that's what's expected, reforming systems I don't understand and jawboning politicians whose names I can't remember. I did not want it. I'm sure I'll make a terrible botch of it and I'm frightened as hell. But it's events again. There's nothing to do but plough on and hope.'

Simmons was jotting a few notes for the morning on his pad. 'While I remember,' he said, 'you've got your vice-presidential nominee at eight.'

'Tell me his name again before I go in,' Rupert said. 'Is it Bobby Deke Williams the Third or the Fourth?'

'It's Robby Deke the Fifth,' said Jenny, scowling. 'And for God's sake don't forget what I told you. His brother-in-law may be president of Louisiana State University, but he's not heading the Morality Task Force. That's my job. It's your mission to cleanse America of moral pollution and my mission to lead your fight.'

Rupert looked over at her and his eyes were still moist. They never made love, these days, but somehow it didn't matter. It was, he thought, her intelligence, her fierce, dogged intelligence, that bound him to her.

Time for the G10 summit and America's turn to play host. Rupert had chosen Bangor, 'in memory of the great son of Maine whose moment this should have been'. Jenny was in Hollywood with her skeleton force, starting to interview studio chiefs about movie-grading reform. He'd glimpsed her on breakfast TV that morning, standing beside Gloria, Task Force deputy director designate. He had Marti by his side on the airport runway. It just seemed the right thing to do.

The Lufthansa jet had taxied to a halt now. There'd been some doubt whether Gross would come. The Free Democrats had bailed out at last. The vote of confidence next Wednesday was lost.

He saw the thin, sallow man edge uncertainly down the steps. He smiled his widest smile. 'Well, Bundeschancellor. We meet again. What goes around comes around, I always say. And welcome to this great country.'

Read on for a taste of Peter Preston's new novel:

Bess

Available now in Viking hardback, £15.99

Every night, on his travels, he would write to her. Occasionally, if time pressed, there could be only a few sentences on the tiny computer he kept in his breast pocket: no more than a reassurance that he was still there, somewhere at the ends of the earth. But at heart he hated the bleeps and flashes and the stumbles of his thick fingers on the keys. The screen in the corner of her room rang a hollow, imperious bell when such messages arrived – just as, long ago, the bell in the servants' quarters at Balmoral had sounded when his great-great-grandmother demanded tea with lemon, or something rather stronger. There was no warmth to such communication. Upstairs: downstairs. Love, as in 'I'd love a gin and tonic.'

Instead he kept a pad of cream vellum in the old leather briefcase his equerry carried. He would ask for a desk and sit there for a few moments, adjusting the light and fiddling with his gold fountain pen, practising to make sure that the ink flowed smoothly from the nib. Then the words would come as he wanted them. 'Dear Lilibet . . .'

He knew she hated the name. 'It's just wet nursery stuff,' she'd say. 'But I'm grown up now. I don't care about what your great-great-grandpa used to call great-grandma. They were them a long time ago. I'm me, now.'

He would shrug and take no notice. It was too late to change. He had been writing the Lilibet letters for thirteen years, ever since she had first learned to read. Usually three pages in his jagged hand, dried with the curved Moroccan blotter before they were fed into the fax; and always, after transmission, folded into the parcel of originals that he would post on to her so that they could be tied, year by year, with red ribbon and stored in the tea chest by her bed.

'Why do you do it?' she'd asked him last summer at the school open day, as they had stretched on the bank of long grass at the end of the hockey pitch and eaten potato crisps from a big yellow bag. 'I mean, I love it. It makes me feel remembered. But it's also a bit strange. I know the other girls laugh at me when I dash out of play rehearsals to check the fax. They think I'm running some kind of dodgy business. One third-former came up to me last week in the gym and asked if she could buy a couple of joints.'

He smiled and then grimaced. 'Honestly,' he said, 'I don't quite know. It just seemed natural when I started. There I was, flying around, taking salutes on every parade ground under the sun, never in one spot for more than five minutes. And there were you two kids when your mother walked out, my little girl and little boy lost and hurried off to boarding school. Out of sight, out of mind. It was all too much like when I was growing up. My brother and I weren't human beings, we were royal objects. We were the parcels Mum and Dad passed between them. This way, at least, you know where I am every day; and you know I think about you and Nicholas and that I care what you're doing. Sorry, does that sound soppy?'

She'd squeezed his hand and brushed the hair back from her eyes. They had watered for a moment. 'No, not at all. Maybe Nicky doesn't like it much. He's such a spotty idiot at the moment. But it sounds just fine to me. Have some more crisps before I change for the match. It's three sets, so tea may be a little late this year.'

Dear Lilibet,
They tell me it's cold and wet in Sussex. Poor you! I'm sitting
on the 24th Floor of the Park Tower in Rio, watching the sun

go down. There are brown girls in unbelievable scraps of costumes coming out of the sea for the last time today, shaking their hair and everything else dry; and men in raggedy shorts selling coconuts along the promenade. When I open the window, you can hear the sound of drums and saxophones. Good evening Ipanema. It feels like carnival every day.

In a few minutes, I think, it will be totally dark. The sun is vanishing like one of those golden balls that float when conjurors cover them with a cloth. Sugar Loaf is etched against the sky and there's a warm blackness spreading, where the lights from the hotels and clubs seem to sparkle more brightly. I've bought myself a disgusting flower shirt from the lobby shop and a straw hat wide enough to pull over my face. Can I get a couple of hours out on the town without the photo hounds by the front door picking up the scent? We shall see. Or rather, you'll see, my love, when you open your paper.

Don't be too jealous, though. This is still the tour from hell. Brother King is confined to barracks on the 25th Floor with some Curse of the Amazon he picked up at the Belem chamber of commerce dinner, and the Viking Queen is staging all her usual strops. Why is the air conditioning too hot or too cold? Who says the ice cubes are safe? Why can't the Little Emperor have fish fingers and beans?

Our Foreign Secretary has gone AWOL again, predictably enough. Locked himself in with a couple of secretaries and enough red boxes to last the night. Affairs of State! The final refuge of politicians who've fouled up. I mean, anyone with their head screwed on could see that carting the entire Royal caravan round Brazil for a week in the sacred name of Commerce wasn't the brightest FCO notion of the century.

'We didn't realize what a big country it was, sir,' they said when they called me. 'We think we've scheduled too much and we'd be awfully grateful if you could fly down and, you know, share the burden a bit.' So I drew a sardine-canning

*factory in Porto Alegre and a fashion show in São Paulo
before lunch while the Top Crowns were getting the squits up
north. And tomorrow, after a delightful working breakfast
with the Minister for Industry, plus a mandatory flip round
the Palace museum in Petropolis, we've got to be in Salvador
for tea with the engineering employers' federation.*

*Solid grind, my love: though they say I can zip back to
Guyana by myself at the end of the week and maybe mix a
spot of fishing with the usual base-inspection stuff.*

*Anyway, that's business and pleasure pending – and you'll
want to get on with your revision. I can't say how proud of
you I am. Oxford in the autumn (cross fingers!) and you've
done it for yourself because you're bloody bright, not just
plodders like the rest of us. I don't know where you get it
from. Not your darling mother, for sure. And it can't be from
me, second-hand Dukey doing second-tier jobs. But I light a
candle every time I think of you.*

Muchest love,
Your devoted D.

She had sat up too late the night before, hunched over her history
notes and drinking mugs of coffee as she tried to get the dates
and names straight in her head. There was bound to be a question
about prime ministers and their chancellors. It came up every
three years on average, and this was year three. Mrs Bowler had
been as positive as ever. 'Of course we can't be certain sure –
but there are themes, strong strands of interest, which are always
resonant. If I were you, I'd make sure that I was specially up on
Macmillan and Selwyn Lloyd, and Major and Lamont, and Blair
and Brown.'

But was that enough? What about Brown and Balls? She could
do the fault lines and the structural bits. But that was no use if
you mixed the details wrong. Somehow everything was getting
too close and too oppressive. She needed air.

It was a morning of free periods. Indeed, nobody kept much

track of them in the last couple of weeks before the exams. They were eighteen, for heaven's sake. Old enough to be married with kids and curlers in their hair, trooping down to the launderette. Too old to be models or swimmers in their dreams. In three months, they'd be far away at universities around the world, with nobody to raise an eyebrow over drugs or sex, or even a cigarette end thrown through an open study window.

The rain had cleared. There was a shimmer of heat to come behind the thinning clouds.

She walked along the cliffs at Rottingdean and looked down to the expanse of Brighton Marina, already beginning to bustle as summer arrived. Doctors sprucing their boats for the weekends away from persistent patients, pausing to answer mobile phones between strokes of paint; estate agents hauling crates of cheap Spanish bubbly aboard their motor yachts for the client cruises yet to come.

No one turned to look at her as she strode right along the cliff path, then down towards Brighton. She was an ordinary girl in a raincoat with a sensible maroon sweater and a sensible charcoal skirt. Her hair needed washing, she knew. One of the many things there wasn't time for last night. So it was pulled back in a tight band, a greasy tug of blonde which left her ears exposed: less obtrusive now than before the plastic surgery her father had insisted on, but still large, still dominant.

She was tall, with wide shoulders which helped to diminish the bosom – the sodding family bosom – but she did not move in the family's way. She was not stiff or tense. She was loose, with an easy, athletic grace. She loved tennis and cricket. She had opened the bowling now for two seasons in the Roedean first eleven. The best action of anyone for the last ten years, they said: real nip off the pitch. Her eyes were green, and sometimes almost seemed gold in the glare of the sun. Her skin was pale, translucent, needing a touch of blood in the cheeks. Her nose, she thought when she looked in the mirror, was too – how would they put it? – too assertive. Hooked, a trifle imperious: a Spencer nose, not the knobbly ski-lift of the Windsor women. She did not think of herself as beautiful.

In twenty minutes she was walking The Lanes, looking in antique dealers' windows, sifting through the tourist bric-a-brac, pausing to watch the coach parties of Japanese chatter their way through the narrow streets and to smile a secret smile. She was lost in her own world.

The postman emptying the box on the sea front felt a twinge in his back and stretched upright for a moment just as the girl in the mac wandered by. 'Good morning,' he said automatically. 'Yes,' she said; and her eyes caught his.

It was an effort to bend back to the open box of packets and brown envelopes. They were wonderful eyes: frank, clear, piercing. And something else. He tied up the neck of the sack. Something memorable. Deep, humorous; with an intelligence which unsettled him and made him turn – haplessly, without choice – to watch her walk away.

'I am not travelling in this plane,' said the Queen. 'It is so old and so disgusting.'

Her jaw, always too square, always heavy with imminent fury, had swelled to an ominous jut, so that her whole face seemed to balance precariously on her thin neck. One more indignity and it would fall of its own volition to the tarmac.

She had never been, nor could ever be, remotely pretty. But she was the available third daughter of the Danish King; and His Majesty's advisers had never doubted what must be done. 'No more commoners, Sir,' they'd said. 'No more horsey girls or simpering virgins from broken homes. No more actresses or television weather presenters. You are royal in a Europe where royalty still means something and there are a few royal princesses who know about duty. You have played on the machines in the gymnasium of life, probably for too long. Now there has to be an alliance and an heir: and this marriage is serious. It cannot afford to fail. Indeed, failure must not be countenanced. We have searched most widely and, we believe, found someone suitable. You may or may not grow to love her. Who can say? If not, then there will always be other pursuits to be followed discreetly. But she is necessary, Sir. This alliance is necessary.'

They had not, of course, mentioned her scrawny buttocks or her dark, contracted eyebrows; they had not mentioned her sour breath or temper.

'See,' she said, bending forward and pointing. 'The seats are filthy and the carpet is old and frayed, and it smells of tobacco. How can a King travel in such squalor? How can a young Prince with a delicate stomach endure such an ordeal?'

The King, as usual, had moved a few yards downwind and, hands clasped behind back, appeared deep in meditation. Do not disturb; do not embroil or consult or appeal to. The little Prince stood by his mother's side, grinning more broadly as her anger grew and giggling with each explosion. No wonder the tabloids were calling him Hamlet already. The Foreign Secretary hugged a red box to his chest as though in protection. The equerries and ladies-in-waiting stood in a defensive ring like the wagons of a train camped for the night.

'Look, Ma'am,' said Emery, bag carrier extraordinary, white-faced beneath the livid insect bite on his forehead. 'Look, we know this is less than ideal and we apologize as profusely as we can. But there are circumstances here . . .' He hesitated. Ah, circumstances! 'You were due to travel everywhere by scheduled Varig services. It is what the taxpayer demands these days. But we had not been told that there are no first-class sections on some of their flights – to Salvador, for instance. And the taxpayer would not, I'm sure, want to see such a distinguished party crammed into economy cabins with Indians and mulattos and their plastic packages and parrots in cages. That would be an economy too far.

'We're all very grateful that the Duke managed to intervene with the MoD and get the Governor's Boeing flown up from the Falklands. I know it isn't exactly palatial and it breaks all the old protocol rules. We specifically asked for two 777s, but one's stuck in the Azores — and London were at their wits' end. Even their emergency budget's bust, and the Expenditure Committee are going up the wall. But please, Ma'am, the flight is only ninety minutes and Captain Cox and his crew will do everything to make you comfortable.'

Her lips set into a thin slit of discontent. Emery swung round in desperation, searching for an ally. The Duke was wearing his RAF uniform, the full Squadron Leader kit. A smear of higher authority.

'Isn't that right, Sir?' Emery implored.

'I believe so,' said the superior officer reluctantly. 'I think we must all make do. Christina, please be so good as to fasten your safety belt. Make sure that the Prince has a paper bag ready. We can't spend the afternoon arguing on a runway in Rio. The press in the terminal will be getting curious. And our engineer hosts are waiting. They will not understand a spanner in the works.'

'That was awfully well done, Sir, if I might be so bold.'

Cox had a puppyish air to him, eager, youthful, wide-eyed.

The Duke shut the flying deck behind him with a firm swing, as though in protection. 'I wouldn't say that. But she can be a bit fierce when roused.'

'Would you like a turn at the controls, Sir?' asked the puppy. 'Flight Lieutenant Crabb here is pretty flaked out. He'd only just got back from Northolt with the Governor when the call came. And it would be a real honour to sit beside an officer of your distinction.'

The young man was trying too hard, he thought. Still, it wasn't a bad idea. Anything to avoid sitting back there with the cowed and the baleful. 'Thank you, Captain. That's a kind notion.'

They were taking the Atlantic route north, heading a score or so miles off the coast, then hugging its outline past Campos and Vitória and Belmonte. There was a light breeze from the east which had cleared the clouds from the sea so that, far below, it glistened and danced. He saw a tuna fleet set in relentless hunt; an oil tanker lumbering south towards Florianópolis; a white cruise liner steaming east with a swimming pool cut into its deck so that, at first glance, there seemed to be a giant blue hole in its heart.

'Coming up to Salvador now, Sir,' said Cox.

It was a sight to remember: a flurry of islands and bold green hummocks rearing out of the water, and then a rocky stretch of coast flanking great bays and wide beaches, with valleys of skyscrapers running back, like veins, up the hillsides.

'Nice-looking spot,' said the Duke.

'Oh rather, Sir. Absolutely. Though they say the low cloud has banked up a bit at the airport.'

'Landing on Automatic?'

'Don't think so, Sir, if that's all right. Crabb said it came down a touch heavy in Stanley. May need a bit of fine tuning. I don't want to give the ladies more of a bump than necessary.'

They swung left in a wide arc and began the final descent. 'Seatbelts please,' said Cox. 'Crew, five minutes to landing.'

The wind was stiffer than they'd been told, piling cloud against the mountain range, hiding the single stretch of black runway and the acres of red earth where another was being built. They were coming in low, roaring over the palm trees and the fields of sugar cane and the desolate townships of shanties and open drains. He could see the faces of children raised upwards.

'I'll take it,' said the Duke suddenly. 'This looks like an easy one.'

Air traffic was burbling away in a thick Portuguese accent, harsh and rising shrilly. 'Airport. Airport.'

'I know it's the bloody airport. What else do you think it is?'

'No, Sir,' Cox cried. 'Not Airport. Abort. ABORT.'

There was a damned little Piper Cheyenne coming in due west, touching down on the earth track and heading slap in front of them. Fucking amateur, the Duke thought. Some bloody playboy taking a spin and zonked out of his brain on coke.

'Climb, Sir, CLIMB.'

The door swung open and he could hear the Queen shouting at the Foreign Secretary. 'So rough. Intolerable. I shall complain to the Prime Minister.'

But the Piper had climbed too and now it clipped the Boeing's starboard wing, spinning it almost lazily on to one side as it hit the runway. The explosion and the burst of fire came five seconds later. On the beach, the brown girls in bikinis clutched their towels and turned, eyes wide, to watch the smoke billowing into the sky.

She was lying on her bed in a track suit re-reading Nigel Lawson's biography, marking the paragraphs that mattered with a blue pencil. Could a Chancellor pursue a policy irrespective of a Prime Minister's wishes? Only if she didn't know he was doing it. But surely that wasn't possible, at least for more than a few months? There was a shuffle and a knock on the door.

'Come in if you've brought a bottle. It's open.'

Christ, it wasn't Emma or Caroline. It was Mrs Granger and she looked impossibly grim.

'Gosh,' the girl said, sitting upright, then scrambling to attention. 'I'm very sorry. I was only joking, Mrs Granger.'

Still utter grimness. The headmistress's face was somehow rigid and her arms were clasped across her stomach. 'No, it's I who am sorry, my dear. And there is no easy way to say it. I've just had a call from the Palace. They can't be quite certain yet. There is awful confusion. But they think the plane your father was travelling in crashed a couple of hours ago at Salvador airport, and they think there are no survivors. Not the King or the Queen or the little Prince. Not your father. They've tried for a temporary news black-out, but they do not expect it to hold. I can't tell you how shocked we all are.'

She moved towards the bed and, awkwardly, put an arm round

the girl's shoulders. 'Would you like to phone your mother?'

The girl pulled herself straight. 'It's not worth it,' she said, the words careful and clipped. 'She's on some yacht somewhere off Antibes. She didn't leave a number. She'll find out long before we could reach her. And then I suppose she will phone me if she wants.'

She stood up and turned to look at the Head. Her face was set, her eyes dry. 'Do you know if they're telling my brother?'

'No. They didn't say and I'm sorry, I forgot to ask.'

'I'll call him myself,' the girl said. 'He's at such an awful school they'll be sure to make a muck of it.'

The office at the south-east corner of the Palace was long and low and panelled in a light walnut from the Dordogne. He had ordered it on the spot at the Riberac timber merchants who'd refitted the library at the Chateau Coumin when his friends, the Foxley-Woods, bought it. No mahogany; no heavy flock; and absolutely none of that plaster and gilt crap left over from Edward VII's Café Royal phase. The carpet was beige and lushly piled to put a spring in his step. The desk – a banana-shaped swirl of matching walnut – had won a Design Centre award five years ago. A single picture hung to the right of his chair, a pleasant enough Canaletto of St Mark's Square he had recently intercepted on the way back from the restorers. He wasn't sure about the gold frame – too obtrusively ornate, perhaps? – but the vividness of the blues gave the room an infusion of colour which his visitors always praised. 'Ancient and modern, Sir Edgar. Such a refreshing contrast.' He was a man of taste.

Edgar Peniston Rowley Fountain, Chief Executive of the Royal Household, welcomed such admiration. He deserved it, he felt, because he had earned it. The last two CEOs, frankly, had been handed the job on a silver platter. They'd been insiders, bit players on the Windsor circuit by marriage, tumbled out of convenient merchant banks after the usual 'soundings' and plonked on the edifice like icing on a wedding cake. But Fountain broke that mould. His father, it was true, had been Lord Lieutenant of Northamptonshire, but only in the last years of his life when the first Blair reforms had tried to spread such appointments amongst what were called 'the ordinary people who are the lifeblood of Britain'. Basically, Dad had made bathroom fittings: top-of-the-range taps and toilet seats. The young Fountain had been to Rugby and Trinity Hall, Cambridge, and Harvard Business School. Decent enough staging posts in their way, but hardly inner circle. He didn't talk much about his twelve years in Shanghai and Harare running British American Tobacco's cigarette distribution networks there. Low tar and lower prestige. He encouraged only cautious remembrance of his term as Administrative Director at the South Bank Centre. Committees under his chairmanship had warned repeatedly of the dangers of flood damage unless Government – or 'those responsible', as he'd said in that unfortunate TV interview on Waterloo Bridge – provided adequate funds. It was not his fault. Nevertheless, he had been distinctly amazed when the ad in the *Sunday Times* – 'Old established family company seeks Senior Exec for Ambitious Modernization Programme' – had turned out to be a front for Whitehall headhunters on the Windsor prowl. 'Must have good grounding in management control systems.'

And he had, hadn't he? Could anyone complain about the profit record of Regal Enterprises 2000 (Malibu) Inc., or the cash flow from Amalgamated Crown Properties plc, or the European sales figures for Saxe-Coburg Franchise Developments SA, or the prospects for the Diadem Experience Hotel and Theme Parks Division? His Clinton Lecture at Harvard last year on Resource Maximization had been specifically praised in the *Wall Street Journal* – 'an object lesson in family corporation expansion without direct family involvement from the new business king at the court of olde England'.

Fountain had been preparing a second address on Royal Risk Management for Yale next semester. But some risks were beyond management. He licked his wet lips. He wiped a distraught hand through the crinkles of white hair which paraded back from his forehead. His head was throbbing and he could hear the constant ringing of phones at his secretary's desk outside. God rot it, the family had fucked up again – as they always did. Killed themselves off this time and left him to pick up the pieces, as usual. He flicked the switch on the intercom.

'Get Chetwode-Belcher to call me the minute he's made contact,' Fountain said.

Emma brought the bottle and Caroline the corkscrew. They sat with her for an hour, chatting and hugging and crying in turns. She kept staring at the fax, silent on the desk.

'I can't take it in. I just can't believe it.'

There was another shuffle outside the door. This time there was a young man in a grey suit beside the headmistress: pink cheeks, brown hair scraped back across a curiously flat head, a pimple of a nose. He did not seem to know where to put his hands. Behind him in the corridor, two more men in suits shuffled in the shadows.

'I apologize for intruding,' said the man in grey. 'We have never met, I think. I am Captain Rodney Chetwode-Belcher, an equerry here on behalf of Sir Edgar Fountain. The Chief Executive of the Royal Household, of course. This is one of those moments when words seem insufficient – but it is my duty, on behalf of us all in the Household and allied enterprises, to record our deepest sympathy for your loss.'

'Of course,' said Caroline sharply. 'But you're talking to the wrong person. She's over there.'

'No, that's all right,' the girl said, walking towards him, pulling the top of her track suit straight, shaking his hand solemnly. 'I haven't been much on Palace show for years. My father wanted to keep me out of it. "She isn't core royal by the rules," he said. "She'll have to make her own way. Let her live her life."'

Chetwode-Belcher licked his lips nervously. 'I'm terribly afraid that's one more aspect of this tragedy that your father was mistaken about,' he said. 'We all face the most awful series of upheavals. We at the Palace find the situation quite terrifying. Press queries have jammed the switchboard. Sir Edgar has cancelled all holidays indefinitely. Just when I'd got a week in Antigua fixed.'

He seemed, for a second, to be about to stamp his feet. The hand flapped petulantly. Mrs Granger coughed. He paused, cheeks flushed, and screwed his hands into tight balls. 'But, by tradition tonight,' he said, 'before anything else can be decided, I am required to ask you one question. What title would Your Majesty be taking?'

She wiped her swollen eyelids and laughed. It was the only thing to do. 'Why, Elizabeth the Third,' she said. 'What other choice is there? But I hope my friends can still call me Bess.'